the reaper's shadow

COLLEGE OF WITCHCRAFT BOOK TWO

ALICIA RADES

ONE

A Year Ago

The coven had lost a child.

Two days ago, a six-year-old boy named Caleb Thomas had gone missing from his bed in the middle of the night. There was no evidence left behind—just an open window he'd been snatched through. He came from a prominent Alchemy family, so the chances he'd run away were slim to none.

But that was all anyone knew. That, and no magic could track him.

We had Seers on every corner, and not one of them had a vision of the missing boy. The coven must've had dozens of psychometrists—people who got visions through touch. They were experts at finding things.

And yet the child was still missing.

I didn't know that was possible.

The dark skies outside the school crackled with lightning, and thunder shook the walls. The Main Foyer was deserted, except for Grant and me. We sat in front of the empty fireplace, balking at the absurdity of it all.

"I don't get it," Grant remarked. He lounged across one of the plush red chairs, his legs hanging over the armrest. He flipped through the school newspaper.

"I know. It's crazy," I agreed. "Maybe you'll get Seer at your Evoking Ceremony this weekend. Maybe we can find him."

"That's not what I meant." Grant shifted in his chair to sit up straight. His eyes darkened as he waved the school paper in the air. "I don't get how the coven can be in an uproar about this whole thing and there's not *one* mention of it in the school paper."

"What?" I balked.

Grant tossed the paper onto the coffee table between us, and it made a hard *smacking* noise as it landed.

I scrambled forward and snatched it up. The paper's name, *The Epitaph*, was scrawled across the top in big, bold letters. Below that was a headline highlighting this year's top fashion for the Midnight Formal.

What the hell? The Formal was two months away. Little Caleb Thomas was missing *now*!

I started flipping through the newspaper, but there was no mention of the boy at all. I crumpled the paper in my fists.

I must've got a look on my face, because Grant narrowed his eyes at me. "What are you thinking?"

I took a couple of shallow breaths, my nostrils flaring. "I think I'm going to have a chat with the head of the paper."

I shot up out of my seat and stomped past the grand staircase.

"Lucas, wait!" Grant called, but I ignored him.

I clutched my copy of *The Epitaph* tight in my fist and stormed down the hall to Professor Carlisle's office. He was my conjuring professor and the faculty advisor for the paper. Rumor had it, he spent twenty years as a journalist at the *Miriamic Messenger* before becoming a professor, and that's how he landed the role as the school paper advisor.

I passed through his classroom and stomped straight through the open door of his office. He sat at his desk, scribbling away at something.

"Your paper is garbage!" I raged, slamming it down on his desk.

The ancient gray cat lounging nearby jumped so high it fell off the edge of the desk. Professor Carlisle gave a start. He looked up to me and adjusted his glasses. His bushy gray eyebrows shot up, nearly touching his hairline.

"Mister Taylor, how may I help you?" He looked delighted to see me, but I was more than a little ticked off.

"I want to know why you're letting the school paper publish this garbage," I demanded. "Why isn't there *one* mention of Caleb Thomas in here?"

"The missing boy?" he asked, looking surprised. "I believe the *Miriamic Messenger* has that topic covered."

"The town paper has shared the facts—which isn't much, to be frank," I pointed out. "Why isn't the school paper doing a feature? Talk about the implications this has on the coven. Analyze what this means for our magic—or run a study on what types of magic might be able to cover this up. Discuss what we can do as students to contribute to the search for the child. The possibilities are endless!"

Professor Carlisle's eyes brightened. He leaned back in his chair, looking intrigued. "Those are all good ideas, Mister Taylor. If you want to submit a piece for consideration, I'm more than happy to look at it."

My stomach dropped. That wasn't my intention for coming to him at all.

"I'm not a journalist," I stated bluntly.

"Well, why not?" Professor Carlisle asked brightly, spreading his arms wide. For a guy pushing eighty, he had a lot of energy. "You seem to have a lot of ideas. The paper could use an opinionated view like yours."

"What the paper *needs* is an investigative journalist," I said. "Someone has to figure out how this boy went missing without a trace."

"That's what the Imperium's for," he reminded me. "Unfortunately, the newspaper club is very small, and I encourage all my students to report on the topics that matter most to them."

My eyebrows shot up. What kind of idiots were in the newspaper club if they thought some stupid dance was more important than a child's life?

"If you're going to go digging on this, I'd love to bring you on board," Professor Carlisle offered.

"That's not what I was suggesting," I told him, rather harshly. "Like I said, I'm not a reporter."

Professor Carlisle shrugged, like there was nothing more he could do about it. "Well, then, I'm afraid we're going to have to leave this matter to the professionals."

"I thought *you* were a professional," I growled before turning on my heel and storming out of the room.

As I walked down the hall, I couldn't get this single thought out of my mind: *Protect the coven.*

I wanted to find this little boy. I wanted to help.

Problem was, I didn't know how.

☾·

Present Day

ANOTHER CHILD HAD GONE MISSING. Same story, different kid.

One moment, ten-year-old Isaac Miller was at home in his bed, sleeping soundlessly. The next he just… vanished. Nothing but an open window beside his bed remained. His family was high-profile like the last, though they were Mentalists instead of Alchemists. Like last time, no magic in the coven could trace him.

After Caleb Thomas went missing, the coven sort of gave up on him. There were no leads, nothing we could do. His case was a total dead end, and we didn't know if he was dead or alive. How could you search for a missing person when the only evidence left behind was their absence?

But this time, I knew something. I was the *only* one who knew *anything*. It wasn't much, but I knew one thing.

Those children were dead.

And whoever killed them was going to strike again.

I'd heard them die. They used the same word, like it was some sort of code.

Caleb's last thought echoed in my mind. It was the child's voice I heard last semester… the one I couldn't match to an obituary.

Is it playtime?

No, it wasn't, and Isaac knew it.

Playtime is over. No child in the coven is safe.

The similarities frightened me to my very core.

I didn't have proof these voices were those of the missing children, but deep down in my gut, I felt it.

At the time I heard the second voice, no one knew Isaac was even missing. It wasn't until morning that word got out about his disappearance. He was older than Caleb by a few years, but the similarities between the disappearances were too coincidental to dismiss.

The one thing that didn't seem to fit—and the thing that frightened me most—was that little Caleb died a *year* after his disappearance. Isaac Miller was killed the same night he was taken.

Don't ask how I knew it was murder. It wasn't like the kids had told me.

But I could feel it in their thoughts—the way my guts twisted when I heard their voices, the way I heaved and shook and felt hot and cold at the same time. It was dark. It was sinister. And it *wasn't* an accident.

As soon as I was discharged from the hospital after my encounter with a reaper, I marched straight up to the Imperium's doors. They met on the top floor of Octavia Hall. I pounded on the heavy door, and it swung open under my weight.

Their meeting quarters looked more like an attic than anything—with a vaulted ceiling, fireplace, and huge window overlooking the town—but it was really big and clean. There were books stacked neatly along all the walls, along with potion vials, crystals, and endless decks of tarot cards. A large round table sat in the center of the room.

The four priestesses were crowded around the table. Each one spoke over each other so loudly that their voices spilled out into the hall. I couldn't make out what they were saying. They stopped abruptly when they heard the door creak open.

"The missing children are dead," I said bluntly.

A woman with a cauldron tattoo on the back of her neck whirled around, eyes wide. Technically, all priestesses held the same power, but she was the oldest of all of them and looked like she naturally took on the role of leader.

I recognized her as Priestess Margaret. She had long silver hair tied into a braid that hung over her shoulder to show off her tattoo, and she wore a gray shawl around her shoulders. Like all the priestesses, she was very pretty.

"Lucas Taylor," she said breathlessly, recognition crossing her features. "The Reaper's Apprentice."

I nodded firmly.

She reached out a hand to invite me inside. "You have heard the child pass?"

"Not just one," I said as I entered the room, my heart racing. "Remember Caleb Thomas, the boy who went missing last year?"

The four priestesses exchanged a terrified glance.

"I think I heard him, too," I admitted.

Priestess Margaret took my hand and dragged me to the table. "Sit. Tell us everything you know."

It wasn't much—and I could tell the priestesses were disappointed by that as I explained to them what I'd heard.

"This makes no sense," one of them protested. She had a wild mane of dark curls and a tree tattooed on her shoulder. I recognized her as Priestess Lilian, Chloe's grandmother. "Why would somebody wait a year to harm one child, only to hurt the other the day they're taken?"

"I wondered the same thing," I told them. "The M.O. doesn't match up. But I know what I heard."

Priestess Charlotte spoke up. She was as old as the others, but her long red hair hadn't started to gray. I noticed the skull tattoo on her wrist. "Perhaps we need to consider the possibility of a third missing child. It could explain the timeline of the deaths. Perhaps Caleb wasn't the child you heard, but it was another one."

"But no others have been reported missing," the fourth and final priestess stated. Priestess Stella was the youngest of the four, but she had this look about her that suggested she was very wise. I couldn't see her tattoo, but I knew she was a Seer.

"Then let's assume it's just the two for now," Priestess Margaret replied. "The first thing we must do is enact safety measures to ensure the children of the coven are safe."

"What about catching the perpetrator?" I demanded.

Margaret shot me a look of sympathy. "With all due respect, we don't know what we're dealing with yet. Our number one priority is keeping the children who *are* alive safe."

"Doesn't that start with explaining what happened to the others?" I demanded. It frustrated me that they weren't launching a murder investigation immediately.

"We will absolutely investigate," Margaret promised me. "The Miriamic Police Department will be informed of what you've told us as soon as we're done here."

"Is there any way I can help?" I asked.

Margaret frowned. "I'm afraid not—not unless you know anything else."

"That's all I know," I replied, regret twisting in my gut. I wished I knew more to help them. I didn't want anyone else getting hurt. I didn't want to listen to another child die. That was something I was determined to prevent.

"There must be *something* I can do," I insisted.

"I'm sorry, Lucas," Margaret said. "Unless you're a police officer or an investigative journalist, I don't think there's anything you can do."

An idea struck, and I shot to my feet. "Well, maybe there *is* something I can do. Thank you for your time, priestesses."

I left the Imperium headquarters and rushed back to school, inspiration sizzling in my bones. If the Imperium Council thought there was only one way to help, then I was taking it. I wasn't here just to sit around and wait for people to die. I could do better to serve the coven.

And I would.

I marched down the hall, through one of the classrooms, and straight to Professor Carlisle's office. He was hunched over his desk, catching up on grades, when I entered the room.

"I'll do it," I announced.

Professor Carlisle looked up from his paperwork, a delightful smile on his face. "Mister Taylor. It's a pleasure to see you. What, may I ask, is it you want to do?"

"I'll take that position on the school paper you offered me last year," I stated.

His face fell. I'd never seen him look so pale before. "I'm sorry, but *The Epitaph* is no longer in print. No one joined the newspaper club this semester."

"Then we'll bring it back," I said confidently.

Professor Carlisle laughed, like he thought I was joking. "And what? You'll write the whole paper? You'll be the only club member?"

I shrugged. "If I have to be."

He kept on laughing, like the idea was hilarious. "It would never work. We'd never have enough content."

"Then I'll start my own publication," I said simply. I hadn't even realized I came up with the idea until I said it. "I guess I won't need an advisor."

I turned around and started to leave, but Professor Carlisle stopped me. "Mister Taylor, wait!"

His laughter had completely died. I turned to face him.

He eyed me curiously. "What exactly is it you'd like to report on?"

"I want to investigate the missing children," I told him.

He adjusted his glasses. "Well, that is quite a heavy topic. Are you sure?"

"Absolutely," I said.

He cocked an eyebrow. "And you'd do this on your own?"

"Yes," I said, my mind made up.

He sighed. "That won't be necessary. The school already has printing resources available, and I must say I've missed advising on the paper. Let's bring *The Epitaph* back."

"Really?" I asked, hope surging in my chest.

Professor Carlisle nodded. "Really. Let me know as soon as you have something worth printing."

I nodded. "I will."

I left the room feeling like I'd seized some sort of power back from the perp who did this. Two kids were gone, and nothing was going to change that. But we could stop it from happening again.

Whoever murdered those kids better watch out…

Because I was coming for them.

nadine

TWO

Returning to Miriam College of Witchcraft after winter break felt like coming home. I'd only spent one semester here, and already I couldn't imagine living anywhere else. The pointed Gothic peaks of Miriam Mansion were like beacons welcoming me back. The deep red carpet spanning the Main Foyer and the dark wood tones of the walls were a comfort.

As Talia and I headed to class on our first day back, I couldn't take my eyes off the magic around me. Even after months living here, I was still entranced by it. Isa and Gus followed at our feet, and even the cats looked fascinated.

At the top of the grand staircase, someone had created a "Welcome Back" banner using orbs—magical lights that twinkled in a beautiful display. A trio of Mentalists used their telekinetic abilities to ride brooms around the iron chandelier. They tossed a black ball around, until a professor yelled at them. The three of them ducked out the double doors on their brooms, zooming out into the snow. Their laughter echoed throughout the foyer.

I smiled as I watched them fly away, but my attention was quickly caught by another group of witches. In the middle of the Main Foyer, a crowd of Mortana necromancers controlled mouse skeletons like puppets in a miniature rendition of *Wicked*. Onlookers gathered around as the Mortana sang an a cappella version of *No One Mourns the Wicked*. Talia started singing along and was still humming the tune long after we'd left the foyer.

In the long hallway, cats prowled beside their owners. A warlock rushed past us holding a toad. Ahead of us walked an Alchemy clique who all had matching cauldron tattoos on their arms. They passed around potions bottles like they were trading cards. A girl with blonde hair took a sip of one, and her golden hair transformed into a dark black with red streaks. Next to her, a guy downed a different potion. I didn't notice anything strange, until he turned a corner and I saw his nose had been replaced by a pig's nose. He snorted a few times, and everyone in his group laughed.

Talia and I passed by a study area. A dozen Seers sat around the tables, gazing into crystal balls and reading tarot. One girl held a piece of photo paper and pressed her hand to it. When she pulled away, an image of a ghostly figure was imprinted onto the paper. I knew the ability as thoughtography, where certain Seers could imprint psychic images onto surfaces. I was taking a thoughtography class this semester as an elective, even though I wasn't a Seer. We were required to take a certain number of electives outside our Cast, to earn our Cast diversity and appreciation credits. I felt thoughtography was a really amazing and unique ability, so I was excited to see someone using it.

We continued toward the stairs that led to the basement. As we reached them, a first-year student looked deep in concentration. He muttered the word *spellbook* under his breath, but instead of conjuring a spellbook, he conjured an entire blown-up river tube. It blocked the stairs and knocked him backward. I was about to ask if he needed help, but he quickly righted himself and subconjured the river tube, muttering curses as he hurried away in embarrassment.

All the magic was amazing to watch, but as we neared my classroom, I got a sinking feeling in my gut. I dropped my gaze.

Talia glanced to me. "Is something wrong?"

I shook my head, but my dark hair fell in front of my face to conceal it. I pushed it behind my ear. "Nothing. Just... feeling a little left out."

Talia frowned. I was the only Curse Breaker in the coven. With my powers, I could manipulate the flow of magic, which made me uniquely qualified to break curses. But I was the only one who could. I didn't have friends within my Cast to practice cool magic with like everyone else.

I tried to lighten the mood and quickly asked, "What do you get when you put a Curse Breaker in an Alchemy class?"

My best friend opened her mouth to answer, but I cut her off.

"Don't answer that," I groaned. "It's a terrible joke."

The answer to the question was: a total freaking disaster. But I didn't need a reminder.

We stopped next to one of the main Alchemy classrooms. Chatter spilled out into the empty hall from fellow classmates eager to brew their first potions. My stomach knotted as I thought about entering the room.

"Do you think they'll realize I'm a fraud?" I asked.

"Don't worry about it," Talia encouraged. "You have the mark of an Alchemist. You have your crystal. You can fool anyone."

I rubbed my fingers over the fresh cauldron tattoo on my forearm. It'd been three weeks since I'd gotten it, so it was healed and convincing. My true mark, the mark of a Curse Breaker, was hidden beneath my shirt, just above my hip. I'd come to really love the crescent moon tattoo, but I had to hide it.

Grammy had warned me of the dangers of being the only Curse Breaker in the coven. People would turn on me, threaten me, and use me to perform spells the coven hadn't been capable of for forty years. I feared that the Imperium would want me to do things I couldn't physically handle. With the way my lupus reacted when I used magic, I'd never be able to keep up with the coven's demands. I had to hide to protect myself.

"You *do* have your crystal, don't you?" Talia asked, noticing my hesitation.

"Yes, of course." I reached into my pocket and held up a small amethyst. Grammy had infused it with her own Alchemy magic before I came back to school. It was the only way to convince anyone I truly had Alchemy powers. But crystals like these were off-limits at school, as students could use them to enhance their powers and cheat on exams. I had no intention of letting anyone know I had it in my possession.

Talia took me by the shoulders and looked me straight in the eye. "Then you have nothing to worry about. You've got this, Nadine. I believe in you. Your grandma believes in you. Lucas believes in you."

Lucas. My heart ached just thinking about him. I hadn't seen him in weeks, and I missed him like the new moon missed the night sky. I'd left right after finals to visit my hometown. It was only an hour and a half drive, but it'd felt like thousands of miles. I barely had a day to get my cauldron tattoo and visit my parents' graves before the weight of my magic hit me. Turns out, my magic and my lupus didn't play well together.

Dr. Yonker had warned me this would happen. He reiterated it in my last appointment, right before I left. He promised things would get better, but that I had to keep using my magic, as that was the only way to train my body to handle it. In the meantime, I was going to feel worse and worse until my body got with the program.

So far, all I'd managed to do was create a few simple orbs and subconjure a tube of Chapstick. That was enough to knock me on my ass for weeks. I'd only just gotten back to Octavia Falls, and I hadn't seen Lucas yet. I couldn't wait to be in his arms again.

"You've all been really supportive," I told Talia. "But if this doesn't work—"

"It's *going* to work," she interrupted. "Now get in there and be the badass Nadine I know you are."

I couldn't help but smile at the compliment, but I didn't move right away.

Talia raised an eyebrow. "Aren't you at least curious to see what will happen?"

"Don't go using my curiosity against me," I warned lightheartedly.

She wrinkled her nose. "But it's so easy."

I nudged her in the shoulder. "Fine, I'm going."

Talia's voice turned serious again. "Good luck. I'll see you at lunch."

"Bye, Tal." I waved, then turned to the Alchemy lab. Steeling my nerves, I took a deep breath and stepped inside.

The Alchemy lab was located in the basement of the school, so there wasn't much light except from a small window set high in the wall. Tables stood in rows, and a black cauldron had been placed atop each one. Along the far wall were endless shelves, housing spell books, herbs, extracts, and other potion ingredients.

The walls were made of stone, with little crystals placed between the larger rocks. The crystals helped raise the vibrations in the room to assist in the alchemy process. Ever since my magic had been awakened, it was as if the entire world vibrated at a new frequency. I could sense magic like I never had before, and it was particularly strong in the Alchemy lab.

I glanced around the room, searching for a friendly face. Most everyone had been paired up at their tables already, and though I recognized my classmates, I didn't know any of them well. Gwen, one of Chloe's back-up bitches, noticed me in the doorway. She tossed her white-blonde hair over her shoulder, displaying the cauldron tattoo on her chest. She shot me a sneer, then turned to her table mate and whispered something under her breath. Scathing, I'm sure.

Whatever. I wasn't going to waste my time with Gwen or any of the Lucky Three. Those girls could go choke on a toad for all I cared.

Isa purred and rubbed up against my leg. I'd brought her along to class for emotional support. She gazed up at me with piercing green eyes, then shot a glance toward the back of the room.

A lone girl sat there, staring down at a spellbook. She had pale skin and thick black hair dyed purple on the ends. Her eyes were rimmed in dark makeup, and her lips were black to match her outfit. Her tight corset top accented her curvy figure. She had two silver piercings on her lower lips, which looked a little like vampire fangs at first glance. She took gothic style to the next level. I loved it.

She didn't exactly look out of place in the coven, but there was something about her—a sort of energy she put off—that made everyone else avoid her. Nobody looked her way. In fact, they all sort of acted like she didn't exist at all. I was equally intrigued by her as I was terrified.

I walked up to the girl and caught her attention. She glanced up at me with a totally bored expression on her face. "Can I help you?"

"Mind if I sit here?" I asked.

She glanced around the room, as if she was about to tell me to fuck off and go find another seat, but they were all taken.

She sighed heavily, half rolling her eyes. "Be my guest."

I sat down, and Isa jumped into my lap. I expected the girl to say something more, but she turned back to her spellbook, like she couldn't care less about her new lab partner.

"I'm Nadine," I offered.

She looked up and frowned, like I was bothering her. "Onyx," she introduced.

"Sweet name," I told her. "I love your nails."

Her nails were black, with a symbol from each Cast painted in deep purple.

Onyx shot me a confused look, like she couldn't figure out why I was talking to her. "Uh, thanks."

"Where'd you get them done at?" I asked. Maybe having one friend in this class would make the whole semester go smoothly.

Some of the darkness in Onyx's eyes lifted, though not all of it. "I did them myself."

"I really like them—" I started to say, but Professor Richards strolled into the room at that moment, cutting me off.

"Quiet down, please," he called. "I'm Professor Richards, and this is Alchemy 101."

It was the same greeting he used my first day in Miriamic History last semester. He'd been an incredible storyteller, so I was thrilled to see he was teaching Alchemy.

"Today, we'll be brewing our first potion," he announced. "It's quite simple, just to get you acquainted with the equipment. Please turn your spellbooks to page three."

All around the room, students conjured their school-issued spellbooks out of thin air. I shyly reached into my bag and pulled out my book. Onyx eyed me curiously, then glanced down at the tattoo on my arm, as if questioning my status.

"I'm still a total newbie," I admitted. "Haven't perfected conjuring yet."

She turned away, like she didn't care for an explanation. At least she hadn't asked any more questions. Conjuring shouldn't be hard, but it used up unnecessary magic.

The sound of students shuffling to open their spellbooks filled the room. I turned mine to page three and saw that we were brewing an elixir for relaxation. Perfect. I could use one of those.

"We'll start with the front of the class," Professor Richards said, gesturing the first row forward. "Once you've gathered your ingredients, you may begin brewing."

While we waited our turn, I read through the instructions. It seemed simple enough. All we had to do was mix lavender oil with sage leaves and speak an incantation. Still, I was worried. When I'd practiced transferring magic from a crystal to a potion at Grammy's house, all I did was burn the water. I didn't even know you *could* burn water.

Grammy said it was a good sign, that at least I was transferring magic.

It was enough to convince my professor I had Alchemy magic, at least. I just hoped it was enough for me to pass.

It finally came our turn, and Onyx and I returned to our table with our ingredients. I sat in my chair, but Onyx stood over the cauldron. Isa sat on my lap, peeking over the top of the table.

"I'll crush the sage," I offered.

Onyx didn't say anything, just started measuring out lavender oil. I figured the cold shoulder was sort of her thing, but she could at least say something, right? I mean, we *were* working together.

Onyx poured the oil into the cauldron, and I added the sage. She turned on the burner and began stirring. Her lips moved to mutter the incantation, but I barely heard her. Dark purple tendrils of magic swirled out of her fingers like smoke and filled the cauldron.

Each member of the coven had their own color of magic. I'd learned that my magic was a dark blue. Onyx's purple magic nearly shimmered. It was mesmerizing.

The strong scent of lavender filled my nostrils, and I could sense the buzz of her magic activating the potion. I watched in awe as she worked effortlessly. Maybe being Onyx's partner wouldn't be so bad, since she was willing to do the work herself.

Professor Richards walked around the room with his hands clasped behind his back. He was ancient, but he moved with grace. He stopped at our table to observe Onyx's magic. The purple tendrils separated from her fingers, then floated down seamlessly into the cauldron.

"Very good, Miss Foxe," he praised. He leaned over the cauldron and took a deep breath. "It's effective, but could use slightly more potency. Should we give Miss Evers a chance to try?"

I stiffened at the suggestion. "You want me to add more magic to the brew?"

"The more magic in the potion, the stronger it will be," Professor Richards said simply.

"I'm not very practiced," I admitted. "My Evoking Ceremony was only a few weeks ago."

"Everything you need is right there in your spellbook," he said, stabbing the page with his index finger. "What more do you need, Miss Evers?"

In front of us, a student caught his attention with a question.

"Excuse me a moment." Professor Richards gave us a polite nod, then headed a few tables away.

Onyx looked down at me and held out the mixing spoon. "Here," she said impatiently.

I stood to look over the cauldron and sighed heavily. If I could pull this off, I'd convince the whole school I was a true Alchemist. This potion was my one chance to thwart off any suspicion.

Discreetly, I reached into my pocket and pulled out my amethyst crystal. I clung to it tightly in one hand and held the other over the cauldron as I'd seen Onyx do. I glanced down at the incantation in the book.

Light of sun and songs majestic
Make this potion soothe the restless.

I didn't need the incantation. My magic didn't work the same as Alchemists did. As a Curse Breaker, I could control the flow of magic—take it from one place and put it in another. That's why I could use the Alchemy crystal. All I had to do was transfer Grammy's Alchemy magic from the amethyst into the potion.

But if I didn't speak the incantation, I'd come off as a fraud. So I began muttering it under my breath while trying to focus my energy on the crystal. I felt the magic buzzing inside of it. When I focused intently on it, I could taste a sugary sweetness on my tongue, with a citrus aftertaste.

I followed the instructions Grammy had given me; envision the magic as a water current. I pictured it flowing through my veins, and used that to control the pathways through my body. Then, I directed it outward through my hands.

Dark blue magic began to swirl out of my fingers. My heart surged in triumph, but I'd barely gotten started. I imagined the magic flowing down into the cauldron, and it followed my command.

The arm I held above the cauldron began to weaken with each passing second. It felt as if I was holding a fifty-pound weight out in front of me. My knees shook beneath me as a wave of fatigue hit. The fatigue was a symptom of lupus—it was my body reacting to the magic flowing through it. I longed to drop my hand, to collapse back into my chair, but I'd be damned if I gave up so easily. I pushed past it and steadied myself against the edge of the table with the hand that grasped the crystal.

"Whoa, you okay?" Onyx's voice cut through my concentration. "You look really pale."

"I've got this," I told her through gritted teeth.

But I was lying. One moment I was staring down at the blue smoke coming from my fingers. The next it flickered a blinding white, like a crack of lightning. A huge *boom* sounded through the room, and a blast shot Onyx and me backward. I hadn't even processed what had happened before I was lying flat on my back on the floor.

The sound of Isa crying loudly from my side was the only thing to ground me to the present. My vision became dark, but slowly and surely, the room came back into view. My heart hammered rapidly. I struggled to my elbows to see that the cauldron had split clear in two. A huge purple cloud of smoke hovered above it. Our elixir was running all over the table and down into the flames. A gag-inducing smell of burnt lavender assaulted my nose, and people started pinching their noses and complaining loudly. A few girls at the front of the room even ran out into the hall, claiming the stench was going to make them puke.

"Dear Goddess!" Professor Richards cried. He hurried to our station and quickly shut off our burner, then came to my side.

Onyx was already getting to her feet. She didn't say anything, but the dark glare she sent me as she dusted off her black skirt was enough. This girl may have been the loner when I walked in the room, but I was the real freak in this class.

"Miss Evers, are you all right?" Professor Richards asked.

"Fine," I lied, pressing my palm to my pounding head. "I'm sorry about the cauldron. I'm not feeling well."

Professor Richards didn't inquire further. It wasn't a secret that my father was human, and it didn't take much to deduce that I was sick. It didn't happen to all half-witches, but according to Dr. Yonker, autoimmune diseases were common among mixed children. My lupus wasn't a huge secret around here.

"Why don't you head back to your dorm?" Professor Richards suggested.

"But the cauldron—" I started.

"We'll get this cleaned up," he assured me. "Miss Knight, can you get some towels from the supply closet?"

Gwen's jaw dropped. "*Me?*"

"Yes, please hurry," Professor Richards said sternly as he helped me sit up.

Gwen poked her table mate in the side. "Come on, Stacey."

Stacey followed beside her. Gwen sneered as she walked by me. She leaned over and whispered to Stacey. "That's so unfair. Is he just going to let her out of class every time she fucks something up? She'll be gone every class period."

Stacey snickered under her breath.

What the hell, bitch? This girl didn't even know me.

By the way Stacey looked down her nose at me, I could only guess Chloe had been talking about me behind my back—and whatever lies she made up must've been pretty nasty.

Professor Richards pulled me to my feet, though I could barely stand. I immediately collapsed into my chair.

"Will you need help back to your room?" he asked.

"No," I replied, still trying to catch my breath. I didn't like being coddled, even if I could hardly walk sometimes from fatigue.

"Are you sure?" he pressed.

"I'll be fine," I nearly snapped at him. "I just need a moment."

I was aware of all my classmates' eyes on me, but I'd used up so much energy trying to do that spell that I had no fucks left to give. I leaned my elbows on the table and buried my face in my hands.

Why? Why? Why? I cursed my body. That spell was literally the easiest one in the book. If I couldn't do that, I had no hope of passing this class.

"Here," Onyx said, pulling me from my thoughts. I looked up to see her holding out my amethyst crystal. "You dropped this."

Her eyebrows knitted together as she stared down at it, like she could sense something wasn't quite right.

I quickly snatched it out of her hand. "Thanks."

Gwen and Stacey returned with the towels, and Professor Richards started mopping up the spilled potion.

"She's not even a full witch," Gwen whispered loudly to Stacey, like having only one parent from the Miriamic Coven made my magic less valid.

"I'm not surprised," Stacey whispered back. "She doesn't look like she knows what she's doing."

I wasn't going to sit here and listen to this. On any normal day, I'd tell the bitches to fuck off, but I didn't have the energy right now. I grabbed my spellbook and shoved it in my bag, along with my crystal, then started out of the room. Isa followed, but she stopped at Gwen's row and growled at her.

Gwen threw her head back in laughter. "Oh, like I'm scared of a *cat*."

Gwen hissed at Isa in distaste.

"Isa," I called, before my cat got herself into trouble. Her ears perked up, and she hurried along beside me.

I was relieved when I made it out of the room, but I could hardly keep myself upright. I had to steady myself against the wall. When I reached the stairs, it felt like they stretched a mile above me. I sat on the bottom step to catch my breath before climbing them. I had a grudge against stairways.

But I held a bigger grudge against failure. I was going to figure out my powers—and I was going to make one hell of a convincing Alchemist.

I stayed to catch my breath a few minutes longer, but I wanted to be long gone by the time class let out. After I managed to drag myself upstairs, I returned to my dorm room. I didn't have long until my next class, but I snuggled up with Isa and looked over my schedule. Once I sat down, I didn't want to get back up.

Eventually, I convinced myself that skipping the first day of class was no way to start the semester. I just hoped I didn't have to use magic the rest of the day.

Isa purred lightly and had fallen asleep on the cushion beside me. I gathered my things and left without her.

Meditation and Inner Magic was held in one of the yoga studios. When I walked in, I found Professor Wykoff sitting cross-legged on a yoga mat at the front of the room. Her eyes were closed, and she held her hands together at her chest.

"Welcome, Miss Evers," she said without opening her eyes. She spoke in a quiet, melodic voice. "Please take a seat wherever you feel comfortable."

I hesitated and glanced around the room. Ten other students were already here, each getting comfortable on their own mats.

"How'd you know it was me?" I asked.

I'd had Professor Wykoff last semester for Introduction to Tarot, so we were acquainted well, but she hadn't opened her eyes to look at me.

"You have a distinct walk," she said lightly, still taking deep breaths. "You tread softly, on the balls of your feet, and slow, like each movement is calculated."

I began setting up my yoga mat in an empty space near her. "Can you tell all your students by the way they walk?"

"Not everyone," she admitted. "Some I can tell by the energy of their breath; others by the magic they give off. You will learn to do the same in this class. There is much to learn in the stillness. The more you discern your inner energy, the more you can understand the external."

"It all sounds very exciting," I told her genuinely.

As soon as everyone arrived, Professor Wykoff began leading us through a guided meditation. All we had to do was lie flat on our backs and listen to her voice. I ended up drifting off pretty quickly. When I woke at the end of class, I felt much better, like some of my energy had returned. Meditation and Inner Magic was officially my favorite class.

I left class with my mat strap over my shoulder. I was passing through the Main Foyer on my way back to the dorm when my eyes caught a lock of brown hair. My heart stopped for a moment, before kicking alive and hammering like crazy.

Lucas stood at the fireplace, looking sexier than I remembered. My eyes roamed over his long legs and broad shoulders. I noticed the chain from the key necklace I'd given him poking out from beneath his shirt. One of his hands rested on the fireplace mantle, while the other was shoved into the pocket of his jeans. He stared down into the burning coals with a deeply contemplative look on his face. His arms were covered in his signature gray zip-up hoodie, but his t-shirt was lifted slightly, showing off a sliver of skin above his waistband. All I wanted to do was run my fingers along it, and do other things I probably shouldn't be considering.

Slowly, Lucas's gaze lifted until his eyes landed on me. It was as if he had sensed me enter the room, like he was drawn to me by some inexplicable force—the same that drew me to him. His mesmerizing green eyes sparkled, and for a moment I was starstruck, frozen in place. A smile touched the corners of his lips, and I beamed back.

Lucas dropped his arm from the fireplace and approached me. When he walked, I swore I could hear a choir singing somewhere in the back of my mind. He was like an angel on earth. An angel of death, perhaps—but an angel nonetheless.

Lucas reached me, and it was in that moment I realized I'd been holding my breath. I sighed, feeling relieved.

"Nad," he said breathlessly as he reached out to catch a lock of my hair. "My little miracle."

"Miracle?" I asked.

He shrugged and tucked my hair behind my ear. "You came back from the dead. You're my miracle."

My heart swooned, and I realized I very much liked him calling me that. If it weren't for Lucas, I wouldn't be here. He'd saved me from death. I owed him my life, but I'd gladly give up anything for him. I'd been willing to give up my soul in exchange for his, and I'd do it all over again if he asked.

"I missed you so much," I whispered, before flinging my arms around his waist.

He winced, and I pulled back. I'd forgotten for a second he was still healing from fighting the reaper the night of my ceremony. He'd literally fought off a reaper to keep me from being taken to the Abyss. He could take my life, my heart, my *everything*. I was his now.

I bit my lower lip. "Sorry."

He wrapped his arms tighter around me and stared into my eyes. "Don't worry about it."

I didn't waste a second before standing on my toes and pressing my lips to his. Lucas gasped in surprise, like he didn't expect me to kiss him in front of the whole school, but I didn't care. He relaxed quickly and brought his hands to my face, cradling it as the passion surged between us.

My stomach flipped, like taking the deep dive at the top of a roller coaster. My heart felt like it was floating in my chest, but it pounded furiously at the same time. I could swear the floor had dropped from beneath our feet, like the only thing keeping me grounded in place was Lucas's hands on mine. All I wanted to do was get him alone.

Far too soon, we drew away from each other. Lucas's eyes remained closed, like he was drinking in the high from the kiss for a few moments longer. I felt lighter than I had all month. Drawing him closer, I pressed my nose into his shirt. His spiced pumpkin and apple scent filled my nostrils. It was stronger than I remembered, like being away from him so long had left me ravenous for his scent. A wave of serenity washed over me, permeating down into my bones. It was amazing the effect he had on me.

Lucas held me tight and pressed his nose into my hair. "I missed you, too. Winter break was hell without you."

"I'm sorry," I said as I drew away. "I wanted to see you sooner, but I got sick."

Lucas reached up and ran his fingers through my hair. "Hey, don't apologize for being sick."

I winced. "Habit."

Lucas's hands trailed down my arms, until they stopped at my hands. I entwined my fingers through his. Just touching him sent me spiraling upward on this high I thought I might never come down from.

He gazed down at me longingly. "You have no idea how much I missed you."

"What?" I teased with a smirk. "Texting wasn't enough to satisfy you?"

To be honest, it was a little more than just *texting*.

He smiled back. "Was it enough to satisfy *you*?"

"Hell no!" I said without thinking about it. I pressed my lips together as a blush rose to my cheeks. "I mean…"

Lucas leaned in close to me. His warm breath brushed across my ear, sending tingles down to my toes. "There's so much I missed doing with you."

I glanced around the foyer. Several people sat in study areas, and others headed up and down the stairs, but no one paid us any attention.

"We can fix that," I whispered.

Lucas's eyes blazed with hunger as I took his hand firmly in mine and dragged him down the hall. My eyes darted around for a private location and landed on the glass doors of the greenhouse. I dragged him inside. It was warm inside, and the shelves were lined with all types of magical plants. The nearest one had black flowers shaped like potion vials. Another had bright pink buds with tentacles that moved. In the center of the greenhouse was a huge Venus fly trap. A bee buzzed by, and the plant snapped at it, consuming it within its leaves.

Lucas and I were alone, but our hands did all the talking. The moment we were concealed inside the greenhouse, I dropped my yoga mat at my feet and grabbed Lucas by the collar. I dragged him toward me, and our lips connected. His hips pressed into mine, until I was backed against the wall. I raked my fingers through his hair as his tongue slid into my mouth, sending heat pooling between my thighs. If I thought my heart was going crazy earlier, it was nothing compared to making out with him.

Lucas's hands roamed up and down my body, like he wanted to savor every inch of me. Slowly, he pushed the hem of my shirt upward, and his hands settled on my hips. His thumbs moved to caress my skin. My nipples hardened beneath my shirt, and I arched my back to invite his hands up further—

But he didn't get the hint. Lucas drew away breathlessly.

"Hey," I teased. "I wasn't finished."

He chuckled lightly, but when I reached up to draw him closer, he pushed my hands away. "We can't get carried away," he reminded me.

I dropped my hands at my sides and spoke softly. "We won't. I will *never* make you do anything you don't want to do."

"I know. It's just… the Reaper's Shadow curse is real, and I don't want you getting hurt."

The Reaper's Shadow was a curse upon the mate of the Reaper's Apprentice. In other words, the further Lucas and I went, the more we risked.

"The lines are clear," I replied. "If we have sex, I come down with a terrible illness. Anything before that should be safe. But we'll stop at whatever lines you want to draw."

"I just don't know what's safe," he admitted. "Are we counting oral?"

I nudged him playfully. "Do you really think I'd blow you right here?"

Truth was, I would if he asked me.

He chuckled, like he enjoyed the picture in his mind. "No, but you still didn't answer my question."

"I was *hoping* we'd get that far some day, but if you don't want to, we won't." I reached out to take his hand in mine. "We'll only go as far as you're comfortable with. But I don't want you to be scared of the Reaper's Shadow curse, either. The stages are sex, marriage, and kids. There's a consequence for each, but we don't have to go that far."

"Do you really want that?" Lucas asked, sounding hesitant. "Can you really live with not ever having kids?"

"If it means I get you, yes," I said honestly. Kids were great, but they were never high on my list of must-haves. Before Octavia Falls, I'd planned to become a homicide detective. Kids had never really been a part of that picture.

"But you still want to have sex," he stated.

"Of course I do. I want to be with you in every way possible." I ran my fingers across his chest, admiring the shape of his body. It wasn't so much about the sex. I could die a virgin if I had to. It was the sex with *him*. I wanted him so badly I'd gladly lay down my life for his. I couldn't keep my desire for him bottled up forever. I could take a little illness to show him just how much I cared.

He grabbed my wrists to stop me. "You already have one disease. Cursing you to another could kill you."

I dropped my gaze. Illness, I could deal with. But now that he put it that way, I wasn't sure.

"We'll avoid anything you're uncomfortable with, until I learn how to use my gift and can break this curse," I promised.

Lucas raked his fingers through his hair. "This curse is dangerous for you, though. Remember that the guy who cast it murdered his own *mother*."

"I know, but Mother Miriam chose me for a reason. I *have* to be able to break this curse somehow."

Lucas squeezed my hand. "I wish it were that easy, but the magic could overwhelm you. You have to understand. I just want to protect you."

When he put it that way, it was hard to argue. Problem was, I wasn't going to give up on this curse. I wanted to be with Lucas without fear of slipping up. That was the worst part—the fear. It felt as if we were chained down, unable to get close enough to touch. Lucas and I needed our freedom from that fear if we were to make this work long-term. And we *would* make this work, because there were no other options. He was it for me, the only person I ever wanted to be with. And I knew he felt the same way about me.

But he asked me to take things slow, and I would honor that.

"We don't have to do anything," I told him. "I just need to know where you draw the line, so we don't cross it."

Lucas thought about it for a moment.

"I don't need your answer now," I offered. "You can think about it as long as you want."

"I don't have to," he said, sounding confident. "I want to be with you in every way we can. We draw the line at sex. I'm comfortable with everything before that."

Lucas leaned in, and my pulse quickened. He pressed his lips to mine, and though the kiss was gentle, heat flared in my thighs. He trailed his lips across my skin, ending at the sensitive area below my ear. His breath sent tingles down my spine. "I can't wait to try it all out."

I laughed as he kissed me again. "Me either, but probably not right here in the greenhouse."

He drew away, smirking. "You're probably right."

He took my hand, and we left the greenhouse. "I hope you kept busy over break."

I shrugged. "If binge-watching TV and cuddling my cat counts."

"You must've done more than that."

"I read some good mystery novels, and did *lots* of oracle card spreads."

Lucas cocked an eyebrow. "Learn anything interesting?"

The truth was, most of the spreads were regarding him. I'd pulled so many cards over the last few weeks I couldn't make sense of what the readings meant anymore.

"I'm still trying to decipher the cards," I admitted. "What about you?"

He glanced around the hall, but no one was watching us. "I've been waiting to tell you until you got back. I talked to the Imperium Council about the missing boys."

My eyebrows shot up. "Do they know anything?"

He shook his head. "Just that these cases are crazy weird. Anyway, I talked to Professor Carlisle, and he's willing to bring back *The Epitaph*."

I shot him a curious look. "*The Epitaph*?"

"The school paper," Lucas clarified. "I want to report on the missing kids."

My jaw dropped. "You're going into investigative journalism?"

"You sound surprised."

"I just… didn't picture you as a reporter, though you do have a way with words," I said. "Gotta admit, I'm a little jealous."

"Jealous?" he questioned.

I smirked. "Out of the two of us, who would you think is more likely to launch an investigation?"

"You," he admitted without missing a beat.

Surely he hadn't forgotten how I'd followed the Treacherous Tarantulas to their hideout last semester. I was itching for an adventure.

"You're welcome to help me," Lucas offered.

"I wish." I sighed. "I'll be lucky to drag my butt halfway across town until I figure this whole magic thing out and what it's doing to my body."

Lucas got a concerned look on his face. "How are you feeling?"

I shrugged. I wasn't about to lie to him. "Same as usual—kinda shitty."

"Nad, you have to tell me these things. Don't leave me guessing. If you need anything, you have to ask." Lucas placed his hands on my shoulders and stared down at me with a gentle gaze. "Let me take care of you."

I didn't want anyone taking care of me, but when Lucas offered, my stomach flipped a hundred times over. If anyone were to take care of me, I wanted it to be him.

"Okay," I agreed. "I'll make sure to ask."

"Good." He placed a kiss on the top of my head. "Do you need anything right now?"

"Lunch?" I suggested. "Talia and I were going to meet up."

"Lunch sounds perfect." Lucas took my hand, and we walked to the cafeteria. We filled up our plates and spotted Talia and Grant waving us over to their table.

I noticed Grant's hair was wet. "How was your morning swim?" I asked.

He leaned forward with bright eyes. "Fantastic! I made my best time yet. I'm going to try out for the swim team this year."

Talia moved a stack of lyrics from beside her to make room for me.

I tilted my head. "The college has a swim team?"

"Sort of," Lucas said as he sat.

Grant shot him a look. "I mean, it's more of an individual sport. We don't compete against other schools, but I'll swim against other students —if I make the team. There are only so many competition slots."

"It sounds like fun," Talia said brightly, popping a tater tot in her mouth.

Grant beamed. "You should try out!"

She laughed lightly. "Uh, no. I'm not a swimmer."

"Then try out for the diving team," Grant suggested. "We could, you know... *hang out*." His voice dropped at the last few words, like he felt self-conscious about suggesting it.

Talia didn't seem to notice. "I'd rather focus on music, but thanks for the invitation. I'll watch you from the stands."

Grant looked pleased by the offer.

"So, how was everyone's break?" I asked.

Grant slumped in his chair, like he was trying to look cool. "Visited my *abuela* in Costa Rica, so you know. Beaches, babes, the whole shebang."

Lucas shot him a look. "I thought you said you spent the whole time running the front desk at your grandmother's hotel."

Grant's face paled, and he straightened in his chair. "Yeah, but it's like *on* the beach. And there were a lot of hot girls."

Talia snickered. "Did you get any of their numbers?"

Grant huffed, like he was so done with this inquiry. "I wasn't interested in a long-distance thing."

"In other words, you tried, and they turned you down," I teased.

Grant rolled his eyes playfully.

I was still chuckling as I brought my water to my lips. Just then, someone walked by our table and kicked the leg, jostling everything. My water splashed up into my face, and Lucas's drink spilled everywhere, getting all over his pants.

"Watch it, douchebag!" Lucas snarled.

The guy scoffed, and I looked up to see it was Ryan—prime asshole of the school.

"Didn't see you there," Ryan said in a fake-ass voice. He turned away and joined up with his buddies, who were all laughing wildly like it was the most clever prank on the planet. Ryan coughed and muttered *losers* under his breath.

I rolled my eyes at them. "Real mature!" I called.

Ryan caught my eye and scowled. Meanwhile, Grant flipped them off, but none of them noticed. Talia rushed to grab napkins and helped Lucas clean up the water.

"Sorry about those guys," Lucas muttered.

"Don't apologize for them," Grant said. "Those jerks are high or something."

I snorted. I mean, it wasn't untrue.

"Grant's right," Talia agreed. "They're totally not worth your energy."

Lucas wiped up the last of the water. "I can handle them. I just don't need you three getting caught in the crosshairs."

"That's sweet, but we're fine," I assured him.

"For sure." Talia lifted her gaze, and her eyes caught something across the cafeteria. "Oh, there's Cody!"

Grant shot a scathing look over his shoulder at Talia's boyfriend. She waved him over. Cody was a total hottie, but I hardly knew him.

"Hey, Cody," Talia said brightly.

"Hi, beautiful," he practically sang. He leaned down to peck Talia on the lips and pulled something from behind his back when she wasn't watching. It was a bouquet of red roses.

She squealed when she saw them, then took them in her hands to smell them. "Goddess, I love them. Why don't you join us?"

Cody's dark eyes roamed the table, until landing on the pile of wet napkins in the center. His face fell. "It looks like your table's full. Why don't you sit by me?" He cocked his head toward a larger table, where a bunch of couples sat around sucking face.

Talia glanced at us, as if asking permission. None of us responded. I mean, what were we supposed to say? *No, you can't go sit by your boyfriend?*

"I, um... was eating with my friends," she said.

"I've got a seat reserved just for you." He leaned over the table, close enough to whisper something in her ear.

She snickered and pushed him away playfully. "*Cody!*"

He smirked down at her. "I'm not giving up. I want you to sit by me, babe."

Cody reached over and snatched up Talia's stack of lyrics. He held them behind his back, and she grabbed for them.

"Cody, give it back," she laughed.

He smiled, like he enjoyed the game. "I'll give it back when you come sit by me."

Talia sighed and dropped her shoulders. "Fair enough. Next time, we'll get a bigger table we can all fit at. Sorry, guys."

Talia grabbed her plate and shot us an apologetic expression.

"Bye, Tal," I said.

Grant gave her a half-hearted salute as she left the table, but his expression soured as Cody draped an arm around Talia's shoulder.

As soon as she was out of earshot, he leaned forward and whispered. "*I'm* the one who feels sorry for *her*. Anyone else hate that guy?"

I poked at my food. "Hate's a pretty strong word."

Lucas shrugged. "I don't really know him."

"Come on, you guys," Grant begged. "He steals Talia away every chance he gets. He doesn't like any of us."

"He hasn't had the chance to get to know us," I pointed out. "As long as he makes her happy, I don't care."

Grant raised an eyebrow. "*Does* he, though?"

Lucas nudged Grant's arm. "Sounds like someone's a little jealous."

Grant frowned. "Yeah, yeah. We all know I've got the hots for her. That's not what this is about."

"Sorry," I said. "But it's Talia's choice."

Grant sighed and turned back to his food, but I didn't miss the daggers he kept shooting at the back of Cody's head.

After lunch, Grant and Lucas both had class, so I headed back to my dorm by myself. It was when I turned the corner at the top of the stairs that I nearly ran into someone. It was a raven-haired girl in a tight black dress and thick tights. I took a step back, and the girl turned around.

My hands curled into fists when I saw it was Chloe. I didn't know why clenching my fists was my go-to response now, but every time I saw her face, I just knew some shit was about to go down.

Chloe had it out for me because of the curse over our families. Forty years ago, our grandfathers got into a brawl. Her grandpa murdered mine and cast a curse that allowed only one family to stay within Octavia Falls each generation. From what I'd heard, Jeb Olson had died a few years back, after serving out his prison sentence for murder. But still, the curse lived on.

One of us had to leave town… or die. If we didn't sort this out ourselves, the curse would do it for us. As soon as Chloe's magic awakened, the curse would be activated. We were locked in a battle over our home.

Chloe's features darkened when her eyes met mine. She stood next to Gwen and Camille. In unison, the three of them crossed their arms, like they'd practiced the coordinated move in private.

Chloe pursed her lips and stuck out her hip. "Nadine. I have to admit, I wasn't sure you'd come back this semester."

I cocked an eyebrow. "Why? Because I beat you to my Evoking Ceremony?"

Chloe scoffed. "Just because you're a few months older than me doesn't make you special."

"It does give me the upper hand," I said coolly.

Chloe eyed me up and down, chuckling lightly. "What are you going to do, use defensive magic on me? According to Gwen, you passed out performing the *simplest* of spells. So by all means, I'd love to see what you've got."

"Sorry," I shrugged. "I don't waste my magic on people who don't matter."

Chloe's face paled. I went to step around her, but she blocked my path.

"I told you not to go through with your ceremony," she warned.

"Whoops," I said flatly. "Forgot I was supposed to be taking orders from you."

"I mean it," she growled. "You don't want to mess with this curse that's over our families."

She eyed me with a burning threat in her eyes, but I wasn't scared.

"So, what? You're going to kill me to keep your place in the coven?" I asked. "That's a real good way to get kicked out."

Chloe opened her mouth, but the words halted on her tongue. She snapped her jaw shut and recovered quickly. "You're *going* to leave."

I placed a hand on my hip and lifted my chin. "Is that so? Octavia Falls is *my* home, too. So maybe *you* should get out of town."

Chloe took a step forward and gritted her teeth. "I'm not going anywhere. My ceremony is the beginning of May. You have until then before the curse activates."

It was clear this was quickly becoming a deadly game of chicken. Neither of us were willing to give up our home.

"I guess we'll see how I feel about it then," I said nonchalantly, though I knew my feelings wouldn't change. I'd risk the curse to stay here.

"Don't make me do this," Chloe warned.

"Do what?" I asked innocently, though I knew exactly what she meant. She'd do anything in her power to drive me out of town. "I'm not *making* you do anything."

I pushed past her and headed down the hall to my room.

"You'll regret this!" she called after me. "One way or another, you *will* leave."

I turned back to her once I reached my door. "Have fun trying to drive me out of town."

I waved like I didn't have a care in the world. Gwen and Camille both stared after me with mouths agape, but I stepped into my room and closed the door before the Lucky Three could say anything else.

Problem was, the second I slipped inside, all my confidence dropped at the door. I slumped against the wall, worry knotting in my gut. Chloe was ruthless and unforgiving. And I just gave her an invitation to come at me.

I knew the coven had rules, and they just might protect me… for now.

But I couldn't say with certainty that Chloe wouldn't take things too far to get what she wanted.

I had to learn how to break curses—before either Chloe or I ended up dead.

THREE

I wanted Nadine more than I wanted anything in the world. Seeing her again was like a rain cloud had lifted from above me. She wasn't just a ray of sun to brighten my gloomy days. She was the whole damn sun—and she lit up my world. No, she *was* my world, the reason for my existence.

That was why I had to do everything I could to protect her. Nadine had tried to give her life for mine, and I could never thank her enough. I could never let anything bad happen to her. That started with making sure Octavia Falls was safe for her—for *everyone*. I had to catch the murderer still roaming these streets.

"What'd Nadine think when you told her about your article?" Grant asked. He lounged on his bed, flipping through his textbook for *Alchemy 202: Transfiguration Potions.* "She loves a good mystery."

"She was curious," I said as I grabbed a fresh notebook from my desk and subconjured it. "But she has enough to focus on without me asking for her help with this case."

"I'm sure that's not all she's curious about," Grant teased, wiggling his eyebrows.

I rolled my eyes.

"I wish Talia would get curious about me," he added.

"You haven't even made a move on Talia," I pointed out.

Grant shifted uncomfortably. "I'm waiting for the right time. It'll happen."

To be honest, I wasn't sure it would. Grant was all talk and no action. It was starting to get irritating to watch.

"I hope it does," I said honestly. I wasn't holding my breath.

I scoured the desk for a pen or pencil, but couldn't find one. "Do you have a pen I can borrow?"

"Sure." Grant sat up to grab one from the cup on his desk. "What for?"

"I have my first interview for my piece on the missing kids," I told him.

Grant's eyebrows shot up. "The families are going to talk?"

"I guess so," I said. I could hardly believe it, either. "I called Caleb Thomas's parents, and they were thrilled to hear someone was investigating again. I'm finally feeling better after my run-in with that reaper, and I managed to set up a proper interview."

Grant's shoulders fell. "Do you really think you can find out what happened to the kids?"

I pressed my lips together. "I don't know. But I'm going to try."

I didn't care what it took. I had to do everything in my power. I didn't know what exactly that looked like yet, but I had a duty to protect this coven. Mother Miriam wouldn't have given me this gift if she didn't want me to use it for good. I'd heard more than once that the coven was in danger, and I wasn't about to ignore those warnings.

The first dying thought had come from Nadine's mother. *The coven's in danger. Stay safe, Nadine. I love you.*

I ran her message over again and again in my mind as I left campus. Faith Evers hadn't said *how* the coven was in danger, but this had to be it. It was almost like she knew something about Caleb's disappearance. I didn't know *how* she knew. She'd been an Alchemist, not a Seer who might've actually had a vision about it. Either way, I couldn't ignore this.

Isaac Miller had given me a similar warning when he died. *Playtime is over. No child in the coven is safe.* I'd be damned if I didn't do something to protect the coven's children.

The walk wasn't long, and it was nice out for the end of January. It was Saturday, but the street was quiet. I stopped at the end of a shoveled walkway, looking over the house. The Thomas' house was tall and narrow, with two stories and a sharp, peaked roof. I eyed the property for clues, but nothing stuck out at me as suspicious.

I approached the door and hesitated a moment before knocking. The sound of my knuckles was barely audible over the pounding of my own heart. I wasn't much of a people-person, and I had zero experience in journalism. I'd be lucky if I managed to pull off this interview.

The door swung open, and a woman with dark bangs and a ponytail stood behind it. She looked like she'd been expecting me.

"Krista Thomas?" I asked. "We spoke on the phone."

"Yes, hi," she greeted brightly. "You're the journalist?"

It took me a second to process the answer, because no one had ever called me a journalist before. I cleared my throat. "That's me. May I come in?"

"Of course." She pulled the door open wider, and I stepped inside.

"I'm Lucas Taylor," I introduced, reaching out to shake her hand. It felt really awkward and formal. Like I said, I was *not* a people-person. "I'm working on a piece about your son for the school's paper, *The Epitaph*. I was hoping I could ask you and your husband a few questions."

"Yes, anything." She gestured to the couch, then called down the hall. "Keith, sweetie! The journalist is here."

There was no response.

"Hang on a second," she said kindly. "He's probably in the garage. I'll go get him."

Krista left the room, and I shifted uncomfortably on the couch. I glanced around the room, as if I might find clues there. Their house was big and tidy, with a homey feel to it. They obviously had a sense of artistic taste I completely lacked, because all the colors matched in shades of brown and red. There was a big, ornate clock on the wall, across from a display of family photos that were arranged atop a huge wall decal shaped like a tree. In a hutch sat a collection of alchemy supplies, which wasn't unusual, since both the parents were Alchemists. They seemed like a positively normal family.

As my eyes roamed over the family pictures on the walls, I noticed a young boy in most of them. *Caleb*.

I found myself drawn to the photographs, and I stood from the couch to get a closer look. The first photo showed the young boy being pushed on a swing at the park. The man pushing him looked at least ten years my senior. I guess that was his dad. Another showed the two at the pool, with the young boy in a floatie while his dad looked up at the camera.

I noticed Krista didn't appear in most of the photos. I thought that was kind of weird, until I glanced across the room and noticed a camera bag on the entertainment center. Then it hit me that she'd been the one to *take* the pictures.

I looked back to the photos and spotted one where Caleb sat in front of a birthday cake. There were six candles on it. Poor kid. That was the last birthday cake he ever had.

"He's cute, isn't he?" a male voice asked.

I whirled around to see a man standing there. He was the guy in the photos—Caleb's father. He held a dish cloth in his hands and looked to be polishing something. His pants were covered in sawdust.

"Sorry, I didn't hear you come in," he apologized. "I was doing some woodworking in the garage."

"Oh?" I asked curiously. "What are you working on?"

He pulled a small object out of the cloth and showed me a wooden carving of a chess pawn. I took it from him and eyed it. It was really smooth, and though it was a simple design, it looked really nice.

"You carve these yourself?" I asked, impressed.

Keith nodded. "I'm making a set for Caleb. He always was a bright kid."

"Making it *for* him?" I asked, handing the pawn back.

At first, I thought he meant in his honor, but Keith answered, "For when he comes back. The Miriamic Police are going to find him. Now that the other kid is missing, they've reopened the investigation. That's why *you're* reporting on it, isn't it?"

My tongue felt like sandpaper. I didn't know how to break it to him that his son was dead. I mean, I didn't have a body. But I'd heard Caleb's last thought. I didn't need more confirmation than that.

Krista entered the room then, saving me from my foolish gaping. She carried a tray of cheese and crackers. "Why don't we all sit down, and we can talk?"

She gestured to her husband, then to the couch. She set the snacks on the coffee table between us, and I took a seat on the opposite chair.

"Do you mind if I record this?" I asked.

"No, of course not," Keith answered. He clutched the pawn tightly in his hand, like it was a beacon of hope for his son's return.

There's nothing more horrible than sitting in the presence of a hopeful parent, knowing their hope was futile. My guts twisted in my abdomen at the thought of being the one to break the news to them, but I couldn't do it. I couldn't be the one to tell them their son was never coming back. I couldn't sit here and watch their hearts break like that.

I conjured my phone and started recording, then pulled out my notebook and pencil to jot down notes. They stared back at me expectantly, and I cleared my throat. "What can you tell me about your son's disappearance?"

Ouch. The question stung coming out of my mouth. That wasn't a question any parent should ever have to answer.

"Well, it's like you probably already know," Krista said. She seemed tense, but she spoke clearly, like she'd grown accustomed to talking about it. "A year ago, we put Caleb down for bed, and when we woke up, he was just… gone."

"You never heard anything that night?" I asked.

Keith shook his head. "Nothing."

"When did you realize your son was missing?" I questioned.

Krista's gaze dropped. "It was a Saturday, but Keith had gone into work to catch up on some paperwork. He works for the city. Caleb usually wakes around seven-thirty on weekends. I was doing laundry, cleaning up, and I lost track of time. By eight o'clock, I realized he hadn't woken up yet, so I went into his room and—"

She choked up and placed her hand over her mouth. Keith leaned over and wrapped an arm around her. I didn't say anything, just waited for her to compose herself.

After a few moments, she cleared her throat. "When I went into his room, it was empty."

"You mean that your son wasn't in his bed?" I asked.

She nodded.

"Was there anything else missing from the room?"

She shook her head and wiped her nose. "Nothing. The only thing missing was Caleb."

My brow furrowed. "Early reports said there was a window open in his room. Is that correct?"

Keith held his wife close as she answered. "Yes. That's the only thing that was strange. His toys were still out, like they'd been the night before. Everything was in order except that window."

"You didn't open it?" I asked.

"No," Keith answered. "It was cold out, the end of autumn. We left all the windows shut."

I pressed the end of my pen to my lips, wondering how I was going to figure out what happened to these kids. I had to cover all my bases. "What were his sheets like when you found him missing, Mrs. Thomas?"

She tilted her head. "What do you mean?"

"Was his bed made?" I asked.

She shook her head. "No. They were tousled, like he'd been sleeping in them all night."

I scribbled a few things down in my notebook. "Do you believe there's any chance he could've run away?"

"No," Keith said firmly. "Caleb had a very happy life here. He was never a flight risk."

"I don't believe he was," I stated, trying to ease his nerves. "I'm just covering my bases."

I took a deep breath before continuing. "Do you know if your child ever had contact with Isaac Miller, the other missing boy?"

"We don't think so," Krista answered. "They were in different grades at school. Even their recess time was different."

I tapped my pen against the paper. What was it exactly that these two boys had in common?

I decided to focus less on that at the moment and learn everything I could about Caleb Thomas while I was here. "Do you mind if I see his room?"

"By all means," Keith invited. He stood and gestured down the hall. "But I doubt you'll find anything the police didn't."

I doubted it, too, but I had to at least try.

The hall was decorated with the same homey touch as the living room. Family pictures lined the walls, and there was a big cabinet on the end with keepsakes and trophies in it. My eyes caught the nameplate on the biggest one, and I noticed it was a championship trophy in swimming.

"You're a swimmer?" I asked Keith, eyeing the trophy.

"I swam a little in college," he said proudly.

"Oh, don't be so modest," Krista countered. "He spent five hours a day training. He was *always* at the pool."

Keith pulled Krista close and planted a kiss on the top of her head. "What can I say? It won me that trophy."

"He won that the night he proposed," Krista told me.

"How long have you been married?" I asked.

Krista took a deep breath, like it'd been so long they'd stopped counting. "Eleven years. Wow, I can't believe it's been that long."

The two shared a deep look, and I instantly felt a pang of jealousy hit me. I wanted that for Nadine and me. I wanted us to last that long, and longer. But I knew we wouldn't get the chance—because of the damn Reaper's Shadow curse. It was more heartbreaking than I cared to admit. I'd sooner die than give her up, but protecting her came first—at all costs.

I gestured to a closed door. "This is Caleb's room?"

"Yes, it is," Keith said.

I opened the door and held my breath. I wished I could say I was impressed by what I saw, but I wasn't. It looked like a regular kid's room, with a twin bed, a bookshelf, closet, and a few toy boxes. Everything was clean, and his bed was made. The curtains had been drawn over the window. For a second, I was half surprised it was closed—like I expected to walk in here with it looking exactly like it had the day he left.

I walked further into the room, my eyes roaming over Caleb's dinosaurs and cars. I saw nothing out of the ordinary. "Have you had Seers come into this room?"

"Yes," Krista said from the doorway. "No one can tell us what happened to him."

I bent down to inspect his toys. He seemed to be really into cars, as he had a whole stack of them on a shelf. I picked up an old black Chevy Impala and looked it over. "Have you had any other Casts come in?"

I knew other Casts could prove handy with their abilities, too. Some Mortana could read the auras of the room and see if anyone had died there. Gifts like that might be useful in a situation like this.

"Believe us," Keith stated sadly, "we really have tried everything."

"And there's just… nothing?" I blew an exasperated breath and set the Impala back on the shelf.

Krista's eyes watered. "Nothing. It's the same with that other boy, isn't it?"

I swallowed. "I have yet to interview his family. If I find anything, I'll let you know. Is there anything else you can tell me about Caleb?"

I stood and began pacing around the room again.

"He was so sweet," Krista praised. "He was kind, well-behaved. No one could possibly have anything against our little boy. He loved cars and puppies and playing at the park—all the things a little boy should love."

My eyes landed on an old cast sitting atop the desk. "What's that?"

Keith looked sad when I asked. "Caleb was a little… accident-prone."

Krista winced at the comment. "He broke his ankle *three* times."

My brow furrowed. "Is there a reason for that? Brittle bones, perhaps?"

Keith shook his head. "No medical reason. The doctors say that after the first time he broke his ankle, it weakened the bones, so they're more prone to breaking again."

So… what did I have? A clumsy kid who was too nice for his own good and liked toys? It wasn't much to go on.

I stood there awkwardly and glanced around the room. I gestured to the closet. "Do you mind if I look around?"

Keith shook his head. "No, not at all. Take your time."

Keith started to leave the room to give me space, but Krista stayed a moment to observe. Her husband nudged her in the arm, and the two of them walked down the hall. I could hear them whispering to each other, but I was glad for the distance. I felt a little weird being watched.

I went to the closet first, but there was nothing there besides clothes and more toys. I made my way around the room, inspecting under furniture like I might actually find something. The truth was, I was way out of my element here.

The bed was next to the window, and I approached that last. I got down on all fours and checked under it. It was dark, so I conjured an orb and used it to illuminate the space. Besides a few dust bunnies, I found nothing. I sat on the bed and glanced around the room hopelessly.

After a few beats, I turned to the window and pushed the curtains aside. I inspected the frame closely, but I found no signs of forced entry, though I didn't expect to. The Miriamic Police Department would've noted that by now.

I'd be damned if I left here with *nothing*. I'd search every inch of this room if I had to. Problem was, I'd pretty much covered it all already.

I got off the bed and lifted the mattress—my last-ditch effort to find a clue. Something clinked against the wall, and my heart lurched. Quickly, I dropped the mattress back into place and flattened my belly against the floor. I used my orb to check underneath the bed again, and my magical light glittered against a small golden object that had fallen from behind the mattress.

I reached beneath the bed, stretching my arm as far as I could. A sharp pain stabbed through my finger, and I drew back. A single drop of blood dripped from the end of my index finger. I wiped it on my jeans, then reached for the small object again. My fingers wrapped around it, and I pulled it out from under the bed.

It was a pin, like one someone might wear on a letter jacket. As I inspected it closer, I saw that the design was of the Miriam College crest —a five-point star with each of the Cast symbols inside. Beneath the crest was the number twenty-five.

I recognized it immediately. It was a ceremonial pin awarded to professors who spent a certain amount of time at the school. In this case, it was a twenty-five-year anniversary pin. What was a professor's pin doing in little Caleb Thomas's bedroom?

I already knew the answer before I asked the question. Someone at the school had taken the boys. I just didn't know why.

Krista cleared her throat from the doorway, and I jumped. "Did you find anything?" she asked. Keith stood behind her, and they both eyed me curiously.

I hesitated. I almost didn't want to show her the pin, because it felt like pretty damning evidence, but I *had* to ask about it.

"Yeah," I said, holding up the pin. "Did any professors ever come visit?"

Keith stepped closer and took the pin from my fingers to inspect it. His face paled, but it was Krista who answered. "No. We're not close with any of our old professors."

"Then what's a twenty-five-year anniversary pin from the college doing in your house?" I asked. The question was more rhetorical than anything, but I was dying to know the answer.

Krista shared a look with her husband. I couldn't quite read their expressions, but they both seemed very afraid.

"You don't think a *professor* took our son?" Keith gaped.

I took a deep breath. I hated to be the one to break the news. "Unless you have another explanation for why that's here…"

Krista looked closely at the pin, but she seemed to have lost her breath. "No, it can't be. No professor would hurt our child. It doesn't make sense."

I expected Keith to try to calm his wife and rationalize the pin, but he didn't respond. He just kept looking down at it, his features tightening in anger.

"We have to turn this into the police," I said. "They can compile a list of suspects."

The two were hard to read, but I swore I saw wariness in their eyes. Keith cleared his throat. "We'll handle that. Thank you for your help. And, um, if you find anything else, will you let us know?"

I nodded. "Absolutely."

"Thank you," Krista said. "If we think of anything else, we'll call."

"I appreciate that," I replied.

I didn't know why, but it suddenly felt like I was being rushed out of the house. I didn't think the couple wanted me to see them grieve. To learn there was a possible lead was good news, but to think it might be a professor was agonizing. Who knew if it was someone they'd known—someone they trusted?

I left the house still unable to wrap my head around what I'd found. Could a professor really be behind this, or was there another reason that pin had shown up in Caleb's room? Krista and Keith had looked pretty frightened, and that confirmed for me that there was no other explanation. A professor was involved. But… who? It was clear finding answers wasn't going to be simple—

"I wish it didn't hurt this much." A voice cut through my thoughts. The voice was strained, and it sounded like an older woman. Another death.

I stopped on the sidewalk as the nausea hit. I gagged, though I knew nothing would come out. I hated that this woman had suffered in her last moments. It was a terrible way to go.

But at least it's over, I told myself. I wish I could've done something to relieve her suffering.

I was trying to accept my gift, but some days were harder than others. Whenever I could, I tried to find the good in the thought. It was a hell of a lot harder than it sounded.

Once the nausea passed, I ducked down a narrow alleyway and conjured one of my notebooks. I knelt behind someone's back fence and scribbled the thought on the paper. I ripped the page out of the notebook and conjured a lighter. Striking it, I held the paper over the flame. It caught fire, and I tossed it onto the gravel, watching it burn.

This was how I managed now—how I let go of the thoughts I heard. I leaned my back up against the fence and took in deep breaths. I conjured my journal and quickly started writing down my thoughts. When Professor Warren gave me my first journal, I thought the guy was nuts. No way would journaling work for me.

These last few weeks, though, it was the only thing that had kept me sane. I *had* to get my thoughts down on paper, or they built up inside of me until I made stupid, rash decisions—like trying to contact a reaper and damn myself to hell.

I wanted to change, and I knew that started with changing how I dealt with these things.

I'm scared, I wrote in my journal. I didn't even know I felt that way until I wrote it. Was it *true*? I stopped writing and stared down at the words, reading them over and over again. I flipped my pencil over and pressed the eraser to the page, but I paused before I could erase the words. It was like my whole body just locked up, forcing me to stare down at the words and really consider them.

I didn't know what I was scared of, exactly. That I couldn't save everyone in the coven? That I may not be able to accept my gift? I wasn't sure.

I can't be scared, I thought.

I'd made a decision the night of the Reaper Moon that I would find a way to deal with my gift, and I would. *I have to be strong*, I told myself.

And so I'd figure this out on my own.

nadine
FOUR

"How was class today?" Talia asked when she met up with me outside my Alchemy 101 class.

I was the last one out of the room, as I'd been cleaning up yet another mishap from today's lesson. This time, I'd let our cauldron boil over. Professor Richards offered to clean it up himself, but I wasn't about to give the Alchemy bitches more fuel to burn their fire raging against me. I'd take responsibility for my own mistakes.

"Alchemy 101 can suck it," I groaned.

"That bad?" Talia asked as we walked down the dark hall. She clutched an incantations textbook to her chest. After her Evoking Ceremony this weekend, she'd be able to start using it. I hadn't tried incantations yet, as I feared how much magic they required.

At our feet, Isa and Gus batted at a fly. Isa was agile and caught it in her mouth, while Gus was clumsy and tripped over Isa's tail.

I shrugged. "It could be better."

"Maybe I can help," she offered. A smile spread across her lips as she reached into her pocket. She pulled out a small pink drawstring bag.

"Are those the crystals we talked about?" I peeped. I glanced up and down the hall, making sure we were alone. I could still hear Professor Richards arranging potion vials in the classroom; otherwise, no one else was in the basement this time of day.

"Yep. I managed to get one from every Cast," Talia said proudly.

My eyes widened. These weren't ordinary crystals like the calming stones I had in my room. These were infused with magic, and we could get in trouble for having them on school property. I'd asked Talia to help me procure a collection so I could test my magic on them. Grammy had said these stones wouldn't give me any powers from the Cast, but I wanted to make sure for myself. If I was going to learn how to use my magic, I had to start somewhere.

"How'd you get so many so fast?" I questioned.

Talia shrugged. "Everything's easy to find in this town for the right price."

My shoulders sagged. "I hope you didn't spend your life savings to help me."

"Pft," she said, like it was no big deal. "They aren't *that* rare. Just don't get caught with them on you. What do you say we head back to our dorm and try them out?"

I didn't want to wait. I cocked my head and said, "Let's go in here."

Talia and I ducked into a deserted classroom. It was another one of the Alchemy labs. It had rows of tables with cauldrons on top, along with supplies for advanced potions lining the back wall. The jars were full of gross things, like lizard eyes and cat nail clippings. I even saw a dead mouse suspended in a clear liquid in one of the jars. Isa jumped onto the front table and nudged a potion vial with her paw. Typical cat.

"Isa," I hissed. "Don't you dare."

She gave me a guilty expression, but lay on the countertop and started cleaning her paws.

Talia opened her drawstring bag and poured three crystals into her palm. I already had an Alchemy crystal, and there wasn't a Curse Breaker crystal in all the coven that we knew of—which only left three others to experiment with.

"Which one do you want to start with?" she asked.

I tried to imagine which type of magic would be the mildest. I knew Mortana magic could be touchy, and I'd seen Mentalists do some crazy stuff. I decided to try the Seer stone first.

"A good choice," Talia said. She placed a pink stone into my palm, and I curled my fingers around it. "What does it feel like?"

I tested the weight in my hand. Magic buzzed through the stone, but it felt different from the Alchemy stone Grammy had given me. Alchemy had a constant, high-frequency buzz to it, whereas Seer magic felt smooth, like I could feel it flowing over my hand like water.

"It's… different," I stated.

"Are you ready to try using it?" she asked.

I took a deep breath. I hoped this wouldn't backfire on me like the Alchemy stone did on my first day in class. "Doesn't matter if I'm ready. I'm going to try anyway."

I pictured my hand like a funnel, opening up to absorb the magic in the stone. Like warm water rushing into my veins, the Seer magic flowed into me and up my arm, until it settled in my chest. I took a long breath, and it felt really light, like I was floating.

Then I let the breath out, and my chest twisted into a tight knot. The warm water-like sensation started to heat, until it felt like it was burning a hole through my ribs. I gasped, and Talia started to freak.

"Goddess, what's happening!?" she cried.

I gritted my teeth. I thought I was going to choke on the magic, but I managed to spit the words out. "It's trying to escape. I need to put it somewhere!"

"Back in the crystal!" Talia insisted through shallow breaths. "Put it back in the crystal!"

I reacted quickly, directing the magic out through my hand again and into the crystal. The knot in my chest eased, and I felt like I could breathe again.

Talia's eyes widened. "It worked?"

I nodded. "It worked. The magic's back in the crystal. At least, I think so…"

I swore I could feel some of that smooth energy lingering in my chest. It made me a little lightheaded. I hobbled over to the nearest chair and sank into it.

Talia tilted her head to the side. "What do you mean?"

"I put some of the magic back, but I don't think I put back all of it," I admitted. I tightened my grip on the crystal and tried to push the last bit of magic into it, but I couldn't. "I'm not sure I can."

Talia pressed her lips together in thought. "You know, one of the traits of Curse Breakers is that they can absorb magic. You must've absorbed some of it."

"What does that mean?" I questioned. "That I *could* get Seer powers?"

"I don't think so," she said. "But it *should* make you stronger in other areas—like conjuration, rituals, astral projection, and things like that."

"Maybe that's why using Grammy's crystal makes me so tired," I theorized. "Absorbing magic means there's more inside of me, so my body reacts to it."

Talia nodded along. "Any psychic visions yet?"

I shook my head. "No. I guess Grammy's right and I can't develop powers from other Casts."

"Do you want to stop trying?" Talia asked.

"No," I decided quickly. "Let's keep going."

She eyed me. "You're sure you're okay?"

I was wiped, but I could handle more. "I want to try."

Talia handed me the next crystal. It was a dark red one, which she said was the Mentalist crystal. Its magic felt electric, like little tiny lightning bolts shooting through my skin. It didn't hurt though—it more or less tickled. I drew the magic into myself, then narrowed my eyes on the crystal in my palm. I tried to get the crystal to move with my mind, but nothing happened. The magic wrapped around me, and I gasped for breath again before quickly channeling the magic back into the crystal.

"Anything?" Talia asked.

I shook my head. "No telekinetic powers, that's for sure."

Talia stared down at the crystal. "It's so weird how good you are at that."

"At what?"

"Transference—transferring magic into something else," she clarified.

"Anyone can do that?" I asked.

Talia nodded. "With their own magic, sure. Crystals are able to harness our powers. But it's quite advanced magic, and you've picked it up like it's nothing."

I shrugged. "It's part of being a Curse Breaker, I guess. At least I'm good at *something*."

Talia chuckled. "You're good at a lot of things."

"Aw, that's sweet," I teased. "Let's try the last one."

Talia hesitated. "You're looking a little pale."

All this magic was making me feel awful, but it wasn't anything new. If I waited until I felt in tip-top shape, we'd never get this done.

"I'm fine," I told her. "Let's see if I can raise the dead."

Talia handed me the final crystal—a purple one so dark it was almost black. Mortana magic was the strangest of all. Unlike the others, it didn't give off a constant vibration. Instead, the electric magic swelled and waned at various intervals. I couldn't find a pattern to it. No wonder Lucas had such a hard time with his magic—it was all over the place.

"Did it work?" Talia asked after several silent moments.

"I haven't tried yet. I'm just trying to get a feel for it."

I held the crystal in my hand for another minute, partially testing it out, and partially waiting to gain some of my strength back.

Finally, I worked up the courage and siphoned the magic into my body. I had my eyes trained on the mouse in the jar at the back of the room, hoping maybe I'd absorb some necromancy magic and make it move.

But before I had a chance to think about it, a stabbing pain shot down my arm. I dropped the crystal and gasped in pain.

It was so intense, I didn't notice where the crystal had fallen. All I knew was I had to get this magic out of me—and fast! I grabbed for the closest item, which was the cauldron on the table in front of me. I pressed my palm firmly to the cast-iron and pressed my magic outward—but it wouldn't budge.

"Shit!" Talia cried as she dropped to her knees to search for the crystal.

"Frick, this hurts!" I growled. Isa's hair stood on end.

Talia found the crystal and slammed it onto the table. I grabbed it as quick as I could and funneled the magic back into it. When I finally took a breath, Talia had her hand over her heart, and she sucked in heavy breaths. "What happened?"

"I don't know," I admitted. I barely got the words out, I was so drained. "I think I just didn't know how to control it. It got the better of me."

Talia started gathering the crystals back into the bag. "I guess this experiment answers our question."

"You were right—using other Cast magic isn't going to give me new powers."

It wasn't that I *wanted* other powers. I just wanted to understand my own, to know what I was capable of. Right now, I felt capable of very little. If I couldn't even handle Mortana magic, how was I supposed to break curses?

"We can be done for the day," I offered.

Talia handed me the bag of crystals. "Don't go using these alone. I don't want you to get hurt."

"I won't," I promised as I slipped them into my bag. "Thanks for doing this for me."

She smiled proudly. "What are friends for?"

We left the Alchemy lab. All that magic had drained me so much I felt like I should be crawling up the stairs. But that'd be super embarrassing to do in front of Talia, so I gritted my teeth and made it to the top.

Isa nudged me in the leg and stared up at me, like she could tell something was wrong. She was right. Like hell I was making it up another flight of stairs.

"I have some studying to do," I announced. "I'll catch up with you later."

"I had plans to meet up with Cody, anyway," she said. "How's my hair?"

I flatted a stray flyaway. "All good. You look great."

She shot me a smile, but kept smoothing down her hair anyway. "Thanks."

I waved and headed off down the hall in the direction of the nearest study alcove. Talia waved back, and Gus looked disappointed as Isa followed me. I scanned the halls for signs of Lucas. I didn't expect to see him, but I hoped. Disappointment weighed me down when I didn't spot him.

I turned a corner and sank into the nearest chair in the study area. Isa jumped onto my lap and started purring. The truth was, I *did* have to study for Alchemy, but I couldn't keep my eyes open. I slumped in my chair and drifted off.

I woke an hour later to someone shaking me awake. My heart swelled when I saw Lucas's face above me. It took a few moments for him to come into focus. I tried to sit up straighter, but my muscles screamed at me. That barely registered when he was here, though. I always felt better when he was around.

"Are you okay?" he asked, sounding worried.

"Fine," I told him. "I must've drifted off."

"If you need a nap, let me walk you back to your dorm," he offered.

I shook my head and checked the time on my phone. "I have class soon. You didn't have to come find me."

I said it to be nice, but the truth was, I was glad he was here. Every moment away from him was agonizing. I could never be happier than if I got to spend every last second with him.

"I wasn't looking for you," he said, taking the chair beside me. "I was walking to class and saw you. I just came from the cafeteria. Are you hungry?"

Lucas held out an apple in my direction that he must've swiped from the buffet line. I wanted to say no, but I really was hungry, and I didn't have time to grab food before Meditation and Inner Magic.

"Thanks," I said as I took it. It was really nice of him to watch out for me.

"After class, do you want to—?" Lucas started.

"Shit!" some screamed, cutting him off.

Lucas and I both looked up and down the hall, only to see a student running. He carried a notebook with pages flying out of it behind him.

"Shields up, Mister Spyre," a man warned.

As he came closer, I realized it was Professor Daymond, my least favorite professor at school—and I hadn't even had him yet. He breezed toward the student in confidence, even though the kid looked terrified.

Before anyone in the hall could react, Professor Daymond lifted his hands, and a freaking *battle orb* shot out of his palms! It crackled with red electricity as it whizzed through the air at the student. The kid dropped his books and thrust his hands upward. The battle orb slammed into an invisible shield and sputtered out.

My jaw dropped, and I went speechless. How was this asshole still working here? Attacking students out in the open had to be grounds for firing.

Professor Daymond's eyebrows scrunched up, and he stared down at his hands like he was confused. "What is the meaning of this, Brayden?"

The kid stammered. "W-what do you mean?"

After a few moments, Professor Daymond righted his shoulders. "Again, Mister Spyre."

The kid lifted his hands again and flinched, bracing for impact. But when Professor Daymond tried to create another battle orb, magic sputtered in his hands.

"What the hell!?" I blurted before I could stop myself. "You can't go around attacking people!"

Professor Daymond whirled toward me. When he recognized me, his eyes narrowed.

"He teaches Defensive Magic," Lucas explained to me. "Catching students off guard is part of the class."

I gaped at him. "That's insane! Someone could get hurt."

"Witches can cast different types of battle orbs, all with varying intensities," Lucas said. "Some will barely hurt you. Others will stun or burn you. He would never use a full-powered battle orb on a student."

Lucas wasn't explaining this for my benefit. It was his way of convincing Professor Daymond to go easy on me, since I was still ignorant to the laws of magic. I appreciated his effort, but I didn't agree with Professor Daymond's methods.

Professor Daymond stomped our way and loomed over me. "What did you do, *girl?*"

"Me?" I squeaked, my heart hammering. I hadn't forgotten the cruel things he'd shown me in my Evoking training last semester. "I didn't do anything. You're the one attacking students in the middle of the hallway."

He frightened me, but it wasn't enough for me to keep my mouth shut.

"Yet you are the only one to protest," he said with a raised eyebrow.

Isa stood, like she was about to jump on this guy's face if he got any closer.

"She didn't mean anything by it, Professor," Lucas assured him, trying to protect me.

"She didn't?" he asked skeptically. His eyes roamed over my Alchemist tattoo. "We'll see about that."

Before I could react, Professor Daymond grabbed my bag. He yanked the zipper open and started digging through my stuff.

"Hey!" I protested. I wanted to stand, but I was rooted in my chair. "You can't do that!"

"Don't forget who you're talking to," Professor Daymond snarled.

Lucas shot to his feet, and his hands curled into fists. "Lay off her."

"I suggest you sit back down, Mister Taylor," Professor Daymond instructed. "Ah, what's this?"

He pulled out the drawstring bag and dropped my backpack to the ground. He opened the bag and poured the crystals into his hand. My mouth went dry as he curled them in his fist and narrowed his eyes.

"Magic crystals," Professor Daymond said.

Lucas's face paled. He didn't know I had these.

"You used these to attack my magic," Professor Daymond accused.

"What?" I squeaked. "No. I didn't do anything! I don't even know how—"

"We'll see about that. Come with me," he demanded.

I glanced between him and Lucas. "What? Where?"

"To talk to the headmistress," Professor Daymond replied. It didn't sound like he was giving me a choice.

"She had nothing to do with this," Lucas raged.

"I don't even know what you're talking about," I said. I literally had no idea what was going on.

"Tell that to the headmistress," Daymond said.

Then the asshole grabbed me by the arm. I jerked away, and Lucas quickly stepped in and shoved Professor Daymond back. "Don't touch her!"

Professor Daymond's eyes darkened. He looked positively stunned that a student would dare touch him—yet how could he think he had any right to lay a hand on me?

"How *dare* you," Professor Daymond snapped at Lucas. "That's detention for both of you—"

"Professor Daymond!" a female voice snapped.

By now, a crowd of onlookers had gathered. I noticed Brayden had disappeared into the sea of people. He was talking lowly to another student I recognized as Gregory Walker. The crowd parted to let Headmistress Verla through. She wore a dark pantsuit like normal, and her fat cat, Odin, followed at her feet. She pursed her lips, looking ticked off.

"What is the meaning of this?" she demanded.

Professor Daymond straightened his spine, looking pleased—like Lucas and I had just been caught red-handed. "I was conducting a lesson with Mister Spyre when my magic sputtered. I believe *she* is the culprit!"

Professor Daymond pointed a gnarly finger at me. From beside me, Lucas looked half shocked, half thoughtful.

Headmistress Verla raised an eyebrow. "Are you suggesting she cursed you?"

"She did *something*," he insisted.

"I didn't do anything," I said quickly.

"She had *these* on her." Professor Daymond held out my crystals. "They're against school policy!"

Headmistress Verla stepped forward. She reached for one of the crystals to inspect it. Her features fell into a frown. "Is this true, Nadine? Are these crystals yours?"

I shifted in my chair. "Well, yes, but—"

"You see?" Professor Daymond accused. "Black magic! She's up to something, I tell you!"

Verla frowned. "False accusations are not taken lightly around here, Archibald."

Professor Daymond gaped at her. "But I have proof!"

He shoved the crystals outward in emphasis.

Before I could defend myself, Headmistress Verla said, "Nadine, if you'd please accompany me to my office."

Shit. I was in trouble. I couldn't deny those crystals were mine, and I'd known they were against school policy.

"The crystals are mine," Lucas rushed to step in. "I asked Nadine to hold on to them for me."

I scooped Isa up in my arms and stood. I placed a hand on Lucas's shoulder. "It'll be fine. You don't have to do that."

"But Nad…" he trailed off as he eyed me.

"It's fine." I gave Lucas's hand a squeeze, then followed behind Headmistress Verla. Isa growled lowly at Professor Daymond as she passed, then hurried to follow behind me.

Verla didn't say anything as we headed down the hall. My stomach twisted into knots, wondering how much trouble I was in. Verla led me into her office, then rounded her desk and set the crystals down between us. Odin jumped into his cat tower and stared down his nose at me. I sat, and Verla's tight lips turned into a frown.

"What are you doing with these crystals?" she asked in a softer tone than I expected.

I couldn't tell her the truth. I'd sworn to keep my powers a secret— even from my mother's best friend.

"I thought they might help with my symptoms," I lied. I had to hold in a wince. Using my lupus to get out of trouble made me sick. I didn't like setting the precedent that I was incapable because of my lupus—because I wasn't.

Verla's features softened, and she finally sat. "Who told you crystals would help your symptoms?"

I shrugged. I guess I had to go along with the lie now. "No one. I just wanted to try it."

"I'm sorry to tell you that they won't help," she said sympathetically. "Unfortunately, we do not allow these types of crystals on school grounds, as they can be used to cheat in your classes."

"I didn't know," I said. I guess I was going to have to start getting used to lying. The coven couldn't know I was a Curse Breaker.

"I understand that you're still learning the rules, but I'm going to have to confiscate these." Verla swept the crystals into her hands and placed them in her desk drawer.

A beat passed, and I realized that was it. I wasn't getting detention or being suspended. "I'm not being punished?" I questioned.

"Not this time," Verla said kindly. "Your symptoms are hard to deal with—I get that. You'd be surprised at the things people do when they're desperate."

Her words hung in the air for several long seconds. It was like there was a hidden message behind her words. Did she know I was desperate to conceal my secret of being a Curse Breaker—that I was using an Alchemy crystal to lie to everyone? She hadn't asked to search my bags any further, and if she had, she'd have found the Alchemy crystal among my belongings.

But she couldn't know… right?

"I guess they do…" I agreed, eyeing her as if she might admit she knew something. When she didn't say anything, I changed the topic. "You don't think I had anything to do with Professor Daymond's weird magic thing in the hall, do you?"

She shook her head. "No, I don't."

"Then why do you let him torment students the way he does?" I blurted.

Verla sighed and crossed her hands over her desk. "For one, Professor Daymond has tenure and is on the school board. Even if I *wanted* to fire him, I couldn't. The school board goes easy on him on account of what happened to his family."

I tilted my head. "What do you mean?"

Verla's gaze fell. "About a decade ago, Professor Daymond lost his wife, Tonya, and his son, Oliver, to a house fire. He's never quite been the same since."

Well, that explained his cranky-ass attitude.

"That shouldn't excuse his behavior," I said.

"I agree," she replied. "It doesn't. But a little compassion can go a long way when someone's suffering."

"I know about suffering," I reminded her. "And so do you."

I hadn't forgotten the stories about what she'd lost—*who* she'd lost.

"It doesn't give us a free pass," I said.

Verla sighed. "I'm not asking you to like him. To be honest, he *is* a good teacher, even though he pushes his students to the limits."

I had to refrain from snorting. I didn't think Professor Daymond *had* limits.

"He's set to retire soon," she added.

I felt like Verla was trying to shift the conversation—probably because it was unprofessional of her to agree with me. I wasn't going to convince her of anything.

I twisted my hands in my lap. "Well, thank you for sticking up for me and believing me."

"Of course." Her features brightened, like she'd never consider doubting me. "You're Faith's daughter. I'll always trust you."

There it was again—an unspoken message, like she knew I wasn't being completely honest with her. But as I eyed her, she gave nothing away. Maybe I was reading into it too much. I was being careful about my magic—no one would find out.

"I appreciate that." I stood to leave, but Verla stopped me.

"Just… be careful, Nadine," Verla added. "Magic doesn't always behave by the rules, and I'd hate to see you get hurt."

I stood there awkwardly for a few moments, unsure of what to say. "Thanks," I finally settled with.

By the time I walked out of the room, I was almost certain Verla knew something. Problem was, if she already figured it out, how long would it take for the rest of the coven to discover my secret?

☽

Saturday arrived, the day of Talia's birthday. But after a long week of classes, I couldn't manage to drag myself out of bed. I gathered enough energy to take a bath, but the rest of the day I spent alternating between reading and binge-watching a witchy TV series. Talia kept throwing popcorn at the screen every time they got something about magic wrong.

"I want to be there for your Evoking Ceremony tonight," I told her.

"It's okay if you're not," she assured me. "My parents will be there, along with my brother and sister, and Cody said he'll try to make it. It will be fine."

"No, it won't," I argued. "You were there for mine. I want to see you get your powers."

"Your magic is taking a lot out of you, and you need to rest. Really, I'll be okay. You just focus on feeling better."

If I could get better by sheer will, I'd be prepping for a marathon by now. But life didn't work that way, unfortunately.

"I'll be there in spirit," I promised.

Talia smiled. "What? You're planning to astral travel to my ceremony?"

"Can I do that?" I asked, considering the idea.

Talia snickered. "Probably not for a few years. It takes a lot of practice."

I frowned. "Well, I hope you get something good."

"I'll get whatever I'm supposed to get," she said. "Mother Miriam knows what's best for me."

"Before you leave, let me give you your birthday present." I reached over to my nightstand and opened the drawer. I pulled out a box wrapped in pink paper.

Talia's eyes lit up as she took it. "You didn't have to."

"Of course I did!" I told her. "You're my bestie."

Talia smiled and ripped open the packaging. Inside was a purse designed with piano keys on it. I'd seen it in a shop window over winter break, and it reminded me of her.

"Goddess, I love it!" she squealed. "Thank you so much!"

She leaned over to hug me, and I squeezed her back.

"Open it," I encouraged.

Talia's eyes went wide, and she zipped open the purse. Inside were all types of items for her altar—two pillar candles with music notes on them, a small keepsake box decorated in treble clefs, and three different essential oils.

"That's so thoughtful," Talia said. "You're the best."

Talia left for home shortly after I gave her the gift. I really did want to go with her, but I felt awful. In the quietness of my dorm room, I scrolled through my phone and read up on astral travel. I wanted to try it as I drifted off, but my spirit didn't leave my body. Instead, I fell asleep and began to dream.

I walked the dark halls of the school. The sconces on the walls weren't lit, and there was no moonlight coming in through the large window at the top of the grand staircase. Somehow, I could still make out shadows in the empty hall.

I didn't know where I was going, but my feet continued to move beneath me. I descended the stairs into the Main Foyer. It was completely deserted this time of night, but my spine tingled, like someone was watching me.

I shook off the feeling and continued down the hall past the cafeteria. The hall seemed to stretch for miles. I must've passed by a hundred classroom doors before I came to the double doors at the end. A candle stick had been placed between the handles.

Slowly, I reached for the doors to the ballroom. Just as my fingers grazed the handle, the door gave a violent shake, and my heart leapt into my throat.

The sound of a door slamming startled me awake. My heart hammered, and it took me a few seconds to realize where I was. The curtains were drawn, but it was bright enough to make out the features of my dorm room. The adrenaline from my dream slowly subsided.

"Sorry," Talia said as she stepped around my bed, carrying Gus. "Did I wake you?"

I yawned and checked the clock next to my bed. It was already well past breakfast time. "You did, but it's fine," I told her. "You're back later than I expected."

I noticed Talia was still wearing the same clothes she'd left in last night, and her hair was slightly a mess. She set her purse on the couch and sat in the cushion closest to me, stroking Gus's fur.

She dropped her head and bit her lip. "I meant to come back last night, but…"

My stomach sank. "Uh oh. Is that a good *but* or a bad *but*?"

Talia blushed a bright pink that matched her shirt. "Well, Cody couldn't make it to the ceremony, but I met up with him afterward, and one thing led to another…"

"You didn't!" I balked. I tried to roll over, but a spasm went up my back. I stayed put and hoped she didn't notice. "You and Cody did it?"

Talia looked so embarrassed, she was practically wincing. "Yes," she squeaked.

"No way!" I squealed. "Congrats."

She chuckled under her breath. "Thanks."

I wiggled my eyebrows. "So, how was it?"

She wrinkled her nose. "It was… a little awkward, to be honest."

"But good awkward, right?" I asked.

"I mean, yeah…" she said, but she sounded uncertain. "It wasn't planned, and I think it might've been more special if it was, like if he took me on a romantic date first or something."

"That might've helped," I agreed. "But being spontaneous can be fun, too. Do I get any more details?"

"I met him in his dorm and stayed the night," she said, like it wasn't a big deal. "To be honest, it was over kind of quick, and we just fell asleep afterward."

I frowned. "That doesn't sound fair. Your first time should be special."

"I know," she sighed. "But I don't think that's normal. Everyone says their first time is bad."

I wished I could give her some advice, but I wasn't exactly experienced in that department.

Talia changed the subject. "Want to see my tattoo?"

"Yes, of course!" I said. "What's your Cast?"

Talia kicked off her shoes and pulled her pant leg up. On her ankle was a perfect tattoo of an eye.

"You're a Seer!" I said cheerfully. "Any idea what your specialty is?"

"I might," she said, sounding really happy about it. "But it only happened once so far, so I'm not sure."

"What happened?" I asked. "Can you show me?"

"I can try. Do you have anything sentimental I can hold?"

I glanced around, but I wasn't sure what exactly she wanted. On my bedside table was a jewelry box. I opened the nearest drawer. Inside was the key to the abandoned mansion Lucas had given me for my birthday. I dug it out and handed it to her.

"Something like this?" I asked.

Talia smiled and took it. "That's perfect."

She closed her eyes and relaxed into the couch. Her eyebrows knitted in concentration. I didn't want to interrupt whatever she was doing, so I didn't talk for a long time. Finally, she spoke. "I see a really beautiful mansion, and a gorgeous brass lock the key fits into."

Her eyebrows knitted tighter, like she was struggling to see anything more. "There's a lot of laughter and smiles. I think the house was really happy."

"That's good to hear," I said. "I'm impressed."

"But it's been forgotten," she added. "It's like the house is waiting for someone to make it happy again." Talia opened her eyes and handed the key back. "I'm *really* excited to see what I can do with this gift."

"How does it work?" I asked.

She shrugged. "I touch things, and I get visions. The first thing I saw was right after I finished my ceremony. I stood up and steadied myself on the piano at home, and I got a vision of myself playing it when I was a kid."

"That's really cool," I remarked. I'd have loved to get visions as my gift. "Can you see visions with *anything*?"

"I should be able to train myself," Talia said. "But it'd only be to a point. I won't be able to see anything I want to. At least, that's what I've heard from other psychometrists in the coven."

"That's what you have?" I questioned. "Psychometry?"

She nodded. "As far as I know, unless I start having random visions. The way psychometry works is that when a Seer touches an inanimate object, they get visions of the object's past. I think it will only work with sentimental things first, because those have the strongest energy signature."

"That's such a cool gift," I told her. "I wish I'd gotten Seer."

"Don't say that," Talia said with a frown. "We're all given the gifts we're meant to have. You'll find your strengths in curse breaking. I know it."

"Thanks." I gave her a half-hearted smile, but it quickly turned to a wince as I tried to straighten myself on the bed. Isa's ears perked in alarm.

Talia gasped. "Are you okay?"

"I'll be fine," I said, but the cramp in my neck ached.

"Let me help." Talia got up from the couch quickly and opened my nightstand. She pulled out my heating pad and plugged it in, then situated it under my neck. I relaxed into it as it started to warm. Talia went to fill my water bottle, then came back from the bathroom with my pill case.

"Here you go," she said, before she started plumping a pillow under my knees to help me stay comfortable.

"I'll be okay, really," I protested.

Talia shrugged. "Doesn't mean I can't help."

I didn't like people taking care of me. It made me feel like I couldn't take care of myself. But to be honest, it felt good to have a roommate who cared. If I was going to get sick every time I used magic, I was going to need some help this semester.

"Thanks," I said genuinely.

A few hours passed, and I kept handing Talia new things to try her gift on. She tried my star necklace but saw nothing, then a few of my keepsakes under the bed. It was fun to listen to some of the memories, but she seemed to grow fatigued after a while and stopped getting any more visions.

"I'm hungry," Talia announced. "Do you want me to grab some takeout from the cafeteria?"

"No," I groaned. "If you're okay with waiting, we should head down together. I can't stay in bed all day."

"Okay," she agreed.

I was grateful Talia was patient with me, because it took me forever to get out of bed. As I was getting ready, I thought I should've just taken her up on her offer for takeout, but I knew it wasn't good for me to stay in the room forever. I touched my star necklace, knowing that even when I felt like shit, I had to make an effort. Besides, I hadn't used magic all day, and I was feeling a little better.

Talia and I fed the cats and left the room. In the cafeteria, we spotted Mandy and Amy at a corner table. They waved us over after we got our food.

Mandy was dressed in her signature black skater dress that showed off her ample bosom and hugged her curves. Her nails were painted bright blue, and her hair was twisted into two braids. Amy wore a black hoodie with a cauldron stitched onto it. I caught a glimpse of her hand, and it was covered in ink lines—like Mandy had been using it as a model to study palmology. I noticed a bracelet around Amy's wrist with all sorts of crystals strung onto it. Beside Amy on the table lay a thick history book.

"Hey, girls!" Mandy sang. "We haven't seen you in weeks. How was your winter break?"

I chuckled nervously. *Hell.* "It was fine," I said.

"I got a lot of songwriting in," Talia added, popping a carrot into her mouth. I noticed she didn't have a lot on her plate, just a salad and a few veggies. "Hey, Nadine. Want my tomatoes?"

"Sure."

Talia started picking the tomatoes off her salad and giving them to me. It'd sort of become a thing with us whenever she got a salad.

"We went skiing over break," Amy said, bouncing in her seat.

"That sounds like fun," I told them as I spread ketchup on my fries.

"Tons of fun," Mandy raved. "I didn't even know I *could* ski."

Amy rolled her eyes. "She's being modest. She was great at it."

Mandy sipped on her soda, then set her drink aside. Her eyes lit up, and she reached for something under the table. "A little birdie told me you just had a birthday, Talia."

"I did," she replied.

"Congrats, girl! Amy and I got you something." Mandy beamed as she set a small box on the table. It was wrapped in pretty gold foil.

"Aw, you guys didn't have to do that," Talia said, but she took the box and started unwrapping it.

Amy and Mandy both watched her closely. The paper fell away to reveal a photo of a harmonica on the outside of the box. It looked like an antique, but the box was still intact.

"Do you like it?" Amy asked hopefully.

"You guys, I love it," Talia squealed. "I mean, I don't know how to play it, but I'll learn. Thank you so much."

"Pft," Mandy said with a wave of her hand. "No big deal. How was your ceremony?"

"I got Seer," Talia said proudly.

"I told you," Amy said, nudging Mandy in the arm. "I said she'd be Seer, didn't I?"

"You did," Mandy agreed. "I was voting for Mortana."

Talia's eyebrows slammed together in confusion. "What makes you think I'd be Mortana?"

Mandy popped a grape in her mouth and shrugged. "I expect the unexpected. You're so bright all the time, I thought it'd be cool to see you become a necromancer."

"I wear pink every day," Talia reminded her. "I'd be like necromancer Barbie."

The four of us laughed together.

Amy was the first to compose herself. "Congratulations to you, too, Nadine. I hear you're a fellow Alchemist!"

I shifted in my seat. Neither Amy nor Mandy knew my secret. They were my friends, but I'd vowed to keep the secret between only those who'd been there at my ceremony.

"Yeah," I said. "It's been… interesting."

"It takes some getting used to, but you're going to love it," Amy said. "If you need any help studying, you know who to call."

"I might have to take you up on that offer," I said. Mandy watched me with a big smile, and I shot her a look. "What?"

Her smile widened. "Don't think we forgot about you. I know it's been a while since your birthday, but we didn't see you all break. We got you something, too."

Mandy set another present on the table between us, and my heart warmed. "Aww, thank you."

"Open it, open it," Amy chanted.

Slowly, I tore open the wrapping. The box was small and opened on a hinge. I flipped the top up. Inside lay a small green crystal. Wire had been twisted around it, and it hung on a chain.

"Wow, thanks," I told them. "It's really pretty."

"It's not just pretty." Amy's voice took on a serious tone. "It's functional. This crystal is said to ward off curses. With your family curse, we thought you might need it."

My heart swelled at the gesture. It made it so much more special now. I pulled the necklace out of the box and put it around my neck. "This is amazing."

"I made it," Mandy said proudly. "Well, not the crystal. The necklace. Amy picked out the crystal."

"Mandy made me this, too." Amy showed off her bracelet. "Turns out she really has a knack for jewelry making."

Talia frowned playfully. "Aw, now I'm jealous."

Mandy snickered. "No worries, babe. I'll make you some, too. How do pink earrings sound?"

Talia beamed. "Perfect."

Just then, a group of giggling girls passed nearby and sat two tables down. I looked up to see the Lucky Three, though they hadn't noticed us yet. There was nothing but an empty table between us. Each of them wore super short spandex that showed off their ass cheeks, along with tight black tank tops that shimmered in the light.

"Goddess, did you *see* Stacey's scorpion?" Chloe mocked. I could picture the dance pose—back arched, and one leg lifted behind the head. "She has the flexibility of a plank."

Gwen snorted. "I give her a week on the team."

I furrowed my brow and eavesdropped. I thought Gwen and Stacey were friends, but it sounded like loyalty wasn't high on Gwen's list of values.

"I'm trying out for the solo routine this year," Chloe said proudly, popping a piece of celery in her mouth.

"You'll totally get it," Camille practically sang. "You're the best dancer on the team."

I turned back to my friends, who were all eyeing the Lucky Three with disgust. "The school has a dance team? And the Lucky Three are on it?"

Mandy frowned. "From what I hear, they basically run it now. Try-outs for this year's recital were last week. I heard it was brutal."

Amy scrunched up her nose. "The girls in the dorm next to mine came back from try-outs crying."

"Samantha almost broke her leg trying out," Mandy added.

"Ouch," I said, wincing. "It's probably best she didn't make it. I wouldn't want to be on a team with them."

"Me, either," Mandy replied. "Not with girls like them and Lena."

"Lena made the team?" I asked. I hated the girl. She'd been trying to steal Lucas from me all year.

Mandy nodded in confirmation.

I shot them another glance, eyeing their dance uniforms. Chloe sipped on a smoothie, like she'd suddenly become some sort of health nut. Her eyes scanned the cafeteria until they landed on me. She narrowed her eyes, as if expecting me to look away first. I decided to test her dominance and held her gaze.

"What?" she snapped.

I spoke without thinking about it. "Did someone slip a bitch potion into your smoothie this morning, or did you put it there yourself?"

"Go fuck yourself, Evers," she said, before literally hissing at me like a cat.

I smirked. Chloe didn't scare me. "Don't mind if I do. It'd be a lot more fun than sitting in the same room as you."

Chloe leaned back in her seat and sipped her smoothie through a straw. "Just don't be thinking about me while you're at it. You're like, obsessed with me or something."

"Gross," I shot back, nearly gagging at the suggestion. "You're a creature of nightmares."

Chloe cocked an eyebrow, looking pleased. "Oh, so you're scared of me. Good to hear."

"Like hell," I scoffed. "Go choke on grave dirt for all I care."

Chloe sat up straighter and smirked. Her tone held a hint of amusement. "That a curse?"

"I'm not a curse-casting type of witch," I said coolly. "Unlike your family."

Chloe's nostrils flared, and she pointed a finger at me. "Don't you dare say a word about my family."

My hands curled into fists, and visions of me ripping her hair out flashed in my mind. It'd be satisfying, to say the least. "What are you going to do? Curse me? Your grandpa beat you to it."

Chloe shot to her feet. Her knuckles turned white as she gripped tight to her drink. "I'll curse your ass again."

I nearly snorted. "With what magic? You don't have any. And once you get it, there's a fifty-fifty chance the curse will kill *you*—"

I barely finished my sentence before Chloe threw her smoothie outward, splashing it all over me. I yelped as the cold chill spread over my face.

"What the fuck, Chloe!?" Mandy screamed. Talia and Amy both rushed to grab napkins for me.

I wiped the thick liquid from my eyes to see Gwen and Camille standing behind Chloe. They all wore an equal look of satisfaction on their faces.

"Next time, it'll be a potion that'll burn your face off," Chloe threatened. She turned back to Gwen and Camille. "Come on, girls. I can't be caught dead talking to the Freak Sisters."

"Freak Sisters?" I gasped as Chloe started to walk away. I started to get up to beat her ass, but Talia grabbed my shoulder and held me back.

Chloe whirled around and started laughing. "What? You didn't notice *everyone* at school thinks you're all freaks?" She turned up her nose at Amy and started listing off each of us in turn. "A squinty-eyed dyke and her fat Spanish sidekick—"

"I'm Indian," Mandy interrupted, shooting her a confused look, but Chloe continued like she hadn't heard her.

"A dyslexic band geek with zero sense of fashion, and a half-blood who can hardly walk up a flight of stairs," Chloe finished, eyeing us each up and down. "It's like the God of Freaks puked all over the four of you."

My fists curled tighter, but Talia didn't let me go, which was probably for the best. I'd get suspended if I got close enough to Chloe to beat her ass. My anger rattled around inside of me, begging to escape, but I pushed it down. The sooner Chloe was gone, the better.

"Anyway, have fun, losers," she said in the most condescending tone I'd ever heard. She tossed her hair over her shoulder and walked away. Gwen and Camille followed like little puppies.

I rolled my eyes and turned back to my friends. Amy handed me more napkins, and I continued wiping my face off. I had to dig into the front of my shirt to get the cold liquid off my chest.

"You guys okay?" I asked.

Mandy gaped. "No! All I am is a sidekick! I want a better freak identity."

Talia started laughing, and soon the rest of us joined in. Amy placed a hand on Mandy's and said, "You're *so* much more than my sidekick. That bitch doesn't know what she's talking about."

"Well, she's right about one thing," I said, popping a fry in my mouth.

"What's that?" Talia asked.

I smirked. "We're freaks, and we're proud of it."

A smile spread across Talia's face. "Well, good to know you guys are my sisters."

"Freak Sisters," I corrected her.

"Exactly," Talia agreed. "Freak Sisters for life."

FIVE

"You're so lucky you got to meet Keith Thomas," Grant raved. "Did you know he was the best swimmer Miriam College ever had?"

It'd been over a week since I interviewed Caleb Thomas's parents, and Grant hadn't shut up about it.

"Yeah, I know," I said on our way to Magical Theory. "You've told me at least five times."

"Aw, man, I want to meet him," Grant added. "I wonder what sort of swimming advice he'd give me."

"I don't know… *choose a better Speedo?*" I teased.

Grant's pineapple-printed speedo was a real eyesore, but he called it *whimsical* and said it kept everyone's eyes on him during competition.

Grant scrunched up his nose. "My Speedo is fantastic, and you know it."

I rolled my eyes as we entered the classroom. The room buzzed with chatter, but Professor Warren didn't seem to notice. He stood at the front of the room, writing out a few things on the board.

Professor Warren taught my Necromancy Safety class last semester and knew his stuff. He was a great guy, but as my mentor, he left a lot to be desired. He didn't know much about my Reaper's Apprentice powers, and I still had beef with him about how he'd hidden the Reaper Moon from me. I wished I could say I understood where he was coming from, but I was still bitter about it. Even if contacting the reapers last December was a bad choice, he still should've given me the option.

I hadn't told him what happened that night with the Reaper Moon. I didn't need a lecture. Honestly, though things didn't go as planned, I was glad I went through with it. It taught me how to deal with the voices better, and I didn't need Professor Warren's help with that. I could deal with it on my own.

Grant and I sat beside each other at a table in the back. We were one of the last to arrive. We'd barely sat down when Professor Warren cleared his throat and turned from the board. The class quieted.

"Today, we'll be discussing *source energy*," Professor Warren announced. He turned to the board and underlined the words, which he'd written out in big letters. "In other words, where do we find the source of our magic?"

Professor Warren looked out over the classroom, and an awkward silence ensued. He stuck his hands into the pockets of his ironed trousers.

"Anyone?" he asked with a raise of his eyebrow.

At the front of the room, Lena raised her hand. I couldn't help the frown that crossed my face. After Lena kissed me last semester to piss off Nadine, we hadn't been on good terms. I saw her shooting me glances in class every now and then, but she never talked to me. It was starting to feel kind of stalkery and annoying.

"The source of our magic is in our blood," Lena answered. "We're born with it."

Professor Warren pressed his lips together. "If that were the case, the same would apply to all magical races, would it not?"

She shifted in her chair. "Well, it does, doesn't it?"

"Not quite," Professor Warren said.

"But if you push your magic too hard, you'll hurt yourself—just like if you overexert yourself during exercise," Lena insisted, like Professor Warren was wrong. "It's the same thing, same type of energy. It comes from the body."

Professor Warren nodded, looking deep in thought. "A good theory, Miss Hahn, but technically incorrect. Any other guesses?"

He looked around the room, but no one offered up their hand.

"Let's take an example," Professor Warren said. "The Elementai in

Northern California draw their power from Familiars, or magical creatures they've bonded with. The fae in Malovia get their magic from their ancestral home, Edinmyre. Vampires get their magic from drinking blood, and Astromancers obtain their power from the stars. Does that help us form any guesses where witches get their power from?"

Grant timidly raised his hand. "Do we get it from the Goddess?"

Professor Warren looked slightly impressed. "What makes you say that, Mister Bryant?"

Grant looked a little nervous. "Well, she awakens our powers, which suggests she has some control over them."

Professor Warren's eyes brightened. "A wonderful point, but it's unfortunately not the answer I'm looking for. Any other ideas?"

"Alora," I muttered under my breath. It came out without intention. I didn't like answering questions during class. All eyes turned toward me.

"What was that, Mister Taylor?" Professor Warren sounded intrigued.

I cleared my throat. "We draw our power from our afterlife, Alora."

"Exactly," Professor Warren said brightly. "This is an important distinction to make, because it governs many magical laws we will discuss later in the semester. Each answer given is correct in its own right, but at very different levels."

Professor Warren held up a finger. "At level one is our connection to magic—our ability to manipulate it. As Miss Hahn pointed out, that connection is within our blood, passed down through the generations from Mother Miriam and the demon Santos."

He added a second finger. "Level two occurs when Mother Miriam awakens your magic during your Evoking Ceremony. But the third level, and the strength of all our power, comes from our afterlife, Alora."

Professor Warren started pacing as he lectured. "Within Alora are various *types* of magic. Each magical frequency is connected with a different Cast. When you receive your Cast assignment and your mark, the magical potential in your blood is secured to a single energy signature."

Grant nudged me in the arm and leaned over to whisper. "Nadine must have some level of access to all of them as a Curse Breaker."

I nodded in agreement. "Yeah, but it has to have limits. She can only move the magic, not use its powers."

Grant looked thoughtful, and I turned back to the board, listening closely to the lesson.

"Think of your body as conduit for magical energy," Professor Warren continued. "The source comes from outside of you and moves *through* you, and *you* get to decide how to transform and shape it into whatever energetic output you're capable of. With this information, we can apply several universal laws to the Miriamic Coven."

Professor Warren turned toward the board and began writing. "Law number one: The Law of Conservation of Energy. As we all know, energy cannot be created nor destroyed—a basic law of physics. However, Alora's energy fields are a renewable source of magic, which means we always have something to draw from."

He started scribbling down notes for the second law. "Law number two: The Law of Limitations. As Miss Hahn pointed out, our powers are limited. We are not just conduits of magic, but *reservoirs*. Certain levels of magic remain with you at all times, but as it is used up, it is replenished. Should you draw too much magic at once, you will overload your body, and magic will come flooding in like a broken dam. This can result in blacking out, serious injury, and even death. In cases like this, it takes time to recover—sometimes even days to regain your strength. That said, your limits can be expanded; you can build a larger reservoir over time. The more you exercise your magic and learn to control it, the stronger you can become."

He continued writing on the next line. "Finally, the third law of magic: The Law of Love. Strong witches and warlocks are driven by love, because Alora was created by the love Mother Miriam and Santos made. Mastering the vibrations of love will allow you to tune into Alora's magical frequencies with astounding accuracy."

Lena's hand shot up at the front of the room the second he finished. "Alora can't be our only source of power. We use crystals, and Alchemists use plants in potions."

Professor Warren nodded. "There are other sources of magic, but to a smaller extent. Magical plants, for example, contain small traces of magic in themselves. Crystals can contain magic you've infused into them, but it's a better example of *amplifying* your powers than a direct source— much like using a wand or performing a ritual. It's a tool for direction and focus, which ties back to our second law, the Law of Limitations. Crystals and wands can help push your limits because they ease some of the energetic burden on your body."

Lena's hand shot into the air again. The girl couldn't shut up. "So, if our power doesn't come directly from Mother Miriam, she doesn't really have any control over our power, right? I mean, all our Evoking Ceremony does is grant us access to Alora's power, right?"

Professor Warren gave it a moment of thought. "That's correct."

"So she could never, for example, take your power back?" Lena asked.

I furrowed my brow. Why would Lena want to know something like that? Had she upset Mother Miriam?

Professor Warren tilted his head, looking confused why anyone would want to know. "I don't suppose so. The only chance your magic could be cut off is if Alora was destroyed, but that's impossible."

"*Hypothetically*," Lena said dramatically, "if Alora *was* destroyed, could witches still perform magic?"

Professor Warren pressed his lips together. "If they found another source, I suppose that's possible."

I didn't like the direction Lena's questions were headed. Mother Miriam had to have a divine reason for assigning each person to only *one* Cast. If witches gained powers from other sources, or knew how to draw from all five Casts, we'd have demigods living among us. The consequences of such power in the wrong hands could be perilous to all supernatural races.

"So, like, we could draw from magical creatures like the Elementai do?" Lena pressed.

Professor Warren tilted his head in uncertainty. "The Elementai's bond to their creatures is unique. If we *could* draw magic from magical creatures, the effects would be minimal."

Lena spoke without raising her hand. "Could you take from another supernatural? I mean, if we're a reservoir for magic, aren't we ourselves a source?"

Professor Warren's features were calculating. "You'd have to be able to overpower another supernatural, essentially stripping them of their control. It'd be nearly impossible. Theoretically, you'd have to be an extremely powerful witch, and even then you'd only be able to draw from a witch—not another supernatural."

Another hand went up at the front of the room. It was Darcy, a student I recognized who worked in the Lounge's restaurant between classes. She pushed her long red curls over her shoulder. "Wouldn't that be considered a form of dark magic? I mean, we're not supposed to draw from living creatures."

Professor Warren shifted his weight, looking a little uncomfortable. He always got that way when people started asking questions that didn't fall within the scope of course material. "That depends on your definition of dark magic. To the fae, all the Coven's magic is dark, because we have demon ancestry and use tools like crystals and wands. To the Miriamic Coven, anything that brings harm to another living creature falls within the realm of dark magic."

"You mean... killing an animal?" Darcy asked, sounding uncomfortable.

Professor Warren nodded. "Yes. Transforming another being's life force into magic is vile and dangerous. This earth is sacred, and we must honor the lives of those we share it with."

"But what about herbal magic?" Lena questioned. "Aren't plants living as well?"

"Yes, of course," Professor Warren said. "But we are able to perform herbal magic with care, through agricultural harvest. That is vastly different than if you were to simply to burn down a forest with no regard to the plant life."

"So, where does defensive magic fit into that?" Darcy asked. "I mean, since we can use battle orbs to hurt other people."

"Defensive magic should only be used to protect yourself and members of the coven," Professor Warren emphasized. "It's designed to safeguard us from outside threats. Rest assured that all materials used in your classes are sourced ethically and the school only teaches defensive magic to protect you."

"There are other forms of dark magic, aren't there?" Lena asked. She sounded far too interested in the topic, if you asked me. But Lena was like that sometimes. She liked to push limits, even when a topic such as dark magic was clearly making Professor Warren uncomfortable.

"Yes, but they all follow the same principles," Professor Warren explained. "Take demon deals, for example. Demon magic itself is not inherently dark, but demons always ask for something in return. Most often..."

Professor Warren gave a shudder. "Most often, a living soul."

"Ew," Lena said, sounding repulsed. It came off a little fake and ingenuine to me.

A silent beat passed, then Professor Warren cleared his throat. "Anyway, moving on."

"I have one more question!" Lena interrupted, shooting her hand into the air.

Professor Warren hesitated, but he seemed curious. "Yes, Miss Hahn?"

"Just so I understand the magical theory behind it," Lena started. "Let's say you didn't pass your Evoking Ceremony, and you were banished from the Coven with no access to Alora's powers. Magical abilities are still within your blood, so couldn't you still use powers through a different source—say, by making a deal with a demon and drawing from the powers of the Abyss?"

Holy shit, Lena. What kind of twisted-ass question was that? How many souls would one have to kill to maintain that kind of power? I shivered at the thought of such evil.

Professor Warren's lips tightened. "That's not something I believe any witch or warlock has tried."

"But people have been banned from the coven before," Lena argued. "They must've tried *something*. I know I would."

Grant and I exchanged a look of disgust. Was Lena admitting she'd have turned to dark magic—to murder—if she hadn't passed her Evoking Ceremony? Thank the Goddess she passed and didn't have to test it out.

Another beat passed before Lena quickly added, "It's all hypothetical of course. But you're our Magical Theory professor. If anyone knows the answer, shouldn't you?"

Lena didn't even try to hide the condescension in her tone. Her total lack of respect for authority said a lot about her.

A moment of offense crossed Professor Warren's face. He composed himself quickly. "I suppose in theory, it may work. But all of you here have passed your Evoking Ceremony, so that's not a topic worth worrying about. Please get out your textbooks and flip to page one-hundred and twelve."

Professor Warren turned toward the board and began erasing the items he'd written. I watched him closely, not looking at the pages as I flipped through my book. He moved slowly, like it was more or less an excuse not to face the class. He seemed really uncomfortable with Lena's questions—like he knew something he didn't want to admit to the class.

The class passed on a lighter note as we discussed the first three laws of magic. At the end of class, Grant and I were the last to leave.

"Mister Taylor," Professor Warren called. "Can I have a word?"

Great. What was this about?

"I'll catch up with you later, Grant," I said, before turning to Professor Warren. "What's up?"

He gave a kind smile. "I just wanted to check in, as your academic advisor."

I shrugged. "I'm doing fine."

"Have you given any thought about your major?" he questioned.

I shifted my weight between my feet. "Not really."

Professor Warren raised his eyebrows. "You're running out of general classes. Applications for majors are open, and it's customary for students to declare a major by the end of their sophomore year."

I raked my fingers through my hair. "I know."

Professor Warren went over to the desk at the front of the room and flipped open a folder. He took out a sheet of paper and handed it to me. "Here's a list of all Miriam College's majors. Give it some thought before the end of the semester, okay?"

I took the paper without looking at it. The truth was, I always figured I'd end up working in one of the breweries in town after graduation. My best bet was a degree in general studies.

"Thanks," I said lamely. "I will."

I left the classroom and headed to the Main Foyer, where Nadine and I met up every Wednesday for lunch. She got out of class before I did, and was usually waiting for me near the fireplace. Today, she wasn't there. I took a seat to wait for her, but I nervously glanced around. The foyer buzzed with conversation as people rushed to their classes. I expected to see Nadine, but I didn't. Maybe she had a meeting with one of her professors that ran late.

I leaned back in the chair, but a moment later, a strange sensation stirred in my gut.

"I've lived a full life. I'm ready for what comes next."

My spine straightened as I took in the sound of the voice. The thought was peaceful and much easier to deal with than others. Still, I had to honor it and let it go. I conjured my journal. I took a couple of deep breaths as I sat there, my pen hovering over the page.

I often wondered what my last thought might be. Would it be sad and depressing, or would I feel fulfilled by the life I lived? I never felt confident in either answer. Today, I had hope that my last days might end in happiness.

I jotted down the thought, before ripping the page out and tossing it into the fireplace. The flames ate away at the paper, until it was nothing but ash. I smiled lightly as I watched the paper burn. I was finally making progress with my gift.

I turned back to my journal and flipped to a page I'd been using to track my triggers. If I knew what set me off, I could deal with it better. Today, I wrote down the opposite—the things that made me feel good, feel *hopeful*.

"Hey." Nadine's bright voice pulled me from my thoughts. I subconjured my journal and pen and gazed up at her. She looked really nice today, with a crop top and high-waisted jeans. A line of skin peeked out between her pants and shirt. I found myself gaping as I pictured my fingers running along her skin.

"How's it going?" I asked, quickly composing myself.

Nadine sat beside me and breathed a puff of air. "It's fine. Sorry I'm late. I ran into Amy on her way out of Verla's Alchemy guest lecture. She wasn't feeling well, so Mandy and I took her back to her room."

"Amy, not feeling well?" I was shocked to hear it. "Can't she brew something for practically any symptom?"

"I asked her that, too, but she didn't feel up to it," Nadine said with a frown. "She said her magic felt... off."

I tilted my head to the side. "Off how?"

Nadine shrugged. "I don't know. That's all she said."

"Hmm..." I mused. "I wonder if something's going around."

Nadine nudged her foot against mine. "Maybe you can write about it in your fancy paper."

I chuckled lightly. "Yeah, if I can get this first article written. *The Epitaph* has no content."

"How's the article coming?" She sounded genuinely interested. "Any new leads?"

I'd told Nadine, Grant, and Talia about what I'd found at the

Thomas' house, but we had no theories as to which professor could be behind it. Most of the staff had been here a long time—it could be anyone.

I took a deep breath. "Isaac's mom keeps rescheduling on me, and his dad won't take my calls. They're divorced, but neither of them seem to want to talk. I need more information for the article. Anyway, are you ready for lunch?"

"Famished."

Nadine and I headed toward the cafeteria. She talked about the plot of the murder mystery novel she was reading, and I couldn't help but become entranced by the sound of her voice. It was like a song I could listen to on repeat for a century and never get sick of.

We filled our plates with food. She chose healthy options, like a salad and a baked potato, while I went all out with three slices of pizza and a mountain of French fries. We found a table in the corner of the room. Nadine sat across from me and glanced at my plate.

"What?" I asked innocently as I sprinkled red pepper on my pizza, then dipped it in ranch dressing.

Nadine scrunched up her nose. "That looks awful."

My jaw dropped. "You've never had ranch on your pizza? What are you, a pineapple pizza kind of girl?"

Nadine ducked her head and blushed. "Actually, yes. But it's not the ranch that bothers me. You used so much red pepper. How are you not gagging on that?"

I took a big bite of pizza and shrugged. "It's good."

She rolled her eyes. "You're such a guy."

I swallowed and dropped my jaw dramatically. "What's that supposed to mean?"

"You talk with your mouth full for one," she teased.

"Does that bother you?" I asked with a full mouth, just for show.

Nadine shook her head, but she was smiling the whole time. "See what I mean? Didn't your mother teach you table manners?"

"She did. I chose to ignore it."

Nadine nudged my leg under the table with her foot. "Men are animals."

I smirked at her. "Get me alone, and I'll show you what kind of animal I can be."

Nadine swallowed her food and wiggled her eyebrows. "Be careful what you dare me to do. I just might do it."

I dipped my pizza into the ranch again but hesitated as I brought it to my mouth. I looked from Nadine to the pizza, then back at her. "I dare you to try a bite of my *disgusting* pizza."

Nadine crinkled her nose. "Ew, no."

I frowned. "I thought you were all about adventure."

She narrowed her eyes at me. "If I take your dare, you have to take mine."

"Fine with me," I agreed with a shrug. There wasn't anything Nadine could dare me to do that I wouldn't. Nothing I could think of, anyway.

Nadine leaned over the table, and I held my pizza out to her. She took a bite and started chewing with a calculating look. There was something sexy about feeding my girlfriend. Nadine kept on chewing, her features changing as she tested out the flavors.

"What do you think?" I asked.

She swallowed. "Not as bad as I thought, to be honest."

A beat of silence passed as Nadine started eating her own food again.

"So, what's my dare?" I asked.

Nadine glanced around the cafeteria. "Not here."

I narrowed my eyes. "What are you planning?"

She smirked proudly. "It's a surprise."

"Says the girl who hates surprises."

"I only don't like them when I'm on the receiving end," she defended.

"But it's okay to keep me in suspense?" I challenged.

"Exactly," she teased proudly. "Glad we're on the same page. I'll tell you when we finish eating."

I didn't have any clue what Nadine had in mind, but that tiny little promise made me scarf down my meal quicker than ever. Nadine finished shortly after, and we left the cafeteria hand-in-hand. She led me down the hall.

"Can I hear that dare yet?" I asked with a smirk. I couldn't lie and say I wasn't curious.

Nadine waited for a few students to pass us in the hall, then leaned over to me and whispered. "I dare you to kiss me somewhere you've never kissed me before."

A smile spread across my face. I glanced up and down the hall, but it was between classes and no one was around. I squeezed Nadine's hand tighter and led her into a nearby classroom. The lights were off, and the curtains were closed. When I shut the door behind us, it was really dark. It was a small classroom that didn't even have desks. Three fireplaces lined each wall, along with two couches back to back that faced the fireplaces. Crystal balls were set atop each mantle.

Nadine furrowed her brow. "What is this room? Some sort of portal hub?"

"Nah, the coven's portal magic is shit and really rare," I said. "It's a Seer classroom. Some Seers get visions in the flames of fires."

Nadine let go of my hand and walked around the room, eyeing the ornate mantels. Even though it was dark in here, there was enough light coming from behind the curtains that I could make out her form. My eyes locked on her perfect ass as she swayed her hips, sending my pulse quickening. It was damn hard to keep my distance from her when I wanted her so badly.

She ran her fingers across the fabric of the couch and sat down. "So... about that dare—"

She didn't have a chance to finish. I couldn't take the temptation. I immediately sat beside her, and my lips connected passionately with hers. She drew a sharp breath. My heart hammered as I wrapped my arms around her back and drew her closer. Nadine arched her back, pressing her breasts against my chest. I tried to hold back, but I couldn't control it. One hand dropped down to settle on her hip, while the other inched up her torso.

Nadine was warm and soft. My hands moved over her skin, like they were built to please her. All I wanted was to be close to her, to melt into her and become one. I was hers for life, and she could do anything she wanted with me.

I stopped when my thumb grazed the underwire of her bra. The amount of self-restraint it took was astounding, when all I wanted was to get rid of the clothes between us. My dick wouldn't calm down, demanding more.

Nadine moaned against me, and I kissed her harder. Her tongue slid inside my mouth, and her hands tangled in my hair. Goddess, she felt amazing—her soft skin, the curve of her body, her lips on mine. This woman could very well be the death of me.

Nadine drew away, her chest heaving. "What are you waiting for? You've touched my boobs before."

"I-I wasn't sure... I—" I stammered.

Nadine's arms wrapped around my neck. "You always have my permission, Lucas."

Her lips pressed to mine again, and her tongue danced inside my mouth. All the blood rushed from my brain to my dick, and I couldn't think straight. My body took over and started doing the thinking for me. It was like I'd been switched to autopilot with a single goal in mind —*Nadine*.

I pushed the fabric of her shirt up, until both of my hands were fingering the lace of her bra. My heart felt like it was trying to beat its way out of my chest, and I practically forgot how to breathe. If anyone tried to convince me that they'd felt this way before, I wouldn't believe them. This wonderful, glorious feeling was reserved just for Nadine and me. It was special, something to be cherished. I never wanted to stop.

Nadine's hands ran up and down my body. She trailed her fingers a half inch into the top of my waist band, nearly grazing the top of my dick. I gasped, but I didn't think she noticed.

Wanting more, I reached to her back and tried to undo the clasp on her bra. I fumbled for a few moments before she stepped in and did it herself.

"Sorry," I muttered.

"Shh..." she insisted, before kissing me again.

I ran my hands up her skin, until her breasts were in my hands. Oh. My. Goddess. I shuddered.

Nadine got to her knees on the couch and pressed her palm against my chest. Our bodies moved in sync, and I lowered myself onto the couch. Nadine climbed on top of me. Her lips roamed over mine, and her hands fisted in my hair. I squeezed her breasts over and over, unable to stop. My dick was rock hard in my jeans.

Nadine finally pulled away, which I was partially disappointed about, and yet glad, because I needed a moment to catch my breath.

"So, where are you going to kiss me?" she whispered.

I tilted my head at her. "What do you mean? We've never kissed in this classroom before."

Nadine rolled her eyes and swatted my chest. "That's not what I meant."

My smile grew wide. "Where do you *want* me to kiss you?"

I dragged her closer and pressed my lips to the sensitive area below her ear. "Here?" I teased. My lips trailed down to her collarbone. "Here?"

Nadine laughed as my lips tickled her skin. "Surprise me."

I pressed my lips against her harder. She tilted her head to the side, welcoming my kiss. She let out little moans that turned me on. I trailed kisses all along her neck and across her collarbone. All the while, my hands squeezed her breasts. Nadine's body moved in little motions across my dick as she ran her hands all over me. I didn't think she noticed what she was doing, and it made my head spin.

We didn't need words to communicate. When Nadine lifted her arms, I slipped her shirt up over her head. Her bra hung loosely on her shoulders, and I slid that down her arms, trailing kissed down to her hands as I did so. My gaze locked on her breasts. Nadine shivered above me.

"Cold?" I asked.

She had her eyes closed and looked totally blissful. "No. Just enjoying you. You're really good at this."

The compliment did something to me I couldn't explain. I didn't have a lot of practice in this department, and to know I was pleasing her made me want to do more—just to see her happy.

I wanted everything I could get from Nadine, because when we were together like this, it felt like I could finally show her how I felt. Words didn't do it, but when our bodies moved in sync, it was a whole new level of communication. Her love poured into me, and mine overflowed into her.

Wrapping my arms around Nadine's naked torso, I drew her closer to me. She went in for a kiss, but I ducked my head instead. This time, my kiss didn't touch her neck—it went *lower*. My lips brushed across the swell of her breast, and she let out a heavy moan. I kissed her again. My lips dipped further, and my heart hammered as I came closer and closer to my target. I didn't think what I was doing—I just acted on instinct. I drew Nadine's nipple into my mouth, and she gasped in surprise, tightening her hands in my hair. My dick jerked in my pants, and I couldn't take it any longer. I yanked her closer until she was lying on top of me. I grabbed her hips and buried my face into her neck, inhaling the rosy scent of her hair.

I thrust my hips upward, pressing my hardness into her. There were clothes between us, but something about it felt so wrong—and so damn right at the same time.

Nadine leaned back, and shock riveted through me when her fingers undid the button on my jeans. She freed my rock-hard dick and wrapped her soft fingers around it. I went as still as a statue, unable to breathe. The only indication I had that it was truly happening was my pulse pounding in my ears.

"Wow," Nadine breathed, staring down at my length. I hoped she was impressed. I couldn't read her features. Nadine's hand tightened around me, and I totally lost my train of thought. I leaned my head back on the arm of the couch.

Creak!

The sound of a door swinging open met my ears, and light flooded the room from the hall. My heart leapt to my throat, and Nadine yanked away from me instantly. For a second, I'd forgotten we were in a classroom and not in the privacy of our dorms. She grabbed her shirt and covered her bosom, while I shoved my dick back in my pants. It wasn't excited anymore—that was for certain.

I whirled toward the door to see Talia standing there, hands over her eyes.

"Holy shit!" she exclaimed. She quickly jumped back into the hall and slammed the door behind her.

I glanced to Nadine, my heart rate finally slowing. Even in the darkness, I could see Nadine's face had gone totally ashen. After a few beats, she burst out laughing. She climbed off of me and doubled over, still clutching her shirt over her chest. I quickly got to my feet and zipped up my pants. My face burned hot with embarrassment. Nadine couldn't stop laughing.

I cleared my throat. "What's so funny?"

"N-nothing," she gasped as she fastened her bra. "I'm horrified. Thank the Goddess that was Talia and not someone else!"

"Yeah," I stated flatly. "Thank the Goddess. What are we going to do?"

Nadine slipped on her shirt. "Walk out there proudly like we did nothing wrong, because we didn't. What do *you* suggest?"

"We crawl out the window and cut all ties with Talia," I deadpanned.

Nadine rolled her eyes. "You can be so dramatic sometimes. Come on."

She grabbed my hand and practically dragged me out of the room. I followed, but I couldn't look at Talia when we stepped into the hall. Probably for the best, because she wouldn't look at us, either.

"Hey, Tal," Nadine said brightly, as if nothing happened.

"Hey, guys," Talia said, though she kept her eyes on the ground. "Um... just so you know, this classroom is used on Wednesdays at one o'clock. Maybe next time you can find someplace that's not... well, not *my* classroom."

Nadine scrunched up her nose. "That ruins the fun."

"Yeah, I'm sure it was... fun." Talia looked the two of us up and down, then quickly added, "I didn't see anything."

Thank the Goddess, but what were we still doing standing around talking about it?

Talia looked about as embarrassed as I was. She quickly whirled around and turned into the empty classroom before any of us could say another word.

I breathed a sigh of relief and turned to Nadine. "Well, that was—"

"Fun?" she asked.

"I was going to say a disaster."

Nadine shrugged. "Who says disasters can't be fun?"

I smirked playfully. "Parts of it were fun."

"Agreed." Nadine pressed a chaste kiss to my lips. "I know you have to get to class, but I can't wait to finish what we started in there."

Nadine squeezed my hand, then started walking away in the direction of her dorm room. I was left standing in the hallway, speechless.

The truth was, I couldn't wait either.

nadine

SIX

On Friday, classes couldn't end soon enough. I was finally starting to get the hang of Alchemy 101—until Gwen slipped a drop of belladonna oil into my lavender-chamomile mixture. As soon as I added it to the cauldron, white smoke hissed out of the pot. Onyx and I both became victims of the vicious prank, and our vision was blurred for the next half hour.

Onyx never said anything, but she looked *pissed*. I didn't think she'd believe it wasn't my fault, so I didn't bother trying to convince her. I didn't have *proof* it was Gwen, either, but when Professor Richards said he suspected belladonna oil, I knew that bitch messed with my potion.

I stomped back to my room after classes. Isa walked ahead of me, swaying her hips and swishing her tail back and forth.

When I entered the room, Talia was sitting on her bed holding a small wooden box. The moment she heard me, she slammed the box shut and shoved it behind her. Her cheeks blushed pink.

I stopped in the doorway and tilted my head. "Everything okay?"

"What?" she asked innocently. "Yeah. Why?"

I set my bag on the bed. Isa crossed to the other side of the room and started licking the side of Gus's face. I gestured to the box behind Talia. "It looks like you're hiding something."

Her shoulders relaxed a little. "I'm not *hiding* it. It's just… a surprise."

"A surprise for who?" I asked.

Talia paused a beat, then said, "You, actually."

"Oh?" I raised an eyebrow. "Can I see?"

Talia held the box protectively to her chest and stood. "Not until we get to your grandma's."

"Damn, I have a lesson today, don't I?" I'd almost forgotten. I was supposed to start my curse breaking lessons weeks ago, but I hadn't felt well enough until now.

"Yes, and Helena asked me to help." Talia stood and set the box on her dresser next to a pile of trinkets I'd never seen before.

"What's all that?" I questioned, walking over to get a better look. The pile was made of small antiques—including a ring with a huge pink stone set into it, an ancient-looking silver teaspoon, and a pin in the shape of a rose.

Talia picked each one up in turn. "I stopped at *Cornerstone Antiques* between classes. It was *really* cool. There's so much history there. My visions were all over the place."

"These all give you visions?" I asked, reaching out to inspect a vintage pocket watch.

"It's why I bought them," Talia said brightly. "These ones all had happy memories attached to them."

"Really?" I was suddenly intrigued. "What do you see?"

Talia picked up the ring and closed her eyes. "I see an old lady with this one. She wore the ring all the time. It was a gift from her husband. I feel really happy when I'm holding it."

"Can I try?" I asked.

Talia placed the ring in my palm. I closed my eyes and concentrated, but there was no magic within the ring. I felt nothing.

I frowned. "I don't feel it."

Talia smirked. "You're not a psychometrist. Speaking of which, are you ready to get started on your Curse Breaker lesson?"

I took a deep breath. It was like asking me if I wanted to go running to train for a marathon. It wasn't something I particularly *wanted* to do—I tried to use magic as little as possible—but I knew I had to if I was ever going to figure it out.

"Ready as I'll ever be," I said.

Talia grabbed the wooden box and subconjured it. "Good. We'll take my car."

Talia checked her hair in the mirror and smoothed it down before we left the room.

When we arrived at Grammy's, the curtains were closed, and the whole house was dark. I stared up at the front door in confusion. "Grammy said she'd be here, didn't she?"

"Yeah, of course she did," Talia said as she climbed out of the car. Gus and Isa jumped out of the back seat and followed behind us. Gus licked the snow, and Isa adopted a silly walk as she tried to fling the water from her feet on the wet walkway.

"Grammy?" I called as we stepped inside.

"In here, dear," she replied.

I peeked into the dining room and found her sitting at the table. An array of scrapbooks and journals were scattered across the table in front of her. Her cat, Cornelius, sat in her lap. She drew a sip of water from a glass and adjusted her reading glasses when we entered the room.

"Ah, just in time," Grammy said. "I've just finished reading a section in one of your grandfather's journals that I think will be very useful to us. Please, have a seat."

I sat next to her, while Talia took the seat across from me. Isa jumped onto the table and began sniffing the open books.

"Talia, I trust you found what I requested?" Grammy asked.

Talia conjured the wooden box from earlier and set it in front of herself on the table. "I sure did, Helena."

Grammy smiled and straightened in her chair. "Perfect. Then let's get started. As you know, Curse Breakers have the unique power to move magic from one place to another. Now, all curses are attached to something, whether it be an object or a person. Once you can identify the curse, you can draw it out."

I leaned my elbows on the table, drinking in every word. "What happens to the curse once I draw it out? I mean, magic is energy, right? Do I... absorb the power?"

"Alora, no!" Grammy clutched the crystal around her neck. "Such dark magic would devastate you."

I shuddered at the thought.

"Technically, you *could* absorb the energy," Grammy clarified. "But you wouldn't want to. That kind of darkness could make you go mad."

I swallowed the lump in my throat.

"Within the Miriamic Coven, dark magic refers to any magic intended to hurt another being," she explained. "That may mean drawing from another being for your own purposes, since stealing their energy harms them. Or it could mean casting your own magic to hurt someone else. Every spell you cast has a unique energy signature. Curses are cast with ill intent, which taints their energy signature.

"Here's what I managed to gather between what Nicholas—your grandfather—told me when he was alive and how he explained it in his journals," Grammy continued in a softer tone. "As you mentioned, magic itself is energy, but the *specifics* of it is held within an intention. Curses are made of dark energy, but the *intention* of the curse is attached to which-ever person or object it's cast upon."

I furrowed my brow, trying to follow along. "So, what does that mean for breaking a curse?"

"Once you draw the magic out of the object, the intention is broken," Grammy explained. "The magic itself becomes… versatile."

"So, I could transform it into whatever I want?" I questioned.

Grammy sighed heavily. "Yes and no. You can change the intention, but not the energy signature."

Talia looked intrigued. "So you're saying that if the magic is dark, it will always stay dark."

"Yes," Grammy confirmed with a nod. "There are some supernaturals who are able to transform magic, but the Miriamic Coven cannot."

"What happens to the curse once I draw it out?" I asked, my pulse quickening. "I don't want that dark magic inside of me."

"Of course not," Grammy said. "But as energy, it must go somewhere."

"Like into another object?" Talia guessed.

"Exactly," Grammy confirmed.

I ran my fingers down Isa's tail. "How does that break a curse, though? It just moves it from one place to another."

Grammy shook her head. "Not exactly. As I said, you can change the intention of the magic. That said, because the magic is dark, it will always result in consequences."

I shifted in my chair as a beat of silence passed. "Consequences like what?"

Grammy took a deep breath. "Let's say you wanted to break the curse attached to a necklace. You could draw out that magic and funnel it into a glass of water. But because the water now has dark magic in it, it would be poisoned."

"So, we're trading one curse for another?" I asked, feeling slightly frustrated.

"I wouldn't go that far," Grammy said. "By poisoning the water, you've used up and dispersed the magic. The curse can't touch anyone again."

I sat still, thinking it over. Grammy and Talia didn't say anything for a long time. It seemed complicated, yet with everything I'd learned about magic, it also seemed necessary. Magic was energy, and it needed to flow.

My gut twisted as I thought about curses, and my mind immediately went to my family curse. I could feel the darkness of the curse inside of me. I always had, ever since I was a kid. Though I could control it, I didn't want it inside of me at all.

Finally, I spoke slowly. "What about breaking a curse on a person? Is it any different?"

Grammy leaned her elbows on the table. "Yes and no. Curses are held within the individual they were cast upon."

"That's why I feel this darkness inside of me," I remarked in a near whisper.

Grammy's lips pressed into a thin line. She looked uncomfortable at the mention of our family curse. Grammy wasn't ignorant to the many fights I'd started in grade school or the years of therapy I went through to manage my emotions. "Yes, unfortunately."

"It probably has something to do with why Chloe's such a bitch, too," Talia stated.

Grammy shot her a look I couldn't read. "Perhaps. You do have to realize that even if that dark magic is there, a person has a choice whether to act upon it or not. I'm not referring to the curse itself—if you are cursed to die, such a thing can't be avoided, save for if there were loopholes placed into the curse itself."

Her features turned stiff then, and she got a faraway look in her eyes. "But outside of the curse, you get to choose the actions you take—how deeply you let that darkness affect you. Nadine has taken it very well, and why I suspect Mother Miriam chose her."

I gave a shy smile.

Grammy's lighter tone returned. "With witch magic, if the curse is upon an individual, drawing that magic out should be easy. However, if the curse is cast upon a group, it resides in each of those individuals. The curse must be broken one at a time."

I felt sick to my stomach thinking about it. How many curses were out there over entire populations? How could I help everybody?

"Is this all making sense so far?" Grammy asked.

I nodded. "I think so."

Grammy smiled lightly. "Good. Then shall we test it out?"

I tilted my head. "Is it safe for you to be around a curse?"

"Depends on the curse," Grammy said.

She nodded to Talia, who slid the wooden box across the table. It was really smooth, and upon closer inspection, I saw that it was engraved with carvings of the moon cycle.

"This is an enchanted box given to me by my grandmother," Talia explained. "It keeps any magic inside from escaping. Helena sent me to *Cornerstone Antiques* to search for lowly cursed objects we could use to practice on."

"How do you know they're cursed?" I questioned.

Talia's lips turned down. "I told you I could feel when objects felt happy. These ones were obviously dark. With my gift, I could look through their past and see what kind of curse was put upon them. I chose the least dangerous objects I could."

"O-okay," I said warily.

Slowly, I opened the box. I didn't feel anything at first, then the magic hit me like a strong gust of wind. Isa hissed and jumped down from my lap, scurrying into the living room. Gus cowered in the corner.

There were three objects set inside the box—a thimble, an old compass, and a broken pearl earring. Each let off a high-frequency vibration that rang in my ears and made me cringe.

"What do they do?" I asked, careful not to touch them.

"The thimble is a curse of pain, but it's more itchy than anything," Talia said. "When I held it, it felt like little pin pricks were poking all over my body. It didn't really *hurt*, but it was super annoying."

I avoided that one to start with. It sounded awful.

"The compass messes with your sense of direction and makes you confused," Talia continued. "Admittedly, not the best curse in the box, but there are far worse curses than confusion."

"And the pearl?" I asked. Out of all three of them, that one seemed to give off the lowest frequency. It seemed the safest bet.

"That one's really petty," Talia said with a light laugh. "The vision I got showed a jealous woman cursing it so when her sister wore the earring, men would avoid her. It's the exact opposite of an attraction spell."

I shrugged. "That sounds safe. It's not like I'm trying to attract anyone right now."

"Except Lucas," Talia practically sang.

I shot a look at Grammy, who wore a hard expression. She didn't say anything, but she *had* warned me about Lucas the first time we met. I suspected she knew about the Reaper's Shadow curse and didn't want me wrapped up in it. I hadn't really told her about what was going on between the two of us.

"Well, he's not here," I mumbled.

I took the pearl out of the box and closed the other cursed objects back inside. The high-pitched ringing seemed distant now.

Grammy slid her glass of water closer to me. "You already know how to move magic from one place to another. Curse breaking will be more difficult, because the magic will resist. Be patient. When you're ready, funnel the magic into the glass of water."

I steadied my breath. "Okay. Let's give it a shot."

My pulse quickened as I reached out for the pearl. I was wary of curses. They were dark and unpredictable, and I didn't know very much about them. But I knew this was the only way to learn. Grammy held her breath, like she feared what the curse might do to me. But she knew it, too —that I couldn't avoid this, only face it.

I closed my eyes and tested the weight of the pearl earring in my hand. It was light, but there was a heavy energy surrounding it, too. It didn't feel like the magic in any of the crystals I'd worked with. The energy was less of a buzz and more of a weight pulling me down. I rested my hand on the table and concentrated harder, trying to get a feel for the curse so the magic might become familiar to me. The more I focused, the more a bitterness entered the back of my throat. It was dark magic for sure, but it wasn't very strong. I didn't think it could hurt me.

I drew another deep breath, then opened myself to the magic within the pearl. I pictured the magic flowing into me, and my chest began to fill with the heavy weight. Breath no longer came naturally to me, and I had to force my lungs to fill with air.

Grammy must've noticed the distressed look on my face, because she shoved the glass of water toward me. "Change the intention, and channel it into the water," she reminded me.

I reached out with my free hand and clamped it around the glass. I didn't really know what she meant by changing the intention, but she'd mentioned poison earlier, so I used that.

Poison the water, I thought.

Magic moved through me, draining into the glass like I was pouring water from a pitcher. There were only a few drops of magic left—

Glass shattered between my fingers, and blood dripped to the table-cloth. I reeled back in my chair as water splattered all over the table and ran down on my lap. The magic I'd been funneling into the water recoiled, springing through me and back into the pearl like a snapped rubber band.

Talia gasped, and Grammy leapt to her feet, dropping Cornelius on the ground. She pushed the journals and scrapbooks away from the water, while Talia grabbed a stack of napkins from the holder nearby. She handed me some for my hand, then started drying up the water with the rest.

"What happened?" Talia asked in a breathy tone.

"I-I don't know," I said, still trying to catch my breath. I lifted the napkins to check my fingers, but the cuts weren't bad.

"It's okay," Grammy assured me. "I saw this happen when your grandpa was learning his abilities. The curse breaking didn't take. The curse resisted you."

I gaped up at her. "That curse was simple, though. I should be able to do it."

To be honest, I felt like shit. I wasn't sure it was as simple as I initially thought.

"It's going to take practice," Grammy assured me as she moved the journals off the table. "I suspected this might happen."

"How long is it going to take me to learn?" I asked.

Grammy shot me an uncertain gaze. "I'm afraid I don't have an answer. Everyone learns their magic in their own time. It could be a week. It could be months."

I sighed. "How do I get better? Just more practice?"

Grammy settled back into her chair once the table was dry. "That's a start."

"There's something else that might help," Talia suggested after she threw the wet napkins away.

"What's that?" I leaned forward, intrigued.

"Well, a lot of witches use tools to focus their magic," Talia explained.

"Like crystals?" I asked.

Talia nodded. "Usually crystals or wands, but you can really use anything that inspires you. I use music."

"Music?" I furrowed my brow. "How does that work?"

"Well, if I'm having trouble getting a vision, I'll hum certain tunes under my breath," she explained. "It helps get me in the right mind space. I've noticed I'm better at incantations if I sing them."

I pressed my lips together in thought. "Do you use anything like that, Grammy?"

"Oh, sure," she said. "I have a collection of crystals I use when brewing potions—different ones for different types of potions. If I'm brewing a healing salve, for example, I'll place rose quartz crystals around my workspace."

"What about wands?" I asked. "I've never seen anyone use a wand before."

Grammy went still at the mention of wands. She swallowed, then said, "Wands are trickier than crystals. Crystals give off certain vibrations that can help you hone your power. With wands... you need to find the right one that can do that for you."

I fingered my star necklace. "So, does it have to be magical—whatever you use to focus your power?"

Grammy shook her head. "Not necessarily. Some tools can prove far more powerful than crystals, as long as they keep you focused and grounded. Something sentimental, perhaps."

I caught Grammy's eyes dart downward at my necklace.

"So it's more of a mental thing?" I asked.

"Yes," Grammy answered. "The magic comes from within you. How you visualize it can change the outcome."

I nodded, taking in the information.

Grammy must've noticed I looked tired, because she quickly added, "I think practicing once a day is a good place to start. Why don't you take these objects back to school with you and see if you can break any of these curses this week?"

I cocked an eyebrow. "You want me to keep these cursed objects with me?"

"I don't *want* you to," she emphasized. "But we need to start somewhere. Mother Miriam gave you this gift for a reason, and I want to help you learn how to use it. It's going to be hard, and there are going to be risks, but I trust that you know your limits. I'm going to have to let you do this if I want to help."

Grammy's eyes watered. I could tell this was really hard on her. She obviously didn't want me to get hurt, but I think she knew there was greater risk in avoiding my magic all together.

After all, if I didn't learn how to break curses—and get rid of my own —she could very well lose me.

☾

I LAY SOUNDLESSLY in bed that night. Isa stirred at my side, waking me. My eyes opened to a dark room. The only light came from the moon outside the window, which cast shadows over Talia's keyboard. Voices out in the hallway had long since disappeared. It must've been two or three in the morning. Isa jumped to the end of my bed and twitched her ears.

"Here, kitty, kitty," I whispered, careful not to wake Talia. It took me a few moments to pull myself out of my slumber. For a moment, I thought I might be dreaming. Then the room came into focus, and I realized it was very real.

Isa didn't seem to notice me calling her. She hopped off the bed and sauntered around the corner, disappearing from view.

I groaned as I tried to sit up, but my muscles protested. "Isa," I hissed through the darkness. "Come back."

She'd barely left my side all week. What was she up to?

Isa didn't respond with so much as a meow. I figured she just had to use the litter box, so I relaxed into my pillow and closed my eyes... until I heard the sound of Isa's paws hitting the floor. It was quiet and graceful, like she was jumping, but it worried me.

I tossed the blanket off of myself and winced when I sat up. I pushed past the ache in my joints and peeked around the corner. Isa stood in front of the door, her eyes fixed on the doorknob and her back feet padding beneath her, like she was trying to find the perfect balance. Her tail twitched, then she launched herself upward. Her front paws clasped the door handle, and it twisted under her weight.

I gasped as the door swung open a few inches. "Isa!" I hissed, but she'd already slipped through the doorway.

Crap!

I got out of bed and hurried behind her. The hall was eerily quiet. A few sconces were lit, but they were few and far between. I could hardly see where I was going.

"Isa?" I called through the darkness.

No response.

A chill spread over my arms, and the hairs on the back of my neck stood. It felt like someone was watching me, but when I glanced behind myself, the hall was completely empty. My pulse quickened.

The tiniest meow cut through the silence, and I whirled the other way. "Isa?"

Silence.

I swallowed the lump quickly forming in my throat. It occurred to me there was a real possibility ghosts were roaming the halls. The halls were creepy as hell this time of night, but I didn't want Isa out here alone. I continued forward, though something felt peculiarly *off.*

Across from the grand staircase, the large window that looked over the forest let in the moonlight. It illuminated the stairs and the foyer with a dull silver hue. Out of the corner of my eye, I saw a dash of black on the level below me. My hands shook as I reached for the railing and began to descend the stairs. I kept alert, my eyes darting every which way. The soft padding of my feet sounded like drums in the silence.

"Isa," I hissed. "This isn't funny."

Another flash of black crossed my vision, this time in the far corner of the foyer near the fireplace. I tiptoed over there and got down on my hands and knees to peek under the chairs.

Thud.

I jumped as something hit the ground beside me. Instinctively, I reached for it and stood to place it back on the mantle, but my heart stopped when the moonlight glistened off the shiny metal end of it.

It was a knife!

My heartbeat pulsed in my ears, and my throat went dry. I glanced around the foyer, as if expecting someone to be watching nearby. It was only when I looked upward that I noticed the painting of Mother Miriam had been ripped to shreds. My stomach plummeted to my toes. Desecrating a sacred image of the Goddess was nothing short of a crime against the coven. It disgusted me to look at—that anyone would insult the coven in such a way. It looked like someone had used the knife to stab it several times, then dragged it along the painting in three equal lines. The painting curled at the corners of the tears, like it was in pain from the assault.

And I was holding the weapon, I realized in horror.

Nadine, what have you done? I asked myself. But the voice in my head was unlike my own. It sounded like me but was dark and sinister, almost like I *enjoyed* the thrill of vandalism—like I was *congratulating* myself.

But I hadn't done it! I was innocent.

"Got you!" a voice cried from behind me.

I whirled around, and a light flashed in my eyes. I heard the sound of a phone click, indicating a picture had been taken.

"Wait, no. I didn't—" I started to protest. My palms grew sweaty on the knife handle.

Three figures stepped forward, and rage ignited deep in my belly.

Chloe chuckled as she swiped through her phone. "Headmistress Verla is going to love this."

"What the hell kind of trap is this?" I demanded, my hands clenching into tight fists. "You really think she'll believe you?"

Chloe smirked, and her two back-up girls mirrored her expression. "We've got all the evidence we need."

"I should stab you," I snarled. *She deserves it,* that sinister voice said.

Camille crossed her arms and stepped forward. She stuck her hip out like she was Queen Bitch. "Touch Chloe, and I'll make your cat walk off a bridge."

My nostrils flared. She was *not* threatening Isa! "You're welcome to try."

Chloe chuckled. "Don't be so naive. How do you think we lured your cat down here in the first place?"

My breath halted in my chest. Drawing Isa downstairs was all part of a ruse to frame me?

"How'd you do it?" I demanded.

"Oh, you haven't heard?" Camille asked in a condescending tone. She lifted her hand to tap her chin, displaying the mark of a Mentalist on the back of her wrist. "I went through my Evoking Ceremony. I'm a Mentalist."

"That doesn't even make any sense," I snarled. "How'd you use telekinesis to lure my cat down here?"

The three girls laughed lightly.

"Oh, honey," Chloe taunted. "You have so much to learn. The Mentalist Cast is diverse as any—and Camille's unique gift allows her to telepathically communicate with animals."

"What the hell!? You can't do that to my cat," I protested. "She wouldn't listen to you anyway!"

Isa crawled out from beneath one of the chairs and began purring against my leg.

Camille shrugged. "Technically, I can. And she didn't exactly have a choice."

Chloe waved her phone at me. "And when everyone wakes up in the morning, they'll know what you did. Good luck staying in school after this."

My fingers tightened on the handle of the knife. "That's your plan? Frame me?"

Chloe pursed her lips and glanced between her friends. "Seems like a solid plan to me."

"Go to hell, you bitch!" I totally snapped. Red-hot anger swept through me as I lunged at Chloe, swiping the blade outward. I wasn't leaving this coven without a fight. Chloe wanted a battle? She was sure as hell going to get one.

Chloe jumped backward, and my blade met nothing but air. Her features twisted into rage as she realized what I'd just tried to do. *Please.* It wasn't like I was trying to kill her—just teach her a lesson.

"If anyone's going to hell, it's you," Chloe snapped.

She kicked toward me, and her foot connected with my hand. The blade slipped from my fingers and soared through the air before landing in the fireplace. I barely took a second to process it before I flung myself at her. I shoved her hard, and she tripped over one of the chairs nearby, landing on her ass.

I would've burst out laughing if Gwen hadn't attacked a moment later. A blast of magic shot out of her hand, and I went flying several feet backward. I landed hard on my back, gasping for air. Before I could take a breath, Gwen and Camille jumped on top of me. Each of them grabbed one of my arms and pinned me to the floor.

"Get off of me!" I growled, but I didn't have the physical strength to fight them both at once. I tried to conjure battle magic, but I'd had no training in it yet. The most I could do was draw from my raging anger and hope for the best, but the second wisps of magic came out of my palms, Camille twisted my wrist sideways, sending sharp pains radiating up my arm. I cried out.

Isa hissed at the girls and jumped on Camille's back, clawing and scratching. Camille gasped, then threw out an elbow. It connected with the side of Isa's head in a sickening *thud*, and my cat went flying and rolled across the carpet. She lay still, as if she'd been knocked out.

I struggled beneath Gwen and Camille's hold. "You fucking touch my cat again and I'll—*oof!*"

Chloe's foot connected with my gut, and I gasped for breath. The girls laughed as Chloe paced around me, eying me from every angle as if she couldn't choose where to beat me first. "That's right, girls," she sang. "Hold her down."

"You'll be expelled for this!" I threatened.

"What do you mean, Nadine?" she asked innocently. "We were in our rooms all night. We don't know who did this to you."

It sickened me how convincing she could sound. Even the headmistress might believe her.

Chloe dropped the innocent act, and a sinister smile spread across her face. She stopped pacing and loomed over me, cracking her knuckles. "This is going to be a lot of fun."

Before I could try conjuring another spell, Chloe kicked me in the side again. My abdomen contracted under the pain, and I curled my legs upward in a shitty attempt to protect myself.

"Fuck you—!" I sneered, but Chloe cut me off with another blow to my side. I kicked out at her, but she easily dodged me. "Help! Somebody he—!"

Gwen threw a hand over my mouth, silencing me. "No one's coming to your rescue," she laughed, before Chloe and Camille joined in.

"She's right," Chloe taunted. She knelt at my side and leaned in close, while I struggled to escape. She wanted to make it *very* clear who was in charge—and there was no question about it. No matter how much fight I had in me, I had nothing to fight back with.

"Nobody cares about Nadine Evers," Chloe laughed. "That's why they won't give a shit when you're banished from the coven."

Chloe drew back a fist, and Gwen dropped her hand from my mouth at the last second. I didn't have a chance to cry out for help before Chloe's fist was pummeling my face.

"H-help me!" I tried to scream, but I wasn't sure it came out as more than a whisper. Chloe's fist connected with the side of my head, and my vision blurred. The room spun around me, and I was almost certain Chloe wouldn't stop until I was two breaths short of death.

Then I heard something—the sound of a door clicking shut from upstairs. To my relief, the blows stopped coming, though the pain continued to meld into my muscles as bruises formed wherever Chloe had beaten me.

"Nadine?" I thought I heard someone call my name, but it wasn't Chloe or her friends.

"Let's get out of here," Chloe hissed. "We have what we need."

I heard the shuffling of feet. I didn't quite know what was going on. I was just glad I was no longer being pummeled. I curled into a ball on the floor, trying to catch my breath and gather my bearings.

The sound of soft footsteps approached, and I heard a light meow. Someone's hand touched my shoulder, but I didn't open my eyes to see who it was. Frankly, I was trying not to throw up.

"Nadine, what happened?" a female voice asked, sounding horrified.

"Talia?" I rolled over, finally dragging my eyes open. The room was still spinning, and I was pretty sure there was blood running down my face.

Talia gasped, and her features finally came into focus in the darkness. Gus was beside her, nudging at Isa as she began to come to. Talia's phone chimed with a notification, but we both ignored it.

"It was the Lucky Three," I rasped. "They're going to frame me for the painting. We have to tell Verla."

Talia's gaze locked on the destroyed painting, and her jaw dropped. "Dear Goddess. We can't stay out here, in case they're still around. Let me help you back to our room, where you'll be safe. I'll call the infirmary and get a nurse to look at you."

"And Verla," I insisted as Talia draped one of my arms over her neck. "She needs to know what happened here."

"She will," Talia promised. "Up you go."

Talia helped me to my feet, but I barely had the strength to stay upright. I slumped against her, and she stumbled to the side. Tears rose to my eyes as I realized how weak I was. How could I think I had it in me to take on three witches at once?

"I tried to fight them," I explained to Talia. "But I wasn't strong enough—"

"Shh…" Talia said as she led me to the grand staircase. "It was an unfair fight. There's nothing you could've done. You can explain it all to me once we're back in the room. Gus, you've got Isa?"

Both cats responded with a meow.

My feet felt like cinder blocks as I dragged them up the stairs. I knew Talia wanted to get me back to the room because the Lucky Three couldn't get inside. She was only trying to protect me. But all I wanted to do was go after Chloe, to deliver the payback that she deserved.

But I couldn't even drag my own ass up a flight of stairs. Kicking her butt was out of the question.

Talia helped me down the hall and into our dorm room. "How'd you know to come after me?" I asked.

"I woke up and saw your bed empty and the door open," she said. "I heard a commotion, but when I got to you, the Lucky Three were already gone."

I winced as I sat on the bed. "You believe me, don't you? That I didn't do it."

"Of course I do. Lie down while I call a nurse."

I did as I was told, and Isa came to my side to snuggle up with me. Talia had her phone to her ear in moments, but took off to the bathroom while it rang. I didn't hear what she said, as I was already starting to drift off.

"Don't fall asleep," Talia said when she returned. She had a warm washcloth in her hand and dabbed it on my face. "You could have a concussion. Looks like the bleeding has stopped, though."

My insides felt so tender I was certain there were bruises everywhere. "Is there a nurse coming?"

"Yes, and they promised to call Verla right away. I don't have her personal number."

Bang! Bang! Bang!

A loud knock came at our door, startling me. My first thought was that it was a nurse already, but the banging continued. This was no medical visit. I turned into a statue, though my heart must've been beating a million times a minute. Isa jumped off the bed and stood guard in front of the door, hissing. A collection of voices could be heard outside, all sounding pissed.

"We demand Nadine Evers show herself!" Ryan's angry voice came through the door.

My jaw dropped. "Chloe's turned this whole thing into a witch hunt."

Talia scrambled for her phone, and her hand shot over her mouth. "It's all over the school page, but it was posted by an anonymous account. That painting was blessed by the priestesses over fifty years ago. People are calling to have you expelled."

"That was fast," I growled. "Even if I don't get expelled, Chloe expects people to come after me. She wants *them* to do the work driving me out of town."

Bang!

The knock came at the door again. It was so loud that it made me shudder. "Admit what you did, you coward!" Ryan shouted.

I wanted to open the door and give these jerks a piece of my mind, but Talia beat me to it.

"Nobody messes with my friends," she huffed. She stomped over to the door and yanked it open. I couldn't see the confrontation from where I lay on the bed, but I heard Talia snap at the mob. "Listen up, assholes. Nadine isn't going anywhere. So you might as well—ow!"

"Where is she!?" Ryan's deep voice boomed as he shoved his way into the room. My whole body shook as he stopped at the foot of my bed, flanked by at least half a dozen other angry warlocks. If I couldn't fight off the Lucky Three, there was no way in hell I was fighting off these assholes.

"You've insulted our Goddess," Ryan sneered. "We'll make you pay—"

"*Excuse me!*" a stern voice snapped.

Ryan already had a battle orb forming in his hand, but he stopped dead when he heard the voice. I didn't recognize the woman, but she was like a blessing from Mother Miriam herself.

Ryan dropped the battle orb as the woman stepped into the room. She wore scrubs, and I realized it was the night nurse from the school's infirmary. She was an older woman with a wise look in her eyes. Her lips pressed into a thin line, a clear message Ryan and the others to *back the fuck off.*

The nurse planted herself at the foot of the bed, between Ryan and me. She placed her hands on her hips. "None of you belong here."

Several voices protested, but I couldn't make out one voice over the others.

"I mean it," the nurse snapped. "Head back to your dorm rooms, before I report each and every one of you for breaking into another student's room."

Ryan narrowed his eyes, though he knew he didn't have a choice. Attacking a staff member was a good way for him and his gang to get expelled along with me. He shot daggers my way. "You're the one who doesn't belong here. It won't be long before the school board realizes it, too."

He left the room with his mob in tow, his threat hanging in the air. The second they were gone, Talia shut the door and hurried to my bedside.

"They didn't hurt you, did they?" she asked quickly.

"No," I assured her. "She got here just in time."

I looked up at the nurse, who gave me a kind smile. "You can call me Patty," she offered, before conjuring a bag of medical supplies and setting them down at the foot of my bed. "Now, let's take a look at your injuries."

Patty was really nice and didn't prod about what happened. She checked my vitals and assessed me for a concussion, but said I didn't have one. Most of the damage was just bad bruising. She gave me a potion to help with the swelling, but said the bruises wouldn't disappear for a few days. I could already tell the next few days were going to be hell, with how sore I was.

As Patty was nearly finished, a light knock came at the door. "Nadine? It's Headmistress Verla."

"I'll get it," Talia offered as she stood.

"I apologize for the wait. The infirmary called and said there was an emergency." Verla entered the room, and she gasped at the sight of me. She'd obviously been in a hurry when she left her house, because she wore a bathrobe as a coat, and her cat's fur was sticking up at all angles.

Patty packed her things away and subconjured them. "She's a bit beat up, Headmistress, but she's going to be okay."

Verla looked a bit shaken at the sight of my bruises. She shot a glance at Talia. "Miss Murphy, may we have a moment?"

Talia hesitated, then started following Patty out of the room. As she passed by Verla, she said softly, "Go easy on her, will you?"

Verla nodded, and the door clicked shut softly. When we were alone, Verla turned to me. She let out a breath, though I couldn't read what she meant by it. Her tone, however, came out soft. "I understand what you've gone through recently. I know loss perhaps more than most."

The thought of what she'd lost always struck me. Not only had she lost my mom—her best friend—but she'd also lost her sister and child.

"You saw the picture?" I guessed with a frown.

Verla nodded. "Yes, but loss is no excuse to destroy school property."

I gaped at her. Of all people, I thought Verla would be the first to question the authenticity of the photo. She didn't actually believe I did it, did she?

"How can you look at me lying here and think I had anything to do with this?" I burst. "I didn't touch that painting!"

Verla's features shifted, but she was very good at hiding what she was thinking. "I—"

"You assumed," I bit. She thought someone like Ryan had found me after the fact and beat me up. It was exactly what Chloe wanted her to think. I thought Verla would be able to help, but I felt betrayed that she'd ever think I would do something like this. "I swear I didn't do this."

Verla sighed, like this was more complicated than I realized. "Then what *did* happen?"

"The photo was fabricated," I told her.

"Using what? Illusion magic? We don't have that kind of magic within the coven."

"No," I sighed, exasperated. "The photo was real. I *was* in the foyer, but only because the Lucky Three lured me down there. I didn't know what the knife was when I grabbed it."

"The Lucky Three?" Verla asked. "You mean Chloe, Camille, and Gwen?"

"Yes," I insisted. "Chloe doesn't want me here. She tried to frame me."

I looked up to Verla, holding my breath. She *had* to believe me. It was the truth, after all.

Finally, her shoulders dropped. "I believe you, but I'll need you to produce proof to convince the school board."

My nostrils flared. "I don't have proof. But the photo isn't proof I did it, either! Can't a Seer look into the past and see who the real culprit is?"

Verla's features softened. "We can give that a try, but you interacted with the painting. It's like leaving your fingerprints at the scene of the crime. A Seer might get visions of you there and misinterpret the vision."

"I'm telling you I didn't do it," I promised. "I have no motive."

If there was anything I learned from mystery novels, it was that motive was *always* central to the story.

"You don't have to convince me," Verla said. "But the rest of the school board will not be so easy to convince. Something must be done."

I gaped at her. "So you're going to punish me to placate everyone else?"

"I'd rather that than to see them hurt you," she countered.

"I just don't want to be expelled," I said in a small voice. Miriam College was my home. It was where my friends were, and my boyfriend. Learning to hone my magic was my one ticket toward remission. I wouldn't let Chloe use Verla as a tool to get rid of me.

"I will fight for you as hard as I can," she promised. "You're not going anywhere. I will put together a team of professors to work on a repair spell to fix the painting. In the meantime, I think detention is the best option until this blows over."

My eyebrows shot up. "Are you kidding me? I didn't do anything."

"This isn't a punishment," she assured me. "This is to protect you. I believe you, but until we have proof otherwise, the students are going to blame you. If I don't do something, they *will*."

It took me a few moments to realize what she was saying. Chloe's witch hunt had turned out just the way she wanted it, and people would want to see me punished one way or another. Verla was protecting me by ensuring she had control over the situation. Honestly, detention was better than a lynch mob.

I swallowed. "Fine, but know that I'm firmly against this."

"Neither of us have to like it," Verla said. "But this will all be over soon. I promise."

I hoped so.

Verla started for the door, but I stopped her. "Headmistress?"

She turned back to me, her eyebrows raised. Odin mirrored her.

"Thanks for believing me," I told her.

She smiled brightly. "Of course. I'm really sorry this happened to you. If there's anything I can do, let me know."

"You could expel the Lucky Three," I joked.

Verla smirked, though I knew it was unprofessional of her. "Without proof, that's unfortunately overstepping my power. But I'll see what I can do."

She winked at me, then started for the door. I heard voices outside, and though I didn't have the energy or the strength, I stood to see what was going on. I hobbled across the room and caught the door before it swung shut. Several girls had emerged from their dorm rooms to see what the commotion was all about.

Talia stood a few doors down, whispering to Mandy and Amy, who looked on with concern. Amy's cat, Stormy, nudged her leg, like she sensed Amy's unease. I shot them a reassuring look, then noticed a goth girl nearby. Onyx crossed her arms and eyed me, but I couldn't tell what she was thinking. Everyone else had looks of disgust on their faces, but Onyx's features were calculating. It was like she wasn't quite sure I would do something like this—which was weird, because she hardly knew me.

Finally, my eyes landed on Chloe. She stood next to her dorm room, leaning against the frame and wearing a look of satisfaction. Several other onlookers had hung around, but they were further down the hall.

Heat flared in my belly at the sight of the bitch. I hobbled out of the room, my eyes set on Chloe and my hands curled into fists. I had the ungodly urge to suckerpunch her in the face.

"I hope you enjoyed the witch hunt," I snapped in Chloe's face.

She looked mildly pleased to see me pissed off. "Oh, I enjoyed it very much."

"In case you didn't know, things don't work like that around here anymore," I growled. "Verla's going to investigate, and you can guess what she's going to find—the *real* culprit."

Chloe scoffed and tossed her hair over her shoulder. "Like I care what *Verla* thinks. No one wants you here anymore. They never did."

"That's not true," I snapped. "If you think a few bullies are going to drive me out of town, think again. You'll have to hang me before I leave."

I turned and headed back toward my room. Though I hadn't got a punch in tonight, I'd managed to get a word in, and that felt almost as good.

Chloe's sinister laugh echoed behind me. "Gladly."

The word should've given me shivers, but I didn't think Chloe was serious. When I reached my door and turned back toward her, she was gone.

"Nice move, Chloe," I mumbled under my breath. "Now it's my turn."

LUCAS

SEVEN

Nadine was devastated. She hid in her room all day. Usually, the two of us were inseparable outside of class, but this was different. She wouldn't even leave for food.

"I need the weekend alone," she said when I visited her. "At least to give people a chance to cool off."

My lips tightened. "Chloe can go to hell. She can't hurt you like this."

"Don't worry about me," Nadine said gently. "Don't you have an interview today? Focus on that."

I frowned as I twisted her hair in my fingers. "Isaac's mom canceled on me again."

Nadine narrowed her eyes. "His parents are avoiding you. At this point, you can't take no for an answer. You have to make an impromptu visit."

"And what if that keeps them from talking to me at all?" I pointed out.

"You want answers, don't you?" she challenged.

"Yes."

She pushed at me. "Then go get them. I'll be fine."

She was persistent, and I really did want answers. I understood that Isaac's parents were grieving and all, but if it was my kid who'd gone missing, I'd want to do whatever I could to make sure the asshole who took him was caught. I *had* to interview that family. Nadine was right, and I decided to follow her advice to see what I could learn.

I'd asked Talia to come along because of her gift. The car ride was quiet. I couldn't look Talia in the eye after she'd walked in on Nadine and me the other day.

She sighed and shifted her hands on the steering wheel. "This doesn't have to be awkward."

I crinkled my nose. "Doesn't it, though?"

"I saw nothing," Talia assured me again. "How about some music?"

Talia flipped on the radio, even though we didn't have a long car ride. An upbeat pop tempo came on, and she started singing. She nudged me in the side. "Come on. Dance!"

"You know I don't dance."

She cocked an eyebrow. "That's not true. You danced at the Midnight Formal."

"Because Nadine was there," I pointed out.

"So you *only* have fun when Nadine's around?" she questioned.

I furrowed my brow. "No. I can have fun without her."

Talia narrowed her eyes. She didn't believe me.

I huffed. "Okay, so I like her because I have fun around her. Is that a bad thing?"

Talia didn't answer my question directly. Instead, she said, "I know she wants to see you happy no matter what."

"I'm trying," I said. "Really, I am. I'm doing much better than last semester. I'm starting to feel like my old self again."

"Good," Talia said with a smile. She started moving her head from side to side on the beat. A smile spread across her face, and she watched me, waiting for me to join her.

"You should keep your eyes on the road," I said.

Her smile widened. "Not until I see you dancing."

I pressed my lips together and waited a few beats, but she didn't look away from me. This girl was going to crash the car just to get me to dance. Fuck it. I sighed and started moving my head the way she did.

Talia started snapping on the beat, and I joined in. "There ya go!" she exclaimed. "Lucas has rhythm!"

"Do I?" A smile touched my lips. I kept on dancing, putting my shoulders into it as well.

Talia started drumming on the steering wheel and sang along to the song. "Lucas, take it away!"

Talia pointed to me just as the drum solo hit. I slapped my palms to my knees and finished off by slamming the visor upward on the cymbal crash.

Talia threw her head back in laughter. "I guess I was wrong. You *can* have fun."

I was laughing, too, but I quieted when I realized where we were. "We're almost there."

Talia pulled up outside of a black Gothic house with white trim. It was two stories, with a tall turret that stretched to a third level. A huge porch wrapped around the side of the house. She gawked out the window. "Wow, this house is amazing."

"I heard they own one of the cider mills in town," I told her.

Talia whistled. We exited the car and made our way to the door. I knocked, but we were met with nothing but silence.

"Think they're home?" Talia asked skeptically. She looked up and down the street and shivered in the cold.

My brow furrowed, and I knocked again. "I hope so."

After a few moments, I heard shuffling behind the door. A woman answered. She had long blonde hair, but wore no makeup. A thick black shawl was draped around her shoulders, and she clutched a pile of tissues in her hand.

"Hi, Michelle?" I greeted kindly. "I'm Lucas Taylor, from the school paper, and this is my friend Talia. I was hoping you'd have a moment to talk."

The woman's features darkened. "I thought we'd rescheduled."

"Actually, you cancelled on me," I stated bluntly, and Talia nudged me in the side. I softened my tone. "Do you have a moment to talk now?"

Michelle hesitated with her hand on the door. For a moment, I thought she might slam it in my face. Instead, she spoke bitterly. "It's not right for you to show up here out of the blue. My family is grieving. What do you want?"

"To help," Talia promised her.

Michelle's expression softened. I was glad I'd brought Talia along, because she was a lot more personable than I was. She was good at soothing people, whereas I was great at pissing them off.

Michelle sighed. "There's nothing I can tell you that the police don't already know."

"If we could just ask you a few questions. We won't be long," Talia offered.

Michelle looked us up and down and seemed to decide it wasn't fair to keep us waiting in the cold. She stepped aside and gestured us into the entryway. The hall was lined with tons of pictures, and I could see the sitting room through a doorway, housing Victorian furniture. Michelle didn't invite us any further into the house.

She crossed her arms. "What exactly will your article cover?"

I placed my hands in my pockets. "I'm trying to gather as much information as I can about your son's disappearance. My intention is to simply report the facts."

"What do you want to know?" she asked a bit harshly.

Who took your son, I thought.

Michelle chuckled under her breath, but it didn't sound like she found anything funny—more like she was uncomfortable. Talia furrowed her brow in confusion.

"I'm afraid we *all* want to know who's behind this," Michelle said. I reeled back a bit, and she shrugged her shawl off one shoulder to reveal a tattoo of a twisted tree with no leaves—the mark of a Mentalist. "I can read minds."

My eyebrows shot up, and I suddenly felt really self-conscious. What had she heard so far?

"I can't hear everything," she quickly added. "Only what you want me to hear."

She shot a look at Talia, which I thought looked slightly *amused*. "Yes, I heard that."

Talia's eyes lit up. "Very cool!"

Michelle sniffled. "Anyway, I only have a few minutes. I was just headed out the door."

I had a feeling she was lying to hurry us along. I decided to get this over with quickly. "Can you think of any reason someone might want to take your son?"

Michelle shook her head. "No reason at all."

"And there's no chance he ran away?" I asked.

"No. Isaac would never do that," she assured me.

"Do you have any connection to the Thomas family?" I questioned.

Her face paled a little. "You mean the young boy who disappeared a year ago?"

"Yes," I said.

She didn't answer for a moment. After a beat, she dropped her gaze to her hands. "Mark and I knew Krista and Keith in college. I was on the diving team, and Keith was on the swim team, so we hung out sometimes. But after college, everyone got married, we started having kids… we all drifted apart."

"So your son has never met Caleb Thomas?" I asked.

Michelle shifted uncomfortably. "Maybe at school. I don't really know for sure."

I pressed my lips together. Michelle's story seemed to match up with what the Thomas family told me.

"Would it be okay if we saw his room?" I asked.

Michelle hesitated, then finally cocked her head. "It's this way. Though I'm not sure what you expect to find."

As she led us down the hall at a brisk pace, I had the thought that she was only showing us his room to get rid of us faster.

Isaac's room was a total disaster. The bed was unkempt, and the curtains were haphazardly tossed over the curtain rod. There were so many toys on the floor I couldn't even see the carpet. Most of them looked broken. Talia stopped in her tracks, looking shocked at the state of the room.

Michelle sniffled and wiped her nose. "I've been grieving too much to clean up."

"Is his room always like this?" I asked. It looked like a tornado had gone through it. Could it have been foul play?

Michelle nodded. "Always. Isaac never could keep his room clean."

Or his toys intact, I thought.

Michelle frowned. "I heard that."

"Can we look through his room?" Talia asked.

Michelle's eyes looked calculating. "Just be careful where you step."

Talia turned and tiptoed over broken toys and piles of dirty laundry to reach the bed. She ran her hands over the sheets, and I could see the concentration in her eyes as she worked her powers. While Talia busied herself with visions, I turned to Michelle. I still couldn't help but think the boys had some sort of connection beyond age and gender.

"Mrs. Miller, did Isaac ever spend any time in the hospital?" I asked. After hearing Caleb had broken an ankle, I wondered if maybe the boys had met there.

"No." Michelle sounded shocked. "Never. Why would you ask?"

"I'm just trying to think of everything," I assured her kindly. "Is there anything unusual you can tell me about the night he disappeared? You didn't hear anyone in the house, no thoughts or anything?"

Michelle's tone got harsh. "No. It's like I told the police. I was asleep. When I woke, Isaac was gone. The only thing out of place was an open window."

It wasn't anything I didn't already know.

"Any other questions?" Michell's lips tightened. She didn't sound willing to answer any more, but I burned to find a clue.

"So you were home alone that night?" I asked.

"Yes," she answered harshly. "Isaac and I live here alone."

"Of course," I said, like I'd just remembered. "Is there any chance your ex-husband wanted to hurt your family?"

Michelle gawked at me. "No, of course not! He sees Isaac every weekend."

I was reaching the end of my rope here. I only had a few more questions before she kicked me out. "And there's no one else… a colleague, an old boyfriend, a teacher, perhaps?"

Michelle's features darkened, and her nostrils flared. "I told you, I don't know who took my son," she snapped.

"Of course," I replied, but the way she responded made me wonder if she didn't suspect something herself. "Thank you for your time, Mrs. Miller."

"Yes, thanks for stopping by." She sounded anything but grateful.

Talia's shoulders fell as she left the bed. By the look on her face, I didn't think she'd gathered any concrete visions. I didn't expect her to, considering no one else had found anything.

"I'll let you know if we learn anything new," I told Michelle as she ushered us down the hall.

"Please do—" she started to say, but she cut off as I stopped in my tracks.

One of the pictures on the wall caught my eye. It showed three boys, all different ages, standing in the grass near the park. The tall one in the middle must've been Isaac, because he had his mother's features and blue eyes. Isaac's arm was wrapped around two shorter boys. The one on the left I didn't recognize, but the short one on the right was Caleb Thomas.

"I thought your son didn't know Caleb Thomas," I pointed out.

Michelle gaped a moment. "This is an old picture. They must've met on the playground—I hardly remember it. Like I said, I have places to be."

Talia shot me a glance, but neither of us said anything. I was careful with my thoughts, too, because I didn't want Michelle reading me. She ushered us out the door without another word. Talia and I stood on the porch, staring at the door Michelle had slammed behind us.

"She's lying," Talia said bluntly.

"I know," I agreed as we headed back to the car. "No one hangs a picture of some kids you just met at the park. The question is, why are the families lying about the kids knowing each other?"

Talia slid into the driver's seat. "I think the better question is, who is that third boy in the picture, and is he going to become the next target?"

My stomach plummeted as I sat in the passenger seat. "Fuck," I mumbled. "You could be right."

Talia started the engine and shifted into reverse. "I'm starting to wonder if maybe the kids picked up a cursed object or something."

"I don't know," I said thoughtfully. "It's possible, but why haven't the police found it, then?"

Talia pressed her lips together. "That's true—they would've found it. Did anything else stand out to you?"

I shook my head. "The only other similarities I can think of is that the moms were both home alone the night it happened. If they know each other, maybe it was some sort of… pact, or something?"

Talia's face paled. "Make it look like an abduction, like someone else is to blame? But why would they do that to their own kids?"

I shook my head. "I have no idea. For black magic, maybe? They've lied already. What exactly is it they're trying to cover up?"

Talia stared ahead at the street in disbelief. "I have no idea."

I sighed in exasperation. "Did you find anything?"

Talia shook her head. "I tried, but every vision came up fuzzy. It's like someone's *blocking* my powers."

"That could explain why no one else is getting any clues," I said. "But who could block someone's powers like that? Not a Mentalist or an Alchemist, right? So that takes the moms off the table as suspects."

Talia pressed her lips together. "It could be a Mentalist, with the right type of powers. Maybe it's some sort of protection spell. Could an Alchemist brew something to mess with someone's magic?"

"I've never heard of anything like that," I said.

"So… we're at a dead end?" Talia asked.

"No," I stated firmly. I refused to believe that.

Talia glanced over to me. "How do you propose we find out what the families are hiding?"

"I don't know," I admitted. "But there's something more important we have to do."

Talia tilted her head. "What's that?"

My hands curled into fists in my lap. "We have to find the third boy, and protect him—before he dies like the others."

nadine

EIGHT

Lucas's investigation was driving me crazy. It was like reading a mystery novel without having enough clues to piece together the answer. I was usually so good at it, but when Lucas confided in me about what he'd found, all I could offer were outlandish theories.

I wished that I could give him more, but after the beating I took from Chloe, my symptoms had flared drastically. All I could focus on was making it through the flare-up. Forget about studying curse breaking or solving Lucas's mystery.

I must've daydreamed a thousand different ways to get back at Chloe, but there was no way to do it when I was stuck in bed. I couldn't fight back physically, and magic drained me every time I used it. I wasn't entirely sure what other options I had. But I knew I'd figure it out one way or another—as soon as I had the energy.

Every inch of my body ached, and the bruises only made my muscles even more stiff than normal. I felt like a statue as I dragged my ass out of bed each morning and hobbled to the bathroom to pee. I winced every step of the way.

By day three, I found myself standing in front of the mirror, holding myself up by the edge of the sink. The potion Patty had given me had helped reduce the appearance of the bruises, but I was still tender everywhere. It made me want to go after Chloe even more.

I eyed myself in the mirror, taking in my pale complexion and the bags under my eyes. I only had so much energy to give. I could go after Chloe, or I could take a freaking bath. I didn't have the energy for both.

It was a tough decision, but I had to be real with myself. No way was I standing up to Chloe in this condition. I broke down and turned toward the tub.

Waiting for the tub to fill felt torturous. I was desperate for the relief of the hot water. I poured Epsom salts into the water and eyed the crystals as they began to dissolve. It would never be enough to take care of this stiffness and swelling.

"To hell with it," I told myself.

I dumped the rest of the container into the tub, since it was nearly gone anyway, then I stripped down and climbed in. I winced as I lowered myself into the tub, the muscles in my back and legs protesting.

I didn't want to move. I closed my eyes and took in deep breaths, waiting for the cramp in my wrist to let up. I was used to the cramps, but my wrist had been acting up ever since Camille twisted it when I'd tried fighting back. Eventually, the cramp eased, and I wiggled my fingers to help ease the tightness in my tendons.

I sank deeper into the water, letting it envelop me completely. This was no spa resort, but I was grateful to have a tub in my room. It didn't wash away my symptoms, but it made them easier to deal with.

Eventually, the water became cold, and my fingers had turned to prunes. I got out of the bath in stages, because doing it all at once was taxing on my body. I sat up and waited for my joints to adjust to the new position, then dragged myself out of the water and sat on the edge of the tub. I dried myself off there, then stood and wrapped a robe around myself, before returning to bed where I hoped my body would heal.

The next few days passed in a similar manner, each day a little easier than the last. I went from doing nothing but taking a few trips to the bathroom, to finally making it down to the dining hall to grab my own lunch, rather than asking Talia to grab me something three times a day. I was relieved when I finally had the energy to get back to class.

My Thoughtography class was small, with merely a dozen students, and I was the only student in the class who wasn't a Seer.

"We've spent the semester reviewing thoughtography theory and history," Professor Clarke stated. He was one of the younger professors and had a unique sense of style—long hair, suspenders, and mis-matched socks with intricate designs on them. "Today, we'll be putting our knowledge to the test."

He started handing out papers. When he reached my desk, I saw that the papers were blank and glossy—film paper. Isa sat on my lap and sniffed it.

"Your assignment today is to think of a place that was special to you as a child," Professor Clarke announced. "It could be your childhood bedroom, a park, a store you loved—anywhere. Transfer the image of that location onto the photo paper. Any questions?"

"Yeah." My hand shot into the air, and Professor Clarke cocked an eyebrow at me. "I'm not a Seer. I can't complete this assignment."

All eyes turned to me, and a few students across the room began chuckling under their breath. A girl named Avery Mitchel tossed her blonde curls over her shoulder and sneered, "If you're not a Seer, what are you doing in this class?"

"This class is open to all Casts, as a Cast diversity credit," Professor Clarke said before I could respond. "The assignment is not mandatory or graded, but I would like those of you who can to try the exercise."

Avery huffed. "Well, then this class should be an easy A. There's no reason to *skip* all the time."

My hands balled into fists, and Isa let out a low growl. This bitch didn't know anything about me or why I'd missed so much class. She could take her insults and shove them where the sun didn't shine.

"What the hell's your problem?" I demanded.

Avery narrowed her eyes at me. "Maybe you should be asking yourself that question. I'm not the one who vandalized school property."

"I didn't—"

"Ladies," Professor Clarke scolded. "Save it for another time."

Avery held my gaze a moment longer, but she eventually backed down and turned to the front of the room.

By the time class let out, I was fuming. Chloe was winning. She was turning everyone against me. I couldn't let her get away with this.

I held my textbook tightly to my chest and wasn't really watching where I was going. I turned a corner and nearly rammed straight into someone. Isa *did* run into them, and she hissed. I stumbled back and raised my gaze to see that it was Headmistress Verla.

"Nadine," she said brightly. "Just the person I was looking for."

She shot a look at Isa, who was giving her the stink eye, but Isa's attention was quickly stolen by Odin. The two cats stared each other down, their fur on end.

"Isa," I scolded. She could get quite territorial. She backed down, then I turned to Verla. "You were looking for *me*?"

"Yes. I wanted to let you know that the school board has concluded their investigation on the vandalism."

My mood instantly lifted. "So they know I didn't do it?"

Verla frowned. "Unfortunately, the investigation was inconclusive. That said, we found evidence of Chloe, Gwen, and Camille's involvement, and they've been given detention as well. I am suspending any further detention you have to serve."

"Really?" I felt I could breathe easier. Maybe this was enough to get people off my back.

Verla glanced around the hall. A few students passed by, but they ignored us. Still, she took me by the shoulder and led me into an empty study area. "Your mother was my best friend. I will always fight for you."

Verla's words should have been reassuring, but they left a bad taste on my tongue. I didn't know what it meant, but sometimes, this woman felt too good to be true. I feared she expected something of me in return— something I may not be able to give to her. I just didn't know what it was.

But at least I had an ally.

"Thank you, Headmistress," I said.

"No need to thank me." Her gaze flickered down to my textbook. "What are you carrying that heavy thing around for? Do you need help with conjuring?"

I bit my lower lip. "I can do it. It just… tires me out."

Verla's features fell. "Well, that's not fair to any witch. May I give you some advice that might make it easier on you?"

"Sure," I agreed brightly. I'd take anything.

"A mistake most witches make with conjuring is that they picture their stash as separate from themselves—a universe that cannot be accessed by touch," she explained. "When you see it that way, you create resistance. But conjuring is much simpler than that."

"How so?" I asked.

"When we subconjure an item, we more or less bend space around it," she said. "We already know how to manipulate our environment. Everything you touch is changed when you interact with it. Conjuration is simply a magical manipulation rather than a physical, but one is as simple as the other. Subconjuring your textbook should be no more difficult than setting it on a table."

She made it sound so easy, when to me, conjuring felt like running up six flights of stairs.

"How do I do it?" I asked.

"Well, how do you set a book on the table?" she asked.

"I set it down and let gravity do the work…" I answered, unsure what she was getting at.

"Exactly. You do not have to force the textbook to stay on the table, in the same way that you do not have to force conjuration. You simply let magic do the work."

I pressed my lips together. "I think I get what you're saying. I'm being too forceful and overdoing my magic, and that's why it's tiring me out."

Verla nodded. "Would you like to try it?"

"Yes. I'll need a moment." I closed my eyes and repeated in my mind what Verla had said. *This shouldn't be any harder than setting the textbook on a table.* Taking a deep breath, I allowed my magic to blossom out of my chest, twisting it around the textbook in my arms. I focused on letting it work intuitively, rather than forcing it. My fingers opened, and the textbook fell out of my arms.

But the *thud* I'd been expecting never came. When I opened my eyes, the textbook was gone.

I blinked a few times. "Wow. I don't feel exhausted at all."

"That's good!" Verla praised. "You see how you let magic do the work for you?"

"Yes! Thank you so much for the advice."

She patted my shoulder. "Anytime. I unfortunately have a meeting to get to, but my door is always open."

Verla hurried off down the hall with Odin at her heels. I watched her go, until Isa's meow pulled my attention away from the headmistress.

"Well, Isa. This changes things," I said, holding my head high. "Come on. We have work to do."

I returned to my dorm room, but I stopped in my tracks when I reached the top of the grand staircase. Down the hall, a group of people gathered in the hallway. At first, I didn't think anything of it, until I realized they were *in front of my room*. All eyes were on my door.

"What now?" I groaned under my breath.

I made my way over to the crowd. A couple of girls noticed me and squeezed together to let me through.

"What's going on—?" I started to ask, but I cut off when I saw what they were all staring at.

Big, bold letters were sprawled out across the door in deep red paint. At least, I assumed it was paint, because who the hell would use *blood* to mark my door? Long streaks of liquid dripped ominously down the door, spelling out the word *half-blood*.

Grant knelt in front of my room. He dipped a rag into a bucket at his side and scrubbed fiercely at the letters. No matter how hard he scrubbed, the word wouldn't wash away.

My nostrils flared, and my hands curled into fists. Angry magic rattled around in my chest, begging me to slam a battle orb into a bitch's face.

Grant kept scrubbing as he glanced nervously up and down the hall. He did a double take when he saw me, and his features fell.

"Nadine," he said breathlessly. "I-I didn't want you to see."

I crossed my arms and stuck out my hip. "Chloe can choke on the paint for all I care."

"I don't think it's paint—" Grant started to say, but I cut him off.

I whirled toward the crowd. "What are you all looking at? Nothing to see here."

People started whispering, but the crowd slowly dispersed.

I turned back to Grant. "Thank you for trying, but it's not a big deal."

"Aren't you bothered by this?" he asked.

I was, but I wasn't about to admit it, not in front of everyone.

When I didn't say anything, Grant added, "This isn't a harmless prank. It's a threat."

I pressed my lips together tightly. "I can handle her."

"I hope that's true," Grant said. "But this is low, even for Chloe."

I frowned. "Everything she does is low."

"You don't understand. In Miriamic culture, *half-blood* is very offensive. We *all* have Miriam's blood in our veins. And this…" He gestured to the stain on my door. "I tried a cleansing spell, but it didn't work. Someone used magic to do this."

"You mean Chloe got one of her side-kicks to do it?" I couldn't say I was surprised. "If you think I'm afraid of her, you're wrong. I doubt she'll even pass her ceremony."

Grant sighed. "I just don't want to see you get hurt."

"I'll be fine," I insisted, but I was only trying to convince myself. The truth was, I was terrified of what lengths Chloe would go to by the time her magic awakened. If I didn't feel like passing out every time I used magic, then maybe I had a chance to get back at her. Isa rubbed up against my leg, like she was worried.

I knelt beside Grant and reached for the rag. "Let me help."

He drew away. "I've got it. You shouldn't have to worry about stuff like this."

I stopped in my tracks and eyed Grant as he kept scrubbing away at the letters. At first, I wasn't sure what he meant. Did he think I was some frail soul who couldn't take a little bullying? Grant's hard features suggested something else. He was angry, like he took the attack personally. That's when I realized that Grant had seen this kind of thing before. He didn't want anyone else experiencing what he had.

"Go inside," he said calmly. "I'll take care of this."

"Grant…" I didn't know how to thank him for trying to protect me. "You're a really great friend."

He smirked. "Eh, I try to be. We *half-bloods* have to stick together."

I smiled, glad that he was reclaiming the word instead of letting it weigh him down. "Thank you."

Grant wouldn't let me help and practically shoved me inside the room. I stopped just inside the door and turned back to him. "Hey, you wouldn't happen to know how to brew poison, would you?"

Grant smirked. "Only if I want to get expelled."

Getting my friends into trouble was the last thing I wanted to do. I wouldn't let Chloe target them, too.

"Best we avoid that, then," I said, before shutting the door behind myself.

As I collapsed onto my bed, a sense of overwhelm overtook me. But I was also motivated more than ever—motivated to work on my magic, and motivated to stop Chloe.

I reached into my nightstand and pulled out the box of cursed objects Talia had bought for me to practice on. Maybe Verla's advice would help me with curse breaking, too.

When I flipped open the top, I could feel the energy buzzing off the objects. Isa hissed and buried her head under the blanket. I quickly snapped the top shut again, then went to the bathroom to fill a cup of water. I returned to the bed and set the water on the nightstand. I opened the box again and eyed the objects—the thimble that caused mild, itchy pain; the compass that screwed with your sense of direction; and the pearl earring that repelled men.

I'd tried the earring before, so I decided to try the compass this time. I held it in my palm and closed my eyes, concentrating on the magical curse inside of it. I drew the magic into myself and redirected it into the glass of water like Grammy had taught me. This time when I worked the magic, I focused on letting it flow through me naturally like Verla had suggested with conjuring. The magic left my body and funneled into the glass of water. As it left me, I breathed a sigh of relief.

"Holy crap," I whispered to myself when I opened my eyes. "Did I just break my first curse?"

Splash!

No sooner had I said it did water come exploding out of the cup, spraying all over the walls and down on my face. I flinched, and my whole body tensed. Magic buzzed through me as the curse went flooding back into the compass.

Anger bubbled up inside of me. My lips pressed into a thin line, but the longer I sat there, the more frustrated I got.

"This is stupid!" I growled. My nostrils flared as I inhaled deep breaths.

Isa hissed.

"I thought it would work this time," I said with a frown.

"Damn it!" Grant's voice came from outside the room, then came a loud *thud*, like he'd pounded his fist against the door in frustration.

That only made me more mad, because I wasn't just angry about my magic. I was pissed at Chloe. She wasn't just messing with me, but she was messing with my friends. I hated her for it.

She deserves to be cursed, a voice said in my head. It sounded like my own, but I didn't know where the thought had come from.

She's already cursed, I thought. *Same as me.*

What could one more curse hurt? the voice responded. *Or three...*

My gaze traveled to the curse-safe box, where all three cursed objects sat inside. The thought to dump them on Chloe crossed my mind, but I shoved it out of my head as soon as it came.

That will only make things worse, I thought. *There's no need to fuel this fire. I need to focus on learning curse breaking so I can break our family curse. That's the only way to stop this. Petty revenge will accomplish nothing.*

But it will feel good, I argued with myself.

Damn it, I was right. But I was conflicted, too. Dealing with Chloe's retaliation would only distract me from real solutions.

But I can still have fun in the meantime, the voice countered. *Chloe deserves it.*

Hell yeah, she did. But I had to deal with this properly—

And properly, I would. I snatched up the box of cursed objects and left the room, abandoning Isa. Grant must've seen me leave, but I hadn't even noticed him. In fact, I was halfway down the hall before I realized I'd left my room at all. It crossed my mind to turn back, but the thought of revenge pushed me forward.

I heard Chloe's voice down the hall before I saw her. She was seated in an alcove, laughing with Gwen. Both of their backs were to me. I pressed myself to the wall and peeked around the corner.

"No way am I going to get Seer," Chloe said, like Seer powers were some sort of insult. "Seers think they're better than everyone else. So you can see the future. So what? I could slice you in half with a battle orb."

Gwen threw her head back and laughed. "Seers can be *so* selfish. Like, okay you can sing, but how does that help the coven?"

"Exactly," Chloe emphasized. "Like, go do something with your life that actually means something. Your paintings aren't going to fix the coven."

"Goddess," Gwen sighed, rolling her eyes.

I surveyed the area from my hiding spot. Chloe's designer bag sat next to her chair, only a few feet away from me.

"In class last week, Talia Murphy said art and *self-expression* were the best way to serve the coven," Gwen teased. "Like no, bitch. We need to *educate our people*, not give them a box of crayons and let them run wild."

My hands curled into fists when I heard Talia's name. These girls didn't get to talk about my friend behind her back and get away with it.

Chloe laughed. "No kidding. If everyone just pushed themselves to be successful, the coven would thrive."

I got angrier the more they talked. Talia was entitled to her own opinion, and if she thought the coven was better off when people worked on becoming the best versions of themselves by following creative passions, then she was right. Talia was one of the best people I'd met in all of Octavia Falls, and she was one of the reasons I wanted to stay. The coven would be nothing without her.

All my reservations about cursing Chloe fell away. I wouldn't let her talk about my friend like this.

When Chloe and Gwen weren't looking, I ducked into the alcove and silently snuck behind the plush chair Chloe was sitting in. I held my breath, but the two were talking so loudly that neither of them had heard me. As my breath calmed, I leaned over and began unzipping Chloe's bag. My heart hammered at the chance of getting caught, but I wasn't about to walk away from here without trying. The zipper sounded like gunshots going off, it was so loud. But neither Chloe nor Gwen seemed to notice. Once the bag was open a few inches, I quickly tossed the cursed objects inside. I held my breath again and forced my pulse to slow. Chloe and Gwen kept on chatting like nothing happened.

"I have to get to class," Chloe announced, reaching for her bag.

I crouched down lower behind her chair so I wouldn't be seen. When she stood, I heard the sound of her fingernails against fabric. She scratched her legs, and I smiled. The thimble was already working its curse on her.

"I'll see you later," Gwen said, before stopping her. "Um… Chloe?"

"Yeah?" Chloe sounded like she was already out of the alcove and in the hall.

"Isn't your class that way?" Gwen asked.

My smile widened, and satisfaction settled deep in my belly. The compass was working, too.

"Oh, yeah. You're right," Chloe said. "I don't know what I was thinking."

I wanted to laugh, but I held my hand over my mouth so I wouldn't give myself away.

A few moments after Chloe's footsteps faded, Gwen rose from her chair and left the study area as well. I couldn't help it when a big grin spread across my face.

I'd done it. I'd cursed Chloe.

She was finally going to get what was coming to her.

NINE

Valentine's Day arrived, and I told Nadine to meet me outside at six o'clock, though I didn't tell her where we were going. I wanted it to be a surprise.

I dressed in a button-down shirt and nice slacks. I didn't like how it looked on me—too formal—so I rolled up the sleeves to expose my forearms. It didn't feel like *me*, but I thought Nadine would like it. I slipped on my jacket, but I was so nervous about the date that I was practically cooking in it. I took it off and subconjured it.

Grant had taken off a half hour ago to hang with Amy and Mandy, who were hosting a singles party. It sounded like there was going to be a lot of drinking, and Grant was holding out for strip poker. I was so glad I had a date, because I'd be damned if Grant managed to drag me to that thing.

I headed down the hall toward the Main Foyer. Orbs shaped like hearts floated above my head. Pink love letters folded into paper airplanes zoomed down the hall, propelled by telekinetic powers. As I reached the grand staircase, the Main Foyer below came into view. Downstairs, a group of Seers were giving out free relationship tarot readings. In the corner, two witches whispered quietly. One girl handed the other a vial filled with pink liquid, and I witnessed money exchange hands. I noticed a cauldron tattoo on one of the girl's wrists. My guess was she was selling unauthorized love potions.

I descended the stairs and headed outside. There was a large group out there already, all holding tickets identical to the one I had in my pocket. I glanced around for Nadine, but I didn't see her.

I shoved my hands in my pockets and waited. It was cold out, and the air turned to fog when I breathed, but I didn't mind. Something about the cold felt comforting—familiar.

A few minutes later, the door to the school opened behind me. I turned, and I swore I lost my breath. Nadine was dressed in a sparkly red dress that fell to her knees but had a slit up one side. It had spaghetti straps and a low-cut neckline, showing off her smooth skin. Her hair was down in waves, and she wore bright red lipstick. She held a black clutch in her hands, and she practically glowed. I was so entranced, I couldn't take my eyes off her.

Nadine glanced around, and her eyes lit up when she saw me. I beamed and finally managed to drag my jaw up off the sidewalk. I walked to her, taking her hand to help her down the stairs. Her high heels clicked against the stone, and I couldn't help it when my eyes traveled up and down her body. I didn't care what Nadine looked like. She was my everything for other reasons. But I'd be damned if her curves didn't make me go wild.

Nadine smoothed down the front of her dress. "I hope I'm not over-dressed."

"No, not at all," I said, quickly gathering my breath. "You look amazing."

Was there ever a time she didn't? But today was different. What I wouldn't do to rip that dress off her...

I glanced down and saw Nadine's nipples had hardened beneath her dress. She wasn't wearing a bra. My pulse quickened. She shivered, and I rushed to drape an arm around her.

"Sorry it's so cold," I said.

She shrugged. "You can't control the weather."

"Our ride should be here any minute," I told her. In the meantime, I got to hold her close. I pressed my nose into her hair to inhale her rosy scent. My knees went weak, and I never wanted to let her go.

Nadine leaned into me closer and glanced around. "What are all these people doing here?"

I smiled. "Waiting."

She nudged me in the side. "Waiting for what? You know I don't—"

"Like surprises," I finished for her. "I know, I know. But trust me on this one."

Just then, a limousine pulled through the gates surrounding Miriam College of Witchcraft. Nadine's jaw dropped as she watched the sleek limo pull up to the crowd outside.

"The Hearse?" she asked, sounding starstruck.

"They host a Valentine's Day dinner every year," I explained. It was for ticket holders only, since there were only so many tables. "There will be a four-course meal and live music."

"Dear Goddess, I love it already," Nadine squealed. "Thank you."

"Don't thank me just yet," I teased.

The limo stopped, and the chauffeur climbed out to open the door. Couples shuffled forward. I guided Nadine in front of me and handed our ticket over at the door. We ducked our heads, but with the space-bending spell, we could stand up fully once we were inside. Nadine's eyes sparkled as she took in the beautiful space. Red carpet spanned all the way to the back of the limousine, meeting up with a stage where a man played a smooth melody behind a grand piano. There must've been a hundred tables lined in a single aisle between us and the back window. The lighting was dim and roman- tic, and orbs hovered above our heads in the shape of chandeliers. Each table was set with shimmering black cutlery and rose centerpieces.

"This way, please," a host said to get our attention. Nadine and I followed, and we were offered a table next to the window.

"This is beautiful," Nadine said as she sat. Her gaze locked out the window, and she watched the school as we began to drive away.

"May I offer you something to drink?" the host asked.

I grabbed the drink menu off the table and flipped it open. The first item caught my eye. "Two glasses of marmoscot, please," I said, before shooting a quick glance at Nadine. "Unless you wanted something else."

"No, it's fine," she said. "I'm always up for something new."

The host nodded politely. She held her hand out, and a glass bottle appeared in her hand from out of nowhere. She poured a sparkling pink liquid into our wine glasses.

"Have a lovely evening," she said, before walking off.

Nadine smiled as she pulled her wine glass to her mouth. She sniffed it curiously. "What is this?"

"It's more or less a non-alcoholic wine," I explained. "It's an alchemy brew made from a blend of flower petals. It's said to be an aphrodisiac."

Nadine's eyebrows shot up as she took a sip. "An aphrodisiac?" she teased. "Lucas, are you trying to seduce me?"

I tried to keep the smile off my face. "Would I be doing Valentine's Day right if I weren't trying?"

She chuckled and set her glass down. Her eyes roamed over me, across my chest and down my exposed forearms. "No, you wouldn't. I like the wine, by the way."

I took a sip of marmoscot and enjoyed the sweet, bubbly taste on my tongue. As my eyes locked on Nadine, I started to get turned on—and I knew it wasn't the wine.

"How was your week?" I asked, to take my mind off my dick.

"Ugh," she groaned. "Can you not ask?"

My shoulders fell. "I'm sorry. I only meant it as small talk. Grant told me what happened."

Nadine rolled her eyes. "People are mean."

"I'll kick their ass for you," I offered.

"That's not necessary," she said. "I hear people whispering about me in the halls, and yesterday someone slipped a note under my door saying I should leave the school."

My hands curled into fists. "That was probably Chloe."

"Doesn't make it any less annoying." Nadine sighed. "But you don't have to worry. No one is going to drive me out of the school."

"You tell me if they try," I insisted. "I mean it, Nadine. I won't let anyone hurt you."

She blushed. "Thanks."

Just then, our waiter arrived to take our order. There wasn't much on the menu, but we got to choose between soup and salad for the first course, a range of appetizers, an entree, and a dessert.

"Ooh, I've never had duck before," Nadine said as she looked over the menu. "I think I'll try that."

"I'll have the chicken," I told the waiter.

Nadine rolled her eyes at me after we ordered.

"What?" I asked innocently, taking another sip of marmoscot.

"Chicken," Nadine teased. "You're so… adventurous."

"Sure I am," I defended. "It's chicken primavera. I don't even know what primavera is."

Nadine chuckled. "You are way too comfortable inside your comfort zone."

"That's why they call it a comfort zone, Nad," I teased.

She leaned forward, elbows on the table. I could practically see down her dress. *Damn.* If she could hear my heart right now, she'd insist I go to the emergency room. Her mere presence did things to me I'd never experienced before.

"Yes, but you never push the boundaries," she said.

I sighed. "Believe me, I get outside my comfort zone more than you know."

"Oh?" she asked. "Example?"

I shrugged. "The investigative journalism. Dating you."

Nadine shifted in her chair. "I'm outside your comfort zone?"

"Not in a bad way," I rushed to clarify. "In a *this is a totally new experience for me* kind of way."

Nadine raised an eyebrow. "See what I mean? It can be fun to step outside your comfort zone."

"Sometimes, I guess," I agreed.

Our first course arrived, and the waiter set a bowl of broccoli cream soup in front of each of us. Nadine and I started eating as we continued talking.

"What kinds of things do you do outside your comfort zone?" I questioned.

"Tons," she answered simply.

"I doubt that," I chuckled. "I don't think your comfort zone has limits. You'll do anything."

She leveled her gaze on me. "Because I'm willing to step outside those limits. Being a witch isn't exactly inside my comfort zone, but I do it anyway because it's the best opportunity of my life. I *want* to learn to be comfortable with it."

I swallowed a spoonful of soup. "Makes sense. How do you manage to… push those limits?"

Nadine shrugged. "You just decide to go for it."

"Like?" I questioned.

Nadine pressed her lips together and glanced up and down the length of The Hearse. "Like if I wanted to play the piano, I'd just go up and ask the guy if I could. What's the worst that could happen? He says no? People laugh at me when I play? Why should any of that scare me, as long as I have fun doing it?"

"*Would* you have fun?" I asked.

Nadine sipped her soup. "Sure. Why not?"

I leaned forward and whispered across the table. "Then I dare you to ask."

Her jaw dropped open. "What? No—"

She cut off before she could finish protesting. She knew I was challenging her to prove her point. She narrowed her eyes at me. "You think you're so sly, Lucas Taylor. You know I don't back down to a dare."

I finished my soup and leaned back in my chair, a smug smile on my face. "Prove it."

Nadine wiped her lips, then threw her napkin on the table. She stood, then started walking toward the back of The Hearse. I couldn't take my eyes off her ass as she walked, hips swaying in a way I swore was meant to turn me on.

Nadine reached the stage and tapped the pianist on the shoulder. He continued playing his soft melody but leaned over to hear her. Nadine said something in his ear, and he nodded politely. He played a few final notes, then stood from the piano bench and gestured to Nadine.

I straightened in my chair, blown away that he actually took her request. Nadine smiled brightly and took a seat. The pianist held a microphone out in her direction, and she spoke into it in a soft, seductive tone.

"This one goes out to my boyfriend, Lucas," she announced.

Nadine began playing, but it was obvious she had no idea what she was doing. The notes she played clashed, and people around us cringed. I loved it, though. She kept her eyes on me the whole time, and I couldn't help it when a wide smile spread across my lips. It didn't matter how bad the song was—she'd composed it for *me*.

Nadine's song barely lasted thirty seconds. When she finished, she thanked the pianist profusely, then turned to the rest of the restaurant. A few people sighed in relief, but Nadine didn't give a shit what they thought. She curtsied like she'd just played a whole symphony to perfection. Damn it all if that wasn't the cutest thing I'd ever seen.

Nadine returned to our table snickering. Our appetizers had arrived—a sampler of fried ravioli, butter shrimp, and stuffed mushrooms.

"That was amazing," I said.

"See what I told you?" Nadine laughed. "Getting outside your comfort zone can be fun."

I poked a mushroom with my fork. "I wouldn't do it, but it looked like you had fun up there."

"So, you liked it?" she challenged.

I couldn't help but smile. "You dedicated a song to me. Of course I liked it."

Nadine beamed and popped a shrimp in her mouth. "Then it was totally worth it."

Our entree arrived, and Nadine challenged me to try a bite of her duck.

"No, that's your meal," I insisted. "You eat it."

"I want to share."

I tried it, and it actually wasn't bad. Nadine pressed me the rest of the meal about foods I'd never tried.

"You've never had sushi!?" she balked. "We have to get some sometime."

She was already starting a mental list of all the foods we had to try. At this point, I was starting to think she was planning a round-the-world trip for the two of us just so we could blow all our money on food. Not that I would mind spending any extra time with her. She could take me to the damn Abyss if she wanted.

By the time we'd finished our chocolate cake, I was having a lot of fun. Nadine had managed to take my mind off the case, and we were laughing over the idea of ordering Rocky Mountain oysters.

"Bull testicles are *way* outside my comfort zone," Nadine admitted.

"Ah, so I finally found something you won't try," I teased.

"I didn't say I wouldn't try it," she insisted. "I just might puke afterward."

I laughed. "You're so great."

She went quiet at that. "What? Why?"

I shrugged, but my eyes remained fixed on her. "You just are. You make me feel…"

I couldn't find the words. My chest felt lighter than it had in… ever. And just being in her presence sent tingles all over my skin. But it was more than that.

"Like maybe I can take chances," I finally said.

"Well, I'm glad," she replied with a smile. "You're great, too."

My chest warmed. "In what way?"

"I guess when everything else feels uncomfortable… you don't," Nadine admitted.

My breath left my chest. It was a compliment beyond any other.

"I feel good around you," she continued. "You make this whole *learning I'm a witch* thing bearable."

The table went silent, and I reached over to take her hand. "Same, Nad. I don't know if I could be a reaper without you."

She smiled, and my heart swelled. When I was around Nadine, I felt like I could truly be happy.

"I'm glad we did this," she whispered.

I smirked. "The night isn't over."

"Oh?" she asked.

Nadine turned her gaze out the window as The Hearse pulled up outside of *Starlight,* the local performing arts center. "We're going to see a show?"

"If you want," I told her.

"It sounds like fun," she said. "What's playing?"

"It's a musical revue of Broadway's most romantic songs," I told her. I thought it sounded lame, but tonight wasn't about me. I wanted Nadine to enjoy herself.

"I didn't know you were into Broadway," she remarked as we stood.

I took her hand and followed the line of people exiting The Hearse. "I'm not. You don't hate it, do you?"

"No," Nadine assured me. "Talia blasts Broadway on her phone every chance she gets, so I might know a couple of songs."

I chuckled. "Figures."

"What do you mean?" She looked up to me as we stepped into the cold.

I draped my arm around her again and led her toward the theatre. "Can I make a confession?"

She poked me in the side and smiled. "Always."

"Grant's the one who suggested the tickets."

Nadine laughed. "Of course. He'd want to bring Talia."

"You don't sound like you're into this."

"No, it's fine," she assured me, but I heard the lie in her voice.

"It's not fine," I said. "I want you to have fun. We'll do something else instead."

"I think we'd both enjoy that more," she agreed.

Instead of following everyone else into the theatre, I took Nadine's hand and led her down the street. The theatre was only a block down from the main shopping district, and we could see the bright lights from boutique shops and restaurants ahead. Nadine shivered. I remembered my coat and conjured it, then draped it around her shoulders.

She relaxed and pulled it around her. "Thanks. Aren't you cold, though?"

I shook my head. It *was* chilly out, but Nadine sent my pulse pumping so hard it actually felt nice. I entwined my fingers in hers. "I'll be okay."

Nadine looked thoughtful as we walked. "So, tell me. What is Lucas's idea of a romantic night?"

"The Hearse was good, but I can think of something that would've made it better," I said.

"What's that?"

I smirked. "A murder mystery—the fake kind."

Nadine's eyes lit up. "That would've been amazing."

"I know you would've loved it, but I couldn't find anything like that tonight."

"It's okay," she said. "I loved the atmosphere on The Hearse, and the food was amazing—"

I couldn't take my eyes off of her. I stopped on the sidewalk and grabbed her around the waist, cutting her off. Before she could catch her breath, my lips were on hers. Heat pooled deep in my belly, and the air left my lungs. I felt like I was floating as Nadine's hands trailed up my torso. She inhaled a deep breath, and her breasts pressed against my chest. Her lips parted, and I ran my tongue along her bottom lip. Goddess, what I'd do to kiss this girl forever.

Eventually, the moment ended. My heart hammered as we drew away from each other.

Nadine swayed on her feet. "Wh-what was that for?"

Heat rose to my cheeks. "I couldn't resist."

She lifted her hands to run them across my face. Her eyes roamed my features. "I'm glad you didn't. Resist, I mean."

Nadine eyed me like she wanted me. Without thinking about it, I placed my hands inside her coat and wrapped them around her waist. The fabric of her dress was so thin, I could feel every curve of her body. I pulled her closer to me and rested my forehead on hers. I needed a moment to catch my breath.

My hands seemed to have a mind of their own. I couldn't resist moving them downward, until I was cupping her ass. The coat was long enough to cover what we were doing.

"Maybe there's something I can do to make this night perfect after all," I whispered.

"Is there?" Nadine asked suggestively, never taking her eyes off me.

My eyes trailed over her collarbone and downward. I got hard looking at her cleavage and couldn't help it when I started undressing her with my eyes. She was so freaking hot in that dress.

"Come on. I have a surprise—a good one," I quickly added. "Trust me."

She smiled brightly. "I do trust you."

Somehow, I managed to peel myself off of her, and I took her hand. Nadine followed beside me with a quick step. I wasn't sure if it was because she was excited or cold—probably a bit of both.

We reached the end of the block and turned down the next street, where there was a vendor with three black sleighs. Each was led by a velvety black horse. There were no drivers, as the horses were commanded by Mentalists who could communicate with them at a distance. Several couples stood in line, waiting their turn for a sleigh ride.

"Oh my gosh," Nadine breathed. "A sleigh ride?"

I shrugged. "Sleigh rides are popular in town this time of year."

"It sounds perfect."

We approached the vendor and got in line, but it wasn't long before more sleighs pulled up and the couples on them got off. Eventually, it was our turn. I paid the vendor and helped Nadine into the sleigh.

"Hot chocolate?" one of the employees asked, holding up a cup to Nadine.

She took it politely. "Thank you."

I grabbed a hot chocolate of my own, and we settled in beside each other. The sleigh lurched as the horse took off, and Nadine jumped as her hot chocolate sloshed in its cup. She went back to sipping on it as we started down the road.

"You okay?" I asked.

She shivered. "This hot chocolate is amazing."

I eyed the goosebumps on her exposed legs and couldn't help it when I reached over to touch her knee. She felt like ice. "I'm sorry you're so cold. I didn't plan on being outside so long."

"It's fine. Nothing we can do about it now… unless you have a blanket?"

I perked up. "I might!"

I mentally searched my stash—which was more or less based on instinct. I sensed something warm and fuzzy and conjured it. To my surprise, a dark blue blanket appeared in my lap. "I totally forgot I had that."

Nadine laughed. "Well, it's a good thing you did."

I had Nadine hold my hot chocolate while I draped the blanket over both of us. "Better?"

Nadine relaxed into the seat and closed her eyes. She held her cup close to her lips, just enjoying the heat coming off it. She looked so blissful when she did that. "Better."

The horse pulled us off the main road and down a secluded street. A path carved out in the trees appeared ahead. I leaned over and pressed my nose into her hair. "I can think of a few ways to make it even better."

It was bold. It was way outside my comfort zone. But Nadine had challenged me to get outside my comfort zone—and I wanted so badly to accept the invitation right now. I placed a hand on her leg beneath the blanket.

"Lucas," she scolded playfully. "In public?"

I glanced to the single horse pulling us along, then to the trees we were about to enter. "I don't see anyone else around."

Nadine's eyes widened, and she chugged her hot chocolate. "Is this my Valentine's Day gift?"

"One of them," I whispered. My hand inched up her leg, stopping just at the hem of her dress. "If you want it to be."

Her breath wavered, like she too was having a mini-heart attack. "I want it," she said breathlessly.

When she said that, I couldn't stop myself. Slowly, my shaking fingers roamed her body, feeling every curve, and teasing her. Nadine's breath quickened as I reached her breast. I felt her hot breath cross my neck, and I couldn't help but pull her tighter to me.

We locked in an embrace as my hand cupped her breast. Her nipple hardened beneath my touch, and I lost all inhibitions. My dick started thinking for me, and my hand seemed to move to its own accord. I pushed the fabric of her dress away, until my hand was touching her bare skin. Nadine gasped in pleasure, and I dared to glance downward. The sight of her breast in my hand was the hottest thing I'd ever seen.

Nadine tilted her head up, and I couldn't take it any longer. I kissed her passionately, my tongue moving in and out of her mouth, and hers roaming over mine. I couldn't take the temptation any longer. If I thought I was teasing *her*, I was kidding myself. *I* was the one desperate for more.

I placed my hand beneath the blanket again and pushed her dress upward. I waited momentarily for her response, making sure I wasn't pushing things too far.

She didn't say anything—didn't even open her eyes. But damn the desire that overcame me when she parted her legs slightly, welcoming me in. I moved up her dress...

My whole body turned to a statue, except for my heart trying to beat its way out of my chest. If I thought second base was something, it was nothing compared to touching her *there*. She wanted this, and so did I. I didn't even care that we were in a sleigh in the middle of the woods. No one else was around to see. What better place was there?

Nadine grasped the edge of the bench as I pushed the fabric of her panties aside. I kept my eyes on her, watching her features as I explored her sensitive areas. My fingers slid over her with ease, as she was really turned on, which only turned *me* on more.

I didn't have a lot of experience with this, but by the way Nadine closed her eyes and tilted her head back, I figured I must be doing something right. I slid a finger inside of her, and Nadine moaned. She was soft like silk and really warm. As I worked my fingers inside of her, I used my thumb to massage her elsewhere. I wasn't sure if she liked it at first, until I shifted and she gasped. I smiled in triumph and kept massaging her there, since she seemed to really be enjoying herself.

"Lucas," she moaned, grasping my sleeve.

I pressed my nose into her hair and kissed her jaw. "Yeah, Nad?"

Nadine's breathing rate increased, though she didn't open her eyes. "Lucas…"

She didn't explain, but I knew what she wanted to say. She liked it. *A lot.* I could feel it in how wet she was, and see it in the way she tilted her head back. My coat sagged around her shoulders, showing off her heaving chest. Dipping my head, I pressed a kiss to the top of her breast. She gasped again and shifted on the seat, pressing herself into my hand so that I went into her deeper.

Holy fuck. I was so turned on.

I moved my fingers in and out of her and continued circling her pleasure centers. Nadine's fingers tightened on my sleeve, then everything changed. A moan broke out across the forest, but Nadine grabbed on to me and kissed me hard to silence herself. She squirmed in her seat, but my fingers hadn't moved. She contracted around me. It was so hot I started making out with her more. My free hand roamed every inch of her body I could reach.

All too soon, Nadine drew away and slumped into the seat. Her eyes were still closed, but a blissful smile spread across her face.

"Did you like that?" I teased, though it was obvious.

Nadine chuckled as I wrapped her in my arms. "Could you tell? Fuck, Lucas. You can do that to me any time you want."

I smirked and reached for the hem of her dress again. I kissed her neck and asked, "Like right now?"

Nadine laughed and lightly pushed me away. "Um… not now."

"Why not?" I teased. "You seemed to like it so much."

"Because we're coming back to town," she chuckled.

I instantly became alert. I looked up to see we'd made a loop through the trees and were approaching the vendor's station again.

"Damn," I muttered.

Nadine straightened her dress. "Damn, indeed."

I pressed my nose into her hair again, enjoying her floral scent. "Before we get back, do you want your *other* gift?"

She laughed, seemingly at the memory of her first gift. "Sure."

I drew away from her and conjured a small red envelope. Nadine opened it and pulled out the gift certificate inside. Tears beaded at the corners of her eyes when she read it.

"What?" I asked, alarmed. "It's a dumb gift, isn't it?"

"No," she assured me quickly. "A massage gift card is *exactly* what I need. It's really good for my lupus. I can't think of a more thoughtful gift. I love it."

I relaxed as she leaned over to kiss me.

"Now it's your turn," she announced. She opened her clutch and pulled out a small box that fit in the palm of my hand.

"You didn't have to get me anything," I told her.

"I know. I wanted to."

Curiously, I unwrapped the box. Inside sat a single tea bag.

"This is only a sample," she explained. "Grammy will have the rest ready for you on Monday."

My eyebrows shot up. If this was what I thought it was, it was crazy expensive. "Helena didn't have to go through the trouble."

"Well, I paid her to," she said with her chin held high.

I lifted the bag and smelled the sweet scent. "This is matus tea."

"I know," she stated. "I thought you'd like it, since the raw leaves help your anxiety. Grammy says the tea is a lot more potent."

"It is, but matus shrubs are rare," I pointed out. "The tea isn't cheap."

"Forget about the price," Nadine sighed. "I got it at a family discount."

"Still…" I couldn't find the words. I finally settled with, "Thank you."

"Thank *you*," she replied. She leaned into me, laying her head against my shoulder as we approached the vendor station. The whole side of my body warmed where she was touching it. She sighed and spoke in a dreamy tone. "Tonight was a lot of fun."

I cocked an eyebrow. "Well, we'll have to do it again sometime."

"We will indeed," she agreed.

I didn't know about Nadine, but I sure as hell meant it. Getting outside my comfort zone—touching her in places I hadn't touched her before—was fun.

Curse or no curse, we were going to make this relationship work.

TEN

I rode in a horse-drawn sleigh beside Lucas, reveling in the amazing high of our date. It felt amazing to relive it over and over.

"Lucas," I moaned. One second his hands were on me. The next, they'd vanished. I looked over to see that Lucas himself had disappeared. My heart began to hammer.

Ahead of me, the trees cleared, and the high peaks of Miriam Mansion came into view. The soft snow falling around me quickly turned to a blizzard. As the sleigh came to a stop in front of the school, I jumped out and ran inside to escape the cold. My knees shook as I heaved heavy breaths.

"Nadine... Nadine..." a sinister voice echoed through the Main Foyer.

Instinct took over, and I began running down the hall. I didn't know where I was going, just that I had to get as far away from the voice as I could. The hall in front of me seemed to never end. When I glanced behind myself, there was nothing but darkness. I had to keep moving forward.

Except the further I walked, the louder the voice became.

"I'm coming for you, Nadine," the voice laughed.

My heart hammered, and I began running. "Leave me alone!" I shouted.

The laughter continued. I sprinted down the hall, feeling the hairs on the back of my neck rise.

Suddenly, the hall came to a dead end, and I halted in my tracks.

"Nadine!" the voice cried, and my pulse quickened.

I whirled around, and my heart stopped dead at the sight of my own face staring back at me.

"Boo!"

"Oh my god!" I cried as I startled awake. It took a few moments for me to realize I'd only been dreaming. My heart rate began to slow.

"What's wrong?" Talia's breathless voice came from across the room. I'd been napping after a long curse breaking study session, but Talia was still buried in books.

Isa stood on my leg, pressing her paws into me like she'd been trying to get me to wake. The curtains were closed, probably because Talia thought it would help me sleep, but dusk was quickly approaching.

I took a deep, calming breath. "It was just a bad dream."

"About what?" Talia set her textbook aside and shifted on the couch. "Is there anything I can do to help?"

I shook my head. "No. I just need to get rid of this damn curse."

A scratch came at the door, and Talia stood to open it for Gus. A scream tore out of her lungs, and my body stilled in alarm.

"What?" I asked in a rush.

I saw it before Talia answered. Gus came trotting into the room with a dead bird in his mouth. Blue feathers were missing from the wings, and a drop of blood hit the carpet.

"Ew!" I cried.

"I'll handle it." Talia grabbed Gus by the scruff. "Drop it."

Gus growled, but he reluctantly dropped the bird. He looked ashamed as he stared up at Talia.

"Look, Gus. I appreciate the gifts," she said. "But you can't bring dead birds into the school!"

Gus turned away, leaving the dead bird sitting in the middle of the room. Talia hurried to the bathroom to grab a wad of toilet paper, then wrapped the bird in it and tossed it in the garbage.

"I'll take that out when we're done here," she offered, taking a seat on the couch. "There has to be *something* I can do to help."

"What can you do?" I asked. "You can't break the curse for me."

"I can help research it," she said. Gus shoved his butt in her face, and she gently pushed him aside.

"We know how curse breaking works," I reminded her. I'd been researching as much as I could, but I wasn't learning anything new. "I just don't know how to break this one."

"You have to find the source of the curse," Talia mused.

"Yeah, my darkness," I said. "But how do I draw that out? I see it in my mind, but I can't feel it like magic."

"We'll figure it out," Talia promised. "But I don't want you to push yourself too hard, either. If you overdraw your magic, you could get hurt."

I bit my lower lip. "Believe me, that's the last thing I want."

Gus came toward me, sniffing the air. He looked like he was searching for food. He climbed on top of my nightstand and stepped on my oracle card deck. It slipped out from under his feet and fell to the floor.

Talia rushed to pick it up before I could bend down. "Hey, why don't we ask your cards what to do?"

I shrugged. "I've tried, but the messages have been unclear. I guess it doesn't hurt to try again."

Talia handed me the deck, and I opened it. I shuffled through the cards while she spoke.

"I'm thinking about petitioning the school to start a Curse Breaking Theology class," Talia said. "It'd be open to all Casts, so you could take it without blowing your cover."

"That'd be amazing," I agreed. "But who would teach it? I'm the only Curse Breaker alive."

"Someone *must* be able to teach the basics," Talia said. "Your grandma was helpful, but there has to be more to it. We need to figure out the theory behind breaking curses on people. It's gotta be way more complicated than a cursed object."

"Agreed," I said as I drew a card.

The card was a familiar one—the Mirror card. It depicted a painting of a beautiful woman standing in front of a mirror. Her expression looked content and happy, but the reflection's features were hard—full of resentment and anger.

I sighed. "I always seem to pull this card."

Talia moved on the couch to get a closer look. "What does it mean?"

"It's the card of reflection," I told her. "I'm supposed to look inside myself and face my fears. The card is so vague, though, and I don't think I'm avoiding anything. What does it want from me?"

"Maybe there's something you're missing," Talia suggested. "Maybe you're afraid of something you don't even know you're scared of."

"I don't think so—"

Talia's phone chimed, and she reached over to grab it off her bed. She quickly scanned the text message and stood. "Cody wants to hang out. I'll catch up with you later?"

My jaw dropped. "Is it an emergency?"

She shook her head. "No."

"Well, we're kind of in the middle of something."

Talia sighed. "We can read cards anytime."

And you can hang out with Cody anytime, I thought.

"Cody and I need to talk," she said sheepishly.

"About what? Anything I can help with?"

She shook her head and began gathering her things. As she grabbed her binder, several pages slipped out and fluttered to the ground.

I leaned down to grab them. As I was doing so, I caught sight of a few lines on the front page. At the top was written today's date.

You said you'd risk it all for me
This is starting to feel like a one-way street
I want to talk, but I can't breathe
If I walked away, I'd lose everything

My eyes went involuntarily wide as Talia held her hand out expectantly. I reluctantly set the sheet music into her hands, and she rushed to tuck it out of sight.

My stomach sank. "Are you *sure* I can't help? What's going on with you two?"

"Nothing," she assured me. "We just have to talk."

"Well, I didn't mean to look, but those lyrics sounded really sad."

Talia finally looked at me. "They're just lyrics. I write songs for my brother's band. I have to come up with stuff that will appeal to their fans."

"So everything's okay with you and Cody?" I asked warily.

"Well… we kind of had a fight earlier, but it's okay." She quickly brushed it off.

"Do you want to talk about it?" I offered.

Talia bit her lower lip, stalling. "We're just not on the same page about some things."

I didn't want to push her, but I wanted to know what was going on, so I could help. "You don't have to tell me right now, but I'm here to talk whenever you're ready."

"That's sweet of you. I just don't know how to put it." Talia sank back down on the couch. "It wasn't really a *fight*. I don't want you to think Cody's a bad guy, because he's not. He just…" She sighed. "He's such a guy. It's like we speak a totally different language."

"About what? Maybe I can help."

Talia stared down at her hands. "I love him so much and want to make him happy. I know he has needs, and I do everything I can to meet them. But I have needs, too, you know? I tried to bring it up, and it turned into a whole thing."

My mouth felt like sandpaper. "Do you mean… *sexual* needs?"

She dropped her gaze, her voice barely audible. "Yeah."

"Wait… so you wanted more from sex, and he got mad about it?" I asked, trying to understand what she was saying.

"Not *mad*," she insisted. "Just… confused, I guess?"

My features hardened. "What's confusing about it? You want something from him, and he either says *okay, let's do it*, or *no thanks, I'm not comfortable with that*."

Talia still wouldn't look me in the eye. "It's not that simple. I'm asking him for something he can't give me."

"Can't, or won't?" I was suddenly very skeptical of Cody. Talia made it sound like it wasn't a big deal, but I could tell there was more to it.

She looked up from under her lashes, giving me a sheepish look. "I want him to make me orgasm, but I guess it's harder for some girls."

I recalled my date with Lucas last Friday, and how it'd been so easy with him. I knew everyone's bodies were different, but the way Talia spoke rubbed me the wrong way.

"Maybe he's not doing it right," I suggested.

"No," Talia assured me. "Everything down there is working. I'm just bad at it or something."

My jaw dropped, and my indifference toward Cody suddenly turned into an intense distaste.

"Did Cody tell you that?" I practically fumed.

"No," she answered quickly, but there was something in her tone. It wasn't a lie exactly. He may not have said it in those words, but she hadn't come to the conclusion on her own.

"Can you do it yourself?" I asked.

"I have… a couple times," she admitted.

"Then you're not the problem," I insisted. "He probably doesn't know what he's doing. What kinds of things does he do that you like?"

Talia shrugged. "I don't know. We just, you know, have sex. Then he's done, and I can't finish."

My nostrils flared. Her lyrics instantly came to mind, about the *one-way street*. "That's not fair. Most women can't orgasm from penetration alone. He should be trying to please you in other ways."

Her brow furrowed. "They don't? But he said his other girlfriends—"

"Screw his other girlfriends," I interrupted. "They aren't the ones having sex with him, are they? You need to communicate with each other —tell him what you like."

"It kind of ruins the moment," she admitted.

"Really?" I asked flatly. "Being pleasured *ruins* the moment? Tal, don't let him put all the blame on you. Sex is a two-person activity."

"Sometimes it doesn't feel that way." She spoke so quietly I barely heard her. She looked so sad, I couldn't stand it.

"If you don't want to be with Cody, you *can* break up with him," I pointed out.

"No," she said, alarmed. "I could never. I love him so much. If we weren't together, I'd… I don't know what I would do."

I was starting to hate Cody more and more the longer this conversation continued.

"I know what will cheer you up," I encouraged. "What do you say we head to the cafeteria and grab some of that chicken you love?"

Talia shook her head. "I'm not hungry."

"All semester?" I balked. It was clear what I was getting at. I wasn't about to hold back the hard truth with my bestie.

She frowned. "I like the way I look. I've lost five pounds this semester."

My jaw dropped. "You don't need to lose five pounds!"

Talia had always been petite, and was one of the skinniest people I knew.

"You don't have to do this for Cody," I said. "If he really loved you, he'd take you at any size—like Grant."

The mention of Grant slipped out before I could think about it.

Talia's features darkened. "I don't want to be with Grant."

I scrambled to collect myself. "I didn't mean that, exactly. But if I can ask… why not?"

She pushed her hair behind her ear. "Grant's too good to be true. Even if he *did* like me, I don't deserve him."

My eyebrows shot up. How had she not realized that Grant was totally head-over-heels for her?

"You deserve someone who treats you right," I said firmly. "I know if you were available, Grant would ask you out in a heartbeat."

"Well, I'm not available," Talia said coolly. "How did Grant get involved in this conversation, anyway? Honestly, I just want Cody and I to be on the same page. That's all. And we'll get there. I know it."

My stomach dropped, because I wasn't so sure about that. I'd always thought Talia was happy with Cody, but the more I thought about it, the more I realized the red flags had been there all along. She wouldn't eat, and was constantly asking how her hair looked. Her self-esteem had taken a serious hit these last few months. Not to mention how she would rush away to meet up with him the instant he messaged her. It was like he wouldn't let her have her own life.

And I got it—on some level. I wanted to be with Lucas every second of the day, too. But if Talia needed me first, Lucas would understand.

Cody didn't seem to acknowledge Talia had a life outside of him. He was dragging her down. I didn't like it one bit, but I also didn't know what to do about it. She wasn't going to listen.

"I just want you to be happy with whoever you're with," I said softly.

"I'm happy with Cody," she promised, though I wasn't sure whether she meant it or if she was trying to convince herself of it. "I gotta go. I'll see you later."

Talia quickly gathered her things and subconjured them, then hurried out the door with Gus at her feet. Isa and I both watched her go. I hadn't noticed until now how much weight she'd lost. Five pounds didn't sound like much, but on her tiny frame, it was. I made a mental note to buy her some of Barry's Enchanted Muffins later. I knew she wouldn't be able to pass them up.

Isa turned to look at me and blinked.

"What was I supposed to do?" I asked her. "Beg her to stay? Yeah, I'd like to spend more time with her, but…" I didn't know how to finish the sentence. "But I'm talking to a cat, so it doesn't matter."

I returned my attention to the oracle card, contemplating its meaning for several long moments. Maybe the card wasn't telling me to face my fears or do some inner reflection. Maybe it meant to face myself—literally. I had to face my darkness.

I crossed my legs on the bed and got comfortable. Closing my eyes, I inhaled a deep breath. "Okay, Dark Nadine," I said aloud. "How do I find you?"

I focused on every inch of my body, starting with my fingertips and moving up my arms, then down my body. I could feel magic buzzing inside my chest, the same I felt my heartbeat or breath if I focused closely. All I had to do was find the curse and draw it out…

Resistance hit deep in my belly. The moment I noticed it, a chill spread down my spine, and my fingers shook from where they rested on my knees. The resistance was calm at first, almost unnoticeable, but the more I focused on it, the more it chilled me to the bone.

I smirked proudly. "Ah, is *that* you? Well, you can go fuck yourself."

I tugged on the energy swirling in my stomach. It was heavy and felt different from the rest of my magic. I squeezed my eyes shut tighter and willed my magic to circle the area of resistance. I wanted nothing more than to crush it, but my magic did nothing against it.

I realized I couldn't rid myself of my darkness by sheer force. It was a curse—I had to draw it out. Taking a deep breath, I drew my magic upward, tugging on the dark ball of energy in my belly. It fought against me, but I fought harder.

The energy rose to my chest. My throat closed, and the room spun around me. Dark shadows passed across my vision, moving so quickly I couldn't make out the shapes. My pulse quickened, and a sense of urgency hit. I wanted to rush to my feet and sprint out of the room, but I remained rooted in place, as if held down by chains.

My head lolled forward, and I realized a moment too late what a terrible mistake I had made. I hadn't drawn it out quick enough, and I wasn't strong enough to fight it.

The resistance bloomed inside my chest, until it didn't resist at all.

Instead, it seemed to merge with my magic, flowing through my veins and taking over my entire body. Panic wept through me, and I tugged harder and harder, trying to reel it in. The energy yanked out of my grasp, exploding down through my extremities.

A beat of silence passed. I tried to assess the energy inside of me, but I couldn't stay focused long enough.

An evil laugh bubbled out of my throat. I felt lighter when I didn't fight back. My magic seemed to flow through me easier, and my whole body came alight with energy. I felt *strong*.

Perhaps strong enough to combat Chloe.

I clicked my tongue, and words that didn't feel like my own slipped out of my mouth. "Maybe this curse isn't so bad."

Isa growled at me, but I ignored her.

A fly buzzed around my head, and I opened my eyes to see it land on the nightstand. Without thinking about it, I shot my hand out and slapped the fly. It went completely flat, and I drew my hand away to see a smear of blood on my palm.

Magic swelled within me. I felt like I could do anything. At the thought, a purple orb formed in my hand. It crackled like lightning, and I had the urge to throw it. I drew my arm back, and the orb flew across the room. It fizzled out before it hit the wall, but a sense of victory filled my chest nonetheless. I'd just conjured a *battle orb*. I couldn't believe it!

I stared down at my palms, waiting for the fatigue to sit in, but it didn't. That's when I noticed the blood smear on my hand had disappeared. I looked over to the dead fly, and that was gone, too. In its place was nothing more than a tiny pile of ash.

Holy shit. Realization slammed into me. Had I just used *blood magic*? Is that why the spell was so easy to cast—because I'd pulled the magic from the dead creature rather than myself? The implications of this type of magic thrilled me. I could use this to perform magic without nearly passing out every time. It changed everything.

A thought suddenly struck, and I got out of bed. I bent to the garbage can, where Talia had thrown away the dead bird and had forgotten about it. A sly smile spread across my lips as I lifted its limp corpse. I glanced around the room, and my eyes landed on a pack of matches on my altar. I took them, then gathered a few candles from my nightstand and situated myself on the floor in the center of the room.

I didn't think about what I was doing. I hadn't even realized I'd made the decision to try it. I struck a match and lit three candles, one by one. The bird felt soft in my hands. I didn't mind when I felt its warm blood trickling onto my fingers. I studied the bird, wondering how best to use it. Pinching one of the twisted blue feathers, I plucked it out and held it over the flames. The feather caught fire. Laughter that didn't sound like my own filled the room as the burning scent entered my nostrils.

"Shadows cast in the fading light. Turn this creature as dark as night." I muttered the incantation on the spot. My eyes widened as I witnessed the bird's shiny blue feathers darken to a pitch black. It lasted only a few moments before fading back to blue. Still, I never felt more accomplished.

The feather between my fingers burned to ash, and the flame died. A wicked sneer tugged at the corners of my lips. I hadn't felt a thing.

"Perfect," I chuckled.

Isa growled again, but I barely heard her. Already, all the possibilities were rushing through my mind. Gripping the bird tightly in my fingers, I lowered its limp head toward the candle.

"Graveyard stones and ghostly cry. Chloe's wicked soul must—"

A screech tore through the room, and Isa jumped down from the bed and onto my shoulder. Her claws dug into my neck and tore through my skin as she fell to the ground.

"Ow, what the fuck, Isa?" I cried as I pressed my fingers to the fresh wounds. My hand came away with three lines of blood on it.

I snapped back to attention. The warm bird still lay in my palm, but I dropped it the second I noticed. What I'd just been doing hit me like a punch to the gut, and I doubled over as all the air left my lungs. Had I just been about to *curse* Chloe using dark magic? What the fuck?

I sucked in deep breaths of air. It was almost like I'd been possessed, except I hadn't been. I knew what I was doing. I even *wanted* to.

But all rationality had been thrown out the window when my darkness took over. A heavy weight settled in my gut, making my stomach feel hollow and full of bricks all at the same time. I suddenly realized the candles were still burning, and I quickly blew them out so they wouldn't tempt me. My heart raced, and my breath wavered.

"Dear Goddess, Isa," I cried. "What's wrong with me?"

Nothing, a voice in my head told me. It wasn't like I'd *killed* the bird. It was already dead when I tried to perform the spell. If anyone was going to get hurt, it would be Chloe, and she deserved it.

I was so conflicted.

I pressed my face into my hands as I went back and forth with myself, but something sticky touched my skin. I pulled my hands away and realized the bird's blood was still on them. I got to my feet and went to the bathroom. Clutching the edge of the sink, I sucked in a deep breath and looked in the mirror.

"Why would you do that, Nadine?" I questioned myself, shaking my head. Cursing Chloe wouldn't solve anything—and with dark magic no less. Talia had warned me about the dangers of dark magic. It was banned within the coven. If I used it, Chloe won. I'd be banished for sure.

Only if I get caught...

I reached for the faucet to wipe the blood off my face, but my hands shook. Instead, I waved my hand over my face and spoke a cleansing incantation.

"Red, orange, yellow, blue. Make my face fresh and new."

The bird's blood faded from my face, but no sooner had I cast the spell did a sharp pain shoot up through my wrist.

"Ah," I cried.

I grabbed the aching wrist with my other hand and massaged it, but it took a full minute for the spasms to stop and the pain to ease. Tears welled in my eyes, though they refused to fall.

"I can't do this," I whispered to myself.

Black magic was easy. It didn't hurt at all. How much longer could I keep drawing from myself? Even the simplest spells took their toll.

I forced my breath to slow and lifted my gaze to stare at myself in the mirror. My reflection was full of judgement. I hated the way I looked at myself.

I squeezed my eyes shut so I wouldn't have to, but that didn't help. All I saw from behind my lids was my own face, but it wasn't quite my own. It was the one I'd fought in my Evoking Ceremony. She wore dark makeup and a smug smile.

I hated her.

But how could I… when she was me?

She was right about what she'd said during my Evoking Ceremony. I was weak. My body couldn't even take its own magic. I was a burden to those around me. It's why Talia spent so much time with Cody—so she didn't have to deal with me. How could Lucas love me like this? My parents must've died because they didn't want me.

"Shut up!" I screamed.

I knew everything that had just gone through my mind was a lie. So why did I even think it at all?

I have to get out of here, I thought.

I turned around, only to realize Isa had been standing in the doorway to the bathroom the whole time. I stumbled past her and noticed the candles and bird were still on the floor. I moved as quickly as I could to get everything back in its proper place. All that was left was the bird…

It didn't seem right to throw it in the garbage. I knew *I* hadn't killed the bird, but I hadn't treated it with respect, either.

Perhaps that was the answer. If I cast black magic with honor and respect, it wasn't *really* black magic, was it? As long as I didn't intend to hurt anything, there was no harm in it.

I wrapped the bird in tissues. Isa sat on the floor, watching me.

"Come on, Isa." I gestured for her to follow me. "We're going to give this guy a proper burial."

I slipped on a coat, and Isa followed me outside. We walked into the forest behind the school. I could just barely make sense of the trail in the setting sun. I didn't stop until we were far enough away from the mansion that I couldn't see the building anymore. I turned at a thick oak tree and ventured off the path a few yards.

I knelt in the snow and set the bird aside. Isa sniffed the bundle of tissues, then sat beside me and purred her approval. I began digging with my hands. The ground was cold and frozen, but I managed to dig a shallow grave. My fingers felt like icicles when I finally pulled away. Gently, I set the bird in the hole.

"There you go, little birdie," I said. "May you rest in peace."

At that, I scooped the dirt into the hole, burying the bird. When I finished, I smoothed out the top of the grave and placed a rock I'd found nearby on top of it.

My chest felt lighter now that I'd given the bird a proper burial. Coven culture told me that I should feel awful about using black magic, but I didn't. I felt *strong*.

This was how I beat Chloe, I realized. I was too weak without it. And I refused to be weak any longer.

☾·

I WOKE EARLY the next morning and was out of bed and ready for the day in forty-five minutes, a near record for me. I even had time to make it to the breakfast buffet before class. I ate a stack of pancakes and a bowl of fruit, then dumped my tray. I was thrilled when I spotted Lucas passing the cafeteria on my way out.

"Hey, babe," I greeted, pinching him playfully as I came up behind him.

He jumped a little, then relaxed when he saw it was me. He draped an arm around me and noted, "You're looking good today."

I ran my fingers through my hair for show. "Thanks. I feel good."

He eyed me curiously. "What's your secret?"

I glanced up and down the hall, but there were too many people nearby. I wasn't sure how to tell him I'd used black magic. I didn't know if he'd be proud of me for casting new magic or disappointed in my methods.

"Let's go for a walk," I suggested.

Lucas and I conjured our coats and headed outside. We started for the trail that cut through the woods behind the school. The freshly fallen snow left the forest quiet, and the wind was still.

"Can I be honest with you?" I asked.

He squeezed my hand. "Always."

"All my life, I've grown up with what I can only describe as a *dark energy* inside of me," I told him. "I mentioned it to you before, but I never *really* explained it. I think it has something to do with my family curse."

He furrowed his brow. "Should I be worried?"

"No, nothing like that," I said quickly. "It's just… sometimes she breaks through."

Lucas studied me. "Breaks through how?"

"I dumped some cursed objects on Chloe, and I used a bird Gus killed to perform a spell," I admitted.

Lucas's face paled. "Nad, tell me you didn't use black magic."

It was hard to tell exactly what he was thinking. I bit my lower lip. "Kind of. The bird was already dead, so I'm not sure it counts."

"It counts," Lucas pressed. "Nad, you can't do that. It's against coven law."

"But I didn't hurt anyone. And I cast magic without getting sick." My eyes searched his, and I noticed his features deepening with concern. "You're not scared of me, are you?"

He shook his head and stared down at me. "How could I ever be scared of you? This darkness you mentioned, it isn't you. You would never hurt a fly."

But I did, I thought. *Literally*.

"Are you disappointed in me?" I asked. I didn't know what I'd been hoping for by telling Lucas all this. Perhaps I needed some form of validation.

"I'm worried," he admitted, taking my hands in his. "This curse could seriously hurt you. But I know you. You won't stop until you've broken it. Then you'll be free of this darkness—"

Lucas cut off as the sound of commotion came through the trees. We both went as still as statues, listening. I heard a growl first, followed by a roar. Then came the sound of heavy footsteps pounding on the path.

"Holy shit," I cried, my spine straightening. "Are there bears around here?"

His eyes went wide. "I don't think that was a—*fuck!*"

The creature came barreling out of the trees, sprinting and rearing its head like it was some sort of rabid animal. That, or it was *seriously* pissed off.

My heart leapt to my throat, and though every instinct told me to run, I couldn't move my feet. The monster skidded to a halt on the path when it noticed us. It studied us as if considering us for its next meal. I shuddered. The creature was unlike anything I'd ever seen before.

Scratch that. I'd seen it *once*, in a drawing shown in my demonology class. It was a three-headed lion with a black coat and golden eyes. I knew it as a creature of lore—a type of monster created by demons. My gaze roamed every inch of it, taking in the terrifying creature. A scar marred its right paw, and its skin hung tight to its bones. Saliva dripped from each of its three mouths, and it bared its fangs in our direction. I'd wager a guess the monster hadn't eaten in days, and it looked *starving*.

"Nad, get behind me," Lucas demanded. He didn't give me a choice. He grabbed me by the shoulder and shoved his way in front of me.

"Shouldn't we run?" I asked as the creature stared us down.

Lucas kept his eyes on the three-headed lion. "If we run, it will chase us down. I'm not risking it catching us."

"Then what do we do?"

Lucas opened his palms, and purple battle orbs formed in his hands. "We fight back."

No sooner had he said it did the creature begin charging. My heart hammered so hard I could feel my blood pulsing throughout my whole body. I tried my damndest to conjure a battle orb, but nothing happened.

Luckily, Lucas was prepared. He threw battle orbs at the lion in quick succession. They each hit their target square on, slamming into one of the three heads in turn. The lion was blasted backward. I poised to run while it was distracted, but it dug its claws into the snowy dirt and shook its heads like the orbs were nothing but a minor inconvenience.

"Any other ideas?" I squeaked.

"Uh…" Lucas thought quickly and conjured a potion. He flung it at the lion as it charged toward us a second time. But the potion did nothing but spill across the dirt as the vial exploded at the creature's feet.

"Lucas!" I screamed.

The lion lunged, and Lucas shoved me out of the way. I stumbled backward to the forest floor as Lucas threw up a shield. The magic shimmered in the morning light. The shield was no match for the monster, though. The lion's claws reached out and swiped straight through Lucas's magic, shattering his shield spell. He didn't have time to react before the lion had tackled him to the ground.

"Lucas!" I shrieked.

I didn't think about what I was doing. I scrambled to my feet and flung myself on top of the lion. My arms wrapped around the middle head, and I yanked backward. But I was too late. The monster had already taken a swipe at Lucas. The sound of his jacket ripping tore through the forest. My stomach hollowed in response to Lucas's pained cries. Without hesitation, I sank my fingers straight into the monster's eyes, and it reared backward. I held on tight, pinning my legs to its sides. The creature's roar filled the forest and echoed through the trees.

"Nadine!" Lucas cried. He formed another battle orb but hesitated. He didn't want to hit me.

My pulse pounded in my ears, and my joints began to ache with the force I used to keep myself on the creature's back. The monster's jaws snapped at me, but it couldn't crane its necks back far enough to reach me. I had to think of something—and *fast*.

I could feel the monster's magic pulsing through him. I didn't know if he had any special abilities, or if I was simply sensing the magic that created him. But I knew if I could sense it, I could take it for my own. It would at least slow him down... right?

I didn't allow myself to question it, because I didn't have time. If I sat around thinking about it, I'd be ground meat before I made a decision.

I tightened my hold around its neck and squeezed my eyes shut tightly. At my command, my magic tangled with the monster's. I opened my channel, and his magic flowed into me. The magic was unlike anything I'd ever felt before. When I channeled it, a heaviness settled in my chest, and my skin stung like I'd been attacked by a hive of wasps. The taste of copper filled my mouth, and the scent of burnt flesh entered my nostrils. It was dark magic like I'd never known—forged straight in the fires of the Abyss.

The monster roared again, but this time it barely made a sound. It spun in circles, trying to fling me off, but I went nowhere. I kept tugging at its magic, and its footsteps slowed.

Finally, the creature slumped to the ground. I wasn't sure if it was dead or unconscious, but I couldn't check. The monster's dark magic rattled around inside of me, begging to escape.

"Nad." I heard Lucas's voice, but it sounded miles away. My vision blurred as I stumbled over to a nearby tree and caught myself on it.

"Nad," Lucas repeated. He knelt beside me and placed a hand on my back, but it felt like fire on my skin. "What's going on?"

"I have to... get rid of it," I told him between gritted teeth. I could barely talk, the magic hurt so much.

I didn't know what I was going to do with it—or how. If I let this magic go just anywhere, it'd spring back into the creature, and it'd be back to finish the two of us off. I had no choice but to get rid of it for good. Failure wasn't an option.

My hands splayed across the tree trunk, and my fingers curled, nails digging into the bark. I opened my channel once again, this time allowing the magic to flow out of me. I pressed it into the tree, filling up the earth with the dark magic. I focused my intention on death. This creature from hell had to die, or it would kill us both.

Tears rolled down my cheeks as the bark began to shrivel beneath my hands. Above me, healthy branches twisted and curled, as if the tree was in pain. The bark transformed from a healthy brownish-gray to a deep, burnt black. Lucas's eyes widened as he watched.

Slowly, the fiery pain across my skin eased. The burning smell in my nostrils drifted away in the wind, and I smelled Lucas beside me. When it seemed like the magic was gone, I kept going. My channel opened even wider, and magic I didn't realize was still lingering continued to flow into the tree. I continued until there seemed to be no magic left—and even then, I didn't stop. But I didn't force it. It was like Verla had taught me. I had to let the magic work *for* me.

Soon, my vision began to darken at the corners, and my arms became so weak I could no longer keep them up. My head spun, and my whole body collapsed to the side. Lucas caught me.

I took a moment to take in my surroundings. The tree had withered away and was nothing more than a burnt skeleton in a forest of healthy trees. It was as if a fire had come along to claim a single life. I glanced at the monster just in time to see its body appear to sink into the earth. It was gone a moment later, but the earth hadn't moved at all—like the monster never existed.

"Wh-what just happened to it?" I stammered.

Lucas swallowed. "It's been reclaimed by the Abyss. It belongs to hell."

I shuddered. "H-how did this happen? How did it get here?"

Lucas helped me sit up, though I felt like I could hardly move. I leaned against him for support.

"I don't know," he answered in a shaky breath. "The only entrances for monsters into our world are in Malovia, the home of the Arcanea. The fae have magical borders to keep them contained, though. I have no idea how the monster got here, unless someone else sent it."

I groaned. "Another prank from Chloe. Or literally anyone else mad at me about the vandalism. "

Lucas looked thoughtful, but he couldn't seem to make sense of the creature's sudden appearance. "The good news is… you did it."

I blinked at him a few times. My head was clouded, and I wasn't sure I heard him right. "I did what?"

"You killed the monster." I swore I heard admiration in his tone. "You transferred his magic into the tree. And that creature is *dark*. If you can do *that*, you can break any curse you want."

My head began to clear, and I realized what a magical feat it was. It only confirmed for me what I could do with dark magic. I'd *killed* a creature in the process of transferring its magic—that had to fall under the realm of dark magic.

I drew away to look him in the eyes. "I guess you're right. I can't believe I—Lucas!"

My breath stalled when I caught sight of his arm. Blood dripped from the gashes torn in his sleeve, pooling into the snow below. I reached out for him, but he yanked away on instinct. It was the first time I noticed how pale he'd gone. "Goddess, you're really hurt."

"I'll be fine," he said. "Just need some antibiotics and gauze."

"Let me see," I demanded.

I didn't wait for an answer. I yanked on the fabric of his sleeve, opening the hole wider. My guts twisted when I saw the damage underneath. Three gashes ran across his arm and were torn so deep I saw bone. Rivers of blood trailed down his arm.

"We have to get you to the infirmary *now*," I insisted.

Lucas tugged his sleeve over the wounds and pressed down hard. "It's not that bad—"

He didn't get a chance to finish his sentence. His face went totally ashen, and his eyes rolled back into his skull. I only barely caught him before he crashed to the ground, unconscious.

ELEVEN

I woke in the infirmary hours later, wondering if the monster attack had been a dream. Something warm squeezed my hand, and I turned to see Nadine sitting at my bedside. My unease instantly washed away at the sight of her.

She looked tired, as if she had only woken when I stirred. I tried to sit up straighter, but pain shot through my arm. I glanced down to see my forearm wrapped tight in gauze.

"Nad…" My voice came out dry.

Nadine quickly reached for a glass of water and handed it to me. "Here. You should drink something."

I sipped water through the straw but quickly realized how parched I was and drank half the glass in a matter of seconds. Finally, I set the drink on the table beside my bed. "What happened?"

"What happened, *Mister It's Not That Bad?*" she teased. "You passed out, so I ran to get help. They wouldn't let me in the room while they cleaned up your wounds, but they said it should heal within the week. They must've put some sort of magical salve on it."

I sucked a breath through my teeth. "How bad was it?"

Nadine cocked an eyebrow. "Pretty bad. That monster… whatever it was… it tore down to the bone."

I sighed. "I'm sorry."

"Sorry?" she asked. "It's not your fault. Whoever summoned that thing is to blame."

"I should've been able to fight it," I insisted. The sight of her jumping on the back of the monster played over and over in my mind. I'd been so frightened for her. I didn't ever want to put her in that kind of danger again. I couldn't live with myself if I ever let her get hurt.

She ran her thumb over the back of my hand. "Don't worry about it. The monster's gone. It's over now."

My guts sank. I didn't want to jump to conclusions before we had any evidence, but something told me that this—whatever it'd been about— was far from over.

"You did amazing out there, Nad," I told her softly.

She smiled, but it looked forced.

"Seriously," I assured her. "Don't underplay it. Your magic is stronger than you realize."

"Thanks," she replied softly.

I started to get up, but Nadine gently pushed me back into bed. "Where do you think you're going?"

"It's Thursday," I pointed out. "I have class."

She frowned. "Not today, you don't. You're staying in bed until your arm heals."

"I can *walk*," I argued.

"You could also hurt yourself even more," she pointed out. "I'm helping you until you're better. I won't leave your side."

Nadine kept true to her promise over the weekend, only leaving my dorm to grab food or sleep. I hated having her care for me, because *I* was the one who was supposed to take care of *her*, but I found it endearing nonetheless. As if I could fall for the girl even more.

By the following week, I managed to convince her I was fine, and I returned to classes. The Divination classroom buzzed with conversation when I arrived. I was one of the last ones there and quietly slipped into an empty seat in the back—my usual spot. My fingers trailed over the gauze on my arm, as I couldn't help but fiddle with it.

Professor Wykoff stood at the front of the room with her back to us, organizing a few supplies I couldn't see. It was a new unit today, like every week. It turned out there was a lot more to divination than I ever realized.

We must've studied a dozen techniques already, trying to discern messages about the future through various means. We'd already covered alomancy, or divination by salt; abacomancy, or divination through dust or ashes; and ichnomancy, where we read our futures from our footprints.

Divination was a skill all witches and warlocks could learn, and it was a required credit. But I wasn't a Seer. I didn't possess a knack for discerning images from abstract things like salt crystal patterns. I'd quickly learned that the key to passing this class was to make shit up. Professor Wykoff approved of any interpretation, no matter how bogus.

"Welcome, class," Professor Wykoff said in the calm tone she always used. The class quickly quieted so we could hear her. "Today, we will be studying carromancy."

She waved her hand, and a box at the front desk began to hover mid-air. It trailed behind her as she walked around the room, passing out supplies as she explained. "Carromancy translates from Greek as *waxen divination*. It involves the interpretation of melted wax to tell your future. There are many forms of carromancy. One of the most common is to drop hot wax into a bowl of cold water and interpret the images formed. We will be performing that ceremony later this week."

Professor Wykoff reached my desk and set a small candlestick and a matchbook in front of me. "Today, we will start with a simple method. All you have to do is light your candle and interpret the flicker of the flame and the shapes of the melting wax. As always, divination begins with asking a question—whether you choose to focus on relationships, money, or something else. It may take the full period for your candle to burn down, so I suggest you get started."

Professor Wykoff breezed to the front of the room as she finished handing out candles. She was a Mentalist, but highly perceptive. If I hadn't seen her perform telekinesis before, I wouldn't have believed she wasn't a Seer.

I turned my attention to the candle and decided to set a generic intention—what the hell did my future hold? I lit my candle and focused on the flame. It flickered erratically, but I didn't put a lot of stock in the symbolism. There were a lot of people in this class, breathing and interrupting the air currents.

The clock ticked on the wall, and my classmates remained silent. Some of them closed their eyes and started meditating. My mind wandered—

first to Nadine, then to the Magical Theory paper I had due and hadn't worked on yet.

My thoughts settled on the case of the missing boys. I'd done everything I could to identify the third boy from the photo at Michelle's, but the coven was sensitive to information on minors. I hadn't even found a name, and I didn't know where to go next without more information. Neither the Thomases nor Michelle wanted to tell me the truth.

"What an interesting pattern," Professor Wykoff mused, pulling me from my thoughts.

I glanced down to my candlestick to see it was almost completely melted. I hadn't realized how much time had passed. My candle looked nothing more than a blob of wax, so I wasn't sure what she found so interesting about it.

"How would you interpret the flickering of the flame?" Professor Wykoff asked, eyes sparkling.

"Um…" I cleared my throat and made something up on the spot. "It flickered a lot, which might mean I have some conflicting energy. Perhaps the road ahead is going to be difficult for me."

She drew a breath and clapped her hands together at her chest, sounding delighted. "A very perceptive interpretation, Mister Taylor. What can you interpret from the dried wax?"

I eyed the candle from various angles, though nothing stood out to me. It was just melted candle wax, after all. "The wax melted into teardrop shapes, further confirming I have a difficult path ahead."

"Precisely," Professor Wykoff said brightly.

I might've felt a sense of pride, if she hadn't bought every bullshit interpretation I'd come up with this semester.

"Your wax has hardened on the side of the candle." She pointed at the various tear-drop shapes. "This means that you will have a difficult time overcoming your burdens—but rest assured you will achieve your goals."

I sank a little in my seat. Just the fortune I wanted to hear. "Thanks," I scoffed.

I hadn't meant to sound so ungrateful. As my breath left my chest, the air blew the candle out, but it was only out for a second. A moment later, the wick began burning again.

"Oh, my," Professor Wykoff gasped, placing her hand over her heart.

I raised an eyebrow curiously. "What?"

"Your flame! It appeared to burn out for a moment, but it was only an illusion." She pressed her lips together and murmured, "This means something…"

It wasn't that I didn't believe in divination. I just wasn't good at it myself. So when Professor Wykoff got that look of intense interest on her face, I was practically on the edge of my seat.

"What does it mean?" I pressed.

"I have my suspicions, but let's consult the cards for further analysis." She lifted her hand, and a deck of tarot cards flew to her from across the room. She used her telekinetic power to shuffle them, then had me draw a card.

Her shoulders fell when she saw it. "As I suspected. The Seven of Cups is the card of illusion. Something is not as it seems, Mister Taylor. Something… or *someone*."

No shit, I thought. Someone in the coven had gotten away with murder. That was an illusion if I ever saw one.

"Tread carefully," she warned. The woman wasn't a Seer, but I'd be damned if her ominous voice didn't hold the same chilling warning as someone with clear divination powers. "The path you are on is not as clear as you might think. You are about to uncover many secrets. Someone is deceiving you, and you must be careful who to trust."

A chill spread down my spine. When it came to this case, I trusted no one.

☾

AFTER CLASS, Grant invited me to the fitness center for rock climbing. It was still early in the day, so we were the only ones there, apart from a student desk attendant across the gym. It felt good to get back in a harness. Grant acted as my belayer, controlling my safety rope as I climbed. We attached our gear and gave our commands.

"On belay?" I asked.

Grant tugged the rope tight. "Belay is on."

"Climbing," I announced. I rubbed my chalked hands together as I assessed my route over the wall.

"I did that research you wanted me to," Grant said as I began climbing.

"On the potions?" I was already several feet off the ground and glanced down at him. Hope surged in my chest. Finally, I might have some sort of answer.

"Yeah. Turns out, I can't find anything that would mess with someone's powers—not unless you administered the potion directly."

I pressed my lips together as I turned back toward the wall. "Well, Talia didn't eat or drink anything while we were at Michelle's, and her visions were still messy."

I hesitated on the rocks a moment, before finding a better route and climbing quickly. I called down to Grant. "Do you think her powers are just too fresh? Maybe she doesn't know how to use them yet?"

He sounded unsure. "I think if Talia felt a block, it was probably there."

"You're right," I agreed. I trusted Talia to know the limits of her powers.

I reached the top of the wall and touched the ceiling, then announced to Grant, "Ready to lower."

"Lowering," Grant called up to me.

I kicked off the wall, and Grant slowly lowered me to the mat below. I unclipped my gear, and we switched places. As Grant was tying his figure-eight knot, I rolled my shoulders. It'd been a long time since I'd climbed, and it was going to take some practice to work up my climbing muscles again. But damn, did it feel good.

"Oh, I almost forgot," Grant said before stepping up to the wall. "I passed Professor Carlisle in the hall after Magical Plants and Herbs. He said if I saw you to let you know he wanted to talk."

I furrowed my brow. "Talk?"

"Something about the article you're writing," he clarified.

"Right. Thanks for the heads-up."

After we finished climbing, I headed toward Professor Carlisle's office. The door was open when I arrived. Professor Carlisle held a small vial and brought it to his lips. He tipped it backward, but startled when I knocked on the door frame. A light green liquid spilled over his chin, and he hurried to wipe it up.

"Sorry, Professor—" I said before cutting off. The potion sparkled blue in the light, catching my attention. I'd never seen anything like it. "If you don't mind me asking, what is that?"

"Oh, it's nothing," he replied nonchalantly, grabbing a stack of napkins that must've been left over from his lunch. He dotted the potion off his tie. "It's just a potion to help curb symptoms of…"

He trailed off as he looked up at me. There was skepticism in his eyes, like he wasn't sure whether to tell me or not.

"Symptoms of what, Professor?" I asked carefully. "Are you ill?"

He took a deep breath. "It's cancer, I'm afraid."

My stomach turned hollow. "I'm sorry. I had no idea."

His tone brightened. "No reason to be sorry. It could happen to anyone. The potion helps, but I'm afraid there's no cure. Please, do come in."

He sounded like he was trying to avoid the subject, so I didn't push it. My throat turned dry thinking about him living with incurable cancer. I wondered how long he had. I hoped it would be a long time before I heard his last thought.

I shut the door behind myself and took the chair across from his desk.

"I presume you're here about the article," Professor Carlisle said. "I wanted to see how far you've gotten."

I slumped in my seat a little. "Not far, to be honest. I interviewed Isaac's mom, but his dad still isn't returning my calls."

Carlisle's eyebrows shot up. "And did you find anything interesting?"

I sighed. "The parents are lying."

"Oh?" Professor Carlisle leaned closer, looking intrigued. "Lying about what, exactly?"

I glanced toward the door, and though we were in the privacy of his office, I lowered my voice anyway. "The parents told me their kids didn't know each other, but I saw a picture in Isaac's house. In it, he was standing next to Caleb and another boy. I don't know what the connection is exactly, but I think the third boy might be in danger."

"A third boy?" Professor Carlisle asked curiously. "Any idea who the boy is?"

I shook my head. "Michelle didn't say. I wish I would've snapped a photo of it before I left. Then maybe I could ask around and get a name. I've looked through some old copies of the *Miriamic Messenger*, but I haven't seen him."

"Hmm…" Professor Carlisle looked deep in thought. "Perhaps my gift can help."

I tilted my head. It was the first time I realized I didn't actually know what Professor Carlisle's gift was. I knew he was a Seer, but I didn't know anything beyond that.

"What exactly is it you can do?" I questioned curiously.

"Many things," he said humbly. "My gift is… multifaceted, if you will. Most Seers receive their own visions. My gift works differently, in which I'm able to open others' minds to visions, based on their personal experiences."

I stilled. "You can make me have a vision?"

Carlisle nodded. "Perhaps, if you are willing to receive it."

"It sounds like Professor Daymond's gift, but he's a Mentalist," I said thoughtfully. Nadine had told me how he'd used his gift to imprint visions in her mind to train her for her Evoking Ceremony.

Professor Carlisle waved his hand. "It's a similar concept, but a different execution. Professor Daymond plays with your mind as Mentalists do—makes you see what he wants you to see. As a Seer, my gift works alongside divination."

"What might I see?" I asked.

"Think of it like a movie theatre, in which I'm the projector, but you're the ticket-holder. I cannot control what is played on the screen, but I can press *play*, and you can view it."

"This could help us learn who's behind this!" I burst with enthusiasm.

Carlisle pressed his lips together. "It's certainly something I've considered, but as I said, the visions are based upon your personal experiences."

He tapped his chin thoughtfully. "Now that you have more information about the case, perhaps we can use your experiences to uncover more details."

"Then let's try it," I said without hesitation. "How does it work?"

Carlisle laced his fingers together on his desk. "It's simple. Close your eyes, and focus on the case."

"That's it?" I asked. It was almost too easy.

He nodded. "That's it. I will project my power onto you, and if there is anything to learn, you shall see it clearly in your mind."

I closed my eyes and tried to relax in the chair, but I was bursting with energy. If this worked, we could learn who was behind this. We could bring the case to a close and save any future victims.

"Okay, I'm ready," I announced.

I focused my mind on the details of the case—what the boys had said to me in their last thoughts, the pin I'd found at Caleb's house, and the photo of the boys together. As I imagined the photograph in my mind, I honed my attention on the third boy. I recalled the roundness of his face and the freckles across his nose. I pictured the deep brown of his eyes with such precision that they began to take life in my mind. His features became so detailed, I swore I could reach out and touch him. My breath wavered in surprise at how vivid the vision was.

Professor Carlisle didn't speak, and I didn't open my eyes to look at him. I wasn't sure if he could tell what I was seeing.

The boy was still to begin with, and then his features began to move. The image zoomed out and showed him running around a playground. His arms were spread wide, and he made *whooshing* noises like he was an airplane. There were other kids nearby, but they were more or less shadows in the vision. I couldn't make them out, as I was focused solely on the young boy.

"Travis!" a woman's voice called from offscreen.

The boy didn't respond, as if he hadn't heard. Instead, he ran for the playground equipment and started climbing it.

"Travis!" the voice called again. She was more stern this time, obviously annoyed. "Travis Bennett, it's time to go."

Travis reached the top of the playground equipment, and his shoulders sagged. "Coming!" he called back. He headed for the slide and started down it, and that's when the vision ended.

My eyes fluttered open, and I took deep breaths to slow my racing heart.

Professor Carlisle eyed me curiously. "What did you see?"

I drew another breath. "I got a name. Travis Bennett."

Carlisle's eyes brightened. "Well, that's wonderful. What do you plan to do with this information?"

I hesitated. What *could* I do?

Finally, I said, "I'm going to protect him."

"I'm happy to speak to the family myself," Carlisle countered.

"With all due respect, Professor, this is my article," I replied. "I'd like to explore every angle I can."

"I understand that," he sighed. "I just fear what may happen if the kidnapper discovers how much you know. He could be highly dangerous —we can't know for sure. Let me take care of this."

Carlisle wasn't going to budge. He really seemed worried about the perp, and I didn't blame him.

"Okay, Professor," I agreed. "I'll keep my distance."

But it was a lie. I only said it to placate him. The truth was, it didn't matter how dangerous this case got. I was going to do everything in my power to make sure no one got hurt again.

And that started with talking to Travis Bennett's family.

nadine

TWELVE

Several weeks passed, and I was relieved that nothing had happened since the lion attack—no pranks from Chloe, no dark episodes. I was proud to say my curses were working on Chloe. I'd seen her in the hall several times, trying to talk to guys, only for them to turn around and ignore her. One day, I overheard her complaining about her arms itching.

"Maybe you should visit the health center," Camille had suggested. "I'm sure there's a potion that can help."

"I tried a potion," Chloe sneered. "This is different. It's like someone… someone cursed me!"

I whirled around and hurried the other way before she could spot me. If she saw me standing there, she'd think I was spying. She'd know it was me.

I'd been doing better in Alchemy, too, and Onyx was warming up to me. My magic was growing stronger. I didn't always need to resort to dark magic to conjure orbs or perform minor incantations anymore. It still had its side-effects, though. On days I was recovering from spell-casting, I'd curl up with a book in the library. I'd found a few promising curse breaking legends in old texts, but nothing that would help me break this curse yet. I was beginning to feel more at ease, but I feared it wouldn't last long.

Talia and I walked beside each other after class a few weeks later. We spotted Grant and Lucas talking with Mandy and Amy in the Main Foyer and made our way over to their study corner.

"I'm all set," Grant said.

"Set with what?" Talia asked, taking a seat beside Grant. There weren't any seats left for me, so I sat on the arm of Lucas's chair, and he wrapped an arm around me.

"They're talking about their majors," Lucas explained.

"What major did you declare, Grant?" Mandy asked.

"Culinary Alchemy," Grant said proudly. "I'd love to open my own place. I haven't decided whether it'd be a bakery or a brewery yet."

"That major sounds incredible," I told him. "I didn't know there was such a thing."

"Oh, yeah," Grant raved. "It's one of the most popular Alchemy majors. Most people go on to become Alchemists for the breweries and cider mills in town. It's pretty easy to make a career out of maple syrup, too. Culinary Alchemy is Octavia Falls's biggest industry. All the ciders and syrups we export are infused with magic. It easily makes us the best in the country."

"No wonder the food here is so amazing," I said with a laugh.

Grant leaned forward. "What are you thinking about majoring in, Mandy?"

She sighed. "I can't decide between palmology and counseling. I know I don't have to pick yet, but I'm trying to accelerate my coursework and graduate early. I'm going to have to get serious at the career fair next week."

Amy stroked Stormy's fur, who was curled up in her lap. "Do both. I'm thinking about double majoring, too, but I don't know. Magical History is so complex as it is."

"You're majoring in Magical History?" Talia sounded intrigued.

Amy smiled. "I want to know everything I possibly can about other supernatural races. I think we could do so much more to understand the Great Supernatural War and prevent anything like that from happening again."

I furrowed my brow. Everyone else seemed to know what she was talking about, but I hadn't run across it in my classes yet. "The Great Supernatural War?"

Amy's face lit up, like she was thrilled to talk about it. "Eighty years ago, a war broke out between the supernatural races. The Arcanean fae wanted to expose supernaturals. They thought our magic was strong enough to control them. The coven feared modern technology was enough to kill us, so we wanted to stay hidden. The Arcanea attacked the coven, and we retaliated."

My jaw dropped. "You must've won, right? I mean, we're still secret. But how? You guys have made the fae sound so strong."

"Oh, sure," Amy said. "Individually, they're much stronger than we are, but when all the coven's magic comes together, our magic rivals theirs. Besides, we didn't fight the war alone. Vampires and angels took the Arcanea's side, but we had mermaids and enchanters on ours. The Elven Union fought with us, too… until the Arcanea slaughtered them to extinction."

I shivered.

"Until then, the Elementai remained neutral," Amy continued. "But once the Elves were killed, they finally stepped in and took our side. They helped us win the war and get the treaty signed."

"That sounds horrible," I breathed. "You don't think it could happen again… do you?"

Amy bit her lower lip. "I think it's possible. The Elementai are fighting a civil war right now, and I've heard rumors of unrest in Malovia. The Astromancers are on the verge of a rebellion, and don't even get me started on the others. Supernatural races tend to keep to their own outside of trade, but who's to say we won't step in and take sides in one of these wars again? I think it's only a matter of time."

"I hope it's long after we're dead," I said softly.

Amy got a sad look in her eyes. "I hope so, too."

She didn't sound confident about that. It was clear what she was saying—if we didn't get involved with the next Great Supernatural War, our kids would.

Amy cleared her throat, breaking through the momentary silence. "Anyway, what are you majoring in, Lucas?"

"I'm not sure yet," he admitted.

"Well, you still have a couple of months to decide," Talia pointed out.

Mandy checked the time on her phone and stood. "Amy and I have to get to class. Let us know when you decide on a major, Lucas."

"Will do," he said, waving as the two of them left.

Grant sighed and sank in his chair.

"You okay?" Talia asked.

"I'm thinking about skipping the rest of the day," he said. "Does anyone else feel like taking a break?"

"A break sounds great," Lucas agreed.

"I'm actually done with class for the day," Talia said. "So I'm in."

I was feeling decent today, so I was up for anything. "What did you have in mind?"

"Whatever you want," Grant offered.

"I haven't been to town much," I admitted. "Are there any magical or witchy things I need to see?"

"Absolutely," Grant said. "Most of the good stuff happens in autumn, though—the trail rides and orchard tours. We could tour a brewery or cider mill if you want. Otherwise, there are some cool shops I'm sure you haven't seen yet."

"What kind of shops?" I asked.

"There's *Wicked Alchemy*," Grant replied. "I love that place."

"An alchemy shop?" I mused. "That sounds like fun."

We took Talia's car. Lucas and I sat in the back with his arm draped around me. My insides got all warm and fuzzy as I leaned into him.

Talia turned down a quiet street. Trees hung over the road, and the houses looked like small cottages tucked back into the forest. Each had a sign out front, but Talia turned into a parking lot before I could read them.

"This is the Catwalk," Talia announced as she parked the car.

"The Catwalk?" I asked.

"It's the name of the neighborhood," Lucas explained. "This is the site of the original Octavia Falls settlement. The homes have been restored and converted into shops. Since there's not much room for parking, the shops are all connected by trails—hence, the Catwalk."

"Ah, I get it," I said as I got out of the car. "Clever."

Lucas took my hand and led me toward the trailhead. The walkway was paved in stone and completely surrounded by trees. I bet it was really pretty in the summer. It was warm out, but I pulled my coat tighter around myself anyway.

We arrived at the first cottage, which had a sign out front that read

Wicked Alchemy. Beautiful colorful jars hung from the trees. The sunlight hit them, and their colors sparkled off the snow.

"I love it already," I said.

Lucas tugged on my hand, sending electricity up my arm. "Let me give you the grand tour."

When we stepped inside, an array of scents I couldn't place hit my nose. I would've thought they'd be overwhelming since there were so many overlapping one another, but they seemed to complement one another. A soft melody in a minor key played over the speakers. I found it soothing.

The shop was small, but there were so many things to look at on the shelves that it seemed I could spend days in here without getting bored. Potion ingredients lined one wall, with obscure items in jars. I skimmed over the labels to see things like *dracavern saliva* and *kelpie scale*. But I barely took a second to look at the otherworldly ingredients, because my attention was stolen by the centerpiece in the middle of the room. It was a large fountain with endless flowers carved into it. A hundred tiny spouts shot different colors of liquids, each aimed at one of the carved flower leaves. The liquids didn't mix, but funneled down the leaves and disappeared into the fountain again.

"This is the alchemy station," Grant said proudly. He walked up to the fountain and took an empty vial from a nearby table. He held it under one of the spouts and caught the liquid inside. He only let a few drops enter, then pulled the vial to his nose to smell it.

"What are these?" I asked. "Potions?"

"They're dyed oils," Grant answered as he held his vial under another spout. "You can build your own aromatherapy mixture. Grab a vial and try it."

I took an empty vial off the table and held it under the closest spout. When the bottle was half full, I lifted it to my nose to smell it. My shoulders instantly relaxed as I inhaled the sweet scent.

"Mm… eucalyptus," I mused. "What should I mix it with?"

Grant shrugged. "Experiment with it. You really can't go wrong."

I added a few drops of two other liquids, and my mixture turned out smelling like mint and honey. It made me crave a good cup of tea. Beside me, Lucas and Talia were creating their own concoctions. Lucas mixed four oils together and smelled the mixture.

"This one turned out great," he said, holding it out to me. "What do you think?"

I inhaled and got a whiff of cinnamon. It reminded me of him. "I like it a lot."

Lucas sniffed it again, then pressed the cork on. Talia already had three vials filled and made me smell each one of them in turn. They all had a floral scent to them.

"Ew, gross!" Grant turned up his nose as he sniffed his second mixture.

"What's wrong with it?" Lucas asked, leaning over. Grant shoved the mixture toward Lucas, and he jumped back, pinching his nose. "Gross, man. That smells like dirty socks and burnt leather. What did you do?"

"I-I don't know," Grant stammered. "I tried to add some magic to it. I thought it'd smell more potent. I guess I screwed up."

"Let me smell," I requested. When I took a whiff of it, I started gagging.

Talia snickered. "What are they teaching you in your Alchemy classes, Grant?"

He quickly shoved the cork on the vial. "Apparently not enough. Let me give it another shot."

Grant took another vial and chose his oils carefully this time. When he finished, his mixture smelled of cedarwood and rose. He held it out to Talia. "This one I made special for you."

Talia blushed. "For me?"

He nodded. "Unless you don't want it."

Talia smelled it. "No, I do. It smells amazing."

Lucas and I exchanged a glance the others didn't see. Grant was being totally obvious, and Talia barely acknowledged it. Lucas and I were waiting to see what might happen between the two of them.

"What should I try next?" I asked him.

Lucas smirked. "I dare you to try that one and that one together." He pointed to a deep blue oil and an amber colored liquid.

I eyed him curiously. "What kind of danger are you leading me into?"

"Nothing bad. I swear," he promised.

I raised an eyebrow. "So no burnt socks?"

"No burnt socks." He crossed his heart with his finger.

I mixed the two together and brought the vial to my nose. To my surprise, it smelled really sweet and made me feel energized. "What is this?"

"Juniper and frankincense," he said. "One of my favorites."

"Well, in that case, I dare you to try that one and… that one." I pointed to a purple spout and a red one, choosing my scents carefully. They were my favorites.

Lucas eyed me. "Lavender and rose? Why those two?"

He was already filling the vial. I waited until he finished and smelled it to answer.

"So that every time you smell it, you think of me," I told him softly. I ducked my head, and my hair shifted to conceal my features.

Lucas's shoulders fell as he stared down at me. "I will."

He reached out to push my hair out of my eyes. My cheek tingled where he touched me. Our eyes locked, and for a moment, I forgot we were in the alchemy shop. I got so lost in his eyes I could've been standing in the Main Foyer for all I knew.

"Oy," Grant called, pulling our attention away from each other. "Everyone done?"

I looked down to the three vials in my hand. Talia must've had a dozen. "I'm ready," I said.

We paid for our oils, then left the shop and continued down the Catwalk. The trail twisted through the forest and sloped downward toward an open body of water.

"Is that Lake Santos?" I asked.

"It is," Lucas said. "Do you want to get a closer look?"

"What's there to see?" I asked. "It's just a lake."

Talia's eyes lit up. "You haven't seen Pinewood Manor, have you? There's a perfect view of it from here."

I furrowed my brow. "What's Pinewood Manor?"

"It's the most haunted house in all of Octavia Falls," Grant said. "It's so haunted they won't even allow ghost tours."

I was instantly intrigued. "Lead the way."

The trail split off in two directions, and we took the one that led to the lake. At the end of the trail was a scenic outlook. I took a seat on one of the benches at the edge of the frozen lake. Lucas sat beside me and draped an arm over my shoulder, warming my insides.

I rested my hand on the bench, and something crunched beneath my palm. I looked down to see a beetle carcass lying next to me. The bug had been dead a while already, but I had the thought that it might prove useful to me. When no one was watching, I took the beetle in my fingers and subconjured it. If killing a fly had helped me cast a battle orb, then surely I could use this small creature to cast magic, too.

I turned my attention back to my friends and the creepy mansion they wanted to show me. Along the shore atop a rocky peninsula stood a huge house made of brick. It looked like it was once the most beautiful building in town, but it had weathered over the years. From here, I could see the broken windows and withered vines that grew up the sides. The roof sagged along one corner, looking like the house was about to cave in. It gave me the chills just looking at it.

"What's the story?" I asked. "Why is the house so haunted?"

"Legend has it, twenty-six people were murdered in the house forty years ago," Grant said in an ominous voice.

"Dear Goddess," I gasped. "What happened?"

Grant shrugged. "Nobody really knows. It's said that Leroy Pinewood went insane in his old age. He went into a murderous rage while throwing a party. Used a steak knife to kill all the guests and staff—saving himself for last."

"There were no witnesses?" I asked.

Grant shook his head. "That's why the stories are left up to legend. Now the manor is said to be haunted by all twenty-six victims, who seek revenge on the Pinewood family to this day. No one who visits Pinewood Manor makes it out alive."

"That can't be true," Lucas argued. "If it were, where do all the stories come from?"

"I don't know." Grant sighed, dropping the ominous tone.

Talia shivered as she stared over the lake at the manor. "Either way, if people are dying in that house, I'm not going anywhere near it."

"You don't think surviving it would be a fun challenge?" I teased.

Talia turned away from the manor. "Could we get back to shopping? This place is giving me the creeps."

"Agreed." Lucas stood and held his hand out to me.

"Well, *I* think it's intriguing," I stated. "I want to know what really happened there."

"What do you mean?" Grant asked as we started on the trail again.

"People don't just go murdering all their house guests," I pointed out. "What made Leroy go insane? Who else had a motive?"

"You think someone else killed all those people?" Talia asked.

I shrugged. "It's a possibility, isn't it?"

"Wouldn't the police have questioned that at the time?" Lucas pointed out.

I cocked an eyebrow. "I don't know. You tell me."

We reached the main path again, and Grant asked, "Anyone been up to anything fun lately?"

"I cursed Chloe," I admitted. "That was fun."

"You what?" Talia balked.

I bit my lower lip. "I might've dumped those cursed objects on her."

"Good for you," Grant snickered.

Talia frowned. "I spent so much time finding those for you."

"I know," I replied. "I don't know what came over me."

"What kind of curses are we talking about?" Grant's eyes sparkling with intrigue.

"They're low curses," Talia explained. "One of them causes you to itch, and another makes you confused. The third one repels men."

Lucas snorted. "Believe me, Chloe does not need to be cursed. She handles that one on her own."

Lucas may have not been attracted to Chloe, but I'd seen plenty of guys checking her out in class.

"It was petty," I admitted. "But I just can't control myself when it comes to Chloe."

Talia eyed me curiously, like she was trying to decipher what I was saying. "Is this about your dark side you fought during your ceremony?"

I nodded. "Sometimes, I just want to slit Chloe's throat or run Ryan over with my car."

Grant snorted, but he was smiling, like he appreciated when I'd saved him from the Tarantulas last semester. I *had* almost run Ryan over.

"Sometimes I don't even feel like myself," I told them. "It's like Chloe activates that part of me."

Talia pressed her lips together thoughtfully. "Well, she is tied to your curse. I think the darkness you talk about is a manifestation of your curse. That's why Mother Miriam chose you as a Curse Breaker. It's like I said the night of your Evoking Ceremony. You were able to fight your darkness, which means you can fight the darkness of a curse. You've been training with this curse your whole life."

I mulled over what she said, before Grant's squeal pulled me from my thoughts.

"The Gingerbread House!"

I looked up to see a small cottage. It was shaped like a gingerbread house, with accents made to look like candy canes and gumdrops leading up the pathway. In the window were rows upon rows of lollipops.

"I *loved* this place as a kid," Grant groaned. "Too bad I can't indulge like I used to. Though now that I think about it, maybe my diabetes is Mother Miriam's way of telling me to slow down..."

"How's that sweet tooth coming?" Talia teased.

Grant nudged her, and she nearly toppled over into one of the candy canes. Lucas and I both chuckled under our breath.

When we entered the candy shop, the sweet smell of caramelized sugar hit my nose. There were so many colorful candies that it was as if a rainbow had exploded inside the shop. My gaze flickered from treat to treat, unable to decide what I might want to try. There were endless lollipops, caramels, cotton candy, lemon drops, gummies, peppermints, and so much more.

The shop was packed. I noticed an older woman with an Alchemy tattoo helping a few customers by the door. She must've been pushing seventy, but she had long white hair and a young energy about her. She wore an employee nametag that read *Sandy.* I swore I'd seen her before, but I couldn't place her.

Grant grabbed a basket immediately and started filling it with gummies of all kinds. He nearly trampled a group of elementary-aged kids to get to the gummy bears.

"Whoa, man," Lucas laughed. "Slow down."

"Can't," Grant said. "Need. All. The. Candy."

"You're going to go into a diabetic coma!" Talia cried.

Grant shrugged. "Totally worth it. Besides, I never said I was going to eat this all at once."

"We *can* come back, you know," Lucas teased. "*The Gingerbread House* isn't going anywhere."

"You don't know that." Grant glanced around at the other patrons, then lowered his voice. "The ladies who run this place have to be ancient by now. I'm not risking this shop shutting down when the three of them croak off. I'm getting in my fill now."

Lucas rolled his eyes. "I'm sure it's not going to shut down. Maybe you could buy it after graduation."

Grant's eyes lit up. "Not a bad idea…"

"What do you recommend?" I asked, already reaching for a pack of chocolates.

"Not those." Grant took me by the shoulders and turned me around. I came face-to-face with an endless shelf of rock candies. "May I introduce you to the best damn thing on the planet."

I laughed. "I've had rock candy before."

Grant's eyebrows shot up. "Not like this, you haven't. Buy some. Trust me."

I turned to Lucas and crinkled my nose. "I don't know. Can I trust him?"

"On this? Yeah." Lucas grabbed a few rock candies for himself and started filling his arms.

Talia came over with a second basket. "Don't blame me when you all get sick like a kid on Halloween."

"Halloween," I realized. "That's where I've seen that lady before."

I glanced at the woman named Sandy by the door.

"Oh, yeah," Talia said. "They're super popular at Halloween. They set up a gingerbread booth at the festival every year with free candies."

"Don't forget about the free candies here!" Grant practically sang.

He walked up to the front counter, and the rest of us followed. A line of samples were set out, though there were so many I couldn't choose just one. A young girl grabbed a handful of candy corn and shoved them all in her mouth at once. Her mother scolded her, but it was already too late. The girl's hair instantly turned shades of white, orange, and yellow.

"The candies are enchanted?" I was suddenly more intrigued to try them.

"Some of them." Grant popped a hard candy in his mouth, and his features instantly began to shift. His ears grew to the size of dinner plates. "Look. I'm an elephant!"

Talia laughed, but Lucas just rolled his eyes.

"I much prefer these." Lucas handed me a gummy.

I hesitated, but when he popped one in his mouth and nothing happened, I figured it was safe. I chewed the gummy and swallowed. Immediately, I felt like I was floating. I looked to the ground, but my feet were still firmly planted on the floor.

"What's happening?" I asked.

Lucas closed his eyes, enjoying the euphoria. "You're floating. Can't you tell?"

"But I'm not," I pointed out. "Not for real."

"Does that make it any less fun?" he challenged.

"No, I suppose not." I closed my eyes and basked in the feeling of floating. It didn't last long, though.

When I opened my eyes, I saw Talia was chewing on something. As soon as she swallowed, little smoky hearts started coming out of her mouth every time she breathed.

"Whoa," she said. "That's really cool. I'm definitely bringing some of these home."

After Grant filled his entire basket with candy, we checked out and subconjured our recent purchases. It was snowing when we stepped outside, and the air had gotten chillier.

"Where to next?" Grant asked.

Lucas looked to the sky. "I don't know. What's the weather supposed to do?"

Talia checked her phone. "It looks like a storm's coming in. Damn, I missed a text from Cody. Maybe we should head back."

"What, for *Cody*?" Grant couldn't hide the disgust in his tone. "Tell him you're busy."

"I can't," Talia groaned.

"What do you mean, you can't?" Grant demanded.

"Nothing," Talia said. "I just want to see him is all."

Grant narrowed his eyes, but Lucas cut in before he could say anything. "We should head back if a storm's coming through."

"Fine," Grant huffed. "Anyone want to bowl in the Lounge?"

Lucas and I exchanged a glance. "I think Nadine and I are going to take it easy," he answered.

"Sorry, but I'm going to meet up with Cody when we get back," Talia announced.

Grant's shoulders slumped, and he leaned over to whisper, "Forget about it. If Talia's not there, it's not worth it."

"Don't be like that," Lucas insisted. "You can hang with us."

Grant's eyes flickered down to our entwined fingers. "Nah, it's fine. Really. I need to get my swim hours in anyway."

When we returned to the school, Grant hurried off toward the pool without a word.

I turned to Lucas. "Why doesn't he just tell her how he feels?"

He frowned. "Because she's dating someone else."

"And?" I cocked an eyebrow.

"And he's afraid of rejection," Lucas said simply.

I sighed as we started toward the dorms. "I think they'd be so good together."

"You don't think Talia and Cody are good together?" Lucas asked.

"I never *see* them together," I stated. "That's the problem. It's fine if she's happy with him, but I worry. I think she could be happy with Grant, too."

Lucas took my hand as we climbed the stairs. "I know Grant would be happy with her, but we can't force it. They have to figure it out at their own pace."

I really hoped they would.

☾·

THE FOLLOWING DAY, I was happy to enter my Meditation and Inner Magic classroom. This class had started as a blow-off class, but I'd noticed that it had really been helping me this semester. Grounding myself seemed to help me control my magic and minimize the side-effects.

When I arrived, Professor Wykoff was kneeling on a pillow at the front of the room, her hands pressed together in prayer in front of her. Normally, she opened class with a short yoga session, so it was jarring to see her try something new.

A few students had taken pillows from the stacks at the back of the room and were arranging themselves in rows. I followed what my classmates were doing and found a spot at the back of the room with my pillow. Isa curled into a ball beside me.

"Welcome, everyone," Professor Wykoff practically sang. She opened her eyes and took a deep breath, then spread her arms out wide on the exhale. "I hope you're all feeling comfortable. Today, we will be venturing into a new unit. As you may have noticed, we've tried many different forms of meditation in this class already. However, we have yet to put a name to them. The first is movement meditation, which we do daily with our opening yoga practice. We've also worked with focus meditation—or using your senses to ground yourself to the present. Last week, we performed mantra meditation, when we practiced the mantra *om*. Today, we will explore spiritual meditation."

The class stayed quiet as Professor Wykoff stood and lit a bundle of sage. She started walking around the room, smudging the air above each student as she spoke. "I'm sure you all practice spiritual meditation daily."

My heart gave a jolt. I glanced around the room to assess other students' reactions, but no one else seemed nervous. I hadn't learned any sort of spiritual meditation. Was this an unspoken custom within the coven?

"Spiritual meditation is a very diverse practice," Professor Wykoff continued. She reached me, and the soothing scent of sage filled my nose. I found my nerves easing slightly. "For some, it may involve deep silence. For others, it may involve prayer. Either way, the goal is to deepen your connection with Mother Miriam."

She moved on to the next student and continued. "Spiritual meditation is a crucial practice. We tend to think of inner magic as coming directly from ourselves, but we can seek strength from outside sources as well. After all, if we do not believe in ourselves, we cannot perform the great feats of magic we are all capable of.

"Spiritual meditation is not as easy as it sounds. Many students jump into prayer before they are ready—screaming out their desires to Mother Miriam without really feeling the intent in here." Professor Wykoff pressed her fingers to her heart.

She reached the front of the room and set her sage in a bowl, where it continued to burn and fill the room with its sweet scent. "I suggest three steps before you begin to pray. The first is to clear your space. That's why I've smudged the area with sage—to clear each of you of any negative energies."

I hadn't realized until she said it that I was feeling better than when I entered the room. I made a mental note to keep a stash of sage with me at all times.

"Next, release any tension you might be holding," Professor Wykoff continued. She knelt on her pillow and began shaking out her shoulders. "Release tension from your body, but also from your mind."

I focused on the tension in my shoulders, but it wouldn't budge by sheer will. I squirmed on my pillow, trying to get more comfortable, and a few people nearby shot me glances. I realized I was distracting them. I focused my meditation on compartmentalizing my tension and joint pain, so that I could ignore it and focus on the prayer instead.

"You do not want to go into prayer holding any anger or resentment," Professor Wykoff said. "And finally, be yourself. Mother Miriam loves you for who you are. You don't have to pretend with her—she'll know when you're forcing it."

The room went silent for a few beats. All I heard was my classmates' breathing as we soaked in Professor Wykoff's lesson.

"You do not have to ask anything when you pray," she added. "But if you choose to, try to think of how it might benefit others. It is selfless prayers that have the most impact."

"What if I need help myself?" a girl at the front of the room asked in a calm voice.

"Well, why should that be selfish?" Professor Wykoff asked. "If you are able to overcome your own struggles, you will be more equipped to help others."

She took another long breath. "Today, I'd like to try an exercise that I hope you'll all find spiritually uplifting. It is ungraded, so you do not have to report back to me. But if you choose to participate, I ask that you do so with an open mind."

Professor Wykoff went quiet again, allowing us each to open our minds. "Today, we will pray and ask Mother Miriam for a sign. Whatever sign you choose is up to you, and you may assign whatever meaning you want to it. Just know that when you see the sign you've prayed for, you begin to trust that Mother Miriam is listening."

"Will she respond?" I asked without thinking about it.

"Oh, yes," Professor Wykoff answered. "Mother Miriam always responds, though perhaps not always in the way we like. She may not be able to speak to us directly, but she will always be there to lead you on the right path."

A lump rose in my throat, but I swallowed it. I knew Mother Miriam was real—I'd seen her with my own eyes. But trusting she was there to hear every coven members' prayers was a lot to wrap my head around.

"Let's begin with a prayer for the coven," Professor Wykoff suggested. "Then I will give you the rest of the period for your own prayers."

I glanced around the room to see what everyone else was doing and saw they all held different stances. Some knelt high on their pillows, while others leaned back on their heels. Some held their hands at their hearts, and other students kept them rested at their sides. Two friends a few rows ahead of me held hands.

It didn't seem like there was one single way to pray, but I felt like I should do something, so I pressed my hands together at my heart.

"Dear Goddess," Professor Wykoff said. "May you bless the coven, that we may all be strengthened by your grace and live according to your will. So shall it be."

"So shall it be," the class murmured in response.

"You may now say your own prayers," Professor Wykoff announced. "When asking for your sign, be sure to be specific so that Mother Miriam may honor your request."

The room went silent. It felt awkward sitting there, not really sure where to start. I hadn't really prayed to Mother Miriam before—mostly only when I ate dinner at Grammy's. This was all very new to me.

Dear Goddess, I thought. *It's me, Nadine.*

She knows it's you, I told myself. *Be cool.*

My hands shook at my heart. I wasn't used to talking to people I couldn't see—let alone a freaking Goddess. I knew she was out there, but it was still new to me—just the fact that she could hear me and answer my prayers.

I didn't know what to say to her. I'd been keeping a lot of uncertainties buried deep, but maybe it would help to be vulnerable.

I took a deep breath and tried again. *Dear Goddess. I am struggling here in Octavia Falls. This place feels like home, but sometimes it feels like I have to fight so hard to be here—fight against Chloe, and against my magic. I have nowhere else to go, and it's where Grammy and Lucas and Talia are. But if I'm supposed to be here... why does it have to be so hard? I know you granted me magic, but sometimes it feels like... maybe I'm not cut out for the coven. Maybe I shouldn't be here. Please, Mother Miriam—send me a sign. Let me know that this is where I'm meant to be. Let that sign be...*

I paused for a moment, contemplating what sort of *specific* sign Professor Wykoff wanted us to ask for.

A bat, I thought, because it was the first thing that came to mind.

Send me a bat, I prayed, *so that I may know that this is where I'm meant to be. So shall it be.*

I took a deep breath and dropped my hands to my sides. When I opened my eyes, Isa was purring softly below me. I stroked her, then spent the rest of the class doing a mindful meditation, focusing on the thoughts that came into my mind. I noticed I was holding a lot of anxiety and fear around this sign—that perhaps it wouldn't come. And if it didn't... would I leave?

I didn't know.

THIRTEEN

I left class on Wednesday and spotted Nadine passing through the Main Foyer. Isa prowled at her side. I'd memorized her schedule and knew she'd just come from Meditation and Inner Magic. She saw me first and quickly caught up with me. I felt at ease in her presence.

"Hey, Nad," I greeted. "Classes done for the day?"

"Yeah. What are you up to?"

I took her hand, and she relaxed under my touch. "Spending time with you."

A light smile touched her lips. "What do you want to do?"

I shrugged, but the look on my face obviously suggested much more. She nudged me playfully in the side, and I laughed.

"Behave," she teased.

"It's a nice day. Are you up for a walk?" I suggested.

"Sure. How's the case going?"

I sighed. "I've tried everything to get in touch with Travis Bennett's family, but they're even harder to contact than Michelle was. Every phone call and email goes ignored. I tried stopping by their house, and they weren't there. I'm still trying to find the connection, but I've got nothing so far."

"You'll figure it out," she said. "I believe in you."

"You do?"

"Of course," she told me. "When you put your mind to something, you don't give up."

"Mm…" I gazed down at my feet.

We exited the school, and I instinctively conjured a coat and wrapped it around myself. Nadine did the same. The sun sparkled off the melting snow, and the air felt nice.

"What is it?" she asked.

I shrugged. "No one's ever said that to me before—that I don't give up. Dad just says I'm lazy, and Mom never disagrees with him."

Her jaw dropped. "Your parents can go screw themselves, because they're wrong. You're going to get this guy. I can feel it."

I sighed. "It's harder than you think."

"What is?" she asked, like she could sense there was something more.

I took a few moments to answer, wondering how to word it. "It's not easy protecting everyone."

"That's not your job, you know," she pointed out. I wasn't sure I believed her.

A thought broke through my mind. *This too shall pass.*

I stilled, and Nadine glanced at me. "Are you okay?"

"Fine. Just another day in the life of the Reaper's Apprentice."

"You heard a thought?" she asked.

I nodded. "It's no big deal. It happens all the time. Do you mind if we take a moment?"

"Take all the time you need."

I conjured my journal and wrote down the thought. Nadine had never seen me do this before, and she watched curiously.

"This one wasn't bad," I explained to her as I tore the paper out of the notebook. "Most aren't bad, to be honest, but it took me a while to realize it. Last semester, the bad ones were all I focused on, and so I had this idea in my head that *all* of them were bad. But now the good ones come in clearer, and they're all easier to handle."

I subconjured my notebook, then conjured a lighter. I held the paper over the flame and watched it burn a few seconds, before letting the paper flutter into the snow. Isa sniffed at the ashes.

"I'm glad it's gotten easier for you," Nadine said.

"It's a work in progress. The bad ones still get to me, but not like they used to." I waited until the paper burned completely, then took her hand again. "Shall we keep moving?"

"Where are we headed?" Nadine asked.

"I thought we could visit the Protection Tree," I offered. "It's not too far."

"That sounds nice."

It wasn't long before we arrived at the Protection Tree. The park was secluded, which I found relaxing. Sunlight filtered between the long, gnarly branches of the giant oak and sparkled off the snow. Calm energy pulsed through the clearing. Nadine stepped closer to the tree, looking entranced.

"What is it?" I asked.

She eyed the tree curiously, then looked back at me. "It feels different than the last time we were here."

I watched her as she began to circle the massive trunk, her cat following her every step. "It's the magic. You didn't have magic the last time we were here. You can sense it now."

She reached out and brushed her fingers across the bark. I knew the feeling. The trunk was rough on the hands, but smooth on the heart.

"What do you feel?" I asked curiously.

Nadine closed her eyes and concentrated. "It's soft and warm, like a blanket. I don't feel like anything bad could happen here."

A hint of a smile touched my lips.

"Is that the wrong answer?" she questioned.

"No," I said quickly. "It's just interesting that the magic feels like a warm blanket to you. Everyone gets a different feeling with the Protection Tree, based on whatever makes *them* feel safe."

"Oh?" she asked. "What do *you* feel, then?"

I began circling the tree with her, running my fingers lightly over the bark. "I feel… my brother."

Her gaze fell. "I'm sorry."

"Don't be." I shoved my hands into my pocket. "It's nice. It's like he's still here, protecting the town with the rest of our ancestors."

Nadine smiled at me, but she looked like she didn't know what to say. Sometimes, the silence was easier when it came to the loss of a loved one. She knew all too well.

Nadine instantly stopped pacing and bent to inspect an abnormality in the tree.

"What'd you find?" I came to her side and noticed a collection of thick cuts near my hip, just barely half an inch into the tree. It had started healing over.

She bent and looked closer. "Mm… maybe bad things *have* happened here. It looks like someone took an ax to the tree or something."

I frowned. I'd heard the stories. "That was Nicole Verla."

"What?" She straightened at the sound of Verla's name.

"The headmistress's twin sister," I clarified. "You haven't heard this story, have you?"

She shook my head. "I haven't heard anything about her at all, just that she died a while ago."

I nodded. "Nicole had some sort of mental breakdown a few years ago. Rumor has it, she was a Seer who couldn't handle her visions."

Nadine's hand flew over her mouth. "Dear Goddess, that's horrible. What happened?"

I shot an uncomfortable glance at the wound in the tree. "A few years ago, she started calling the Protection Tree a *murder tree*. She wouldn't say why or what it meant. When no one listened—because how could they without explanation—she came out here with an ax and tried to cut it down."

Nadine's jaw hung slack.

"The Imperium caught her in the act, before too much damage was done," I continued. "She was trying to break the town's protection spell."

"Why?" Nadine's brows pinched together. "I mean, she must've had a reason."

I shrugged. "No idea. By that point, she'd gone so mad no one could make sense of anything she said. But attacking the Protection Tree—that's treason. The Imperium hanged her for it."

"*Hanged her!* What is this, the fourteen hundreds?"

I winced. "I don't agree with it either, but most of the town did. She was a threat to our people. Persecution is the coven's greatest threat, and the tree keeps us safe from that. If we were exposed, the coven could be destroyed."

"But… hanging? That seems extreme."

My eyebrows shot up. "For a witch? Of course it is. I think the Imperium should've gotten her help, not hanged her. But if you believe the legends, most people agree she got what was coming to her."

"What legends?" Nadine asked.

"Her corpse disappeared the night of the hanging."

Her eyes were calculating. "Which means... what?"

"Some say monsters appeared to drag her down into the Abyss—that her soul was so rotten even her body was taken with it."

Nadine tilted her head. "Do you believe that?"

I took a long breath. "I'm not sure what to believe. She could've walked off in the middle of the night as some necromancer's puppet, or coyotes could've come to eat her corpse. We'll never know—she was never found."

Nadine braced herself against the tree and shook her head.

I reached out for her. "Are you okay?"

"Tired." She stood straighter and stepped away from the tree, then plopped down on a bench nearby. Isa jumped into her lap, kneading her paws at Nadine's legs.

I sat beside her and took her hand. Instinctively, I began massaging it. "Lupus flare-up?" I questioned.

She glanced upward at the bright blue sky. "I'm really sensitive to the sun. It tires me out."

"Is it always like that?"

She shrugged. "Symptoms come and go. It's normal."

"I'd like to hear more about that," I requested.

She furrowed her brow. "About what?"

"Your normal," I stated. "I don't understand what it's like for you having lupus."

She sighed. "It's different for everyone. For me, my lupus slows me down—a *lot*. Especially when it comes to magic. Every time I use magic, my lupus flares. I get really tired, like I'm pulling my own body's energy to perform the spell. Verla taught me a technique with conjuring, but I'm still struggling. I feel like I have to wait for remission to do anything worthwhile... like actually breaking a curse."

I ran my fingers over her arm. "I hope that's not true. It will come with more practice."

She cocked an eyebrow. "Will it? Every time I use magic, it turns every single task into a monumental chore. Even without it, things like taking a bath are difficult. Getting ready for the day can take hours. Walking to class can knock me on my ass."

Before I could respond, she rushed to explain. "It's hard for you to understand, because to you those kinds of things are non-activities. They're just things you do without really thinking about them. But me? I have to plan every step out and make sure I'm not going to expend all my energy. I only have so much every day, and when I use my magic, that threshold decreases. I have to be really careful."

"I'm so sorry," I whispered. "You don't deserve this."

"No one deserves to be disabled," she stated matter-of-factly. "But life isn't fair, and it's just something I have to live with. I have no choice."

"You're wrong to wait until your lupus goes into remission," I added. "You killed that monster. You're already stronger than you know."

She looked unsure. "I guess. I'm doing pretty good today."

I gazed down at her hand thoughtfully. "What's a bad day like for you?"

"You don't want to hear me complain," she assured me.

I looked her in the eye. "I really do. I want to help."

She sighed. "My worst days were before my diagnosis, because I didn't know what was happening or how to deal with it. I'd wake up in agony and couldn't move. Even walking to the bathroom made me feel like I might pass out. I'd get really bad pain in my chest and couldn't breathe very well. I was gaining weight, and my doctors told me I was just out of shape—that I should exercise more and I'd get my energy back. Being thirteen years old, I believed them. But I could barely walk to the front door, let alone around the block."

"That sounds hard," I remarked.

Nadine scoffed. "Honestly, there was so much more to it than the physical pain. The headaches and mental fog were really bad, and I was staying home from school so much I was falling behind. It was when my hair started falling out that my doctors started to take me more seriously. Even with that and my mom pushing them toward an autoimmune diagnosis, it took two years to finally get an answer."

I gritted my teeth. "Our healthcare system sucks."

She chuckled. "Tell me about it. My lupus got so bad I passed out *walking up the stairs.* I finally developed a rash, which confirmed my diagnosis."

She ran her fingers over her nose and cheeks, outlining the shape of the rash. "It looked like a butterfly, which is an indicator of lupus. They finally got me on immunosuppressants, and it helped put me into remission. But when my parents died, my symptoms came back."

My eyes remained fixed on the hand I was massaging. "I'm really sorry. I wish you didn't have to go through this."

She shrugged. "I wish I didn't, either, but it is what it is. I can't change it. I can only deal with it."

"I wish I could wave a magic wand or brew you a potion and make it all go away," I whispered.

"That's sweet of you to care, but I don't even know if I'd want that," she admitted.

"You wouldn't want a cure?"

Nadine fiddled with the star charm hanging around her neck. "Yes and no. I'd like to go back into remission, but I wouldn't change where I've been. My lupus taught me a lot about myself. I don't think I'd be who I am without it."

I stopped massaging her and took her hand in mine. "That's really cool that you're so comfortable with your illness."

She must've noticed something darker in my tone, because she placed her free hand over mine. "I've been at this longer than you have. You'll figure it out, too. If you need help, you just have to ask."

I gave her a shy smile. Neither of us said it out loud, but it was clear we were both talking about my depression.

"I'm figuring it out," I promised.

She smiled. "I'm really glad to hear that."

I stood and tugged on her hand. "We should probably get back. I don't want you getting too cold."

Truth was, I didn't want her out in the sun, flaring her symptoms.

"Sitting by the fireplace with a cup of hot cocoa sounds good," she agreed.

As she stood, she glanced back to the bench. She stopped in her tracks and reached out to run her hands over a symbol laid into the wood—a manufacturer label. It was made of metal and shaped like a bat. A smile crept across her face.

"What is it?" I asked.

She looked to me, beaming. "Nothing. I just… I feel like Mother Miriam is listening. I feel like Octavia Falls is where I'm meant to be."

I squeezed her hand. I wouldn't want her anywhere else.

Just then, my phone went off. It was tucked away in my stash, but I could sense the subtle vibration of the ringtone through my magic. I conjured the phone and glanced at the screen. My stomach lurched at the sight of the number.

"I should take this," I told Nadine. "It could be about my article."

"I'll see you back at school?" she suggested.

I nodded.

Nadine stood on her toes, then pressed a kiss to my lips. I could've melted right there, but my ringtone distracted me.

As soon as Nadine turned away, I answered. "Hello?"

"Hello, is this Lucas?" a female voice asked.

I cleared my throat. "It is."

"This is Angela Bennett." She was Travis Bennett's mother—the third boy who may be in danger. "You've called a few times regarding the article you're writing about the missing boys."

"Yes," I replied quickly. "I believe you may be able to help me."

She hesitated. "I-I think I can, too. But I need your help in return."

$$\mathbb{C}$$

THE INTERVIEW with the Bennetts couldn't come soon enough. I could hardly concentrate on my lessons Friday morning, as I went through everything I knew about the case. Isaac's father, Mark, had completely blown me off. I'd never gotten an interview with him—which made me think he had something to hide.

But the Bennetts? They *wanted* to talk to me, which meant I might actually find out what I was missing.

The Bennetts chose to meet me at a café on Maple Street. I hurried to *The Cozy Cat* after class and ended up there an hour early. I didn't know what to do with myself, so I ordered a *Cozy Caramel Cappuccino*. Everything here was made by Alchemists, and the cozy cappuccino was supposed to calm my nerves. It worked—except every time the door opened. I kept glancing up, waiting for Travis's parents to arrive. I'd waited so long I was starting to think they'd backed out.

Finally, a couple arrived. The woman was tall, and the man had a thick beard. She untied her scarf and glanced around the café. Her eyes lit up when she saw me, and I waved them over.

"Lucas Taylor?" the woman asked.

I shifted in my chair. "That's me."

She stuck out her hand to shake mine. "I'm Angela, and this is my husband, Jude."

Jude shook my hand next and gave me a polite nod. He had this look on his face I couldn't quite read—anxiety, perhaps.

"If you don't mind me asking, why didn't you contact me sooner?" I asked politely.

The two exchanged a glance as they slid into the bench across from me. Jude glanced around, but we were in the corner and far enough away from the other patrons that they wouldn't hear us. Still, he lowered his voice and leaned forward.

"Michelle asked us not to," he admitted.

I narrowed my eyes. I knew Michelle was hiding something. The question was… what? "Why now, then?"

Angela leaned her hands on the table. "Michelle was persuasive, but we decided we couldn't sit back any longer. We need to know… is our son in danger?"

I felt the blood drain from my face. "I'm not entirely sure. That depends on what you can tell me."

"Why did you contact us?" Angela begged. "What is it that you know about these cases? Do you have any suspects?"

I tried to keep my cool, but it was obvious the couple was very worried about their son. I wanted nothing more than to put their minds at ease.

"Not yet," I admitted. "But I'm hoping you can help with that."

"What is it you think we know?" Jude asked.

I took a deep, stalling breath. Everyone else involved had been lying to me from the start. I wasn't sure I could trust this couple, either. But I had to give them something and hope I got information in return.

"I'm not sure of the connection yet," I said. "What I do know is that Caleb's and Isaac's parents lied to me about their kids knowing each other. Michelle Miller had a picture of the boys together… and your son was in it."

Angela swallowed, and she shared a look with her husband.

I instantly sat straighter in my chair. "You know why they lied, don't you?"

Jude got a worried look on his face. "We have an idea. But if we're going to tell you, we need to know everything you know."

I hesitated. As a journalist, I wasn't supposed to give up information like this. But damn it all if I wasn't curious to know the truth. If it could help me save just one boy, then it was worth it. Besides, it wasn't like I didn't know anything the police didn't.

"That sounds like a fair trade," I agreed. "But I'm afraid I don't know much. What I do know is there's a connection between the missing boys that their families are keeping secret. They both said they hadn't met each other before, but the picture in Michelle's house proves otherwise. We know that the kidnapper has a pattern—taking the boys in the middle of the night and leaving with the window open and no other traces. Well, except for the pin we found at the Thomas' house."

"Pin?" Angela asked.

"We found a pin under the window—a professor's anniversary pin," I explained. "The Thomases turned it into the police. I thought people would know by now."

Jude's eyes went wide. "We've been following this case closely, and nobody said anything about a pin."

Angela threw her hand over her mouth. "Goddess, they hid it."

I furrowed my brow. "What do you mean?"

Angela's shoulders fell. "If Krista and Keith are lying about our kids knowing each other, they never turned that pin into the police. They know it could hurt us. It's just as we feared."

Angela turned her face into Jude's shoulder, and he held his wife close as she sobbed silently.

"How can this pin hurt you?" I was practically at the edge of my seat now. "What is it that you know?"

Jude glanced around the café again. When he turned back to me, his features had gone ashen. "We know who the killer is, and this means our son is in danger."

"You know!?" I burst, my heart hammering. I realized how loud I'd been and quickly lowered my tone. "Who?"

Jude pressed his lips together firmly. "We need your help. You're the only person we can trust."

My mouth hung open, but I quickly snapped it shut. "Why me?" I asked warily. I was only a student reporter.

"Because you're the only person investigating this case who isn't law enforcement," Jude said. "We can't go to the police. You have to help us protect our son."

"Yes," I said without thinking about it. "I'll do anything to make sure this guy doesn't strike again."

I had a sinking feeling in my gut I was about to break the rules, but screw the damn rules. If it saved Travis Bennett's life, then I didn't give a shit.

Angela sniffled and wiped her nose. "We've never told anyone, but if this keeps our son safe, we have to come out with the truth."

I glanced between them. "And what *is* the truth?"

Jude took a deep breath, but his hand shook on the tabletop. "The truth is we're all involved, and he's coming after our kids for revenge."

"Revenge?" I breathed. "Revenge for what?"

Angela's voice shook. "Promise this stays between us, and you'll use the information *only* to catch him."

I wasn't sure I was comfortable with this, but I found myself nodding anyway. If this was the secret that broke the case, I had to go by their rules.

"Your secret is safe with me," I promised.

Angela and Jude exchanged a glance, and the two of them looked satisfied.

"We were only kids," Angela whispered. She didn't look at me, as if the memory pained her. "We met each other through the swim team at school. It was normal for all six of us to hang out after practice. But one night—"

Angela choked up, and Jude took over. "One night, everything changed. We went out drinking and ended up in the forest. We didn't think anyone lived nearby. We were messing around with battle magic and... we didn't mean to hurt anybody."

My stomach sank. I realized then why they didn't want to go to the police—because giving up the suspect would incriminate them. Whatever had happened that night must've been horrific. "What happened?"

Angela swallowed and blinked back tears. "One of our battle orbs went off course. We never figured out whose it was, but it didn't matter. None of us were being careful."

I leaned closer. "Who got hurt?"

Jude's features hardened. "The orb hit our coach's house. It must've hit the gas line, because the next thing we knew, an explosion went off. We could see the fire through the trees. We tried to put it out, but it was too late. His wife and son were already dead."

The air left my lungs. This confession changed everything about this investigation. It explained the connection between the missing boys. Their swim coach must've found out they were to blame and waited until they had families of their own—so he could finally take from them what had been taken from him. It was the perfect motive for killing those boys.

"So your coach is after your families," I thought aloud.

Jude and Angela nodded in unison. The two looked so choked up that it seemed they were at a loss for words.

"Who was your coach?" I asked, dying to finally uncover the killer.

Jude's nostrils flared, and my heart stopped dead when he answered.

☾

THE NAME he'd given me echoed in my mind, and all I could think was I had to tell my friends. This was too big to keep to myself.

I couldn't get back to school fast enough. I checked the foyer and the cafeteria, but I found my friends sitting in the Lounge. They were seated at one of the tables in the restaurant, with a pile of appetizers in front of them. Mandy and Amy sat across from Grant, Talia, and Nadine. The food was barely touched, as their attention was on a jock named Frederick James, though most people just called him James. He looked down at my friends with disgust.

"So, are the rumors true?" he laughed.

"What rumors?" Mandy snapped.

"The rumors that you're all involved with the hex on the school," James said casually. He reached for a French fry and popped it in his mouth. "I hear it's your fault I failed my exam today."

Amy crossed her arms. "There is no hex on the school."

"Yeah," Grant agreed. "If you believe that, you're delusional. Blaming us for your failed exam is low, man."

James shrugged. "The evidence is all there."

Nadine rolled her eyes. "Evidence of what? Let me guess. Something Chloe Olson made up?"

James chuckled. "It's not made up. Magic has been acting weird ever since you moved here. Chloe's just the one who made the connection."

"Acting weird how?" Talia demanded.

Nadine spoke at the same time. "I didn't even have magic when I moved here. Your evidence is flawed."

I reached the table and crossed my arms. "What's going on?"

James reached for another fry, but I grabbed his wrist before he could touch it. He stared me down, but I only squeezed tighter. "That's not yours. And my friends would never hex the school."

James narrowed his eyes at me. "That's what someone guilty would say."

"Fuck off, James," I growled. "If you're failing exams, maybe you should spend more time studying and less time blaming innocent people."

James ripped his arm out of my grasp and got up in my face. "Don't act like you have nothing to do with this."

"I don't know what you're talking about," I said coolly.

James lunged at me, but I didn't flinch like he wanted. He backed up immediately and walked away, laughing.

I watched him go, then pulled up a chair next to my friends.

"What the hell was that about?" Nadine asked. "You don't think there's really a hex on the school?"

Amy bit her lip. "I don't know. I *have* been hearing people say their magic feels drained."

"Like that day Professor Daymond reported Nadine to Headmistress Verla," Talia realized.

Nadine frowned. "Yeah, but I didn't do anything."

"Well, is it just the professors?" Grant asked.

Amy shook her head. "I don't think so. Remember that day I got sick? It wasn't like the flu—it was more like my magic just didn't want to work. I thought I was sick, but maybe it was something else…"

"So what's happening?" Talia asked. "Some sort of curse?"

"No idea," Mandy replied, before turning to me. "You're looking a little pale. Are you okay?"

I took a deep breath. "I finally got an interview with the Bennetts. I know who killed the missing boys."

All of my friends' faces shared a matching look of shock. The silence that settled over the table was eerie, and a shiver traveled down my spine.

"Who?" Nadine whispered breathlessly.

I swallowed the lump in my throat. "Professor Daymond."

FOURTEEN

I couldn't say I was surprised to hear Professor Daymond was behind the kidnappings, but the evidence was circumstantial at best. Though the story of the house fire fit, Lucas had no way to prove any of it.

"That pin I found would've proven it," Lucas told me when I brought it up at lunch the following Thursday. "It was a mistake to let the Thomases turn over the pin. I contacted them, and they say it must've gotten lost in evidence, but they're lying. I know they never handed it over in the first place."

"Can't you go to the police?" I asked. "At least tell them of your suspicions, and have them look into it."

He shook his head. "Not without hard evidence. He's a highly-respected professor. If I have nothing to back up my claim, no one will believe me. You have to remember that our coven lived through the witch trials. Accusations without basis aren't tolerated around here."

Lucas made it sound worse than I could imagine. Though once he mentioned the witch trials, it made a lot of sense. He couldn't go starting a witch hunt of his own. He'd be burned at the stake himself. Writing this story really seemed to be helping him. I think he was starting to feel like he had a purpose again, and I wasn't about to ruin that by pushing him too far.

"As far as motive, I promised the Bennetts I wouldn't share their secret with the police," he added. "It's the only reason they confided with me in the first place. I wouldn't be a journalist if I went tattle-tailing on my sources."

"I'm glad you're getting into this journalism thing, but we have to do *something*," I urged.

"I'm trying. I've been following Daymond around. I'll find my evidence," Lucas stated confidently. "You need to focus on your curse breaking practice. Don't worry about this case."

I glanced at the clock on the wall, and I realized how late it was. "Crap. I promised Talia I'd meet up with her for the career fair."

Lucas smiled, but it didn't reach his eyes. I could tell the whole thing was still on his mind. "Have fun."

"Thanks." I dumped my tray, then hurried to meet up with Talia.

She was waiting for me in the Main Foyer. "You ready?" she asked when she saw me.

"Yep."

We made our way to the ballroom, where the school was hosting a career fair for undeclared freshmen and sophomores. I had a bag of mixed feelings hanging on my shoulders when we walked down the hall. On one hand, the ballroom brought back fun memories of the Midnight Formal. On the other, the room had starred in my nightmares ever since I'd trapped Dark Nadine in there in my mind.

The ballroom didn't feel like the dark, lonely place I'd trapped her, though. Today, the chandeliers were ablaze with flickering flames, and the room buzzed with chatter. Booths had been set up in endless rows, with various professionals behind them talking to students about possible career paths.

Talia and I started at one end of the ballroom. Most of the booths looked like normal jobs, like mechanics, nurses, and sales agents. But the closer I looked, the more I noticed a magical aspect to each of the jobs.

At the mechanic booth, a warlock showed off his telekinesis by rebuilding a car engine quicker than I thought possible. The students around him stood slack-jawed in awe, before he quickly disassembled it and the pieces lay neatly organized on his table again. I overheard a nurse talking to a group of girls in my Alchemy class about magical plants and how medical botany was an in-demand job right now. The sales agent demonstrated his mind-reading abilities to students to show them how he could sell them anything—even a pen.

Beside that booth was one for the Miriamic Police Department. They had all kinds of flyers lying out, and one of the officers stood behind the booth.

I nudged Talia. "Oh, this looks interesting."

We walked up to the booth, and I started taking all the flyers I could carry.

"Are you interested in law enforcement?" the officer asked kindly. He wasn't much older than me, but he was taller and wore his police uniform.

"I almost got into a police academy," I explained. "I wanted to become a detective. How does the training work in the coven, since we're all required to take four years at the college?"

His eyes brightened. I got the sense that I was one of the first people all day to show interest. He quickly shoved a flyer in my direction. "Here's the information on our program, and the steps it takes to become a detective. Of course, you'll have to complete your officer training first, and a promotion to detective is possible after at least five years on the force. Unlike other police academies, our officer training takes place right here at Miriam College. It's a two-year program taken in your third and fourth years, alongside your magic classes. The coursework involves criminal law, human relations, forensic science, and more."

"Those classes sound amazing," I said, waving my flyer at him. "Well, thanks for the info. I'll take these and come back if I have any more questions."

He nodded politely as Talia and I walked away from the table.

"Do you think you'll major in criminal justice?" Talia asked.

I skimmed through the flyers as we walked. "I want to. I didn't know the school offered it. Have you declared a major yet?"

"Not yet," she said. "I'm definitely doing something with music, but there are a couple of different majors for it."

"Oh? Which ones are you thinking about?"

"I *could* go the teaching route," Talia mused, her eyes roaming over the various booths. I caught sight of a funeral home sign—an obvious job for Mortana. "I think it'd be fun to work with young kids, but I don't think that'd give me much time for composing. The school has a more general course of study, so I could do something like producing. But there aren't any jobs like that around here. I'd have to leave Octavia Falls, and I don't really want to do that."

My eyes fell upon a booth that advertised a local therapist's office. Avery Mitchel, a Seer from my Thoughtography class, stood there with a couple of her friends, listening to the woman's speech.

"Psychology is an excellent field for Seers," the therapist was saying. "As we are very empathetic and intuitive, we can often help others uncover problems patients weren't even aware of themselves. Some Seers are especially gifted in the field of therapy."

I turned to Talia. "Have you considered therapy?"

Her gaze flickered to the booth. "I want to major in music, not psychology."

"I mean combining the two," I suggested. "Music therapy is a thing, right? Like helping people with their emotional trauma through music?"

Talia's eyes lit up. "Yeah, it is. It's not a major offered by the school, but maybe I could double major. I don't know if anyone around here does that."

I shrugged. "So open your own practice."

"That's a really good idea," she said. "I'll have to consider it."

Talia stopped at the therapist's booth to listen to her spiel. I wasn't that into it, since it seemed like a Seer-dominated field, so I turned to the neighboring booth. I recognized it immediately. The table was decorated with a brown table cloth the color of gingerbread, tinsel that looked like frosting, and various cardboard-cutouts of candies. A chocolate fountain flowed as the centerpiece, and all sorts of suckers were laid out for sampling. The three ladies from *The Gingerbread House* candy shop down on the Catwalk stood behind the booth. Two of them were occupied with other students, but the third caught my eye.

She was an older woman with a long nose and salt and pepper hair piled atop her head. She wore her uniform from the shop, with a name tag that read *Betty*.

"An Alchemist!?" she cried, looking down at the tattoo on my arm.

I pushed my hair behind my ear and approached. "Yep, that's me."

"Come, come," she said, gesturing me forward. "Learn the secrets of our trade."

I stepped forward, even though I was already certain I wouldn't be going into candy making.

"We combine culinary expertise with Alchemy magic to produce a wide variety of sweets," Betty explained. "Do you like to cook?"

I shrugged. I'd cook if I had to, but I wasn't into it like my grandmother was. "Occasionally."

"Ah, then you might consider majoring in Culinary Alchemy," she encouraged. "There are many benefits to the job, apart from taste-testing the sweets."

Betty gave a loud laugh, but it came out sounding more like a cackle. It kind of gave me the creeps, until her features returned to normal.

I glanced over to Talia, who looked like she was about done listening to the therapist. "Well, uh, thanks," I told Betty.

"Wait!" she cried. She reached across the table and held up one of the suckers. "Don't forget your complimentary lollipop."

I took it from her, but she stared at me expectantly.

The woman next to her finished talking to other students and turned her attention to me. She must've been older than the other two women by a couple of years, with short-cropped hair and cat-eye glasses. Her skin, however, was impeccably smooth. In fact, all three of the women shared a youthful look, though they were obviously past retirement age.

"Go ahead and try it, dear," she said. I glanced at her name tag to see it read *Agnes*. "It's a Luck Lollipop! If your tongue turns blue when you eat it, you'll have luck the rest of the day."

"Oh, well, how could I pass that up?" I said kindly. I opened the lollipop and licked it. "What color did I get?"

I stuck out my tongue for the ladies to see. Agnes and Betty shared a quick glance I couldn't read. The third woman, Sandy, caught sight of me, and she quickly shut down her conversation with other students to turn my way.

"It's blue!" Sandy cried, elated. Her excitement seemed a little over-the-top for a minor party trick. "You are very lucky, indeed."

"Awesome. I could really use it," I said, before sticking the sucker back in my mouth.

"Don't act so special," a sinister voice came from beside me.

I turned to see Chloe standing there, one hand on her hip. I hadn't noticed her before in the sea of students, but she must've been standing at the booth the whole time, because she too held a sucker in her hand. She wore all black today, with a sleeveless dress, long tights, and black boots. I thought it was supposed to look intimidating, but I was indifferent to it. It matched her black soul.

"I got blue, too." She stuck her tongue out to prove it. All I could think of was how childish she looked.

"Two lucky students at once!" Betty beamed. "You two are very fortunate."

Chloe looked like she was about to roll her eyes, but resisted. "I'd be fortunate if I managed to avoid *her* the rest of the day."

"Same," I sneered, never once taking my eyes off her. She stared me down, but we were both distracted a moment later.

"Free candy!" Mandy cried, rushing up behind me. She was alone, as Amy had already declared her History major and didn't need the career fair to decide.

Mandy poked me in the side when she approached, but her face fell when she noticed Chloe standing there. Mandy narrowed her eyes and draped an arm around my shoulder. Her voice came out sounding harsh. "Am I interrupting something?"

Chloe looked her up and down. "Nothing to see here. Though a word of warning, Mandy, you might want to lay off the sweets."

Mandy dropped her arm from around me. My eyebrows shot up, but it was Mandy who responded. "*Excuse me?*"

Chloe's eyes roamed up and down Mandy's form. "You should start watching your weight—you know, the Freshman Fifteen and all. Or in your case, the Freshman Fifty."

My initial shock morphed quickly into anger. I tried to hold it back, but I shook with rage.

"Bitch, you did *not* just say that!" Mandy snarled.

Chloe smiled sardonically and brought the lollipop back up to her lips. "Oh, I don't mean anything by it," she lied in a fake-ass tone. "It'll only do you good. Everyone knows you're too fat for guys. Isn't that why you hang out with Amy—hoping *she'll* give you a chance?"

A wave of heat billowed up from my belly, and I was done for. I couldn't control the urge to lash out at the insult.

"You rotten piece of grave dirt!" I shouted. I drew my arm back to slam my first into Chloe's face, but a wide smile had formed across her lips. I realized a second later that this is what she *wanted*. She was hoping to get a rise out of me. She wanted me to get in trouble, to paint herself as the victim.

Instead of punching her pretty little nose as I would've liked, I opened my fist and swatted the lollipop out of her hand. It went flying through the air, narrowly missing the three witches who owned *The Gingerbread House*.

Chloe looked slightly shocked, but not because she'd lost her lollipop. She'd *wanted* me to punch her. "What are you waiting for? Don't you want to punch me?"

"To the Abyss and back," I snarled. "But you're not worth it."

The red-hot anger coursing through me didn't cool down. Telling Chloe she wasn't worth it was a bigger blow to her ego than physically retaliating would ever be. I turned on my heel. Mandy smirked proudly at me, while Talia looked on with raised eyebrows.

Apparently, turning away from Chloe was the biggest insult of all, because she lunged at me. Her fingers tangled in my hair, and pain shot through my skull as several strands broke free.

"Ow!" I cried. My hand shot to the back of my head, and I turned to glare at her. People along the whole row had turned to watch us, but I barely noticed them. "What the hell was that for?"

Chloe didn't seem to hear the question. Instead, she narrowed her gaze at me and reached into her purse. "I believe I have something that belongs to you."

She pulled out three small objects, then tossed them at my feet. "Next time, get a little more creative."

It took me a moment to process it, until I realized what she'd thrown at me were the cursed objects—the earring, thimble, and compass.

Chloe stood there just long enough to take in my gaping features, then turned away. She swayed her hips as she left, and the crowd quickly lost interest in us. Soon, the room was buzzing with chatter again. Mandy and Talia were at my side in a second.

"Are you okay?" Mandy asked.

"I'm fine," I told her. "Are *you*?"

"Pft. Chloe can't mess with me."

I reached down to pick up the cursed objects, but Talia got there before I did. She quickly picked them up and subconjured them. Almost instantly, she began itching the back of her hand.

I frowned. "You didn't have to do that."

"They need to be put someplace safe until we can get back to our room," she said. The enchanted box that kept the curses from influencing us was still under my bed.

"Fair enough," I said. "Should we head back?"

We'd barely made it through a portion of the career fair, but it didn't look like any of us were interested in continuing on.

Talia turned to Mandy. "You up for hanging out?"

Mandy smiled. "Absolutely."

We headed back to our dorm room, but we only got halfway there when Mandy stopped me. "Nadine, what is going on with your…"

She trailed off as she reached out to touch my hair. A huge chunk fell out of her fingers and fluttered to the floor.

My hand shot to my scalp. "What the…?"

It took me a second to process it. My heart sank, and I quickly ran my fingers through my hair. Chunk after chunk came out, until a pile started forming at my feet.

"Goddess!" I cried out in horror. "What's happening!?"

I stared down at my shaking hands, where strands of hair were now tangled around my fingers.

Talia's jaw dropped. "Chloe grabbed a few strands of your hair. She must've gotten Camille or Gwen to hex you!"

"Hex me?" I balked, though it wasn't far-fetched at all. In fact, it was to be expected. But my *hair*?

"Come on," Mandy said quickly. She looped her arm through mine and rushed me down the hall to the dorms. She glanced up and down the hall, while I tried to hold back my devastation.

Gus and Isa had been out hunting mice earlier. They were waiting at the door for us, and they rushed inside the second Talia opened it. My whole body shook as Mandy led me across the room and to the bed. I sank into it hopelessly as strands of hair continued to fall to the ground around me.

"It's falling out so fast!" I cried. "I'm going to go bald!"

"I'll get a towel," Talia said as she rushed to the bathroom.

"What's that going to do?" I asked. I couldn't decide whether to be angry or start crying. I was too shocked to even move.

Talia came back into the room carrying a purple towel. "If we wrap it around your head, maybe it will slow the effects, until we can find a solution."

Mandy yanked her phone out of her pocket. "I'm calling Amy. There has to be some sort of antidote."

"But this is a hex—like some sort of curse, right?" My voice cracked. "There's no cure."

Talia started wrapping the towel around my head. I was still as a statue and barely noticed. "Hexes are a lower form of ill-intended spells. They aren't as dangerous as full-blown curses. This one will run its course. Your hair won't be gone forever."

Talia's words should've been reassuring, but there was uncertainty in her tone. I knew what she wanted to say but didn't. A curse like this depended on how potent it was. If the curse was strong enough, I might never grow my hair back. Talia was just *hoping* this was one weak-ass curse.

I was, too.

I began to sob. As my hair fell out in clumps around me, I was taken back to my pre-diagnosis days. Back when I was *really* sick, before I started my meds, I'd wake to clumps of hair on my pillow. My hair had thinned so badly, I had to brush it a certain way to hide the bald spots. I recalled how hard it'd been to grow it back. My hair had become a part of me—the way I styled it, the shampoo I used that smelled like roses. Chloe hadn't just cursed my hair. She'd cursed my whole damn identity.

"Amy's on her way," Mandy stated as she pressed a button on her phone. I hadn't even heard her talking. I was too devastated to hear much of anything.

Tears sprang to my eyes and poured over my lids. "Is she go-going to be a-able to fix it?"

"She'll try her best," Mandy assured me.

I wiped at my nose. Isa noticed my unease and settled herself in my lap, purring loudly. The towel helped keep the hair from falling down around me, but my head itched under it, like it was still falling out.

Mandy sat next to me, whispering words of encouragement, while

Talia worked on cleaning up some of the hair. A knock came at the door several minutes later, and Talia rushed to answer.

"I came as fast as I heard," Amy breathed heavily.

"Come in," Talia said.

Amy rushed into the room, her cat trotting along behind her. She stopped in her tracks when she saw me. "It's going to be okay. I just aced an assignment in hair regrowth last week."

She spoke so calmly I didn't have a choice but to believe her. I wiped the tears from my eyes. "Are you sure this is going to work?"

Amy hesitated a moment. "Well… we're going to try. Let's see the damage."

Mandy reached up and unwrapped the towel from around my head. I gasped when I caught sight of the clumps of hair in the towel. Mandy quickly folded it up and stashed it out of view. All three girls looked at me with wide eyes.

"Is it that bad?" I asked in a shaky tone.

I reached up to touch my head, but Mandy caught my hand. "Best if you don't think about it."

"Do you still have the crystal we gave you?" Amy asked me. "The one that wards off curses?"

I pulled it out from under my shirt, where it hung off the necklace Mandy had made. "I wear it all the time. I thought it was supposed to keep this stuff from happening."

"Not completely," Amy admitted. "But it will help. We'll get this fixed. I promise."

"What do we have to do, Amy?" Talia asked.

"We'll have to let the hex run its course."

"I'm going to go completely bald?" I cried.

"Temporarily," Amy admitted. "Tal, if you could grab Nadine's hairbrush from the bathroom, that might help speed things up."

I started to stand. "I'll get it."

"No," Talia said quickly. "Believe me, you don't want to see this."

I hadn't even thought about the mirror in the bathroom. I sank back into the bed, pressing my face into my hands. *It's not the end of the world. It's just hair*, I told myself.

Hair that I freaking loved.

To anyone else, it might *just be hair*. But to me, it meant a lot more than that. I'd already lost my hair once, and growing it back had been the one thing that made me feel and look normal—when the rest of my body had already broken down. Chloe was taking that from me again.

I was a complete sobbing mess.

Amy conjured tons of alchemy supplies. She set up a portable burner on my nightstand, along with a miniature cauldron that fit perfectly on top of it. She placed various herbs next to it. I only recognized ginseng, though she conjured vials filled with different colors of oils.

"How is this going to work?" I asked, sniffling.

"While we wait for the spell to pass, I'll work on brewing a hair growth potion," she explained. "It will take a few hours until it's done, if that's okay."

"I don't see any alternative," I replied.

Talia returned with my hairbrush and sat next to me on the bed. She began brushing out what was left of my hair. My scalp was sensitive with every stroke, and I could feel the strands falling away. Some broke free and tickled my arm as they fell to the bed. I shuddered.

Mandy placed a hand on my back while Amy got to work brewing the potion. "What are you going to do, Nadine? Curse Chloe back?"

"Hell yeah," I answered automatically. My tears dried as stone-cold resolve washed over me.

"You can't stoop to Chloe's level," Talia protested.

"Well, I can't sit around and do nothing!" I insisted. "Chloe has framed me for vandalism, beaten me to a pulp, painted *half-blood* on my door, and hexed my hair! All I've done is dump a few minor cursed objects on her."

I'd spent most of the semester trying to learn how to break this curse. Meanwhile, Chloe had found endless ways to torment me.

"She can't get away with this," I said. "It's time she sees what *I'm* capable of."

I shot to my feet and went to my dresser, where I rifled through my drawers until I found a scarf to wrap around my head.

"What are you going to do?" Talia asked curiously. "Do you even *know* any hexes?"

I draped the scarf over my head and tucked in the ends, then squared my shoulders. "No, but either way, she's going to get what's coming to her. Aren't you pissed?"

"Of course I am!" Talia cried.

I eyed each of my friends. "Look, I'm not going to ask you to cast spells for me the way Chloe is using her friends. I don't want any of you to become a target. But I'm going to kick Chloe's ass, and the only thing I ask is that you don't stop me. So, are you with me or not?"

"Well, if I can't stop you, then I'm in," Talia offered. "I'm not letting the Lucky Three touch you again."

"Thanks, Tal," I said.

"I'm in, too," Mandy added.

"And me," Amy said.

"Then let's get this bitch." I stomped out of the room, and my friends followed. As I headed down the hall, I conjured a small box I'd been collecting dead insects in, just in case they ever came in handy. Now seemed like the perfect time to use them. I gathered a handful of insects, their tiny dead bodies crunching in my hand, and subconjured the box again. With my hands curled into fists, I pounded on Chloe's door.

No answer came.

"Where the hell is she?" I growled under my breath. She couldn't have gone too far. We'd only just left the career fair, so she had to still be in the school.

I whirled around and started down the hall toward a nearby staircase. Before I could make it there, Mandy grabbed me by the arm. "Not that way," she warned. "That's the Vanishing Stairwell."

I'd heard of it before and had nearly forgotten about it. The Vanishing Stairwell was the product of a spell gone wrong, and it appeared and disappeared at random intervals. No one went down there anymore, not since a student had died after being trapped in there years ago. It was a magical version of Russian Roulette—one you didn't want to test out.

"Then we'll go this way," I decided, turning in the direction of the main stairs.

I barely made it a few steps before I heard a door swing open from behind us and the sound of Chloe's cackle echoing down the hall. A smirk crossed my face as I turned to glare at her.

Chloe stepped out of a nearby dorm room, waving goodbye to whoever was inside. "It's going to be fantastic. I can't wait to see it. Thanks for the help, Gwen."

The door clicked behind her, and she turned. Chloe stopped dead in her tracks when she saw me standing there. After a moment, her lips curled into a sneer. "Nice *scarf*," she mocked.

"My hair will grow back, but you'll always be a raging bitch!" I snapped.

Chloe only laughed. "What are you going to do about it? You're a weak-ass witch. That's why no one wants you here."

"She has us," Talia said, stepping forward. Mandy and Amy did the same, and my chest filled with confidence.

"Like I'm scared of you losers," Chloe scoffed.

"You should be!" My fist tightened, and the insects crushed in my hand. I drew their energy into me, then blasted a defensive spell out of my other palm. A purple orb whizzed through the air and slammed straight into Chloe's chest. It hit so hard her feet left the ground, and she went flying backward, landing flat on her back next to the Vanishing Stairwell.

Talia gasped and threw her hands over her mouth. "Oh my gosh! When you said you were going to kick her ass, I thought you were going to throw a few punches and pull her hair! I didn't think you'd knock her out!"

I froze as I waited for Chloe to move, but she'd gone completely still. I hadn't meant to do anything but maybe leave a few bruises. Had my spell been that powerful? I uncurled my fist to see the bodies of the insects had turned to ash. I let the ash slip through my fingers, and I cautiously approached Chloe. She was still breathing.

I stopped beside her and was caught off guard when she swung her foot out. It connected with my ankle, and I was knocked off my feet. I caught myself, but it was a hard landing. Pain radiated up my wrists, and I realized Chloe wasn't knocked out at all. She'd been *pretending.*

Chloe was on me in under a second. Her fingers tangled in my scarf, and she pressed my face into the carpet. "Like I said," she snarled. "Your magic is weak."

"And it's four against one!" Talia snapped. I heard the battle orb crackling in her palm, though I couldn't see with Chloe holding me down. "Step away from her, or you're going to regret it."

Chloe was momentarily distracted, and I used the opportunity to thrust my elbow up into her face.

"Ow, you bitch!" she cried, covering her nose. I scrambled to get to my feet, but Chloe grabbed for my scarf and yanked it off my head. Strands of hair fell around me, and all Chloe could do was stare at her handiwork and laugh.

A battle orb whizzed between us. I didn't see which of my friends had fired it, but confidence swelled in my chest knowing I had them to back me up. Chloe jumped backward, looking shocked that my friends had the balls to try attacking her.

"Who's the weak one now?" I taunted, shoving her. She stumbled a few steps backward. "You don't even have magic." I shoved her again, and she tripped over the edge of an open doorway, landing on her ass. Her eyes went wide in horror, and I was pleased I was getting through to her. "You don't realize who you're messing with, because I'll—"

Without warning, Chloe vanished from sight, along with the doorway. Where there was an open archway only moments ago, now there was nothing but a wall.

Holy shit. I hadn't realized what I'd done until it was too late.

I'd shoved Chloe into the Vanishing Stairwell.

"Dear Goddess…" My hands shot over my mouth, and I slowly turned to my friends. They all shared a matching look of horror. "Please tell me this isn't as serious as I think it is."

Talia's voice shook. "There's no telling when the stairwell will reappear. It could be minutes… or months."

"I didn't want to *kill* her!" I cried. I whirled back to the wall and pounded on it. "Chloe, can you hear me?"

"She can't," Talia said. "It's a space-bending spell. For all intents and purposes, the stairwell doesn't even exist at the moment."

"Then what's going to happen to her?" I asked. I'd wanted to get back at Chloe, but not like this.

Talia's features turned ashen. "I have no idea."

I turned to Mandy and Amy. "Is there nothing we can do? No spell to open the stairwell back up?"

Amy bit her lower lip. "I've never heard of one."

I began pacing. "Goddess, this is bad. I'll be burned at the stake for this. Chloe will be stuck in the spell for months. She'll starve to death, and they'll find her skeleton and—"

"Somebody help me—whoa!"

Chloe's terrified voice returned as the doorway appeared once again.

She held her fists up, as if she'd been pounding on the wall. As the wall vanished in front of her, she fell forward and caught herself.

I'd never seen Chloe look so scared before. Doors opened all throughout the hall in response to her pleading cry. Students poked their heads out of their dorms curiously. All eyes were on Chloe and her trembling form. She looked up to me, then to my friends, and her body began shaking harder.

"You s-stay the hell away f-from me," she stammered as she got to her feet. Chloe scurried away, obviously traumatized by the matter.

I was relieved the stairwell had reappeared and Chloe managed to escape. But now that she did, the whole thing seemed utterly hilarious. Chloe had never been scared of me before, and I'd finally managed to make her quake in her designer heels. It was a pleasure to watch.

"That was a close call," Talia said as we watched Chloe scramble back to her room. She shot glances our way, as if making sure we weren't planning to attack again.

I crossed my arms. "A really close call, but it got the job done. Chloe's scared of me now."

"Is that what you wanted?" Amy asked curiously. "It may drive her to come after you harder."

"Or leave me alone," I pointed out.

"I think it's best to assume she'll retaliate," Mandy said. "That way you're prepared."

"Mm…" I mused. "What's the best way to keep Chloe at a distance?"

"Show her you're better than her," Talia said thoughtfully. "Chloe thrives on getting under your skin. You have to show her she can't."

"That's a good point," I agreed. "Ladies, I have an idea."

☾

If Chloe thought she could mess with me, she could go choke on a frog. Whatever she threw my way, I'd handle, because I was a bad-ass witch like that.

The following day, I breezed through the halls of Miriam Mansion like a witch about to raise the dead. My brand new shoulder-length hair swayed with each step I took. My girl squad strolled behind me, each of us wearing matching outfits—skin-tight black dresses, makeup as dark as death, and stiletto heels.

I was acutely aware of every pair of eyes on us. People turned in slow motion when they saw us coming. Jaws dropped, and I could practically hear the bad-ass beat playing to the rhythm of our confident footsteps.

I'd never felt so fearless before, and *everyone* took notice.

Each of us had brought our own flair to our outfits. Mandy wore a black choker she'd made herself, while Talia strode down the hall confidently in a black corset with pink ribbing. Amy showed off her legs in fishnet tights.

My signature look for the day consisted of lace fingerless gloves and a temporary tattoo down my right arm that read *Freak Sisters*. Not to mention my new hairstyle.

Amy's potion had been successful. My hair had grown to shoulder-length overnight. It wasn't as full as it used to be, but Amy assured me it'd be back to normal within the week.

People didn't have to hear us coming. It was like they could sense trouble from a mile away. As we descended the grand staircase, I swore every eye in the Main Foyer turned our way, and all conversation seemed to cease.

Gregory Walker and Brayden Spyre stood at the bottom of the stairs, gazing into a crystal ball. When they saw the four of us coming, they went as still as statues, staring. Gregory dropped the crystal ball, and it thudded hard on the carpet before rolling under the staircase.

Chloe, Gwen, and Camille had been gossiping at the nearest sitting area and were the last in the room to notice our arrival. The look of sheer shock on Chloe's face was better than any curse I could put on her. She thought she could mess with me—and I'd just proven her wrong with a giant *fuck you*.

Chloe managed to compose herself. She rose from her chair and tossed her hair over her shoulder. "Nice wig," she sneered.

"Nice try," I shot back. "But it's my natural hair."

Chloe's jaw dropped, but she quickly collected herself and crossed her arms.

I narrowed my eyes at her. "You might as well back the fuck off, because there's *nothing* you can do to scare me."

"That's big talk for someone who needs her loser sisters backing her up just to talk to me," Chloe said.

I scoffed. "Oh, believe me, they only came to watch the fight."

Chloe gaped. "Are you threatening me?"

I smirked. "Unlike you, I don't need to sabotage the competition to win a fight. I'll do it by my own merit. Oh, and it's the Freak Sisters."

I turned on my heel and started toward the hall behind the stairs. Amy, Mandy, and Talia gave the Lucky Three matching death glares before turning to follow me. Chloe had gone totally speechless as we sashayed away, all eyes on us.

As soon as we passed Gregory, he seemed to pick his jaw up off the floor. He hurried behind us to retrieve his crystal ball, then caught us in the hall. Gregory planted himself in front of me. He was at least a head taller than me, and his wild hair made him seem even taller.

"My, you ladies are looking *fine* today," he said, eyeing the four of us up and down. He pushed his glasses up his nose to get a better look. "You just might be the hottest girls in the school."

I stopped in my tracks and placed a hand on my hip. "While I'm flattered, we don't have time to stand around being objectified all day."

He'd been eyeing Amy's fishnet leggings, but quickly snapped to attention. "It's not like that. I wanted to invite you to The Dungeon."

"The Dungeon?" I repeated. "What's that? Some sort of role playing game?"

"Better." Gregory conjured four cards. He flipped them over, and I saw that they were tarot cards. Each was identical to the others. I recognized them as the Devil card, though the image was in an art style I hadn't seen before.

"Are you serious!?" Mandy squealed. She rushed to my side and snatched the cards from Gregory's hands. She inspected them close, as if to see if they were real.

Talia and Amy both closed in, too.

"I don't get it," I said.

"The Dungeon is an elite club in the basement of the school," Talia explained. "It's so exclusive, even the teachers can't get in. You need a card like this to even find it. Where'd you get these, Gregory?"

He shrugged. "A little here, a little there. I know how to get my hands on contraband. I've got some nightshade, too, if you're up for that?"

I gave him a look, wondering what he even meant by that. The other girls didn't seem to hear him, as they were too entranced by the cards.

"We *have* to go," Talia insisted. "Tyler talks about this place all the time, but I've never been."

"I don't know," Amy said, biting her lower lip. "Clubs aren't really my scene."

Mandy looped her arm through Amy's elbow. "They are tonight."

"It's Friday night," Gregory said, like that was supposed to entice us. "The party is going to be huge. So, will you join us?"

I was intrigued, to say the least. I could really use a night where all hell broke loose. I didn't want to give a damn right now anyway.

"What's your price?" I asked him.

"Tell you what," Gregory said, sounding like he'd done this a million times. "Since you ladies look so fine today, I'll give 'em to you for free."

"Free?" Mandy balked. "What's the catch?"

"No catch," Gregory assured us. "Just want to see you there tonight."

He winked at Amy, and she frowned.

"We'll take them," Talia said without question.

"Perfect. Can't wait." Gregory left us with the tarot cards and hurried off.

Mandy turned to Talia. "You know what he's doing, right?"

"What's that?" Talia asked innocently.

"He's roping us in and trying to get us to buy more contraband off him," she said.

"Well, it's not like I'm going to," Talia replied.

"Besides, these are probably counterfeit." Mandy waved the tarot cards in the air.

Talia perked an eyebrow. "And? As long as they work, who cares?"

Mandy smiled. "I like the way you think."

Amy's gaze followed Gregory as he turned the corner. "Um… do you guys think he realizes I'm gay?"

"Doesn't matter, sweetheart." Mandy patted her on the shoulder. "No one can take their eyes off your legs in those tights. You look hot."

Amy smiled sheepishly.

"So, we'll each take a card and meet back here tonight?" Mandy asked. "Say, ten o'clock?"

"Sounds perfect." I took one of the cards from her hand and subconjured it. "I think it's time the Freak Sisters raise some hell."

☽·

LATE-NIGHT OUTINGS WEREN'T easy on me, but I'd be damned if I missed tonight's party. Talia and I experimented with our magic in the mirror, playing with our makeup and hair. She finally settled on black hair with pink stripes—a simple spell that would wear off by the end of the night. I wore my dark eye makeup from earlier but added blood-red lipstick. We met up with Amy and Mandy behind the grand staircase late that night when the halls were quiet and abandoned.

"So, where do we find this place?" Amy asked.

"Ladies, get out your cards," Talia announced.

We all did as she asked. While I was studying the artwork of the devil, Talia flipped her card over to the back, which had an intricate abstract purple design on it.

"The Dungeon is enchanted," she explained. "Each night, the entrance moves so that the professors can't find it. The map is on the back of your card."

I looked closer, and I noticed that the design *did* look like a map—a maze of hallways and rooms. One particular room was blackened out, our obvious destination.

"This way," Talia said proudly.

As she led us down the stairs to the basement, Mandy asked, "How do you know all this, Tal? I only knew you needed a card to get in."

"I've heard stories from my brother," she said. "Not that he's *ever* invited me, the prick."

I eyed her as we walked the long hall. "I thought you liked your brother."

"Oh, I do. But I can't wait to see his face when I show up."

"He'll be there?" I asked.

"Ooh, he'll be there," she assured me as we turned down another hall.

There seemed to be a hidden message in her words. I wasn't entirely sure what she meant.

"We're here." Talia stopped in front of an empty wall. Nothing but black brick stared back at us.

"Um… are you sure this is it?" Amy asked.

Talia glanced at the map on the back of her card, then up to the wall. "I'm sure. The entrance is hidden, so we just have to find the way in."

"Any chance your brother shared that little detail with you?" I questioned.

Talia shook her head.

Mandy flipped her card over a few times. "Well, if these cards are our tickets in, then maybe…"

She stepped up to the wall and pressed the card flat against it. In front of my very eyes, a doorway began to form. The bricks seemed to sink into the wall, flattening and smoothing out until they formed a shiny black door with a red handle.

"Hell awaits, ladies." Mandy twisted the knob, and a pumping bass spilled out into the hall. She gestured each of us forward, and we entered.

A long hall stretched in front of us, draped with red curtains on either side. We reached the end, and Talia pulled back a curtain to reveal a lively nightclub. The music grew even louder as we stepped out of the hall and onto a balcony. Below us, a live band played upbeat music on stage, while students danced under red pulsing lights. The club was incredible, with dark walls and various plush red couches placed in different seating areas. A bar lined one end of the room, where students passed out drinks I could only imagine were brewed by Alchemists, judging by the way fog seemed to roll off them. There didn't seem to be anyone older than twenty-two in sight. The Dungeon was obviously a very well-kept secret.

We descended the stairs in the direction of the bar. A couple sucked face at the bottom, blocking our path until Mandy yelled loud enough over the music that they moved. My eyes continued to roam over the club, allowing the carefree nature of it all to sink into my bones.

I saw a couple people I knew from class, but most of the crowd seemed to be juniors or seniors. In a sitting area nearby, I witnessed Gregory conjure a small vial of liquid. He handed it to a young girl, who unscrewed the cap and used a dropper to place a couple drops under her tongue.

Talia leaned into me. "Drinks first, or dancing?"

"Dancing," I answered. "We have no idea what's in those drinks."

"True," she snickered. "Come on."

Talia took my hand and dragged me out onto the dancefloor. I immediately fell into the beat, tossing my hands in the air and letting my hair flow around me. It was crowded, with barely any room to call my own, but Amy, Mandy, and Talia surrounded me, and we kept close as the rest of the crowd seemed to close in on us. Talia shimmied her butt in my direction, and Mandy started grinding on me. I laughed loudly. I loved being here with my girls and not giving a shit for once.

The song came to an end, and the lead singer announced a quick break. A popular mainstream song came over the speakers, while the band went to grab drinks. A couple of people seemed disappointed and left the dancefloor, but most stayed and continued dancing to the music. Amy and Mandy twirled around, grinding and running their hands over each other. Talia and I got into our own swing of things, twerking and tossing our hair in unison.

"Talia Murphy," a male voice scolded, pulling the two of us out of our funk.

I turned to see a tall male with chestnut brown hair staring her down. He'd been the lead singer up on stage, I quickly realized. He was even more attractive up close, with tattoos running up one of his arms and a light layer of eyeliner on—though that wasn't exactly my type. His arms were crossed, and he looked pissed.

"Just what in the Goddess's name do you think you're doing here?" he demanded.

Talia chuckled, but she didn't stop dancing. "Is that why you stopped playing, Tyler?" she teased, spinning around him.

That's when I realized who he was. This was her brother, the lead singer of the Wicked Warlocks.

"I told you not to come," he said, relaxing a bit. "You're too young."

She scoffed. "I'm not any younger than anyone else here. To be fair, *you're* the old geezer in this place."

Tyler shrugged, totally loosened up now. "Hey, I get paid for the gig. I don't ask questions. So, are you going to introduce me to your friend?"

Talia stopped dancing and gestured to me. "Tyler, this is my best friend and roommate, Nadine. Nadine, this is my older brother, Tyler."

I reached out to shake his hand. I noticed the ends of his fingers were rough, like he spent a lot of time playing guitar.

"I've heard a lot about you," I said over the music.

He cocked an eyebrow. "Only good things, I hope."

"Absolutely," I assured him. "Talia's the sweetest."

Tyler frowned. "Yeah, which is exactly why I don't need her corrupted by The Dungeon."

"Please," Talia scoffed. "You think a little dancing is going to hurt me?"

"There's more that goes on here than dancing, little sis."

"Hey, Tyler," a female voice drawled from behind me. I turned to see Chloe approaching. She wore a tight black dress and high leather boots. A sparkling black clutch hung from her shoulder, and she carried a fizzing drink in her hand. She breezed straight past me and ran a finger over Tyler's chest.

"What are you doing talking to these losers?" Chloe taunted. "Come sit by me and my friends, and we'll show you a good time."

Chloe waved to Camille and Gwen, who sat huddled close on one of the red couches. They ogled at Tyler. I could swear Gwen almost drooled.

Tyler looked down at Chloe with disgust, but before he could say anything, Talia cut in. She planted herself between Chloe and Tyler, pushing Chloe's hand away. "Sorry, but he's kind of busy."

"Well, I think he can speak for himself," Chloe sneered.

Tyler looked like he didn't want to get in the middle of this. Instead, he shrugged and said, "Sorry, Chloe, but I have to get back up on stage."

Chloe looked a little taken aback.

Talia turned to Tyler, completely ignoring Chloe. "Catch up with you later?"

"I'll have my eyes on you the whole night," Tyler replied. It was meant as a threat, but Chloe must've thought he was flirting, because her jaw dropped.

Talia pulled her brother into a hug. He was over six inches taller than her and had to bend to hug her back. "Don't forget the key change on *Dark Whispers*," she teased.

He rolled his eyes as he drew away. "Like I'd ever. See you, Tal. Nice to meet you, Nadine."

Tyler headed back on stage, and Chloe stomped off. Talia beamed.

"Does Chloe have any idea you two are related?" Mandy asked, coming in close.

Talia shook her head. "Chloe barely remembers my name most days."

I laughed. "The look on her face was priceless."

"She was so flustered, she almost tripped on her way back," Amy snickered.

"As long as she leaves us alone," Talia said. "I didn't know she'd be here. I don't want her ruining our night."

"Hell, no!" I cried. "She could never—"

"Nadine?" a voice cut me off.

The sound was like a song, and even though music played over the speakers, the voice seemed to drown it out. My heart skipped a beat, and I turned to see Lucas standing there. He looked really hot, in a button-down shirt that was open on the top few buttons and the sleeves rolled up to his elbows. His hair was in disarray, but in a really sexy way.

"Lucas!" I cried. I stepped away from my friends and flung my arms around his neck. "What are you doing here?"

His hands settled on my hips, and my heart danced to the beat of the music. "Grant dragged me along. Tricked me, actually."

I snickered. "How'd he trick you?"

Lucas frowned. "He told me he needed help with an Alchemy assignment. I should've known it was a ruse."

I couldn't stand here and watch Lucas's lips move without doing something about it. I leaned in and kissed him. The music seemed to fade for a moment, until I drew away and the club returned to normal. Lucas's shoulders dropped, like my kiss had put him totally at ease.

"Is this Grant's first time here?" I asked.

"Must be. I don't even know how he got tickets."

I glanced over to see Grant had quickly melded into my group of friends. He danced with Mandy and Amy, though his eyes remained locked on Talia.

"Where there's a will, there's a way," I said. "I bet Mandy let it slip Talia would be here tonight."

"He *would* go through great lengths for that," Lucas agreed. "Thank the Goddess you're here. I don't know if I'd survive this place otherwise. What are you doing here, though?"

"Girl's night," I explained, taking his hand. "Come dance?"

He rolled his eyes playfully. "If I have to."

"You have to," I joked.

I dragged Lucas through the crowd and back toward my friends. The Wicked Warlocks started playing again, and the crowd roared in excitement. I could hardly hear anything. Forget about talking to Lucas. Instead, I let my hips do all the talking, swaying them to the upbeat tempo. Lucas eyed me up and down, looking hungry.

I never took my eyes off him while I danced. He barely moved, but I didn't need him to. Reading his signals, I ground my body against his. He placed his hands on my waist as my ass shimmied against his frontside. Lucas wasn't a dancer, but I'd be damned if his hips didn't begin to sway in sync with mine.

I turned to face him again, and he was beaming. "You like that?" I shouted over the music.

He leaned in to speak in my ear. "I can't say I'm disappointed I came."

I stopped dancing and took a step away from him, my eyes darting downward. "Oh, you did? Already?"

Lucas's face remained expressionless for a moment, until he caught on to my joke. He grabbed me around the waist and pulled me into him, pressing his hips against mine. "Not like that, Nad. Get your mind out of the gutter."

I smirked. "Too late. There's no saving me now."

Lucas took my hand and spun me around, before pulling me close to him again. "What am I going to do with you?"

"Naughty things," I teased.

Lucas smirked. "Right here?"

"Later," I said. "I gotta give you something to look forward to."

He sucked a breath and joked, "The suspense is killing me."

"Don't die on me!" I insisted. "We have lots of things left to do together."

He cocked an eyebrow. "Like?"

"Well…" I glanced around the dancefloor. "I've never seen your real dance moves—like when you aren't dancing with me."

He scoffed. "My *real dance moves* consist almost entirely of the chicken dance and the bunny hop."

"So show me," I said with a smile, before adding, "I dare you."

He hesitated.

"You don't want to be the first to bow out on a dare, do you?" I challenged.

He scrunched up his nose. "Why do you have to tempt me like that, Nad?"

I laughed, then gestured toward our friends. "A dare's a dare."

Lucas stepped forward, into the circle our friends had formed. Mandy dragged him into the center, and Lucas jumped into the motions of the chicken dance. When he finished shaking his butt, he was smiling. I couldn't stop laughing—not because I thought it was funny, but because I was having so much fun seeing him enjoy himself.

"Good job!" Grant said, clapping him on the back. "You're a pro. Now watch this."

Grant shoved him out of the way, then started doing the robot, which he was surprisingly good at.

Lucas returned to my side and kissed me on the top of the head. "I'm going to get you back for making me do that."

"I didn't *make* you do anything," I argued.

"Well, then you can't claim I did when I dare you to crowd surf."

I looked up to the stage and smiled. "You're on."

"Wait, Nad," he quickly stopped me. "I didn't mean it. It's not an official dare."

I frowned. "Oh. Do I get a dare?"

He hesitated, his eyes shifting from me to the stage. "Fine. Since you seem *so disappointed*..." He winked playfully. "I *officially* dare you to crowd surf."

I shook my head. "You're making this too easy."

I turned away and pushed through the crowd, until I reached the stage and climbed onto it. Tyler spotted me and grabbed my hand, pulling me up while he sang.

I tugged on the bottom of my dress. "I hope this is okay," I said.

Tyler saluted me, and I took that as my cue. I spread my arms out wide and closed my eyes. A part of me feared that no one would be there to catch me when I fell. But the other part wanted the adventure, to find out if I was wrong. I tipped backward...

And the crowd caught me. I laughed as I stared up at the pulsing lights, enjoying the feeling of floating over the crowd. I felt weightless—carefree. For just this one moment, it didn't feel like I had a curse on me. It didn't feel like children in the coven had been murdered. It felt like I could breathe...

I reached the back of the crowd, and a couple of strangers helped set me gently onto the ground. "Thanks!" I called over the music.

I returned to my friends and expected to see Lucas smiling at me. Instead, his eyes were focused on something else. I followed his gaze and spotted Cody. He was dancing with Talia, but had dragged her a few feet away from the group. Unease churned in my gut. Grant, Amy, and Mandy must've felt it, too, because they weren't grinding against each other like before.

"Hey, beautiful," Cody drawled.

Talia blushed. The two of them were totally oblivious to the rest of us watching.

"I like your dress," Cody complimented. "Why don't you dress like that all the time?"

Talia ran her fingers over her corset. "It's for special occasions only. Makes you appreciate it more."

"Oh, I appreciate it," he replied seductively. "Just be careful around *other guys*."

Talia continued dancing but eyed him curiously. "What do you mean?"

"Some of them might appreciate it *too* much. Who was that guy I saw you hugging earlier?"

Talia started laughing. "Believe me, you have nothing to worry about. Tyler's my brother."

Cody seemed to relax. "Oh, your *brother*. Yeah, that changes things."

"Wait, so I can't hug other guys?" Talia tilted her head. She didn't sound offended, more like she was trying to learn the rules.

Cody frowned. "You wouldn't want me hugging other girls, would you?"

Talia pushed her hair behind her ear. "No, I guess not."

Cody's hand ran down Talia's side, until it settled on her waist. "You know I don't like to share, my Chubby Cheeks."

He pinched Talia's cheeks. She blushed and dropped her gaze, but my jaw instantly dropped. Beside me, Grant was shaking, looking ready to explode.

"What's wrong?" Cody asked, like he hadn't realized he'd offended her.

"Please don't call me that," she said in a low voice. I could hardly hear it over the music, but that was the best I could get from reading her lips.

Cody's shoulders slumped. "Don't be sensitive. You used to love that nickname."

Talia opened her mouth to say something, but she snapped it shut before anything came out.

"Look, beautiful," Cody said. "I'm not trying to be mean. I just want you to know how I feel. Terms of endearment are my thing. Would you prefer I call you Little Princess?"

Talia gazed up under her lashes. "I'd prefer neither. Can you just call me beautiful again?"

Cody sighed and kissed Talia's forehead. "Anything, beautiful. I'm sorry. Can I get you a drink?"

"Yeah, sure." Talia's voice came out sounding brighter. "Just a water, though. I don't need anything that will dehydrate me."

Cody winked. "I've got you covered."

Cody walked away, and Talia finally seemed to realize she was no longer standing in our circle. She turned toward us, and I took her by the hand.

"You okay?" I asked.

She furrowed her brow. "Yeah, why wouldn't I be?"

"Cody was kind of being an ass," I pointed out.

She shook her head. "What? No. Cody's going to get me a drink. He's such a sweetheart."

I glanced to Grant, who was staring slack-jawed at Talia.

"Well, if you ask me, I think you could do better," Grant said.

Talia shot him a glare. "I *didn't* ask you."

Cody returned, but instead of water, he came back carrying two drinks in martini glasses. Talia's back was to him, and she continued to sway her hips to the music. Cody came in close and bumped into her. The liquid in one of the glasses jumped out, spilling all over her dress. Talia shrieked.

"Talia, you should've been watching," Cody grumbled.

"Sorry," she apologized profusely. She eyed the glasses in his hands. "Where's my water?"

"I thought you'd like this more. Come on, let's go get you cleaned up."

Cody took Talia's elbow, and the two of them left the dancefloor. No one bothered to clean up the spilled drink.

"Goddess, I *hate* that guy," Grant growled.

"I think we all do," Mandy agreed.

"All the classic signs of emotional abuse are there." Grant started ticking them off on his finger. "First, he lays on the charm and builds her trust. Then he socially isolates her by dragging her away from her friends. Then he compliments her backhandedly."

"Backhandedly?" Amy asked, curious.

"*I like your dress. Why don't you dress like that all the time?*" Grant repeated. "It's an off-handed way of criticizing her normal fashion. Once he's got her roped in with the compliment, he throws out a non-endearing nickname. See, *Chubby Cheeks* is meant to sound like an endearing pet name, but he's using it to call her fat—which Talia is not, and would it even matter if she was?"

My jaw dropped the longer Grant explained. I'd picked up on some of Cody's comments, but not the way Grant had analyzed them. Everything Cody had said seemed calculated to tear Talia down. It made me sick. Dark energy stirred in my gut, begging to escape and give Cody a taste of his own medicine. I already had a dozen insults on my tongue.

"Next, he insults her by calling her too sensitive, then uses that to gaslight her by telling her how she feels or how she *should* feel," Grant continued. "He goes on to deny his behavior and uses his sense of humor to continue to insult her. And when that isn't working, he lays on the charm again by offering to get her a drink. Only he needs to show he's in charge, so he doesn't get what she asked for. Instead, he acts like he's the saint for suggesting something *better*, then further gaslights her by blaming her for spilling the drink."

My eyebrows shot up. "Holy crap. You really have this down to a science."

Grant blushed. "Yeah, well, someone has to know these things."

"Do you think Talia even notices?" Lucas asked, sounding worried for her.

"Nah," Grant said. "Cody's got her so wrapped around his finger. Guys like him are good at disguising their behavior with good intentions and twisting any blame off themselves."

I crossed my arms. "Well, he sounds like a dirtbag—a wolf in sheep's clothing."

Grant frowned. "He is."

"This is why I don't date guys." Amy sighed. "Someone needs to talk to Talia."

"I'll do it," Mandy offered quickly, before grabbing Amy by the arm. "Come on. We've got a girl to rescue."

"Let's never be like that," Lucas suggested before I could leave his side. "You'll tell me if I'm being an ass, right?"

I smirked. "I will. And you'll do the same for me?"

"You can count on it."

"I'm going to go talk to Talia." I hurried off, but I couldn't find my friends in the crowd. The music faded slightly as I stepped into a narrow hall at the back of the club. I caught sight of the ladies' restroom and went inside.

Mandy's voice met my ears before I had the door halfway open. "Talia, please come out," she begged. I entered the room to see Mandy banging on the stall door. Amy stood nearby, looking anxious.

Talia sniffled from where she sat in the stall. "Go away. I don't want to talk to you. You ruined a perfectly good night!"

"What happened?" I asked gently.

Amy sighed. "Mandy opened her big mouth, and Cody stormed off."

My stomach sank. "Why's Talia crying?"

Amy hesitated. "Cody said some… not so nice words before he left."

I gaped. "Did they break up?"

Honestly, it'd be good news.

"No, we didn't break up," Talia sniffled. "He just… got angry."

"That doesn't make it okay," I argued. "What'd he say?"

Talia heaved a couple of breaths. "M-Mandy yelled at him, and Cody wanted to leave. I told him I wanted to stay. H-he said…"

Mandy turned to me, looking annoyed. "He called us a bunch of losers and basically implied that if Talia chose us over him, that made her a loser, too."

My nostrils flared, and I seethed. "Tal, you're not going to let him talk to you like that, are you?"

"That's not what he said!" she defended.

"Well, it wasn't worded *exactly* like that," Mandy admitted. "But it might as well have been."

"You don't understand," Talia insisted, sniffling. "If you hadn't set him off—"

"I can't control what he says!" Mandy defended. "He needs to get his anger in check—"

The stall door swung open, cutting her off. "Maybe *you* need to get *your* anger in check," Talia snapped. Her eyes were completely bloodshot. "What was all that yelling about, anyway? I barely caught half of it!"

"Cody was being a dick," Mandy said. "He needs to know he can't treat you that way."

"Treat me *what* way?" Talia demanded. "We were having fun, and you lost your shit for no reason."

I couldn't believe Talia couldn't see it. Anger continued to bubble up in my throat. "He was insulting you," I pointed out.

Talia's gaze snapped in my direction, and she scoffed. "Like I need your help—any of you! The last time you gave me advice, it nearly ruined everything I have with Cody."

My jaw dropped. "The last time? What advice did I give you?"

"You know," she spat.

It hit me what she meant. The last time I gave her advice, I'd told her to talk to Cody about what she wanted in the bedroom.

My eyebrows pinched together. "You never told me what happened."

"How could I?" she cried, wiping her eyes. "You'd only tell me to break up with him."

"Why would I do that?" I demanded. I heard it in her tone—there was a reason, but one she wasn't willing to tell me. "All I said was you didn't have to be with him if you didn't want to. I was trying to be supportive."

"Well, you can stop it—all of you." Talia pushed past me with her elbow and went to the sink, where she started dotting her eyes with a paper towel.

I stood next to her and crossed my arms. I wasn't letting her leave until I knew the truth. "What are you hiding?"

She avoided my gaze. "I don't want to talk about it."

My blood boiled, because I already sensed I knew the answer. Anger rattled around in my gut, forcing its way up to my throat. "We've never lied to each other before. If Cody hurt you—"

"He didn't hurt me," she snapped, obviously offended. She buried her face into the paper towel and started crying harder.

Shit, this was bad. I didn't have to be an empathic Seer to know that. I'd never seen Talia cry before, and it tore my heart to shreds to see my best friend struggling like this.

I reached out a shaking hand and placed it on her shoulder. "We're all here for you, but we can't help if you don't tell us what happened."

"Nothing," she wailed, but it was an obvious lie. Talia bent over the counter and inhaled deep breaths. Amy and Mandy were at her side in a split second, all of us gently comforting her. The gesture must've broken something inside of Talia, because the confession came spilling out. "We talked like you said we should, but it didn't solve anything. I told him I wasn't in the mood, but he—he—" Talia hiccupped. "He begged until I said yes."

My anger boiled over, and the gentle hand I'd placed on her shoulder curled into a fist at my side. My nostrils flared, but there was no putting this rage back where it came from.

"It's not your fault," Amy whispered.

"Of course it is," Talia cried. "I told him yes. I wanted to see if our conversation changed anything."

"He coerced you!" Mandy exploded.

I'd already reached my tipping point. I wanted to offer Talia words of encouragement. I wanted to cry with her. But more than anything, I wanted to give Cody White a piece of my mind.

I acted without thinking about it. I spun on my heel and fled from the bathroom. I was on high alert when I stepped back into the club, scanning the room for signs of that dirtbag. My eyes fell upon him standing on the balcony, sipping on a beer. He was surrounded by a couple of other guys, who all laughed at something he said—probably a lame joke. I barely noticed the crowd as I stomped across the room toward the jerkwad. Bodies closed in at all angles, but I must've given off one hell of a pissed-off vibe, because people seemed to move to make room for me.

I climbed the stairs and breezed over to him. Cody didn't notice me until I had my fist in his shirt. I shoved him up against the railing so hard that his feet nearly left the ground. He was bent backward over the balcony. Amusement played in his eyes, until I conjured a battle orb and held it threateningly to his face. It was the highest-powered orb I'd ever conjured without dark magic, fueled entirely by my burning rage. All his buddies went dead silent, and Cody's eyes filled with terror. His beer bottle dropped to the ground and shattered.

"I know what you did to my friend," I snarled in a voice that wasn't quite my own. It was dark and seething. "You think you can get away with that?"

Cody's friends all went silent. I could only guess they were staring at me in shock, but I barely noticed them. All my attention was on this asshole in front of me.

"I don't know what you're talking about!" Cody said, his voice shaking.

"You know exactly what I mean!" I screamed. My voice carried across the club and over the sound of the music. I briefly caught sight of Talia, Amy, and Mandy emerging from the hall near the bathrooms. They looked up at me in horror, but I barely processed their faces. I was too fucking angry.

I grabbed harder to Cody's shirt and yanked him off the railing, then spun him around until he stumbled into the wall. He caught himself, but his knees shook. I bent and picked up one of the shards of his beer bottle. His eyes went wide when he saw me approaching. I smirked proudly, glad to see him standing there with his tail between his legs.

"You took advantage of my friend," I growled. "You saw she was in a vulnerable position, and you coerced her, you filthy piece of trash—you *rapist!*"

"I didn't—" Cody started, but he was cut off when I swiped the piece of glass at him.

It cut into the skin on his cheek, deep enough that blood began to trickle down the side of his face. I hoped it left one hell of a scar. His hand immediately went to his cheek, and shock crossed his features, like he couldn't believe I'd dared to take the swing. I didn't give him a chance to compose himself. I dropped the piece of glass, and my fist cracked into the side of his jaw. He stumbled to the side, and I laughed maniacally.

"Oh, did that hurt?" I taunted. My heels clicked on the floor as I took another step closer. "Not as much as it's going to hurt—"

Someone caught my wrist as I drew it back. It had to be one of Cody's friends. I spun and promptly sank my knee into his royal jewels. A grunt of pain came, and I was instantly distracted from pummeling Cody's face in, because it wasn't one of his friends at all…

It was Lucas.

FIFTEEN

I never thought I'd have to drag Nadine away from a fist-fight—or that I'd be caught in the middle of it.

I sank to my knees and groaned in agonizing pain. Damn, Nadine had one hell of a kick. Good to know she could defend herself, but it wasn't looking so good for me. I sucked in deep breaths, but the air had been stolen from my lungs. Bile rose to my throat, and I was almost certain I was going to puke.

"Oh my Goddess!" Nadine cried. "Lucas!"

She knelt by my side and placed a hand on my shoulder, but I didn't have the strength to respond.

"Are you all right?" she asked.

"Peachy," I managed to squeak out.

"I'm so sorry," she repeated over and over. I was trying to focus on not puking that I didn't know how many times she said it.

"Nadine, what the hell!?" I thought the voice had come from Talia, but it was hard to tell over the ringing in my ears.

"I—" Nadine started, but Talia cut her off.

"Don't bother explaining," Talia snarled. "I've seen enough."

Talia's footsteps faded as she stormed off. All I saw was Nadine gaping. After a few moments, she turned her attention back to me.

I was starting to come back to reality now, and everything that had happened in the last several minutes came rushing back. Nadine had gone to comfort Talia, then the next thing I knew, her voice was echoing across the club. I'd looked up to see her practically hanging Cody off the balcony. By the time I'd reached the top of the stairs, she'd already cracked her fist across his face and was ready for another go.

"I'm sorry. Let me help," Nadine said again.

I finally felt stable enough that I let her drag me to my feet. I gripped the banister for support. When I finally looked around, I saw that Cody and his friends had all run off, and Talia and Amy were both gone. Grant and Mandy stood on the level below us, whispering at the edge of the dancefloor. Nadine and I were alone on the balcony.

"Nad," I coughed. "What the hell is going on?"

She began pacing. She wouldn't look me in the eye, and her whole body shook. She mumbled under her breath, but I couldn't make out what she was saying.

"Nadine!" I snapped, trying to get her attention.

She stopped pacing and turned to me. Her expression shifted suddenly. One moment it was dark and sent a shiver down my spine. The next her face fell, and concern was written all over it. She almost looked scared—of what, I wasn't sure.

"What. Happened?" I demanded.

"I-I don't know," she admitted in a shaky tone. "Talia said… she said some things, and I got really mad and I-I…"

I'd never heard Nadine stammer in this way, like something had really frightened her. She began pacing again. After a few moments, her eyes scanned the balcony as if looking for a solution. Her gaze fell upon an abandoned beer bottle one of Cody's friends had left sitting on the railing. She practically lunged for it and started chugging the damn thing.

I gaped. "Nad!"

I stumbled the few steps over to her and snatched the bottle from her hands. It sloshed over the front of her dress.

"Lucas!" she cried.

"What do you think you're doing?" I demanded. My mind raced a million miles per hour. I didn't know how to make sense of everything I'd just seen, let alone know how to feel about it. "You don't drink!"

"I just need to get out of my own head for a second." Nadine thrust her hands into her hair, tugging on the strands.

I grabbed for her wrists so she wouldn't hurt herself. "Stop it."

Her breath wavered, and her eyes got a distant look to them, like she wasn't seeing anything in front of her.

"Nad, look at me," I insisted. When she didn't, I shook her a little. "Look at me."

Finally, her gaze traveled to mine, and her features softened once again. "Lucas," she whispered breathlessly. "I'm sorry."

"Sorry?" I gaped.

Tears brimmed her eyes. "What else do you want me to say?"

I barely heard her over the music. "We need to talk," I insisted.

I took Nadine's elbow and led her down the long hall lined in red curtains and out of the club. She didn't resist, but she stepped away from me as soon as the door shut behind us and vanished. The silent basement hall seemed to stretch miles between us.

"Care to explain?" I tried to be gentle, but my voice came out harsh. It was like I was seeing a totally different person when I looked at Nadine.

"I don't know what came over me," Nadine said, sounding genuine. "Cody is an ass—no, worse than an ass. I don't even have a word for it. And I lost it!"

"Yeah, he was being a jerk," I agreed. "But you don't go threatening people with battle orbs for it!"

"I'm not talking about tonight," Nadine said. "I'm talking about… something else."

It was clear in the way she said it that it was a secret between the girls. I sensed it was something I didn't really want to ask about, and I didn't think Nadine would tell me anyway. Girl code and all that. I could make assumptions of my own.

"That's no excuse for putting yourself in danger," I told her.

"Danger?" she balked. "I could take Cody."

I cocked an eyebrow. "And all his friends? You could've gotten a battle orb to the face, or a curse cast upon you. And drinking? This isn't you."

Nadine's lips tightened. "No, Lucas. It *is* me. You just haven't seen this side of me before."

I stepped toward her. She seemed hesitant, but she let me run my fingers across her arm. "I know my Nad," I whispered. "She doesn't do violence."

"But *she* does," Nadine shot back.

I furrowed my brow. "What?"

"This curse!" Nadine cried. Tears began running down her face. "She's a part of me—the dark part that came out tonight. No matter what I do, I give in to her. When I'm faced with Chloe, or some asshole like Cody, I just… I can't control myself. Lucas, I don't know what to do!"

Hell if I did. Nadine stood in front of me, practically bawling, and all I could do was stand there. Half of me wanted to comfort her. The other half wanted to run in the other direction. I'd barely caught a glimpse of the darkness she spoke of tonight, and it terrified me. I hated to think of what she'd have done to Cody if I hadn't stopped her. She'd already left a mark deep enough for stitches.

Nadine shoved her hands into her hair again.

"Nad, stop!" I demanded. My fingers trembled as I reached out for her, but I only hesitated a second. I wrapped her in my arms, and she buried her face into my shoulder. "We'll figure this out and get rid of her. There has to be someone we can talk to about this."

"Who?" she asked in a muffled voice. "No one knows how to break this curse. I have to figure it out."

"And you will," I promised, running my fingers through her hair.

Nadine took a step back, her features going dark again. "*When?* Before or after I completely snap? I can't keep doing this. I just want it to be over! The only thing we can do is get rid of this curse. And if I can't do it, then I'll have to leave Octavia Falls."

My blood ran cold. I couldn't lose my Nadine. I couldn't.

And so I had to do everything in my power to make sure that didn't happen.

☾

I WAS FUMING when classes resumed on Monday. Nadine had scared the hell out of me, but when she broke down in my arms, I knew she was just as scared as I was—if not more. There *had* to be something we could do, but I had no answers. I wish I did. I wish I could protect her. What kind of boyfriend was I if I couldn't?

Between Nadine's freak-out and my investigation into Professor Daymond, I'd found myself crawling back into that dark hole I'd spent so much effort trying to get out of. Hopelessness settled in my gut. How could I protect Nadine? How could I prove Professor Daymond's guilt? How was I supposed to do a damn thing for this coven?

My mind raced through these problems on my way to breakfast that morning. I didn't want to eat, but I needed to get out of my room. As I was passing the large window opposite the grand staircase, I noticed three girls chatting nearby and laughing.

My eyes locked on the girl in the middle, and my rage flared. I curled my hands into fists and stomped up to her.

"This is your fault!" I snapped, my hands shaking at my sides.

I needed someone to blame. Chloe was a part of this, and she'd tormented my girlfriend one too many times. Maybe if she stayed away, Nadine could handle this curse easier.

Chloe chuckled, and the two girls beside her went silent. "Oh, no," she said flatly. "Did someone's hair fall out again?"

I got up in her face, but I didn't touch her. "Stay the hell away from my girlfriend."

Chloe smirked. "Come on, Lucas. I thought we were friends."

I scoffed. "We've never been friends. All you've ever done is use and manipulate me. I won't let you do that to Nadine."

"Did she send you here to tell me that?" Chloe fake-pouted. "Nadine can't handle me on her own anymore?"

"Nadine doesn't know," I said. "You need to figure your shit out, because Nadine isn't going anywhere. And if you even *try* to hurt her again, so help me, I will summon a reaper and deal with you myself."

Chloe's jaw dropped. I wasn't sure if she believed me or not, but she believed it enough that she went speechless.

Satisfied with her reaction, I turned and headed down the stairs to the cafeteria. I wish I could say I felt victorious, or that I'd done something to help Nadine, but I only felt sick. It was like the case with the missing boys all over again. There was nothing I could do to solve this.

I found Grant sitting at a table alone in the cafeteria. I went through the buffet line and added eggs, bacon, and a slice of toast to my plate, but the portion sizes were scarce. I'd be lucky if I managed to choke half of this down. Grant was eating slowly and staring down at a pile of open books in front of him when I sat.

"Tell me some good news," I groaned.

Grant spoke with a full mouth. "I'm making a vision board using old yearbooks."

I cocked an eyebrow.

Grant swallowed. "I gotta get in the right mindset if I'm going to claim the champion swim title this season. I'm going over stats from previous years, and pictures of previous winners. I'm going to win this season. I know it."

"Well, that is good news," I said.

Grant eyed me curiously as I took a bite of scrambled eggs. They tasted like Styrofoam, and I chewed slowly.

"Everything okay?" he asked. "This isn't still about Friday night, is it?"

"Kind of, yeah," I admitted.

"You just have to be there for Nadine right now," he said encouragingly.

Yeah, sure. I could be there for her. But it didn't fix her problems.

"I'm trying to be there for Talia, but I won't make a move until she's ready," Grant said.

"Have you even talked to her?" I asked skeptically.

"Yes, we *talked*." Grant sounded offended. "Well, I tried. She won't tell me much. But it's fine. I'm here to listen whenever she's ready."

"I *have* listened to Nadine," I said. "And I don't know what to make of any of it."

"Maybe you're thinking too hard," Grant offered.

"I can't stop," I practically snapped. It was nothing against Grant. I was just irritated. "I'm reaching my rope's end here. Nadine is cursed. Kids are disappearing. I still have no evidence against Professor Daymond."

Grant's shoulders fell. "Still nothing? You've been following him around for days!"

I gritted my teeth. "I know. But the guy's a fucking bore. When he isn't in class or in his office grading papers, he's in the halls tormenting students. Not exactly the proof I need."

"What about at home?" Grant questioned.

"Worse," I groaned. "He gets home every night after dark, pops a meal in the microwave, and goes to bed. He's scary lonely."

Grant's eyes went wide, and he lowered his voice. "Just like all the other serial killers you ever hear about on the news."

No freaking kidding.

"Doesn't matter," I said. "My article is useless without proof. The police won't believe me anyway."

I didn't think Nadine had quite understood me when I mentioned how the coven felt about witch hunts. Speaking out against Professor Daymond without proof was a serious offense. But I had to do *something*, or I was never getting my evidence.

"There's gotta be someone you can tell," Grant insisted.

"Who?" I asked. I had no one to turn to—not unless I wanted to break my word with the Bennetts and reveal their secret.

"I don't know," Grant sighed. "Someone who will listen."

I had no one, except for maybe—

I shot out of my chair. "I gotta go."

I abandoned my uneaten food hurried to Professor Carlisle's office. His door was closed when I arrived, so I knocked.

"Come in," his bright voice called.

I opened the door and stepped into the room. He was rearranging a stack of papers and fumbled when he looked up to see me in the doorway. A collection of empty potions vials tumbled across the desk. A few rolled off onto the floor, and his cat's hair bristled. I noticed the remnants of green liquid in the vials—his cancer potion.

"Lucas, what can I help you with?" he asked, straightening in his chair.

I glanced behind myself, but the room was empty. I closed the office door anyway, just in case someone overheard. "I know who killed the boys."

Professor Carlisle's face went paper white. "W-who do you suspect?"

I paced around the room. I couldn't sit with the array of emotions bubbling up inside of me. "It's Professor Daymond. I'm sure of it."

Carlisle's jaw dropped, though a bit of color had returned to his face. "Professor Daymond? What makes you think that?"

My hands curled into fists. "An anonymous tip," I said, leaving it at that.

Carlisle furrowed his brow. "And what did this anonymous tip say?"

I sighed and slowed my pacing. "I can't say, exactly. I have to protect my source."

"That's very admirable of you, but if I'm to help you as your advisor, I need to know the truth," he said. "What evidence do you have against Professor Daymond?"

I raked my fingers through my hair. "Nothing, really. Just… a story. But it *fits*."

Carlisle eyed me curiously, as if wondering what I was hiding. "You do understand what you're saying?"

"I know." I gritted my teeth. "It's not my intention to start a witch hunt —only to find the person who did this, and make sure they get what's coming to them."

Carlisle hesitated a moment, absorbing what I'd just said. "We can't publish this story without undeniable proof."

"But we have to stop him!" I burst. "We have to do everything we can to protect Travis Bennett."

Professor Carlisle raised a hand to stop me. He spoke calmly, an emotion I could barely comprehend right now. "I agree. But if we go public with this, Travis is in even more danger. Who's to say Professor Daymond won't accelerate his plans?"

My breath stalled. "You believe me, then? That Professor Daymond is the one behind this?"

Carlisle took a deep breath. I saw the skepticism in his features, but there was something else there—something I couldn't read. "I'm listening," he finally said. "I'm willing to explore all angles."

I breathed a sigh of relief. I'd half expected Carlisle to blow me off.

"What can we do?" I asked.

"I'm afraid there's little we can do," he replied. He sounded a little irritated.

"We can't sit around here doing nothing!" I cried. "Someone else could get hurt. I won't let that happen."

Carlisle snapped. He shot to his feet and shouted, "It's not your job to solve this case, Mister Taylor. Your job is to report the facts!"

I reeled back a step. I'd never seen him like that.

Carlisle caught the wide-eyed look on my face. He quickly composed himself and sat back down. "I apologize. I didn't mean to shout. It's my cancer advancing—makes me irritable. I just don't want to see you get hurt—like the other boys."

"Daymond won't touch me," I assured him. "I'm not like his other victims."

"Yes, but we can't let him know we're on to him," Carlisle replied. "If he is in fact behind this, you would be putting yourself at risk. Tell me what you know, and I'll take care of it."

"Really?" I finally felt like I could sit. I sank into the chair across from him.

Carlisle nodded. "I'm afraid you are getting too involved in this case. Perhaps you should take a step back."

The suggestion was like an arrow to my heart. "You're pulling me from the article?"

Carlisle sighed, a look of regret written across his features. "It's for your own safety. The more you dig into this, the more danger you're in."

I crossed my arms. "So you're saying even if I *could* prove it, you wouldn't publish the article anyway."

"If it would keep you out of harm's way, then yes," he admitted.

How dare he try to take this away from me! I couldn't just sit around waiting for someone else to arrest Professor Daymond. I knew too much —and I had to make sure everyone else knew it, too.

"Fine," I growled, shooting to my feet. "I don't need this article to prove who's behind this. I'll find my proof, and I'll make sure the Miri-amic Police Department takes care of this murderer."

I started out of the room, but Carlisle stopped me. "Be careful," he warned. "I can only do so much as your journalism advisor. I can't protect you out there. Men like Professor Daymond won't hesitate to harm you to protect themselves."

"Thanks for the warning," I said sarcastically. "But I think I can handle myself."

I stormed out of his office feeling like my magic was about to burst out of my palms. I quickened my pace and shoved my way through one of the back doors of the school before I could accidentally set off a battle orb inside.

The sky was overcast today, and the air bit at my face. I plopped down on an empty bench near the greenhouse and buried my face in my hands. Carlisle could try to protect me all he wanted, but this wasn't about me. It was about taking down Daymond so no one else got hurt. If I had to take the blow instead of another kid, I'd take it.

"Lucas?" Professor Warren's voice pulled me from my thoughts. I looked up to see him hurrying down the path, carrying a briefcase.

"Professor Warren," I greeted, though it came out colder than I intended.

"What are you doing?" He eyed me up and down. "You must be freezing."

I glanced down at myself and realized I'd forgotten a coat. I shrugged. "The cold doesn't bother me."

Professor Warren glanced to the door, like he was running late. He sighed and abandoned his previous obligation to sit beside me. "Lucas, what's going on?"

"Nothing," I lied.

Professor Warren shot me a sharp glare. "We've shared one too many conversations for me to buy that."

I huffed. I didn't want to tell him everything, so I settled with, "Professor Carlisle's kicking me off the newspaper."

"But it's done you so much good!" he cried.

I scoffed. "Tell Carlisle that."

"I just might," Professor Warren said, drawing himself up. "I've noticed a difference in you, now that you have a hobby. I'd hate to see you revert to old habits."

I frowned.

"Have you given any more thought to your major?" he asked.

I shook my head. That was the last thing on my mind right now. "General Studies, I guess."

"You should keep writing," he suggested.

"How?" I bit. "I have nothing to write about now."

"You don't need Professor Carlisle's permission to write," Professor Warren pointed out. "I know you carry the journal I gave you. Why don't you write something in there?"

I cocked an eyebrow. "Is that an assignment?"

"No, just a suggestion." Professor Warren stood. "As a writer, you can't take rejection too hard. You're going to be something great one day. I know it."

"You're not a Seer," I grumbled.

He smirked lightly. "I don't have to be. I just have to trust that you won't give up."

That was all he said before he turned around and hurried into the school. I watched him go, his words echoing in my mind. *You won't give up. You won't give up.*

Nadine had said something similar. *When you put your mind to something, you don't give up.*

I conjured my journal and a pen and flipped to an empty page. My pen scratched across the paper with fervor, as fast as I could come up with the words.

A dark and empty soul
Trapped in midnight shadows
Chained by thoughts he cannot see
Reaching for a door forever closed
No escape from this dark dungeon
Nothing more horrifying
But he'd be damned beyond the Abyss
If he ever gave up trying

The weight on my shoulders seemed to ease as I drew my pen away. I reread the words, feeling the heaviness permeate deep into my chest. Professor Warren and Nadine were both right. I *didn't* give up.

Carlisle's permission or not, I was going to protect this coven's children—the only way I knew how.

☾

"It's unfair," Nadine grumbled.

We sat in the Lounge on one of the big couches between classes. A supernatural drama played on TV, but I wasn't paying attention. I had my arm around Nadine, and she was snuggled up close. Neither of us had said anything for the last half hour. I think we both were enjoying the silence.

"What's unfair?" I asked.

"Professor Carlisle." Nadine shifted on the couch to look at me. "He can't kick you off the paper. Someone has to catch Daymond."

My shoulders fell. "He's the newspaper advisor. He can do whatever he wants with it."

Nadine frowned. "I know he *says* he's protecting you, but…"

I raised a curious eyebrow. "But what?"

"But I think you're smart and you know what you're doing. I think if anyone's going to catch Daymond, it's you."

"I will," I said with firm conviction. "I just have to pivot."

"Pivot?"

"I have some ideas…"

Nadine sat up straighter. "You do? Enlighten me."

I frowned. "You wouldn't like it."

"Tell me anyway."

I glanced around the Lounge, but there was hardly anyone in here this time of day. The closest group was sitting at a study table across the room. I leaned into Nadine to whisper lowly. "You know I've been following Daymond, but I'm ready to switch up my tactics."

Her eyes brightened with intrigue. It was the first ray of sunshine I'd seen from her since the club. It seemed talking about something else helped take her mind off her own problems.

"What are you going to do?" she asked.

"I realized Daymond might have an accomplice. I've decided to watch Travis, in case someone tries to hurt him."

Nadine's features fell. "That's great, but you can't protect him twenty-four-seven. You have class, and you have to eat and sleep."

"You're right. I *don't* have to protect him twenty-four-seven. Just at night, when Daymond's most likely to snatch him, just like the other two boys."

"What if he strikes during the day?" she asked.

I shook my head. I'd given this quite a bit of thought. "It doesn't match the M.O. You should know—you read tons of mystery novels."

"Yeah, but there are only two cases so far. What if some of the similarities are a fluke?"

"I don't think they are," I said. "Daymond's doing this for a reason, and he's already established a pattern."

Nadine sat up straighter, like she suddenly had an idea. "Take me with you."

My eyebrows shot up. "Take you with… Nad, this could get dangerous. If I catch Daymond in the act—"

"Then I'll be fine," she interrupted. "I want in on the action."

"But you're—" I cut off mid-sentence when I realized what I was about to say. *But you're sick.* That had never stopped her before.

"I appreciate that you care. But I can *help,*" she pleaded. "I'm sick of dealing with Chloe and my powers. I need a break from all that. Mystery is my thing. I might notice something you won't."

The tension in my shoulders eased. "I just don't want you getting hurt."

Nadine entwined her fingers in mine. "I'll be fine."

We held each other's gazed for several moments, and my insides melted. Damn it, how could I say no to this girl?

"You're going to come whether I say you can or not, aren't you?" I asked.

She smirked. "You know me well."

Nightfall arrived, and Nadine met me at a door near the back of the school. She strolled down the empty hallway wearing her hair tied tight in a bun at the nape of her neck, along with a black trench coat that tied around the waist.

"Why are you staring at me like that?" she asked.

I rearranged my features. "How was I looking at you?"

She narrowed her eyes. "Like you want me to take this off, but I'm not sure if it's because you hate it or you just want to undress me."

I smirked and grabbed her around the waist playfully, then pressed her up against the wall. My lips stopped a mere inch from hers. "Well, I don't hate it."

She smiled. "Too bad. I was hoping you might take it off."

Hunger for her burned deep in my belly. "That can be arranged."

I pressed my hips into hers, but I stopped when I felt something hard between us. "I'd say I'm happy to see you, but that's not me," I joked.

"No, silly. It's my night-vision binoculars." Nadine chuckled and pushed me away. She pulled them out of her pocket, along with a pile of other spy-like gear.

My eyes fell upon the lock-picking set. "You know you can unlock doors with your magic."

"Not if the lock is enchanted," she pointed out, before placing her things back in her large coat pockets. "I'm ready for anything."

"Okay, but at the first sight of danger, you're gone," I insisted.

She sighed. "I'll be fine. You worry too much."

"What are we worried about?" Grant's voice came down the hall.

Nadine and I looked up to see him and Talia making their way toward us. Talia's features soured when she spotted Nadine. Nadine had mentioned things were difficult between the two of them after what happened at the club.

Talia stopped in the hall and crossed her arms. She was dressed in black from head to toe, with her long brown hair tied into a high ponytail. "You didn't tell me *she'd* be here."

Grant's features fell. "I didn't realize it'd be a problem."

Talia opened her mouth to protest, but Nadine spoke first. "It will be fine. Won't it, Tal?"

"I might as well not come," Talia said bitterly. "You probably don't want me there, anyway."

"Stop avoiding me," Nadine pleaded. "I said I was sorry. Can't we just get along… for the guys?"

Talia hesitated, and her gaze flickered over to Grant. His eyes were bright and hopeful.

She sighed. "Fine, but I'm not coming for you. I'm coming for Grant."

Talia stepped between Nadine and me to get to the door. Grant hopped along happily behind her like a little puppy dog.

I raised my eyebrows at Nadine and lowered my voice. "Still no luck talking to her?"

Nadine frowned and shook her head. "Not yet, but she'll come around."

"I hope so," I told her as we stepped outside and into the cold.

We took Nadine's car into town and parked on a quiet street not far from the Bennetts' house. It was cold out at night, but most of the snow had melted.

"What are we looking for?" Talia asked.

"I'm looking for anything suspicious within a three-block radius of Travis Bennett's house," I told her. "If Travis is in danger, we have to catch Daymond before he can get to him."

"Do you think we'll find anything?" Grant asked.

My gut twisted. On the one hand, I wanted to catch the bastard. On the other, I hoped Travis wasn't a target. "I'm not sure," I admitted.

"Then let's get going," Talia said.

We all stayed quiet as we weaved through the streets. The sky darkened, and the air became colder the longer we walked. The streets were eerily silent.

Then I heard it—the sound of a voice coming from a nearby alleyway. Nadine's index finger immediately went to her lips, and the four of us crept forward.

My pulse quickened as we approached the dark alley. I glanced around and realized we were less than a block from Main Street. That put us right next to the Bennetts' house.

"The Bennetts live on this street," I said breathlessly. I hoped to the Goddess this wasn't related, but the way my heart pounded told me otherwise.

A wooden fence bordered the nearest backyard. I signaled everyone to be quiet and to follow me. We pressed ourselves against the fence and crept closer to the alleyway. I peeked my head around the corner, and my stomach dropped.

Two figures stood there, but hardly any light from the streets made it into the alley. All I saw were shadows, but they were both tall, with broad shoulders—obviously grown men. The shorter one had long hair tied into a ponytail at the base of his neck. I couldn't make out any unique features of the other man.

"Rumors are starting to spread," the taller man hissed. "We have to keep our circle of intel small, or we risk exposing our operation."

"It's only a few kids," the other guy argued.

My blood ran cold, and I turned to stone where I stood. The kids... they were talking about Caleb and Isaac. I *knew* Professor Daymond was working with an accomplice—and it looked like there might be more than one. I scrambled to conjure my phone and begin recording.

"Others will find out," the man snarled in a voice that sent shivers down my spine. "Cover this up, before it gets out of hand."

I witnessed something exchange hands—a wad of cash perhaps, but it was hard to tell through the darkness.

"I'll do my best," the guy with the ponytail promised. "You have nothing to worry about, Archie."

Archie?

It hit me, and my heart slammed against my rib cage. Archibald! The tall guy was Professor Daymond—and he was paying someone to cover up the murders!

I was about to jump out into the alleyway and grab the motherfucker. What I wouldn't give to pummel his murderous face in. But Nadine was peeking around the corner with me, her night vision binoculars to her face. She grabbed me before I could make a move.

"He's coming!" she hissed.

I'd gone so stone cold, I barely noticed Professor Daymond had turned and was headed straight in our direction. His accomplice walked in the opposite direction.

I struggled against Nadine's hold. Fury flared in my bones. "What are you doing? We have to confront him!"

"And get killed?" she snapped. "He teaches defensive magic. We don't stand a chance."

Grant tangled his fingers in my coat and dragged me down the street. He was a lot stronger than Nadine, but I still could've taken him if I wanted. But Nadine had a point. Daymond could fry all four of our asses in one go, and I wasn't going to let Nadine get hurt.

Against all my instincts, I followed my friends and ducked around the corner with them. The sound of a car door slammed, and Professor Daymond drove away.

My shoulders slumped, but my heart continued to hammer. "I can't believe we just let him get away."

"And what would beating him up do?" Talia challenged. "It wouldn't give you any more proof than you already have."

"You all heard him," I argued. "We're witnesses now."

"To a very ambiguous conversation," Nadine pointed out.

"They mentioned the kids!" I cried. I waved my phone at them. "I have him on record."

"Let me see that," Grant said. I gave him my phone, and he watched the recording. "It's too dark to see their faces, and Daymond didn't actually admit to anything. Believe me, I want him hanged as much as the next warlock, but you have to play the system. You can't go on hearsay—only concrete evidence."

I looked around the street corner to confirm Daymond was gone. The car that had been parked there had vanished. "Then let's go find our evidence."

I stomped toward the alleyway, determined to find something to prove that Daymond was tied to all this. My friends followed. I walked to the middle of the alleyway, where Daymond and his accomplice had been standing.

"What are we looking for?" Talia asked.

"Anything," I told her. I glanced around, but my stomach sank. I wasn't sure what I thought we might find. It wasn't like there was going to be a big sign advertising Daymond's transgressions.

"The smallest thing can help," Nadine pointed out. She started along the nearby fence, inspecting every board as if she might find something out of place. Talia turned to the other side of the alley and did the same.

"There's got to be something more," I insisted. My heartrate had slowed, but I was still on high alert. I spun around, looking for something—*anything*.

"Daymond's not going to get away with this," Grant assured me.

Before I could respond, Nadine piped up. "I found something!"

She snapped on a rubber glove—one of the many things she'd come prepared with—and picked up a small object I couldn't make out at first. Grant, Talia, and I closed in on her to get a better look.

"What is it?" Grant asked.

Nadine pinched it between her fingers and held it up. It was a glass vial, no more than two inches tall. "It's empty, but unusual… right?"

Nadine sounded uncertain, like she didn't know whether potion vials were typical litter here in Octavia Falls.

"Odd for sure," I mused.

Talia gasped. "What if Daymond is using a potion on the poor boys? Like a sedative?"

Nadine conjured an orb and held the vial up in front of it. She tilted it a few times, then dimmed her light. "It looks like it had something in it, but there's no more than a few drops left."

"I might be able to reverse-engineer what's left of it," Grant offered. "We could figure out what's in it."

"*If* it was Daymond's at all," Nadine added. "I never saw him drop anything."

"But this is right where he was standing," I pointed out. "It has to be his. This could help us figure out how he's taking the kids and leaving no trace."

"But why is this here tonight?" Nadine asked, challenging the mystery. "You don't think he took Travis, do you?"

My stomach sank at the possibility. "Goddess, I hope not."

"We should go to the police," Nadine suggested.

"And say what?" Grant challenged. *"Hey, we found a potion vial in an alleyway. Can you drug test it for us?"*

"Why not?" she asked.

"Because doing so is begging for a witch hunt," Grant pointed out. "We didn't hear a firm confession, and we have no idea what this is, or if it's even Daymond's. I say we get the results back and go from there."

Talia bit her lower lip. "I agree with Grant."

"This is tampering with evidence," Nadine argued.

I hated to disagree with her, but Grant was right. "We have to be sure about our evidence before turning it in."

Nadine's shoulders fell. "Fine. You guys know how the coven works better than I do."

She pulled a Zip-Lock bag out of her coat and dropped the vial into it, then handed it to Grant. "I hope you know what you're doing."

"I do," he promised. "It's just going to take a while to get the results. But when we do, we'll know for sure if this potion ties to the investigation."

Crash!

Something sounded from the end of the alleyway, and a cat hissed in the distance. Our gazes snapped up in unison to see a shadowed figure sprinting away from the scene. A pile of garbage cans rolled onto the gravel.

"Fuck," I growled, taking off in an instant.

"Lucas, wait!" Nadine cried from behind me, but I barely heard her.

I shot out onto the street but halted in my tracks. I glanced up and down the sidewalk, but the street was completely deserted. "Where'd he go?" I mumbled under my breath.

My friends caught up to me, and Nadine rounded in front of me. "What were you thinking? We don't know who that was! You could've gotten yourself hurt!"

"I think I know exactly who it was."

Grant cracked his knuckles as he looked up and down the street. "Professor Daymond, back for more?"

"I bet he realized he dropped whatever was in that vial," I said. "He was probably coming back to retrieve it."

"While that makes sense, we have no idea if that's true," Nadine pointed out.

My lips tightened. "I guess we'll know as soon as we run the test."

One way or another, I was catching this killer.

nadine

SIXTEEN

Investigating with Lucas had been a lot of fun, but I couldn't help but feel that we'd walked away with nothing. Sure, we overheard Daymond's conversation, but it didn't tell us anything we didn't already know.

At least Travis Bennett was still safe, according to Lucas, who had been in contact with his parents. But Lucas wasn't giving up just yet. He was still patrolling the neighborhood every chance he got, but I couldn't come as often as I would've liked. My body wouldn't allow for so many late nights in a row, and it showed.

I revisited that night over and over in my dreams, but instead of being surrounded by my friends, I was alone. The air was warm in my dream, and I wore all leather as I walked around the neighborhood.

Laughter echoed down a nearby alleyway, and I snuck closer. When I saw a figure standing there, red magic crackling in his hands, I stepped out of the shadows to face him. Shadows cast from his magic flickered off the evil man's face.

"You're not going to get away with this, Daymond," I snarled in a dark voice.

He threw his head back and laughed. "Oh, little girl, I already have."

Blue magic burst from my hands and sped straight toward him.

I woke with a start, never getting to witness the end of the dream. Rage rattled around inside of me, and my hands shook.

Today, Isa snuggled up closer to me, licking the side of my face for comfort. I was still as a statue, waiting for the fear to subside and my joints to loosen up.

"Nadine," Talia gasped. I'd startled her awake. "Are you okay?"

"Bad dream," I told her. "Go back to sleep."

"Too late," Talia said. "My alarm is set to go off in five minutes."

She swung her legs over the side of the bed and stood. "What have you been dreaming about? You've woken up like that more than once over the last week. Is it Chloe again?"

Talia must've forgotten she wasn't talking to me, because she sounded genuinely interested.

"Not Chloe," I admitted. "Honestly, she's left me alone lately, which is kind of a miracle. Maybe I scared her when I went all crazy in the club."

Talia had just pulled out a shirt for the day, and she froze as she held it up. "I thought we weren't going to mention that."

I sighed and shifted on the bed so I could see her. "We need to talk eventually."

She didn't look at me while she spoke. "I don't want to talk about it."

"But that's what friends do," I argued. "I stepped out of line, and I'm sorry. But there are things you're obviously keeping from me. And Cody—"

Talia held a hand up to stop me. "Trust me, Nadine. I don't want to hear it."

"But he's not good for you."

She whirled on me. "I think I can decide that for myself. And I'm working on it. Honestly. Cody and I are on a break right now while we both figure some things out."

I was relieved to hear it, but I didn't like the word *break*. It suggested they were going to get back together, and I didn't want Talia anywhere near him.

"I really do hope you know what you're doing," I nearly whispered. "I just want what's best for you."

She offered a shy smile, but it didn't meet her eyes. "You let me worry about that, and you can worry about your own stuff—like learning curse breaking or something."

Talia turned toward the bathroom to go get dressed, totally blowing me off. My breath grew hot. I wished she'd listen. She didn't even have to agree with me—just let me talk.

But I guess that hurt her too much, and I didn't want to hurt her.

And so I'd do exactly as she suggested. I was going to break some damn curses, because at least then I was doing something productive.

Well, at least I thought I could, until I realized I had no idea where Talia had stashed the box of cursed objects. She'd probably hidden it from me because she was afraid I was going to use them on Chloe again.

Fine. If Talia wanted to be petty like that, I'd make this a day of research.

It was Thursday, so I only had one class and had the rest of the day free. I took a long bath that morning, then headed to class with mere minutes to spare. I sat in the back of Thoughtography and kept my head down. The other girls in the class made a point every chance they got to tell me I didn't belong there, since I wasn't a Seer.

Well, screw them.

I was headed toward the library when an arm came out of nowhere and wrapped around my torso. My heart lurched, and I swung my elbow back. It sank into my assailant's gut.

"Where are you going, my beautiful mirac—oof!"

I gasped and whirled around. "Oh, Goddess, Lucas. I'm sorry! You snuck up on me."

He clutched his stomach and steadied himself against the wall. "I should've expected that," he gasped.

I reached out for him. "Are you going to be okay?"

He sucked a deep breath, then stood up straighter. His voice sounded mostly normal. "I'll be fine. I thought you'd at least recognize my voice."

I grimaced. "I was kind of in my own little world here. I'll make it up to you and you can do it again."

I turned away from him and started walking away slowly. I shot a glance backward and winked.

"Not going to work, Nad," he said with a hint of a smile. "Moment's ruined."

He stepped closer to me and took my hand, then reached up to brush my hair behind my ear. I closed my eyes, basking in his touch. When he was this close to me, all my problems seemed miles away. It felt as if I could deal with them in another life.

"What's going on in that pretty little head of yours?" he asked.

I glanced up and down the hall. A few people walked by, and I didn't want to talk where anyone could hear us. I dragged Lucas into an empty classroom that had the lights turned off. I could make out the shadows of desks and various animal skeletons mounted to the back wall from the light filtering in through the red curtains.

"I'm still researching curse breaking," I told him in a low voice. "I was just headed to the library to see if I could learn more. I'm making some progress, but I still have stuff to figure out."

He wrapped an arm around my waist. "Anything I can do to help?"

I pressed my forehead against his, and my heart pitter-pattered. My head spun every time I got this close to him. "You don't happen to have a magic wand that will rid us of all our problems, do you?"

Lucas smirked. "I've got *one* magic wand that might distract you."

I giggled, probably louder than was necessary. It really helped lighten the weight on my shoulders, though. "Do I get to see this magic wand?"

Lucas glanced around the empty classroom. "Right here?"

I bit my lower lip. Now that he'd mentioned it, I couldn't stop the possibilities from racing through my mind. My breath wavered as my eyes roamed over his strong arms, then down to the bulge in his pants. "I thought it was an invitation."

"There's no lock on the door," he pointed out.

"What about that one?" I gestured to another open doorway that led to a small room. I couldn't see much of it from where I stood.

"Professor Warren's office? Nadine, you are *naughty*," he practically sang.

I stepped closer to him, my lips just inches from his. My chest rose and fell rapidly as hormones raced through my bloodstream. "Do you want to be naughty with me?"

Before I knew it, his lips were on mine, and his hand had come around to cradle the back of my neck. My knees went weak as his tongue grazed along my lower lip.

He drew away, breathless. "You really think I could resist you?"

I scrunched up my nose. "Well, a girl's gotta test her theories."

I grabbed Lucas by the hand and dragged him into the office. The room was small and tidy, with a plush red chair that matched the drapes. I guided Lucas into it, then turned around to lock the door.

When I turned back, his gaze was locked on me. He had a totally starstruck look in his eyes. His hands gripped tightly to the armrests, and his legs were parted, as if inviting me forward.

I gladly obliged and sat myself straight in his lap. I took his face in mine and planted a passionate kiss on his lips. Lucas and I drew a deep breath in unison, like we were afraid we might never come up for air. He wrapped his arms around me. They roamed my body, until finally settling on my ass. Lucas squeezed tightly, then dragged me even closer to him.

I closed my eyes and moved my lips in sync with his, moaning each time his tongue slid inside my mouth. Fuck, I wanted more.

Lucas apparently did, too, because he reached up to push the fabric of my cardigan aside. I dropped my arms from his face and helped him strip the damn thing off. I never once stopped kissing him. To do so would be traitorous—a sin to my deepest desires and to Lucas himself.

His hands moved over my bare skin, then trailed under the straps of my camisole, caressing every inch of me. My heart hammered, as if trying to break out of my chest and offer itself to him. Lucas's hands moved to cup my breasts, and I inhaled a sharp breath.

To my dismay, he drew away. "Did I hurt you?"

"No," I said quickly. My eyes locked on his beautiful face, roaming over his gorgeous green eyes, and flickering down to his cupid's-bow lips. "I like it when you touch me there."

He smiled, but it wasn't the forced smile he often gave that never met his eyes. This was genuine and real, like he had no idea he was doing it at all. His eyes sparkled and turned my insides to mush.

"I like touching you there, too," he whispered.

"Then do it again," I said breathlessly just before my lips connected with his again. Lucas squeezed my breasts, and I shifted on his lap until I was straddling him. My hips moved over his hardness, and he moaned.

"Fuck, Lucas," I breathed as I came up for air. My eyes remained closed, like if I opened them the moment might dissolve in front of me. And I never wanted it to end. "I want you so bad. I wish you knew how much I love you."

Lucas stilled, and I finally dragged my eyes open. He was staring at me like he'd just turned into a block of ice. He didn't move an inch. "You… you love me?"

I blinked a few times. "I thought that was obvious."

"Well, you've only ever said it once," he pointed out.

I ran my hands down his arms, and I could feel his pulse beating rapidly against my fingers. "Really? Then let me make it very clear, Lucas Taylor. I love you."

His whole body shook when I said it. It took him a moment to gather his bearings, though his eyes never left mine. "I love you, too, Nad."

We kissed again, and passion swirled in my belly. The emotion grew, until it felt like the only way to keep it from overwhelming me was to cry. I couldn't explain it, but a tear fell down my cheek.

Lucas drew away in alarm and instinctually wiped the tear from my face. "Everything okay?"

"Perfect," I promised. "I love being with you. And I know there are ways to show you without the physical stuff, but this just feels so... raw and passionate. It's like I can show you how I feel without having to say a word—"

Lucas pressed an index finger to my lips to quiet me. "You don't have to explain it to me. I feel it, too. Words can never do it justice."

"I agree. Is it okay if I try something else?"

Lucas nodded, swallowing in anticipation.

I forced myself to crawl off of him, though it was agonizing. A cool draft filled the distance between us. I smirked as my hands reached for the button of his jeans. "I think I'd like to see that magic wand now."

Lucas chuckled at the lame joke.

"Hey, don't blame me," I teased. "You're the one who came up with it. Is this okay?"

Lucas tilted his head at me, like my question threw him off guard. He reached out to take my hands, forcing me to look him in the eyes. "Don't be scared. I want this as much as you do... maybe even more."

He dropped my hands and leaned back in the chair again, his legs open and inviting. "Do whatever you want to me."

I beamed at the offer. "Gladly."

My heart pummeled against my chest as I knelt in front of him. I undid the button on his jeans, then slid down his zipper. I couldn't stop my hand from shaking as I freed him from his trousers. This wasn't the first time I'd touched him there or witnessed his impressive length, but we'd been interrupted last time. My pulse quickened at the promise of exploring him fully this time.

I curled my hand around his hardness and began pumping it up and down. "You'll have to let me know how it feels. I'm not exactly an expert."

He tilted his head back against the chair, closing his eyes. His features were soft, as if he were in a state of pure bliss. "Could've fooled me. Ow."

I'd squeezed a little tighter and immediately regretted my mistake. I loosened my hold. "Better?"

"Much better," he sighed.

Lucas instructed me how to move my hands over him. He must've really liked what I was doing, because he eventually sat back and took it all in. He kept his eyes closed, but his hands roamed over me, feeling my arms and shoulders, before tangling into my hair. I was having enough fun pleasuring him that I didn't worry about what he was doing to me. I could only focus on one thing.

After a few minutes of drinking in the blissful expression on his face, I dared to increase my speed.

He gasped. "Nad…"

"You like that?" I asked proudly.

He responded only with a moan, which told me all I needed to know. I continued what I was doing, slowly increasing my speed until he gasped.

Lucas curled forward. He wrapped his arms tightly around me and placed his head on mine as moans of pleasure escaped his lips. I beamed as I felt him contract in my hand. A warm liquid touched me, and my smile grew even bigger.

Lucas drew away and slumped in his seat. He barely moved, like he was coming down from a euphoric high.

"I take it I'm a natural," I teased.

"Well, you are a witch," he joked with a laugh. "You should know how to handle a magic wand."

"I think I need more practice," I told him.

Lucas zipped his pants, then leaned over to the desk to grab a few tissues. "You will," he promised. "But now I'm concerned my talent doesn't measure up."

I cocked an eyebrow. "Your talent?"

He smiled. "I need practice, too."

I beamed. Was he suggesting a repeat of Valentine's Day?

"You have to get to class," I pointed out.

Lucas checked his phone, and his shoulders sagged. "Shit. At least let me make you a promise."

"Oh?" I asked curiously, raising an eyebrow. "What's that?"

"Next time, it's your turn."

☾

I STARTED for the library after Lucas and I parted. My head spun as I replayed what we'd done. Unfortunately, it was time to get back to work.

Talia and I had exhausted every resource we could find on Curse Breakers, but the literature focused mostly on lore and didn't talk much about technique. I hoped to find something today that I might've missed.

"Curse breaking...?" the librarian asked me thoughtfully. So far, I'd relied on the computer system to lead me to resources. Maybe the librarian knew about something that hadn't shown up in the computer.

"Yes, curse breaking theory, if possible," I said. I glanced down to see the label on her desk read *Rosemary*.

She pressed her lips together. "And this is for a class?"

"Yes, Magical Theory," I lied. "I thought it'd be an interesting subject matter."

"Interesting for sure," she agreed in a soft tone. "But very little is known on the subject, due to the rare nature of Curse Breakers. You know the last Curse Breaker died forty years ago?"

She obviously didn't know I was that man's granddaughter. I didn't need the reminder.

"Yes," I said with a fake smile.

"Let me see what I can find," she offered. Rosemary pressed her fingers to her temples and closed her eyes. She didn't make a noise, and she was as still as a statue. I wondered if she'd gone into some sort of trance.

I glanced around the quiet library. Tall mahogany bookshelves lined the walls, and a chandelier lit by candles hung from above us. A large staircase led to a second level, carved intricately like the woodwork in the rest of the mansion. The only students I spotted were seated at study tables on the far end of the room, but none of them paid attention to the librarian. Finally, she dropped her hands and took a deep breath as she opened her eyes.

"What just happened?" I asked curiously.

"Oh, I'm sorry," she said kindly, pushing her cat-eye glasses up her nose. "I should have explained. I'm a Mentalist with a photographic memory—when it comes to written texts, at least. I know every book the library has on every subject. I believe I may know of one that can help you. Follow me."

Rosemary led me up the stairs and around the balcony. She stopped at a row of shelves in the corner that appeared like they hadn't been touched in ages. They were all covered in a thick layer of dust.

Her finger hovered over the spines, and her eyes scanned the shelves. She stopped at shoulder level and tilted her head. "Huh, that's weird."

"What is?" I asked.

"It's missing… I don't recall this book being checked out," she said, more to herself than to me.

"Is something wrong?" a woman's voice came from behind us. The two of us turned to see Verla strolling down the aisle, a pile of books in her arms.

Odin waddled beside her and sneezed at the dust. Isa wasn't here to hiss at him, since she'd run off with Gus somewhere earlier today.

"Headmistress," Rosemary greeted kindly, nodding toward her. "Just a misplaced book, I'm afraid."

Verla's gaze traveled over the spines, and something seemed to click. She realized almost immediately what section we were in. "This is… for a school project?"

I nodded, though my guts twisted like I'd been caught doing something wrong. "For Magical Theory."

Verla narrowed her gaze at me. It was subtle, but enough that I noticed suspicion in her eyes. "Why don't you come to my office? I might have something that can help you."

"Really?" I asked, sounding a little too enthusiastic for a simple paper. I turned to Rosemary. "I guess I won't need your help after all. Thanks for trying, though. And I hope you find the missing book."

"Yes, me, too," she said, sounding awfully bothered by it.

Verla gestured to me, and I followed her to her office. She didn't say anything until the two of us were inside. The door swung shut behind me, and she turned toward me.

"Do you want to tell me the truth?" she asked pointedly.

My mouth went dry, and I spoke slowly. "The truth about what?"

"About why you were in the curse breaking section," she stated simply. She didn't come out and accuse me of anything.

"I…" I opened my mouth, but the excuses fell flat on my tongue. There were tons of explanations I could give—some true and some not—that were easily believable. I wasn't sure which one to go with first.

She sat behind her desk. A huge pile of books sat upon it, and she had to push them aside to see me. Verla gestured to the chair across from her, inviting me to sit. "Is this about your family curse?"

"No," I answered automatically, though I didn't know why. It almost felt like I was in trouble, and I was covering my ass. And now I was on to improvising…

"Partially," I admitted.

Verla shook her head regrettably. "I've actually wanted to talk to you about this for a while. I lost your mother to this curse."

For a second, I thought she meant my mother had died because of it, but that wasn't right. This curse had nothing to do with my parents' death. The blame for that fell entirely on the faulty brakes in their car.

"You mean how she left Octavia Falls?" I asked.

Verla nodded. "Yes. I've considered every loophole, and I'm afraid there isn't one. I thought with more time, I might be able to help, but—"

"Chloe and I will figure it out before her ceremony," I said. I didn't want Verla worrying. "But that's not the only curse I have to deal with."

I didn't mean to say it. I'd only meant to redirect the conversation.

Verla's spine straightened. "Another curse? What happened?"

I chewed my lower lip. I couldn't exactly back out now. "Have you ever heard of the Reaper's Shadow curse?"

Verla began to shake her head, but she paused, like she'd realized something. She began shuffling through the stack of books on her desk and grabbed a thick one that seemed newer than the others. She opened to a page near the back of the book and began frantically thumbing through the pages.

Finally, she stopped, her eyes scanning the words. "Samael Davis," she whispered breathlessly. "The son of a Reaper's Apprentice who brutally murdered his mother in cold blood. The incident cast a ripple effect, a curse upon all future mates of the Reaper's Apprentice—for no one could ever love the shadow of a reaper."

Verla's breath wavered as she lifted her gaze to mine.

I clicked my tongue. "That's the one."

"How could I not have realized this before?" she asked herself. "You and Lucas…"

Dear Goddess, don't tell me this was going to turn into a lecture on sex.

"No," I said quickly. "We haven't. But there has to be a way to break the curse."

"Not without a Curse Breaker," she warned.

She sounded afraid, like it wasn't even a possibility—like she didn't know a thing about me. Strange, since I swore she'd caught on to something the last time we spoke. I didn't dare say a thing about my true abilities, not unless I knew for sure I couldn't hide it from her any longer. I hadn't told *anyone* but those who were at my Evoking Ceremony. I couldn't start now, even though I trusted Verla. I knew the moment I caved, I'd run off and tell Amy and Mandy, too—then who else would find out?

"The Reaper's Shadow curse hasn't touched you yet, has it?" Verla demanded.

I shook my head. "We're being careful. But there has to be *something*."

"The only way to avoid curses these days is to run away from them," Verla insisted.

I crossed my arms. "I refuse to believe that. I'm not a coward."

She looked at me incredulously. "It is not cowardly to save yourself! You must have some sense of self-preservation."

Sure, I did. But I also had a chance to break these curses, if I figured out how.

She sighed. "I suggest you reconsider your relationship with Lucas."

I pursed my lips. "That's not really your choice to make."

"I'm saying this because I *care*," she insisted. "I don't want to see you hurt… like your parents."

My chest compressed. "That's not fair."

Damn, did she know how to hit me where it hurt. I wanted to storm out of the room, but my hands gripped the armrests of the chair. It was hard to breathe.

"I have no intention of hurting you," she said gently. "I just couldn't bear to see a curse take you like my…"

She trailed off, like she was afraid she'd said too much. At first, I thought she was about to mention my mom again, but her eyes were filled with the pain of something far more recent.

I softened my tone. "Are you talking about your sister? I didn't know she was cursed."

Verla rearranged her features. "Well, it was never confirmed, but what she did… it wasn't her."

"You loved her a lot," I remarked. It was evident in the faraway look in her eyes and the soft, distant tone she used.

Verla sighed, finally looking at me again. "Of course I loved her. She was my twin sister, and I miss her very dearly."

Verla was incredibly easy to read when she spoke of her sister. It was almost as if I felt her heartbreak as my own.

"You don't think she deserved what the coven did to her," I stated. It wasn't a question.

Verla shook her head, looking like she was choking back tears. "No, she did not."

I hadn't come here to fight with Verla or to make her upset. I quickly changed the subject to distract her. "You said you had something that could help me with curse breaking?"

Verla cleared her throat and began looking through the stack of books on her desk. "I have a book that can help explain the theory, but again, it's useless without a Curse Breaker."

My heart swelled with hope, though I tried to encourage her in a way that wouldn't give me away. "Maybe if I knew the theory, I could make sense of it all."

Verla grabbed a book that looked a lot like the ones on the shelf in the library—leather-bound and very old. She flipped it open and thumbed through a couple of pages until she found what she was looking for. She turned it toward me and stabbed the page with her finger. "This is the chapter you want."

I scanned the page, but the text was really small, and there was a lot to read. "What does it say, exactly?"

"Well, to break a curse on a family, such as the curse over yours, you would have to gather each affected individual together," she said. "The curse could only be broken through cooperation, and by a Curse Breaker, which again—"

"I know," I interrupted. "Doesn't exist."

I grabbed the book and leaned back in my chair, reading over the passages as fast as I could. Grammy had made it sound like curse breaking could be performed individually, but this book said the opposite. Grammy must've been mistaken. Then again, how many family curses had Grampy broken before he was killed at such a young age? Probably none.

How the hell was I supposed to convince Chloe to work with me on this? The answer was obvious.

I had to reveal to her my true power.

SEVENTEEN

ooling around with Nadine had quickly become one of my favorite hobbies since the semester started, but there was far more to our relationship than the physical stuff, and I wanted her to know it. The following Wednesday, I met up with her in the Main Foyer for lunch, a bouquet of red roses in my hands.

Nadine sat in front of the fireplace and turned when she heard me approach. Her jaw dropped when she saw them. She couldn't look away. "What's the special occasion?"

I pressed my nose into them, inhaling the floral scent that reminded me of her. "There's no special occasion. I just saw them and thought you might like them."

Truth was, I'd gone to town earlier to get them. A card was pinned to the bouquet, with a poem inside I'd written especially for her.

Nadine took the flowers in both hands and inhaled a deep breath. "I love them."

I took her hand and helped her stand, before wrapping an arm around her. "And I love you."

She blushed, then pressed a kiss to my lips. I'd never get sick of telling her I loved her—especially when she kissed me like that every time I mentioned it.

"Ready for lunch?" I asked her.

"Yes." She took my hand, and we started toward the cafeteria. "Also, Grammy invited us over for dinner, if that's okay."

"Not a problem," I told her. I hadn't seen Helena in a while, and I'd been meaning to thank her for the matus tea she made me.

That evening, Nadine and I arrived at Helena's house just after six o'clock. Nadine had let me drive, and I rushed out of the driver's side to open her door.

"Thanks," she blushed. "But I can really get the door myself."

"It's called chivalry, Nad," I reminded her. I didn't do it because I thought she was incapable. I helped to show her I cared.

Isa jumped out of the car and onto the sidewalk. Nadine barely noticed her as she smiled up at me. "Thank you."

I shrugged. "What are boyfriends for?"

She smirked. "I can think of a couple of things."

I rolled my eyes. "Let's keep it civil for Helena."

Nadine laughed as we walked hand-in-hand up the sidewalk. "You think Grammy's going to care about a few jokes? She's the one who gave me my first condoms."

I chuckled under my breath. "Your grandma can be quite... unpredictable at times."

"Depends on the situation," Nadine said with a shrug. "I'll bet you anything we're having brisket tonight."

My mouth was already watering.

Helena greeted us kindly at the door, offering us each a hug as we stepped into the hallway. "Nadine. Lucas," she sang. "I'm so glad you could make it. It's been a while."

"Well, you know how college goes," I said. "It's easy to lose track of time. Thank you, by the way, for the matus tea."

Her eyes brightened. "Oh, that reminds me. I have a fresh batch I want you to take with you when you go."

"That really won't be necessary," I protested, but she wouldn't take no for an answer.

"At least let me pay you," I insisted.

"Nonsense," she said with a wave of her hand. "You're family now."

Her words struck me harder than they should've, and my chest suddenly softened. Helena had always been like the grandmother I never had, but I didn't realize she'd thought of me in the same way. It was comforting in a way I hadn't felt in a long time.

"Anyway," Helena said, clapping her hands together. "Food is on the table."

She led us into the dining room, where a whole spread filled the table. It looked like Thanksgiving dinner, though the table was only set for three. A huge brisket that could've fed a dozen people was laid out in the middle of the table, along with roasted potatoes, squash, dinner rolls, and a veggie tray. She must've spent all day preparing the meal. Her cat sat in a chair, peeking over the table with longing eyes.

"Wow, Grammy," Nadine breathed as she sat. "It looks delicious. Are you sure there's no special occasion, because you guys have been spoiling me today."

"Spoiling you?" Helena asked as she took the head of the table. She crossed her hands together and rested her chin on them. "What has Lucas been up to?"

Nadine told Helena about the flowers, and she went on to ask other questions about our relationship as the three of us dug into the delicious meal. It didn't seem like she was prying, but was more or less making conversation. Though she kept throwing glances my way, as if she was wary of something. I barely got a word in, because I couldn't keep shoving mouth-watering, tender brisket in my face.

Finally, Helena broke the facade, and I realized exactly why she'd been giving me strange looks. "You two are being careful about the Reaper's Shadow curse, aren't you?"

I wasn't sure how Helena knew, considering most people in the coven hadn't heard about it. I figured Nadine had told her.

Nadine buried her face in her hands. "Goddess, Grammy. Are you asking if we're having sex?"

"Well, condoms don't save you from curses," Helena pointed out.

I'd gone completely still. Despite how much I'd eaten, my stomach felt hollow. It wasn't like I *was* screwing her granddaughter, but that still wasn't anything you wanted to talk about at the dinner table.

"No, Grammy," Nadine finally said, dropping her hands. "Lucas and I are not having sex. You don't have to worry about the curse."

"Well, until you find a way to break it—" she started.

"We will," Nadine cut in. She was obviously uncomfortable, but she didn't let it show in her tone. "But until then, you're going to have to trust us."

Helena didn't seem to expect that answer, because she gaped for a moment before composing herself. "I'm glad you have it handled. I would like to help, though."

Nadine tilted her head. "Help how?"

"I spoke to Talia—"

Nadine groaned.

Helena shot her a sharp glance. "I didn't go out of my way to inquire about your life. I ran into her while shopping. Anyway, she said you hadn't been able to break any of the cursed objects yet. I thought maybe we could try with something else."

Helena stood and turned to the hutch behind her. She opened one of the top drawers and pulled out a pearl necklace. "This curse is simple—by far the simplest one I've found."

Nadine took it from her and eyed it from every angle. "Where did you get it?"

"A friend sold it to me," Helena said. "Said it had been nothing but trouble in her family for generations. She wanted to get rid of it, and I was more than happy to do that for her."

"What's the curse?" Nadine asked. "I can feel some sort of magic in it, but just barely."

"It's a curse of bad luck," Helena explained. "But it's subtle, so much that the wearer may not even realize it's cursed. You might trip and break your shoe, but you won't be rushing to the hospital with a broken leg."

Nadine straightened, looking more confident the longer she inspected the necklace. "It's worth a shot."

Helena smiled proudly and placed a glass of water in front of Nadine. I hadn't seen Nadine try to break a curse before, though she'd been working on it all semester. Killing that monster was the closest I'd seen, and the closest she'd come.

Nadine noticed me eyeing her and offered to explain. "It works by drawing out the magic and transforming the intention. I can't change dark magic to light, but I can change how it behaves. The theory says I can change this bad luck into poison, which is why I need the water to transfer it into."

I narrowed my eyes in thought. "Those are very different things, though."

"Well, yeah," she said simply. "That's the idea—to transform the magic."

"Right, but the magic required to poison water would be much more than a minor bad luck curse," I pointed out.

Nadine and Helena exchanged a glance, but it was Nadine who spoke. "You're saying I've been trying too hard, pushing the magic beyond its limits?"

I shrugged. I wasn't really sure *what* I was saying. I only wanted to help. "It could be why it hasn't worked yet."

"But her grandfather..." Helena started thoughtfully, though she didn't finish.

"I think Lucas has a point." Nadine stared down at the glass of water. "When I killed that monster—"

"What monster?" Helena gasped.

Nadine winced. "Oh, right. Kind of forgot to mention that. Some jerk at school summoned a monster, but we handled it."

Helena didn't seem pleased, but she let Nadine continue.

"When I killed the monster, I focused its magic on death and pain, and that's what killed the tree," Nadine mused as she stared down at the glass of water. "That magic was comparable to the monster, because it was already trying to hurt us. So if poison is too strong... then I have to think of something else."

Nadine pressed her lips together. Finally, she perked up and began spooning another pile of potatoes onto her plate.

"Still hungry?" I teased.

She shot me a smirk from across the table. "Famished," she deadpanned, before turning serious again. "No, I just want to test the theory."

Nadine clutched the pearls in one hand, while the other hovered over the pile of potatoes on her plate. She closed her eyes, and her eyebrows knitted in concentration. Her eyelids fluttered, and she winced slightly. I straightened in my chair, ready to jump across the table and snatch the pearls from her fingers if I had to, but her features quickly returned to normal.

Helena and I watched intently. Neither of us muttered a word. I wasn't even sure we breathed.

Then, before my very eyes, the potatoes began to dry up, withering until they cracked. Mold sprouted over top of them and grew into a thin, fuzzy layer.

I held my breath, but Nadine didn't move, even moments after the mold had stopped growing. Finally, she let out a breath and opened her eyes. They widened as she stared down at the potatoes.

"Goddess," Nadine breathed. "I-I think I did it. I broke a curse!"

"I'm so proud of you!" Helena shot out of her chair and leaned down to pull Nadine into a tight hug.

I reached across the table to squeeze her hand. "This is great. What'd you do differently this time?"

Nadine looked amazed, like she couldn't believe it. "I thought about what might be comparable to bad luck. Then I thought it'd be unlucky if all the food on the table turned bad. And I had my answer! I transformed the bad luck into rot."

My heart swelled with pride for her, but it was made ten times better by the look on her face. She seemed so relieved, like a huge weight had just been lifted from her shoulders.

"This is fantastic," Helena said. "You remind me so much of your Grampy the first time he broke a curse."

Nadine beamed. "Well, yeah. I'm a badass. I just broke a curse. Who else in the coven can do that?"

I chuckled lightly as I watched her, admiring the smile on her face and the brightness of her eyes.

"Take that, pearl necklace," Nadine teased. She lifted the necklace and secured it around her throat. "I think I'll wear it as a badge of honor."

"Go ahead," Helena said brightly. "You've earned it."

Nadine leaned over to hug her grandmother. "Thank you for all your help, Grammy. What curse can I break next?"

"We've made progress," Helena reminded her, "but you should take time to rest. Let me make you up a dish to take back to school with you. And I'll get you that tea, Lucas."

Helena stood to go to the kitchen, and Nadine turned to me. "Holy shit. I did it! I was starting to think I never would."

I couldn't take my eyes off her. "I knew you would."

She tilted her head at me, brow furrowed. "How could you know that?"

"Because you're my little miracle. You can do anything."

She smiled, but it quickly faded.

"What?" I asked in alarm.

"I just hope you're right," she said. "This was a simple curse, so it was easy to break. I just hope I can have your confidence when I finally learn how to break the curse on me."

☾

NADINE'S PROGRESS should've thrilled me, but what she'd said about her own curse had me rattled. Chloe's ceremony was only a few weeks away. If Nadine didn't break the curse by then, she'd have to leave Octavia Falls. And this wasn't some simple cursed necklace. This was complicated—a curse cast by a murderer. You didn't reverse that kind of thing over dinner.

If she leaves, I'll go with, I decided.

Until I remembered I was on a mission to put a murderer behind bars. Fuck, this wasn't going to be easy.

I was on my way to class on Friday after a meeting with Professor Warren when I saw Grant heading through the door to the pool. I quickly caught up with him.

Grant stopped outside the locker room when he heard his name. "Hey, man. What's up? How'd your meeting go?"

"I finally declared a major," I announced.

"That's great!" Grant said. "What'd you choose?"

"Journalism," I told him.

"Good for you. You'll do great."

I glanced around the pool. There were only a few people swimming laps, but I lowered my voice anyway. "Did you learn anything about the potion we found in the alleyway?"

"Amy and I finished the analysis this morning." Grant's shoulders sagged, and I knew it wasn't good news. "It was just a healing potion. We don't think it was tied to the boys."

I frowned, but I was far less disappointed than I thought I'd be. Part of me sensed it was nothing more than a coincidence. I wasn't sure what kind of answer I'd been hoping for, but I realized Grant had given me the answer I expected.

I clapped him on the shoulder. "Thanks for trying."

"I'm sorry," he replied genuinely. "I want to get proof as much as you do, but this wasn't it."

"We'll find it," I said.

Grant turned toward the locker room, and I left the pool. I couldn't lie and say I wasn't disappointed we'd found no concrete evidence, but I wasn't going to let myself wallow in it. Things got bad when I did that, so I wouldn't even let myself go there.

I passed by a study alcove and ducked into it to kill some time before class. I conjured my journal and started scribbling in it. Professor Warren had pushed me toward gratitude last semester, and I'd found it actually helped. I tried to write down a thing or two whenever I felt myself slipping.

My list started with small things, like how I had a bed to sleep in and warm meals three times a day. Then more and more things started coming to me, until I'd filled the whole page.

I'm grateful Travis Bennett is still alive.

I'd just placed the period at the end of the word when nausea hit. I knew what that meant, but I thought—why not embrace it, at least *try* to be grateful for my gift? I closed my eyes and rested my head on the back of the chair.

"*I should've tried harder,*" the voice said. I didn't know what it meant, as there was no context, but the thought felt sad, like I wanted to cry just hearing it. And yet the nausea seemed to pass instantly, as if it'd never been there in the first place.

I let the thought sink in for a few moments, then scribbled it on a piece of paper and tore the page from the notebook. I couldn't exactly light a fire in the middle of the school building, so I'd taken to tearing up the notes instead. I shredded it into little tiny pieces, until the words couldn't be read, and no one would be able to piece the paper back together.

Then I stood, took a deep breath, and walked over to the garbage can nearby. "You did the best you could with the time you had," I whispered, then let the pieces of paper flutter into the garbage can.

A smile touched my lips as I stood there, just taking in the moment. That thought had been so easy to deal with. And it'd been *sad*.

I was finally starting to feel like I had a hold on my gift.

I didn't have a whole lot of time to think about it, because I had to get to class. I hurried off to Crystal Studies, but I was one of the last ones there. All the desks in the back row had been taken, so I found an empty seat near the middle of the room. The class was small, but it was far from my favorite, considering three of the Tarantulas were in this class with me. Ryan and his buddies sat in the corner, challenging each other to a burping contest.

Professor Poppy stood at the front of the room and waited until everyone quieted. She was an older lady who wore all types of crystal jewelry around her arms and neck. It was so much that she jingled when she walked. Her silver hair was piled into a tight bun at the top of her head.

"By now, you should have a firm grasp on the names and uses of the crystals we've studied this semester," Professor Poppy said. "Today, we'll be learning how to apply your knowledge to crystal grids."

She held up a round piece of wood that had been carved with repeating, overlapping circles that looked like flowers.

"This is a flower of life crystal grid," Professor Poppy explained. "The grid uses a pattern of sacred geometry that will amplify the power of your crystals and help you set powerful intentions during manifestation rituals. By manifesting, I simply mean drawing your desires into your life."

She set the grid on the table in front of her and projected her workspace onto the screen at the front of the room. She smudged sage over the area while she spoke. "Crystal grids themselves do not contain magic. They do, however, assist in manifesting your desires, combined with the power of crystals, how you arrange them on the grid, and the power of your intention."

She gathered various crystals and arranged them in a specific pattern over the grid. "I have chosen these crystals to align with the specific intention of healing, but your grid will look different depending on what you wish to manifest and the stones that speak to you. First, I'm lining the outer edge with fluorite, to stabilize my energy fields. Next, I've chosen rose quartz and alexandrite for healing, as well as turquoise for emotional balance. Finally, we add a quartz crystal point to activate our intention."

The quartz crystal was larger than the others and stood tall in the center. Professor Poppy took another quartz crystal in her hand, but it was longer and pointed. She began outlining the grid, touching the quartz to each crystal. "The last step is to focus on the energy of your intention and charge the crystals with it. We touch each crystal to combine their energy into one."

Professor Poppy finished, then began walking up and down the rows. She conjured small drawstring bags and handed one to each student, along with a piece of fabric printed with the same crystal grid she'd used for demonstration. "Today, you will receive your crystal grid, along with a collection of crystals that I've cleansed under the full moon. You do not have to use all the crystals in your bag. Choose the ones that feel right for you, and experiment with them. Explore different intentions that you might set through this ritual, but be open to anything. Next week, we will write out our intentions and place them beneath the quartz point. Each of you will be responsible for laying out your own crystal grid in your dorms and leaving it sit for a month, where you can revisit your intention daily to amplify your energy. At the end of the semester, you will write a paper discussing your experience with this ritual. Some of you will manifest your desires in that time. Others may not, but keep in mind that this is not a competition."

A girl at the front of the room raised her hand. "What can we use crystal grids to manifest?"

"Anything your heart desires, my dear," Professor Poppy said.

Ryan elbowed Nolan and whispered loudly. "I know what I'm going to manifest."

He made a crude gesture, and Nolan punched him in the shoulder. Of *course* Ryan was going to try using magic to make his dick bigger.

Professor Poppy frowned when she reached him and handed him his crystal grid. "I'm afraid no magic can help you there, Mister Greyson. I suggest starting with something a little more realistic."

Ryan slumped in his chair, and a few girls across the room laughed. He shot a glance at them. "It's a little out of this world to begin with."

The girls giggled harder, but in a way that suggested they were falling for his charm. *Gross.*

"You may begin," Professor Poppy said.

I laid my crystal grid over my desk and emptied the bag of crystals beside it. I inspected each one, trying to recall their names and uses. I knew most of them, but others weren't as obvious. I began laying the crystals out on the grid.

I thought about what intention I might set for the project. The first thing that came to mind was to help Nadine—whether it was to help her into remission or help her break her family curse—but Professor Poppy had told us earlier this year that crystal magic didn't work that way. For these crystals to help Nadine, she'd have to make her own crystal grid.

Maybe there was a way to use the crystals to protect Travis Bennett… If I could use them to amplify my intuition, maybe I'd finally find the proof I needed to put Professor Daymond behind bars—

"What the hell, Nolan?" Ryan sneered.

I looked up to see that Ryan and his buddies hadn't even touched the supplies Professor Poppy had handed out. Figures, considering they never took this class serious in the first place. All they did was screw around.

Nolan laughed and held up a drawing I would've liked to never see. "It's life size!"

The third Tarantula, Corbin, threw his head back in hysterical laughter.

"Maybe for *you*," Ryan snapped. He reached for the drawing, but Nolan held it out of his reach.

"Don't ruin it," Nolan laughed. "We can make posters!"

"Like hell," Ryan growled. He twitched his hand, a gesture that I thought was meant to snatch the drawing from Nolan's hand using telekinesis, but it didn't work.

Ryan glanced down to his fingers in shock, then tried again. Nothing happened. Ryan's nostrils flared. He obviously wasn't kidding around any longer.

"What the fuck did you do!?" Ryan demanded. He shot to his feet, and the whole class quieted.

"Mister Greyson," Professor Poppy warned. "I'm going to have to ask you to sit down."

Ryan twisted his hands around like he was trying to perform magic. "Something's not right! You slipped something in my lunch, didn't you?"

Corbin practically cowered in his seat at the accusation. He scoffed. "If I were going to prank anyone, it'd be Finn, and you know as well as I do that you'd be the mastermind."

"Then it was you," Ryan accused Nolan.

Nolan stood until he was just a few inches away from Ryan. "You might want to shut your mouth before I slam a battle orb into it. I didn't do anything."

"You think I'm scared of one of your battle orbs?" Ryan laughed. "Even with this little prank, I could fight you."

"You wanna bet?" Nolan lifted his hand, but nothing more than a few sparks came out. His features fell. "What the hell!?"

Ryan whirled on Corbin, like he was the one to blame. Before he could accuse him of anything, Corbin held his hands up and tested his magic. A few orbs floated up out of his palm, but they fizzled out quickly.

"My magic isn't working, either!" he cried. Corbin shot an angry glance around the room, as if the culprit was nearby.

All I could do was watch. My mind tried to calculate what was happening, but I didn't know what might cause this.

"Boys. Boys!" Professor Poppy tried to get their attention. "I'm going to recommend you visit Headmistress Verla to sort this out."

None of them heard her. They started yelling and tossing accusations around the room. A few guys in the front row stood and tried to threaten them with magic, but theirs didn't work, either.

Worry knotted in my gut. James had said weeks ago there was some sort of curse on the school affecting people's magic, but I'd written it off. Yet I'd seen it time and time again—first with Professor Warren and Professor Loren last semester, then with Daymond in the hall weeks ago, and that day Amy was sick. It seemed to be spreading.

I tested my magic—just a small orb in the palm of my hand. It worked, no issues. But Ryan caught sight of me and apparently thought I was a threat. He lunged, and I saw him coming with a mere moment to spare. Heart racing, I jumped from my chair and knocked it over. My crystals scattered across the floor. Ryan tripped over someone else's foot and crashed to the ground. Everyone was shouting now that I couldn't make out anything.

I wasn't sure who threw the first punch, but before I knew it, the whole classroom had broken out into a warzone. Half the class seemed to still have their magic, because battle orbs whizzed above my head, and shields shimmered around different students. I threw up my own shield and planted myself in front of a group of three girls who cowered in their desks. Apparently, their magic wasn't doing so hot, either.

A battle orb landed against my shield and exploded. My shield magic wavered, but I pushed more energy into it, and it held.

"Go!" I shouted to the girls.

They practically whimpered as they scrambled out of the room. Professor Poppy tried to calm the other students, but she was a Seer. Her gifts weren't useful in immobilizing the mob, and her voice wasn't loud enough to hear anyway.

Magic continued to fly throughout the room, and if it wasn't magic, it was fists and round-house kicks. I glanced around the room for other victims and spotted a girl and a guy ducked beneath a desk. I threw up my shield around them.

"Get out of here!" I cried.

They didn't hesitate. They raced for the door and were gone in moments.

I looked around for others, but everyone who remained either had magic or had instigated a fist-fight. I ducked out of the room as fast as I could. The students who'd escaped had raced down the hall but stopped at the corner. They watched the room warily, as if waiting for it to explode or something.

I hurried up to two guys near the front of the crowd. "You two make sure everyone gets out of here. I'll go alert Verla."

"You've got it," one of them said. He turned and started ushering students to a safer area while I took off running.

The next half hour passed by in a blur, thanks to the adrenaline-rush that didn't seem to wane until the chaos finally calmed. I'd found Verla in her office, and she came running the second she heard. Somehow, she'd managed to calm the class, and gave the Tarantulas two weeks of detention for starting the whole thing. She never addressed the magical issue that was clearly taking place, though I was sure I heard her mention something about calling in the Imperium Council to investigate.

"You can go now, Lucas," she'd told me.

I found my friends in the Lounge. They sat in plush chairs near the TV with excited looks on their faces. All eyes seemed to be on Mandy, who was showing off something on her arm.

"You'll never guess what power I got," Mandy gushed.

I noticed the tattoo as soon as I joined the group. It was an image of a tree with gnarly branches and no leaves, pressed permanently into her skin with black ink—the mark of a Mentalist.

"Telekinesis," Nadine guessed immediately.

Mandy scoffed. "Too common. Try again."

Nadine noticed me approach and looked up to me. She took my hand and explained under her breath. "Mandy's ceremony was this week, but she only discovered her powers last night. She's making us guess."

"Mm…" I mused as I sat on the armrest beside Nadine, draping an arm over her. "Mind reading?"

Mandy scrunched up her nose. "Like I want to hear all your dirty thoughts. This one is better."

"Better than mind reading?" Grant gawked. He looked to Amy, but she held her hands up innocently.

"Hey, I'm banned from giving any clues," she said, obviously already in-the-know.

"Is it a form of mindreading?" Talia guessed. "Like reading people's memories?"

Mandy clicked her tongue and shook her head. "Nope."

"Pyrokinesis," Grant threw out.

Mandy frowned. "Since when in the history of the coven has anyone had pyrokinesis? You know we can't manipulate fire."

"Then… dowsing," Grant guessed.

Mandy looked confused. "The ability to locate water? Isn't that a Seer power?"

Grant shrugged. "What's the difference?"

Talia looked unamused. "Seer powers are more personal and interpretive, like reading people's emotions. Mentalist powers are more about manipulating other minds, like *changing* someone's emotions."

"I won't manipulate," Mandy promised, crossing her heart. "I'll only use my powers for good. I swear."

"So, what's your specialty?" I asked.

Mandy could hardly contain herself. "I'm a dreamer!"

Nadine cocked her head. "A dreamer? What's that?"

The rest of us looked equally confused.

"It's not an official term," Mandy explained. "I don't know that there *is* a term for it, but I can enter other people's dreams!"

"Whoa," Talia said breathlessly. "That's wicked and could be crazy useful."

"I know," Mandy beamed. "I could literally plant ideas in people's heads, and they'd never know it."

"Like the movie *Inception*," Nadine pointed out.

"Exactly," Mandy said. "But like I said, I'll only use my power for good. Well, there are *some* people I'd like to give nightmares, like Chloe and Ryan."

The girls laughed. I'd almost forgotten Mandy and Ryan dated briefly.

"Speaking of Ryan," I said begrudgingly. "Guess who just started a fight in my Crystal Studies class because he couldn't conjure an orb?"

Grant snorted.

"That was *your* class?" Amy asked.

"Damn," I sighed. "News travels fast. Apparently, a bunch of people are having problems with their magic today."

Nadine's face paled. "You don't think it's like James said—that someone cursed the school?"

"No," I said firmly, though I couldn't be entirely sure. I only knew what Nadine was thinking, because I'd worried about the same thing. If this was a curse, how the hell was my Nadine—the one and only Curse Breaker in the coven—supposed to handle something this big? It could kill her.

No, no. I couldn't think of that. There had to be another explanation.

I just didn't know what it was.

C·

I COULDN'T SLEEP that night and woke to my stomach rumbling. After lying in bed for several minutes, I decided to head down to the vending machine in the Lounge to grab a midnight snack. I needed a walk to clear my mind anyway, as if I might stumble upon an answer—about the missing boys, about Nadine's curse, about anything.

The halls were dark, as was the Lounge. Most of the Lounge was shut down, except the front area with the TVs and vending machines. I stood in front of the vending machine surveying my options when I caught movement out of the corner of my eye. I gave a start and snuck toward the Lounge doorway, where I'd seen the movement.

I peeked down the hall and spotted a figure stalking down the hall. A chill ran down my spine, and I narrowed my eyes. The broad shoulders and confident gait were strikingly familiar.

I drew a breath when I realized it was Professor Daymond. What the hell was he doing at the school at this hour? Nothing good, I could only assume.

I checked the hall and saw no one else, so I slipped into the shadows and followed behind Daymond. I kept my distance and witnessed him turning down a flight of stairs and entering the basement. I snuck down the stairs behind him and peeked around a corner.

Professor Daymond stood outside one of the alchemy storage rooms, his back to me. He jiggled the handle, but it didn't budge. An incantation slipped from under his breath. He glanced up and down the hallway, as if keeping watch. I shrank back into the shadows, my pulse quickening. Whatever Daymond was up to, it seemed sketchy as hell.

I pressed myself against the wall to control my breathing. Daymond cursed and muttered another incantation. The *click* of the lock disengaging sounded, and the door creaked open. I peeked back around the corner to see Daymond sneaking into the storage room.

Definitely sketchy. The alchemy storage rooms contained all sorts of magical items that were difficult to obtain. Daymond wasn't an Alchemy professor and shouldn't have access to those rooms. I didn't even know how he'd managed to override the ward placed on the door.

Then again, he was on the school board. He probably helped cast the protection spell to begin with.

I waited for him to emerge, but the minutes ticked by and nothing happened. Finally, when I thought he might've fallen into some hidden portal inside the alchemy room, the door opened, and he stepped out.

Nothing seemed particularly unusual. He wasn't carrying armfuls of stolen supplies or anything, though he wouldn't need to if he subconjured them. But there was something in his eyes. He seemed to hide it with a firm expression, but there was the slightest hint of worry, like he was afraid he was going to get caught. His gaze darted up and down the hall again, but he didn't see me hiding behind the corner. I swore his fingers shook as he reached for the doorknob and spoke another incantation. Red tendrils of magic swirled out of his fingers, and a *click* sounded, signaling the ward was back in place.

Daymond straightened his suit coat and started down the hall opposite my hiding place. As he turned a corner, I hurried behind him, careful to take silent footsteps and to hug the shadows.

I followed Daymond down three more hallways, each as dark and eerie as the last. I couldn't tell where he was going, as we'd left the class-rooms behind and were headed toward maintenance rooms.

I turned another corner behind him... but he was gone. My pulse pounded in my ears as I slowed my steps and moved forward cautiously. I glanced from door to door, but they were all closed.

Creak!

Shivers tingled down my spine as a door creaked open behind me. I whirled around to see Professor Daymond emerging from a room and pacing the hall casually. My heart leapt into my throat. A battle orb crackled in his palm, and he tossed it from one hand to another like it was a baseball.

It was a *threat.*

My guts sank knowing I'd been caught. But more than anything, anger coursed through my veins. I should've been scared of Daymond, but my rage overpowered any fear.

"I know you're following me, Mister Taylor," he said casually, keeping his eyes on the orb. "This isn't the first time I've seen you sneaking around."

My eyes narrowed. I was banking on the hope that he wouldn't take a victim within the school, but given his moral compass, it was a risk. I conjured a battle orb, not because I thought it'd be any help against him—the defensive magic professor—but to show him I was ready to defend myself if I had to. Isaac and Caleb didn't have that chance, but I wasn't going down without a fight.

"I know what you did," I growled. My whole body shook.

Professor Daymond caught his battle orb in one hand and closed his fist. The orb fizzled out, as if I was no threat to him at all. A sardonic smile crossed his features. It was eerie, like he'd run into me between classes—not sneaking around in the middle of the night.

"Then you know to stay away," he said.

"Not until justice is served." I held my head high, but Daymond looked me up and down like I was nothing more than a joke to him.

"I know what you're up to," he snarled. "You're never going to find what you want."

"And what is it I want?" I challenged, my heart hammering.

Daymond took a step closer, like he hadn't heard my question at all. "I don't like to threaten students, but I won't stand by while you follow me any longer."

I swallowed. "What are you going to do?"

Daymond backed me into the wall, and my mouth went dry. He didn't get close enough to touch me, thank the Goddess. He crossed his hands in front of himself, and somehow, that was even more terrifying. He spoke so coolly, which was unusual for the temperamental old man. "In case you were unaware, I have quite a bit of power at this school. It would be a shame if you failed this semester."

Was that supposed to scare me?

"You don't have the power to do that," I spat.

He raised an eyebrow. "Don't I? I *am* on the school board, and I can ensure they will listen to me."

I shrugged. "So fail me."

Daymond laughed. "Oh, you misunderstand, Mister Taylor. My power goes far beyond changing a few grades. I would really hate to revisit Miss Evers's vandalism charge again. That kind of thing could result in expulsion."

I gaped. He wasn't seriously threatening to expel Nadine? Expulsion from the college was a big deal. It meant the coven rejected you… and I couldn't let that happen to Nadine because of me.

"You wouldn't dare," I growled.

"Oh, no," he said quickly. "Not if you keep your distance. This is your one and only warning to stay away. You don't want to know how far I will go."

He held my gaze a moment longer, and I shivered again. Seemingly satisfied, he turned on his heel and walked away. I longed to follow, but the threat in his tone was clear. He'd already shown how far he would go. If he caught me again, who knew what he would do? I could end up in the same grave as he threw those kids… wherever that was.

And that was exactly why I wouldn't give up. I had to see this through to the end, and I wouldn't stop until Professor Daymond was brought to justice.

That's what brought me back to the Bennetts' neighborhood the following night. I wasn't sure what I hoped to find, but I *had* to make sure Daymond kept his distance. The last thing I wanted was for him to accelerate his plans because he knew I was on to him.

I hadn't brought anyone along with me this time. The streets were quiet, but I was jumpy. Every cat that scurried down the alleyway or crackle of electricity from the street lamps had me on high alert. My gaze darted up and down the street as I made loop after loop around the Bennetts' block. If anyone were awake to see me, they'd wonder if I was crazy.

Movement caught my eye from somewhere up ahead, and I immediately ducked behind a cluster of bushes. I peeked over top of them, my heart hammering.

A cat prowled out onto the street. It moved between the shadows of the street lamps, so that I couldn't make out its features. From here, it was nothing more than a shadow. The hairs on the back of my neck stood, like I was being watched. I glanced up and down the street but saw nothing. My gaze returned to the cat. There was nothing particularly unusual about it—cats roamed all over Octavia Falls—but the way this one moved… It intrigued me. Almost like it was familiar… and it wasn't alone.

The cat perked up, responding to a noise I hadn't heard. Immediately, it went trotting across the street, disappearing into the shadows.

I narrowed my eyes and waited a moment, as if the cat might return. When it didn't, I deemed the street safe and emerged from my hiding space. And yet, it didn't feel safe at all. I crept forward, hugging my coat tight to me.

I reached a crossroads and glanced up and down the next street. Usually, I'd turn here and head around the block again, but something gave me pause. I couldn't explain it, as nothing had changed on the street at all. The air was the same chilly spring temperature, and the street remained eerily silent. And still, I was suspicious.

I need to mix up my pattern, I thought. *I'll circle the block in the other direction—*

No sooner had I thought it did something hard slam into my back. I hadn't seen where it'd come from, but I sure as hell felt the impact. My lungs seized, and my knees buckled. The world spun around me.

Before I could make sense of what had happened, everything went dark.

nadine

EIGHTEEN

"I hope this isn't going to become a habit." I said the words to lighten the mood, but the tension in the air only seemed to grow.

Lucas lay on his bed, a fresh bruise forming around his eye. I'd come running to his dorm room the second I heard from Grant. According to his version of the story, Lucas came stumbling into school this morning disoriented and with this massive bruise over his eye. I pressed an ice pack to Lucas's face and smoothed out his hair.

"You hope *what* isn't going to become a habit?" he asked groggily.

"Passing out," I teased, though the joke felt dry.

"I didn't pass out," he clarified. "I was attacked—some sort of stunning spell."

"What were you doing out in the middle of the night anyway?" Grant asked. He stood nearby, his arms crossed. He didn't look happy with Lucas.

"Same thing we did earlier," Lucas admitted. "I was making sure no one went near the Bennetts' house."

Grant relaxed a little. "You could've told me so I wasn't sitting around worrying. I texted you!"

"I know," Lucas groaned. "But I was trying to be stealthy."

"Not stealthy enough, apparently," Grant said. "We could've helped."

"So you could get hurt too?" Lucas asked. "I'm glad you guys weren't there. Daymond might've done more than knock me out."

My eyebrows shot up. "You think it was Professor Daymond?"

"Who else would it be? He made it pretty damn clear he'd respond if he caught me following him again."

"Did you see him?" I asked. "You can turn him in!"

Lucas sank deeper into the pillow. "No, I didn't see him. I got distracted by some dumb cat."

"This is getting ridiculous," I complained. "Can't you turn him into the headmistress for threatening you?"

Lucas cocked an eyebrow, but immediately winced. "Even if she believed me, Daymond would convince the rest of the school board otherwise."

I lifted the ice pack to check his face. It was purple and swollen pretty bad. "How'd you get the bruise, anyway? I mean, if you were hit in the back?"

Lucas shrugged. "Either I got kicked in the face after the fact, or I hit it on the sidewalk on the way down. I don't remember."

My stomach sank. "I'm so sorry."

"Don't be," he told me, placing his hand over mine. He gently took the ice pack from me. "It's not your fault."

Lucas pushed himself to a sitting position and placed the ice pack on his eye. His lips pressed into a thin line. "I'm sick of sitting around waiting for something to happen. I'm sick of investigating and finding *nothing*. I need to do something."

Grant and I shared a glance. "What are you going to do?" Grant asked curiously.

"I don't know," he admitted. "If I can't prove who the killer is, then I'll… I'll…"

I eyed him. "You'll what?"

An idea seemed to strike in that moment, because Lucas shot out of bed. He tossed the ice pack aside, even though he still really needed it. "I'll catch up with you guys later, okay?"

He headed for the door, but I stopped him. "Wait."

"Really, I'll be fine," he assured us. "I'm just going to stop by the library for a while. Enjoy the weekend without me."

Lucas left Grant and I standing there gaping at each other. I still wasn't sure of it all, long after the door had shut behind him. I finally turned to Grant.

"Any chance you think he has some brain damage?" he asked, half-serious.

"I don't know," I said skeptically. "I don't want to interrupt if he's working on something important, though."

Grant stood there a few moments, as if contemplating going after him. "I guess you're right. Have you had breakfast yet?"

I shook my head. "We can grab something if you want."

Grant took his insulin, then we left the room.

"How are classes?" he asked to make small talk as we headed toward the cafeteria.

"I think I might actually pass Alchemy," I said, which was a relief. "My lab partner spoke two words to me last week, so I think we're only a full sentence away from being best friends."

Grant chuckled. "That bad, huh?"

"No, actually. I like Onyx," I admitted as we descended the grand staircase. "She's quiet and keeps to herself, but she's easy to work with."

We reached the ground level of the Main Foyer and turned toward the cafeteria.

"That's good—ow!" Something whizzed through the air and knocked Grant in the back of the head. He rubbed the area of impact and turned toward the culprit, eyes narrowed.

The Tarantulas stood on the opposite end of the Main Foyer, juggling apples with their telekinetic powers. They must've swiped them from the cafeteria, and obviously had no intention of eating them. Their eyes fixed on us, and all five of them laughed.

"I thought these guys were hit by that weird magic curse going around," I whispered to Grant.

"They were, but it's apparently short-lived. Only lasts a couple days."

Ryan caught me eyeing them. "Sorry," he called, his voice dripping with sarcasm.

I narrowed my eyes at them and bent to pick up the apple they'd thrown at the back of Grant's head. I tossed it in my hand and caught it. "Next time, make sure you can actually *control* your magic before you start showing off."

Ryan's laughter died. "Honey, I can control more than just my magic. You wanna see?"

I scowled at him. "No, thanks."

Ryan scoffed. His whole posse had gone quiet now, and they approached us slowly, as if stalking prey. "What is it, sweetheart?" Ryan drawled. "You prefer this loser to me?"

"Yeah, actually, I do," I stated. "He knows better than to inflate his fragile masculinity by putting others down with lame nicknames."

Ryan smirked, but he looked uncomfortable. Not many girls could resist his charm. "Careful what you say, half-blood," he warned. "You're only here because the coven is generous. If it were up to me, you outsiders would be gone."

"Hey," Grant growled. "She was accepted into the coven by Mother Miriam, same as you."

"And how does she repay us?" Ryan snapped. "By defiling the Goddess's image!"

Ryan gestured to the painting above the fireplace, which had been repaired weeks ago. I couldn't believe he was still bringing that up.

I shrugged. "I'm still here. Why don't you let Mother Miriam be the judge of me?"

Ryan scoffed. "I hope she does judge you. Maybe she'll decide to get rid of you—and send your half-blood friend back to Mexico."

I was ready to lunge at Ryan, but Grant grabbed my arm. "Come on. Let's go. They're not worth it."

I shrugged him off. "We should fight back. They can't talk to you like that."

The Tarantulas didn't hear me. Instead, they started chanting, "Go back to Mexico. Go back to Mexico."

Was I seriously standing here listening to this? It was like arguing with children.

I wanted to start something. *Get your revenge,* a voice in my head whispered. *Do it for Grant.*

But Grant kept tugging on my arm, and the voice seemed to grow quieter.

"I won't fall for your tormenting," I told Ryan. "I'll save my energy for things that actually matter. Have fun, boys."

I tossed the apple back to them and rolled my eyes as we walked away. Once we were inside the cafeteria, I turned to Grant. "Why do you let them walk all over you like that?"

"Those guys are bullies," Grant said. "All they're looking for is attention. They *want* you to fight back. The best way to fight them is ignore them. Trust me."

Grant stared ahead as we got into the breakfast line. His features were tight, and he looked like he was thinking hard.

"How often do they say that to you?" I asked quietly.

"It doesn't matter," he said. "Just forget about it."

I let the subject go for now, but I wasn't going to forget about it. I knew the story about how the Tarantulas had stolen Grant's insulin last year. I was willing to bet he had a lot of stories like that, though he wouldn't admit to them.

Grant and I filled our plates and started for our usual table. I noticed two people were already sitting there. Talia had a bowl of yogurt in front of her and one earbud in her ear. The other hung loosely so she could hear what Cody was saying beside her. Cody didn't have any food in front of him. He just sat on the edge of his chair, staring at her.

Grant stopped in his tracks when he noticed the two of them. I swear smoke came shooting out his ears.

"Relax," I told him under my breath. "Let's just go over there and hopefully he'll leave."

"Yeah, and take her with," Grant said bitterly. "I thought they were on a break."

"They were," I said bitterly.

"I hope they're not back together."

"Me either," I agreed. "But we're going to find out."

As we approached, I caught the tail-end of what Cody was saying. "I don't know why you bother listening to audiobooks. Isn't it easier to just read the textbook?"

Talia blushed and ducked her head. "I'm more of an auditory learner."

Cody reached out to brush her hair out of her face, then pulled the earbud gently from her ear as he drew away. "You don't have to do that here. I'll help you study."

Talia's features seemed to brighten. "Are we actually going to study this time?"

Cody didn't get a chance to answer, because Grant and I set our trays down and sat across from them. Cody's eyes darkened the moment we sat.

"Hey, Talia," I said brightly, like I hadn't heard their conversation.

She hadn't seemed to notice our approach. She tore her gaze from Cody's. "Oh, hey, guys. How was Lucas?"

"Well enough to go to the library," I said. "How are you?"

I shot a glance between her and Cody, hoping she could read my signals.

"Everything's fine," Talia said. "I was just studying while I ate."

Grant didn't touch his food, and he didn't take his eyes off Cody the whole time. Cody shifted in his chair, obviously feeling Grant's eyes on him.

I could feel the tension in the air and rushed to break it. "Do you want to try to get a bowling lane later today, Tal?"

"Sure," she said, shooting a glance at Cody. She sounded uncertain, as if she was waiting for his permission.

"I'll catch up with you later," Cody said. He stood, then leaned down to give Talia a peck on the lips. He must've thought he was being discreet, but Grant and I both saw when he trailed his hand down her back and grabbed her ass. Talia stiffened, though she tried to hide her horror.

That's when Grant totally lost it. He slammed his hands down on the table so hard my silverware rattled off the edge and onto the floor. His chair squeaked back as he shot to his feet. "That's no way to treat a lady!" Grant shouted.

The cafeteria went silent, but Grant didn't even notice. His chest heaved as he stared Cody down.

Cody smirked in amusement. "I don't see her complaining."

"Grant," Talia warned. "Please don't."

"No," Grant argued. "I'm sick of this. You're obviously uncomfortable, and this guy is too much of a psychopath to notice."

Talia gaped, and I went speechless.

Cody's jaw tightened. "What did you just call me?"

Grant squared his shoulders. "Psychopath. A personality disorder characterized by impaired empathy and remorse, along with—"

Cody shoved Grant, and he stumbled back a few steps. "Are you trying to start a fight? You think I don't notice the way you look at my girlfriend?"

Cody shoved him again, and Grant caught himself on the table behind him. There were four girls sitting there, and one of their cups of apple juice knocked over. The girls squealed and left the table before they got caught in the middle of the fight.

"You need to back off," Cody growled.

"Guys, please," Talia begged.

I shot out of my chair and threw myself between the two guys. The last thing I wanted was to see Grant get hurt. "You both need to calm down."

Cody scoffed. "Please, it's not like I need to conjure a battle orb to win a fight against this loser. I've already got Talia. He knows I've won."

Grant gritted his teeth. "She's not a fucking consolation prize, you jackass!"

I didn't even see it coming. Grant swung his fist, and it connected with Cody's jaw. He went down, knocking chairs to the floor where he fell.

"Grant!" Talia cried. She hurried out of her chair and knelt at Cody's side. He was clutching his face and feeling with his tongue to make sure his teeth were still there. I wanted to be horrified, but I was—dare I say it? —*proud* of Grant.

Cody scrambled to his feet, his eyes burning with rage. Grant and I reacted in the same second, each conjuring battle orbs before Cody could take one step in our direction. Fatigue instantly set in, but I steadied my magic, and the orb remained blazing in my palm.

Talia gasped and threw herself in front of Cody. She pushed his chest. "Cody, don't."

He stopped, nostrils flaring. "You're on his side?"

Talia gaped, shooting a glance between Grant and Cody. "I'm not on anyone's side. I don't want anyone getting hurt."

Cody glared down at her. "Your friends are trash, Talia," he spat.

I smirked slightly, as if it were a compliment. I still remembered how it felt to punch him in the club.

"If you can't stand by me, you're not the girl I thought you were," Cody sneered.

Tears welled in Talia's eyes. "What are you saying?"

"I'm saying it's *them* or *me*."

Talia gaped, completely speechless. "I-I…" she stammered.

Cody's eyebrows shot up. "Goddess, Talia. This isn't something you need to think about."

"Yes, I do!" she cried. "This isn't fair."

Cody scoffed. "You're right. It isn't. Find me when you have an answer."

Cody stormed out of the cafeteria. Slowly, I lowered my battle orb, and the whispers around the room turned back into full conversation.

"Tal," Grant said gently. "I'm sorry. I—"

Talia jerked away from him when he reached out for her. "Don't touch me," she snapped. "That whole thing was uncalled for."

Grant's jaw dropped. "I was defending you."

"I don't need your help." Talia snatched up her things from the table and subconjured them, then rushed out of the room after Cody.

"Talia!" I called, racing after her. I caught up with her in the hall.

She whirled around. "Just... don't talk to me right now."

"I want to help," I assured her.

"You almost threw a battle orb at my boyfriend!"

"I was defending Grant. Tal, please let me help," I pleaded. "I thought you and Cody broke up, anyway."

"I said we were on a break," she clarified. "Cody wants to fix things. I should at least give him that chance. And I don't need your help."

Talia abandoned me in the hall before I could get another word in.

I returned to the cafeteria to check on Grant. He sat slumped in his chair and poked at his food. I didn't think he had any intention of eating anymore.

I took a seat beside him, not really feeling hungry myself. "You did the right thing."

He frowned. "You think so?"

"Yeah, Cody deserved it."

Grant sighed. "I'm not feeling very hungry anymore."

"You have to eat something," I said, stopping him.

Grant was already on his feet. He glanced between me and his uneaten food, then grabbed the banana sitting next to his plate.

"Is that going to be enough?" I asked.

"I have food in my dorm if it isn't," he grumbled. "Thanks for caring."

"Is there anything else I can do?"

He shook his head. "I think I just need some time alone."

Grant took his plate to the kitchens and left the cafeteria. I sat alone, nibbling at my breakfast but not really tasting anything.

I eventually sat there so long that most of the cafeteria had cleared out.

It was the weekend, and all my friends seemed busy, so I decided to enjoy the first days of spring and take my studying outside. I was walking near the greenhouse when I spotted the Lucky Three seated in a circle on the grass. Chloe flipped tarot cards over onto a purple scarf in what looked like a complicated spread.

I was already pissed, and seeing Chloe didn't help. My pulse immediately quickened—an innate response to Chloe's presence. I shoved my emotions down, because I knew it was the curse talking. It wasn't like Chloe was doing anything *wrong*. And yet, it felt like I should be shoving her face in the dirt.

We had to do something about this curse. Together.

I walked up to Chloe. "We need to talk."

Chloe eyed me up and down. "Can't you see I'm busy?"

I sighed. "This is more important than tarot readings."

She turned back to her friends and continued flipping over tarot cards, like I wasn't even there. "Okay, talk."

"Not here," I insisted. "This is between you and me."

Chloe scoffed. "What? You want to lure me away from my friends so you can get your revenge? Nice try, Evers."

"This is serious." If what I knew about curse breaking was true, I wasn't going to break this curse without her. "We might as well get this over with sooner or later."

"Oh, so you're walking me to my execution?" she said flatly.

"I want to talk this out," I stated. "There has to be a solution."

Chloe chuckled lightly and gently placed her tarot cards aside. She stood, and Gwen and Camille both snickered under their breath. Chloe stood so close to me our noses were practically touching.

"There is *one* solution to this," Chloe said in a clipped tone. "And that's with you leaving town the second I get my powers."

I crossed my arms. "I've established that I'm not leaving."

I meant to add that there was an alternative—a way for both of us to stay—although I couldn't talk about it in front of Gwen and Camille. Hell, Chloe was the *last* person on earth I wanted to tell about my true powers, but I didn't see how to solve this any other way. I'd have to strike some sort of bargain so she'd keep my secret.

But Chloe didn't let me get that far. "Stop acting like you deserve this," Chloe snapped.

Fuck, it was impossible to play nice with her. "Your grandpa is the one who cast the curse!" I cried. "Of course I deserve to stay."

Chloe scoffed. "Don't you think my grandfather had a reason? Yours isn't as innocent as you might believe."

I had several other harsh words for her on my tongue, but I bit down to keep them contained. "Fighting over who stays and who leaves doesn't matter, anyway. There's a way that we can both stay."

Chloe laughed. "Not in this coven. You haven't learned a thing, and that's why you don't belong."

My hands curled into fists, and my body shook. Dark energy swirled in my gut, bubbling up and about to explode. I pushed it down, but my anger broke through.

"Stop saying that!" I screamed. I shoved Chloe, and she stumbled over her tarot deck. Cards went flying everywhere across the grass. "If you weren't such a bitch, we could actually figure this out!"

"You're not listening!" Chloe shrieked. "There are no other options!"

"*You're* the one not listening!" I spat.

Chloe shoved me back so hard I fell onto the grass. My hand landed on something soft and wet. I looked down to see the guts of a dead mouse squishing between my fingers.

It wasn't unusual to see dead mice and squirrels around campus, with all the cats around to catch them. This seemed awfully damn convenient, and I wasn't about to let the opportunity pass me by. I curled my fingers around the dead mouse, feeling dark power surge through me from its blood.

I jumped to my feet, and a battle orb formed in my palms, more powerful than any spell I'd cast before. I'd become better at magic over the semester, and I had the extra boost from the dead mouse to push me that much further. It was enough to burn Chloe, that was for certain. I hoped it left one hell of a scar.

Gwen and Camille gasped in unison, and they scrambled to their feet. Each stood at Chloe's side and conjured a battle orb of their own.

"Throw it!" Chloe sneered. "I dare you. Show us you *really* belong. Come on, show me your magic."

I drew my arm back and thrust the magic toward her—but it never left my palm. The magic ricocheted back in my direction, blasting me off my feet. My back slammed against a nearby tree, and I gasped for air that had been knocked from my lungs. I slumped to the ground. My whole body trembled, and my palm burned as if I'd just touched a hot stove. I gazed down at my hands in shock. The hand that had cast the magic was red and tender, and the mouse blood on my other hand had turned black.

My magic had betrayed me and backfired. I'd been warned about black magic before, and I'd just experienced first-hand why it was worth avoiding. I hated to think what I could've done to myself if I'd cast a larger spell.

Nearby, Chloe doubled over in laughter. Gwen and Camille snickered as they gathered their things and walked away. The Lucky Three left me slumped at the base of the tree.

"I told you she didn't have what it took," Chloe said to her friends, loud enough for me to hear. They were still snickering as they strolled into the school.

"Nadine!" Talia's voice came across the yard.

I glanced over to her to see her sprinting toward me. Her eyes were bloodshot, and she dashed tears from her cheeks. Whatever she'd been crying about had been immediately interrupted by the sight of me lying there.

Talia knelt at my side. "Are you okay?"

"I'll be fine," I told her.

"What happened?"

I winced as I sat up straight. "That depends. How much did you see?"

"I walked out of the school to see a battle orb in your hand, and then see you blast yourself into a tree!"

"I didn't mean to. I was going to fry Chloe's ass."

Talia pressed her lips together, looking pissed. I wasn't sure if she was pissed at me, or about what happened with Cody earlier.

"What is it?" I asked.

Talia looked at her wit's end. "I can't keep watching you get hurt. You and Chloe need to figure stuff out."

I scoffed. "Great advice. While I work on that, you can figure stuff out with Cody, because he's a jackass."

I wasn't prepared for what came next. A sob broke out of Talia's chest, and she broke down in tears.

"You don't h-have to w-worry about him a-anymore," she sobbed. "We're o-over for good."

My heart sank. "What happened?"

She hiccupped. "I went after him to talk things through. I didn't know what I was going to say, really. I mean, how could I be asked to choose between my best friend and my boyfriend? He had his phone out and was texting someone. I thought nothing of it, and I didn't mean to touch it. But when I reached for him, my hand grazed his phone and I-I s-saw…"

Talia burst into tears again. She spoke so fast I could barely make out what she was saying. "I saw a vision of him sexting another girl!"

I wrapped an arm around her and rubbed her shoulders as she sobbed into her hands. "I'm so sorry."

"No, *I'm* sorry," she cried. "You were right. Cody's a total ass."

She dashed the tears from her eyes. "He said it only started when we took a break, but he was lying. I saw it in my vision. It's been going on the whole time."

"You didn't deserve this," I told her.

She sniffled. "It doesn't feel that way. I must've done something wrong—"

I cut her off immediately. "You did *nothing* wrong. Don't blame yourself for Cody's mistakes."

"I can't help it," she said in a low whisper. "I deserve it."

"No, you don't," I said firmly. I wished I could make Talia see how amazing she was. Cody never deserved her. A thought occurred. "Is… is that why you stayed with him?"

She wiped her nose. "What do you mean?"

"You stayed because you thought you deserved to be treated poorly?" I asked gently.

Talia turned her gaze away and hugged herself. "I don't know. I guess I stayed because I didn't want to admit things were as bad as they were. Even now, that doesn't sound right. I mean, Cody wasn't *bad*."

"You're still doing it," I pointed out.

She blinked a few times. "Doing what?"

"You're justifying his behavior."

"Well, he never hit me or anything. It could've been worse."

"That doesn't make it *good*," I told her. "He never hit you, but he still hurt you—through his words and his actions. He constantly made you uncomfortable, and that's just as bad."

Talia contemplated my words for a few moments. I held my breath, hoping she would understand where I was coming from and not get defensive. I wanted her to see she deserved better.

Talia took a deep breath and twisted her hands in her lap. "I just wanted it to be perfect, you know? In high school, guys never really paid attention to me. I was just some nerd who hung out in the music room all the time. And then Cody took notice…"

"Grant noticed, too," I reminded her.

She frowned, almost looking ashamed. "I thought Grant was joking. He was just… too nice. It felt like he was faking it or something."

"That's just Grant."

Talia dropped her head. "I didn't know that at the time. With Cody, it felt like a fairytale. I guess I was more in love with the fairytale than I was with him."

"He was your first love," I realized. "You just wanted it to be perfect, so you convinced yourself it was."

She nodded lightly. "Yeah. I thought things with Cody were how relationships were supposed to be. But I can't keep pretending."

I wrapped her in my arms. "You'll find your prince, Tal. I know it."

She leaned her head against my shoulder and sniffled. "I hope you're right, but right now, it's too painful to look that far ahead."

"It's going to take time," I said reassuringly. "Cody's betrayal is still fresh. If you need anything, I'm here for you."

She stared into the distance. "I just need some time to process it all."

"So it's cool that I punched him?" I teased to lighten the mood.

Talia chuckled lightly. "Considering he was cheating on me at the time and… other things…"

My guts twisted when I thought of how the dirtbag had treated her… coerced her. I wanted to puke.

"Yeah," Talia said, a slight smile touching her lips. "We're fine."

I hugged her tight. "That makes me really happy. I'm sorry about everything that happened—with Cody, and between you and me…"

"Thanks. I really needed to hear that."

Talia and I embraced, and my heart swelled. I was happy Talia and I had repaired our relationship, but I knew only time could heal her broken heart.

☾

After Talia and I made up, I felt like I could breathe again. But Chloe's Evoking Ceremony was fast-approaching, and I hadn't made any progress in getting her to listen to me. Even if I *could* break this damn curse, Chloe refused to cooperate.

Lucas had hit a dead-end in the library, too. He'd gone to research Miriamic law and explore his options, but there was nothing he could do without hard evidence.

I woke Thursday morning feeling like I hadn't slept all night. My whole body was stiff, and I felt as if I could sleep for another twelve hours. Isa snuggled close to me, and I stroked her tail gently.

"Do you need anything before I leave for class?" Talia asked. She stood in front of her mirror, pulling her hair into a high ponytail. It looked really good on her.

"I'll manage," I said, before quickly adding, "Actually, would you mind bringing me my meds?"

"Sure thing." Talia tightened her ponytail and went into the bathroom.

I sank my head back into the pillow, hoping that if I waited, the fatigue would pass. I knew it wouldn't.

"Here you go," she said. I hadn't even realized she'd returned. Talia placed my pills on my bedside table next to my water bottle.

"Thanks." I uncapped the pills and counted them out, then downed them with a few sips of water. Immediately, my stomach churned. Bile rose to my throat, and my head spun.

Talia must've noticed all the blood drain from my face, because her features immediately shifted to worry. "What's wrong?"

"Trash can!" I barely got the words out.

Talia practically dove for the trash can and got it under me just as I began heaving. I couldn't help the gross noises I made. My throat burned, and I broke out into a thin sheen of sweat. Isa paced back and forth on the bed, worried. I heaved again, spewing my guts a second time.

Even when I thought it was over, I remained hunched over the trash can. Another attack bubbled up, though nothing came out. All I did was dry heave. Goddess, I felt awful.

"Are you going to be okay?" Talia asked when I'd finished.

My head spun so fast, I could barely lift it. I reached for the tissues next to my bed and wiped my mouth.

"I don't know," I admitted. "I wasn't nauseous until I took my pills. What'd you give me?"

I picked up the bottles and inspected the prescriptions written on the outside. Everything I normally took was here.

"They're just your pills." Talia sounded wary, like I might blame her.

"They didn't feel like my normal pills," I said, popping off the top of one of the prescriptions. Everything *looked* in order—until I reached the last bottle. The size, shape, and color of my immunosuppressants looked right, but the logo usually stamped on them was gone.

My guts twisted, this time for other reasons. "These aren't my meds," I said flatly, trying to wrap my head around it.

"What?" Talia's voice shook.

"These aren't my meds," I repeated. "Has anyone been in the room?"

She started to shake her head, but she caught herself. "Lena came by yesterday," she said breathlessly.

"What was *Lena* doing here?" I bit her name harsher than I meant to. That bitch had already messed with my boyfriend. Now she was messing with my meds?

Talia gaped, like she couldn't believe Lena would do something like this. "She heard about what happened with Cody and wanted to talk. They had a thing last year, and I guess things ended in a similar way. She seemed really genuine…"

"Did she go into the bathroom?" I demanded. I couldn't believe someone could be so vile as to mess with my meds.

Talia swallowed. "She was only in there for a few minutes. I didn't think anything of it."

I should kick her ass, I thought, though I knew the voice wasn't my own.

I can't, I countered. *Not when I feel like shit.*

I tried swallowing down the dark energy rising in my chest, but my stomach was so empty, it didn't seem to want to go anywhere. I wanted to stomp down the hall and demand an explanation, but I could hardly move.

"Tell me what you need," Talia said quickly.

My head spun, but I managed to speak. "Call Dr. Yonker."

Talia took my phone and called my doctor right away. While I leaned back on the pillow, she explained to him what had happened. I expected him to make some sort of recommendation or put in a new prescription. I didn't expect him to make a freaking house call.

But that's exactly what he did. "I'll be there as soon as I can," I heard him say from the other end of the phone. "Get Nadine to the infirmary immediately."

"Come on," Talia said as she tried to help me sit up. "Doctor's orders."

Whatever Lena had poisoned me with was quickly working its way through my bloodstream. I couldn't make sense of which way was up and which way was down, and my limbs felt like they were made of noodles. I tried to stand, but my knees buckled beneath me, and I collapsed onto the floor.

"Ugh…" I thought I heard myself groan, but I couldn't be sure.

"Goddess!" Talia cried. She had the phone to her ear a second later.

I didn't move from the floor. Cramps spread throughout my body, creating a twisting whirlwind of pain shooting up and down my extremities.

I couldn't make sense of how much time had passed, but I was aware of several people in scrubs hoisting me into a wheelchair.

"It's going to be okay," one of them said kindly, patting my knee. I thought I recognized her voice. I peeled my heavy eyelids open long enough to see that it was Patty, the nurse who'd come to my aid the night the Lucky Three beat me up. "We'll take good care of you."

I noticed the worry in her eyes. I wondered if Lena knew the prank meds would mess with my lupus this badly.

The nurses wheeled me down to the infirmary, and I somehow ended up on a hospital bed, though I didn't remember them transferring me there. I was out for a while, until Dr. Yonker arrived and administered a prescription to curb the side effects. Finally, the room stopped spinning.

"I'm sorry this happened to you," Dr. Yonker told me kindly. "From now on, I suggest subconjuring your meds, where no one can touch them."

I'd already thought of that. I should've done it sooner, but had held off because I was still learning my magic. Conjuring came easily to me now, though.

"Thanks for your help," I told him weakly.

"If there's anything else I can do, I'm only a call away," he said.

Dr. Yonker stayed a while longer to discuss my symptoms and how I was managing with my magic. He was happy to learn I could conjure things without nearly passing out anymore. Progress, he called it.

Goddess, I hoped so. I'd skipped so many days of school this semester. It was hard to accept things had to get worse before they got better.

I slept the rest of the day and into the next morning. When I woke, I felt like I could move again. Whatever pill Dr. Yonker had given me helped my symptoms immensely.

My friends visited later that day, but the nurses wanted to keep me another night for observation. Lucas stayed until I fell asleep.

When I woke, he was gone—probably kicked out by one of the nurses. I wasn't released until close to dinnertime. I returned to my dorm, made myself presentable, and headed downstairs.

I found Talia and Grant sitting in the Main Foyer, tossing balls of string around for Gus to play with. Talia laughed at something Grant had said, which I was really happy to see. I sank into a chair beside them.

"Nadine, you're back!" Talia cried.

"You look good," Grant added.

"I'm feeling a *lot* better," I told them. "Thanks to Talia. The nurses said it could've been a lot worse if she hadn't acted so fast. What's so funny?"

Talia giggled and rolled up her ball of string. "Grant's just telling me about practice earlier this week."

Grant shifted in his chair. "So I wanted to try out this new Speedo, right? Like, I've worn the pineapple-printed one enough times, everyone's lost interest. This one was cheetah print! Well, I forgot what size I was and I'm thinking, of course I'm a large. No guy wants their package to be anything less."

I snickered as he told the story dramatically.

"So I get them on, and I'm thinking, okay they're not too bad. A little bigger than my last ones, but not too bad." Grant paused for dramatic effect. "Well, I get in the water and I'm swimming laps, and the Speedo starts coming off!"

Talia laughed beside me, even louder than the first time she heard the story. I couldn't help but laugh with her.

"I could've stopped and fixed it," Grant continued, "but I'm up against three other guys. I mean, it's only warm-ups, but we all know we're competing out there in the water. So I get to the end of the pool and turn around—and the Speedo is suddenly around my knees! My whole package is just hanging out there—"

The sound of laughter met my ears, but it wasn't in response to Grant's story. I turned toward the hall nearby, where I heard loud voices cheering and laughing while they passed. At least a dozen girls were walking past the Main Foyer. Each wore matching black sparkly tank tops and spanks that showed their ass cheeks. I recognized the uniform from the many times Chloe had worn it. It was the dance team. They might as well have had *bitches* written across their asses, because it was sure as hell written on their face. Lena and Chloe were hooked arm in arm, leading the girls down the hall as they laughed about something I didn't catch. Gwen, Camille, and Stacey followed dutifully behind, along with a bunch of other girls I didn't know.

My nostrils flared. Of fucking course Chloe and Lena had gotten close over the last semester. I'd forgotten they were on the dance team together. Lena had been acting as Chloe's puppet when she replaced my meds. I just knew it. She was Chloe's best option for getting into my room. Mother Miriam knows we wouldn't let any one of those other girls inside. And they'd manipulated my best friend to do it!

Bitches! I screamed internally. There had to be a better word for it, something even more vile and disgusting, because that's what these girls were. They were worse than scum at the bottom of a sewage drain. They were—

"Nadine!" Talia's voice cut through the sound of my pulse raging in my ears. I stood and started making my way toward them. I'd hardly realized it. But even when she brought it to my attention, I didn't slow down. I couldn't sit by and let Chloe and Lena get away with this.

They have to pay, a dark, sinister voice said in my head.

I didn't even bother countering it. After everything Chloe had pulled this semester, what was the point? I stomped down the hall and pushed my way through the crowd of dancers.

"Tonight's recital is going to be amazing—Ah!" Lena screamed as I grabbed her by the shoulder. She spun around, and I shoved her.

"Bitch!" I roared. "You messed with my meds!"

"Like I'd go anywhere near your stuff," Lena shot back.

I narrowed my eyes. "You already have. More than once."

It was obvious I was referring to Lucas.

Keep it up, Nadine, the dark voice encouraged. *Show her what you've got.*

That's not why I came out here, I snapped internally. *Go away.*

"Goddess," Chloe scoffed, tossing her hair over her shoulder. "There's no need to go psycho."

I whirled on her. "I know it was your idea! How many girls did you get in on it? At least one to make the pills, and you had Lena plant them."

Chloe smirked slightly, but her features remained otherwise passive. All eyes were on us, but I didn't care. "I have no idea what you're talking about," she stated flatly.

She's lying.

"If you use my friends again, I'll—"

"You'll what?" Chloe challenged, raising an eyebrow. "Your threats are empty. I know you don't have it in you to hurt me."

Oh, we've got plenty, the voice said with a click of her tongue.

Chloe's eyes flickered toward the entrance of the Main Foyer. I followed her gaze and noticed Grant and Talia standing there, along with a couple of other people who'd stopped to watch the confrontation.

"Not without your backup, at least," Chloe teased.

"Like you don't have an entourage everywhere you go," I shot back. "At least I'm not getting other people to do my dirty work for me."

Chloe smiled. "Oh, so you *are* dirty. Nice to hear you speak the truth."

My nostrils flared, and I got up in her face. "I am *nothing* like you."

Chloe's lips tightened. Though she tried to keep her cool, I could see the anger rising within her. "You sure, Evers? Last time, you nearly fried me. Too bad Lucas isn't here to save you from yourself."

The way she said it hinted at something more, and my whole body shook. "What did you do?" I demanded. I took deep breaths, trying to calm myself, but my tone wavered.

Chloe waved her hand. "Oh, it was nothing. Just a double dose of those pills you had. He'll be over it by Monday—"

I did everything I could to keep myself from reacting, but I couldn't take it anymore. The heavy, sickening energy swirling around in my belly exploded through me. There was nothing I could do to hold back, not once she started talking about Lucas.

Give her hell.

I snapped, and my fist pummeled into Chloe's face three times in quick succession. I didn't even decide to do it—just one moment I was standing there, and the next I saw a blur in front of me and my knuckles ached. Chloe stumbled backward, and I didn't have to think twice. I took that bitch down.

I jumped on top of her so that she couldn't get away, slamming my fist into her face over and over again. I smiled, finding it satisfying to be in control. When I held her down, she couldn't touch me or my friends. All she could do was beg for mercy—mercy she didn't deserve, and mercy I wouldn't give.

Chloe lifted her hands to shield herself, but my fist rammed straight past them and into her nose. Screams echoed down the hall around me, but they barely registered. All I could focus on was the sweet taste of revenge.

"Somebody do something!" a girl called.

"Nadine's gone psycho!" another screamed.

There were so many voices overlapping one another, I couldn't make them out. They could've been in my head, or they could've been a thousand miles away. It made no difference.

Blood spurted out of Chloe's nose, shooting over the front of my shirt and all over her uniform. I laughed maniacally at the sight of blood. It was so satisfying. Chloe finally knew who she was dealing with, and I dared her to mess with me again.

"Get off!" Chloe shouted, but I punched her again. She screamed, then lifted her hand to shove her fingers into my hair. She tugged so hard that strands broke free, but I didn't give two shits. She'd already made me bald once before. I guess she was ready for another go.

"That's it!" I laughed. "Harder, Chloe."

"You're fucking crazy!" Chloe snapped, tugging once again. This time it was so hard that she yanked my head to the side and I went flying off of her.

I rolled across the ground but scrambled to my feet as Chloe took off running down the hall. I'd just barely stood when a battle orb exploded like a miniature grenade right where I'd been a moment ago.

Shit, that was right. I had fucking *magic*. What was I doing wasting my time on a mere fist fight? Shit was about to get real up in here.

Another battle orb went off, and I realized that Chloe's posse was attacking me. But they weren't messing with ordinary Nadine. I was freaking pumped and ready to take this bitch out. I threw up a shield behind myself, a spell I didn't even know I could conjure until now. Battle orbs exploded against it before they could reach me.

Chloe scrambled over to a table nearby and grabbed a decorative vase off of it. She hurled it at me as hard as she could, but I dodged it. I kept my eyes on her, smiling proudly as I admired the bruises on her face. She braced herself against the table, a terrified look crossing her features.

"I've been waiting too long for this," I taunted.

"Do your worst," she spat. "I hope it gets you kicked out of the coven."

Her words should've halted me in my tracks, but in that moment, they meant nothing. She'd gone after my friends, and that was a sin above all else. The coven was meant to protect each other, and instead Chloe had sabotaged others.

The invitation was too tempting to resist. I lunged for Chloe and pinned her against the wall with my forearm. She scratched and clawed at me until blood began to drip down my face, but I never loosened my hold on her. Instead, I just laughed like a fucking maniac, because what else were you supposed to do when someone was attacking you?

True fear entered Chloe's eyes as I lifted my palm and formed a battle orb inside of it. It burned and crackled with rage.

"Don't ever go near my friends," I growled, before lowering the battle orb to the side of Chloe's face.

Pure satisfaction swirled in my belly as Chloe let out a shriek. The orb was high-powered enough to sizzle against her skin, burning it. I didn't even need black magic to conjure it—*that* was how fucking pissed I was.

"How does it feel!?" I yelled. "How does it feel to be the one getting hurt?"

Chloe's eyes glossed over, as if the pain was too much to bear. I drew back, because I wanted her to feel the pain—to suffer. I couldn't let it be over too soon. She slumped to the ground and looked up at me from behind bruised eyes.

"Get up and fight!" I snapped, kicking her in the stomach. "You're nothing on your own! Prove you belong in the coven! Fight me!"

I swung my fist at her face again, and she completely collapsed onto the ground. Chloe didn't even make a sound as my foot connected with her stomach over and over again.

Strong hands landed on my shoulders and dragged me backward. I hadn't realized my shield magic had failed, and someone had slipped past the spell. I kicked out for Chloe again, but my foot didn't reach her.

"Let me go!" I screamed at whoever it was. I flailed, but I couldn't get out of their grasp. "Let me—"

"Nad!" Lucas's stern voice snapped in my ear. There were shouts and screams coming from all different directions it seemed, but Lucas's voice drowned out all the others. "What were you thinking!?"

I whirled around to face him, and my jaw hung slack. His face was a welcome sight, pulling me back to reality as my gaze roamed over his green eyes and down to his cupid's bow lips. My pulse slowed at the sight of him, taking my emotions down a notch. He was perfect in every way, and yet there was something starkly different about him, too. I'd never seen such disappointment in his eyes. But there was something else there, too—fear unlike I'd ever seen it. At first, I didn't understand why he was looking at me like that. Then I heard the cries of horror from behind me, and I looked over my shoulder.

"Dear Goddess," I breathed. The uncontrollable rage that had exploded out of me seemed to seep slowly back into my stomach again as rationality took over.

I stared at Chloe's bruised and bleeding form as several of her friends helped lift her. She couldn't even stand, and one of her eyes was swollen shut. One whole side of her face was covered in red-hot burns and blisters. Her head lolled to the side, and I realized for the first time that she was knocked out.

The whole hall had gone silent as all eyes locked on me. Chloe's entire dance team shared the same look of disdain, as if they were about to curse me right then and there. Talia and Grant weren't far away. Talia held on to Grant, and he had an arm wrapped around her. I couldn't understand why they were staring at me that way, like they'd just witnessed me grow three heads.

I was about to ask Lucas what happened to Chloe, but it all came rushing back to me a second later. *I* had done that to her. The thought made me sick, and I swayed on my feet. I clutched my stomach with one hand and grabbed Lucas with the other so I wouldn't fall over.

"I-I did that, didn't I?" I realized. It was so much worse saying it out loud, because I wasn't entirely sure it was true until that moment. The whole thing had lasted less than thirty seconds. It felt like a dream.

I remembered how satisfying it felt, and that alone made me want to hurl. I never should've done that. It never should've felt that way. What the hell was wrong with me?

"You did," Lucas said dryly, like he couldn't make sense of what he'd seen.

I let go of him to stare down at my hands, as if that might convince me this wasn't real. But the evidence was right in front of me. My hands shook as I witnessed the blood coated over the backs of them.

"Goddess, Lucas..." My voice broke. "Chloe said you were sick. She said—"

"She was lying," Lucas told me. The way he stared at me made me uneasy—like he didn't even know who he was looking at. "That doesn't make what you did okay."

He looked like he was about to launch into a lecture, but I beat him to the freak-out. My whole body quaked as I broke down in sobs.

"You're right," I cried. I pressed my face into Lucas's shoulder.

He stiffened, like he didn't know what to do when a sobbing girl came to him. Eventually, he placed his arms around me, but it wasn't the welcoming embrace I'd come to know. It was cold and stilted. Nothing about it felt natural.

The hall was quieter now, as some of Chloe's friends had dragged her away to the infirmary, but voices continued to overlap one another. Several people had come out of the cafeteria to see what was happening, and several of Chloe's friends rushed down the hall to find a professor. I knew they'd be coming for me any moment, but it didn't matter. I kept replaying in my mind what I'd done, unable to believe that it'd been real and not some vivid dream.

"I'm a monster!" I cried into Lucas's shoulder. "I never meant to hurt her like that. I don't know what came over me. I-I—"

"What the hell was that, Nadine?" a voice demanded from behind me.

I turned to see Talia standing there, fuming.

"This is wrong," Talia cried. "You and Chloe can't keep doing this. Women need to support each other. You're part of the same coven, for Alora's sake!"

"I've *tried* talking to her," I insisted. "She won't cooperate."

"Then try something else," Talia suggested, her voice growing more intense.

"I did," I said sarcastically. *I beat her up.* I didn't blame Talia for being upset with me, but I didn't know how to explain myself right now—so I got defensive instead. "You fought her, too. Just a few weeks ago, you were backing me up."

"Not like this!" she shot back. "I got caught up in the moment. You've been at each other's throats all semester—"

"Nadine." A voice cut her off. The woman drew out my name, like my mother would when I was a child. It was the sound of utter disappointment.

I swallowed the lump in my throat as I turned toward her. "Headmistress Verla."

"To my office," she said sharply. "Now."

NINETEEN

I couldn't make sense of what it felt like to see Nadine flip out like that. I'd been walking to dinner when I noticed the commotion in the hall. My first thought was to move on and stay out of it—until I heard someone shouting Nadine's name.

"Nadine's gone psycho!" someone screamed.

And she had. Her eyes were void of remorse. There was nothing but satisfaction in them as she seared a battle orb against Chloe's face. It was eerie… and frightening.

Even now that the hall had cleared and Nadine left with Verla, I couldn't wrap my head around it. My Nad was loving and gentle, a welcome calm to the usual storm.

But today proved she was one hell of a storm herself.

And it terrified me.

But it wasn't her, I told myself. There had to be another explanation.

She'd spoken of her darkness before, and I'd witnessed it more than once. The night at The Dungeon, when she'd attacked Cody, stuck out in my mind. Chloe must've given her a good reason to fight back, I decided. Nothing else made sense.

Grant and Talia tried to say something to me as I passed, but I didn't hear it. I felt like I was moving through a fog as I walked to Headmistress Verla's office. I hadn't been invited along, but I wanted to be there for Nadine when she got out.

I ran back what I'd witnessed through my head—Nadine conjuring a battle orb, Chloe screaming out in agony. This was the kind of shit Ryan would pull, not Nadine. How did this happen?

Chloe was in the infirmary now. Something had possessed my Nad.

I didn't know how long I sat outside Headmistress Verla's door. It could've been hours. I fought between the pull I felt behind that door—toward Nadine, my world, my everything—and the urge to run far, far away.

Eventually, the door opened, and I got to my feet. Nadine stopped in the doorway when she saw me. Her eyes were red and blotchy, but she wasn't crying. So many emotions flickered past her features that I couldn't pick out a single one. It seemed to be a mix of shame, loss, and betrayal—as if she had betrayed herself.

"Nad," I whispered.

"I can't." Her voice cracked. "I just can't right now. You deserve an explanation, but I need a moment."

"Then we won't do this right now," I told her. I yearned for answers so I could stop feeling so conflicted, but the second I saw her, all I wanted to do was hold her. Which made no fucking sense. She'd just beat the shit out of another student.

"Let's get out of here," I suggested. It was the only way I could think to cool her down.

She nodded. "Okay."

I took Nadine's hand and led her outside into the warm spring air. It was dark out now, and the stars twinkled above us. The moon wasn't visible yet.

We entered the trees and followed a familiar path, before I veered off course toward the abandoned mansion in the woods. We'd had such a good time there last semester that it seemed appropriate.

"Where are we going?" Nadine asked in a small voice. She wouldn't look at me.

"Don't you recognize where we are?" I asked.

She glanced around the dark forest. "It looks different at night."

"We're almost there," I told her.

Several minutes later, Nadine and I emerged from the trees and into a clearing. The Gothic mansion rose above us, and green ivy grew up the sides. It was similar in style to the school, but much smaller.

"Thanks for bringing me here," Nadine said. "I needed to get out of the school."

I conjured a blanket and laid it in the grass, because it was a really nice night and I thought Nadine might like lying under the stars.

"Do you want to tell me what happened?" I asked as I situated myself on the blanket. The sky was clear overhead, and the Milky Way looked brilliant.

Nadine lay down beside me, though she kept her hands folded over her chest. She was only inches from me, but we didn't touch. I stole a glance at her, and she was staring up at the sky with a thoughtful expression on her face.

"I want to tell you," she finally said. "It's just hard to explain."

"I'll do my best to try to understand," I offered. I didn't know why I gave her the benefit of the doubt. I'd seen what she'd done with my own two eyes. If I hadn't stopped her, who knew how far she'd take things? I could only guess, and though the thought told me to abandon her here and run back to the safety of the school, I didn't want to run. Not when *my* Nad was right here next to me.

Nadine took a deep breath. "I guess it's not hard to explain. It's more… hard to face. I wasn't myself earlier tonight. But I also didn't do anything I didn't want to."

She got really quiet then, like the confession had been everything she was scared to say. It chilled me to the bone, as if I'd been hoping she'd say she was possessed by a demon or something. But this was different, and my guts sank. It sounded like a cry for help.

"I know what it's like to not feel like yourself," I admitted. "Maybe in a different way, but I get it."

She finally turned her head to look at me. "In what way?"

"Some days, I feel like me," I told her. "Other days, it's like I'm just a shell. I go on autopilot and nothing seems to matter. I just go through the motions."

"This is different," she said, turning her gaze back toward the stars.

"I know," I replied. I didn't know what I was trying to convince her of —maybe just assure her she wasn't alone.

"This wasn't just autopilot," Nadine admitted. "Something else took control. I couldn't hold back anymore."

"I'm sorry," I whispered. "That sounds terrifying."

"I shouldn't have lost control," she insisted. "Chloe messed with my meds, and I was pissed, but beating her to near unconsciousness wasn't right. She said she hurt you."

"I told you she was lying."

"I know that *now*. It's like Chloe *wanted* me to lose it..." Nadine's voice fell shamefully. "And I gave in."

I sighed. "What did Verla say?"

Nadine closed her eyes. "I'm suspended."

I pushed myself up on my elbow and gaped. "You're what?"

She looked up at me and frowned. "I'm suspended until the end of the semester. I'll stay with Grammy and take my exams privately. Then the school board will decide if I deserve to be expelled or not."

Sheer horror rippled through me. They couldn't kick Nadine out.

"Did you tell her what Chloe did?" I demanded.

"It doesn't matter," Nadine said quietly. "Maybe I'm better off leaving anyway."

My whole body turned to stone. *"What?"*

Nadine's eyes brimmed with tears. "You know I don't belong here. If I'm not expelled and kicked out of the coven, my family curse will make sure I leave either way."

"Unless Chloe fails her Evoking Ceremony," I insisted. "Or you break the curse."

"I can only do that if Chloe cooperates, and I can't get anywhere near her. And if I thought I could get her to listen before, I've ruined any chance of that."

"You still have time," I pressed.

"I only have a month after Chloe's ceremony before the curse claims a victim," Nadine said. "My two choices are to get her to listen... or leave."

"You can't leave!" I cried. My voice echoed through the trees, and I lowered my tone. "You passed your ceremony. That's proof that you belong."

"I don't know *why* I passed," Nadine said. "Maybe it was a fluke."

"Mother Miriam doesn't make mistakes," I told her. "If you leave, I'm going with you."

She shook her head, like the conversation was too painful. "This is your home."

When she said that, my heart shattered. I reached out and wiped a tear from the side of her face. I choked up. "My home is with *you*."

Nadine forced a smile, but it was short-lived. "That's sweet of you, but you're wrong."

I didn't think my heart could break any further, but it did. "You don't understand! Before I met you, I was numb. I either felt nothing, or I felt anxiety. You brought me to life, made me *feel*. I live for you now. I will always be yours. Your darkness doesn't matter to me, because it was *her* who did this to Chloe. We'll find a way to deal with that together."

Nadine's eyes sparkled, and she sniffled. "You only see the good in me, and that scares me. You say I'm pure of heart, and that's why I'm a Curse Breaker, but I don't think that's true. I hurt people."

"You always do it for the right reason," I argued. "The darkness is terrifying, but you, Nad, you're not dark. You're like the stars above us. You are the light *among* the dark. My starlight."

I pressed my hand to the side of Nadine's face, and she laid hers over top of mine and closed her eyes. We both went silent for a few moments, but I didn't like the quiet. Words began tumbling out of me as I sought to fill the moment.

"*Darkness falls in the dead of night. But it can't drown the starlight*," I whispered.

"Did you just make that up?"

I nodded. "For you."

Her features softened as she gazed up at me. "I don't deserve that."

"Yes, you do," I insisted. "It's the darkness inside of you that's trying to convince you otherwise. I know exactly what that feels like."

Nadine furrowed her brow. "Because of your depression?"

I nodded. "Before you say anything, I know it's not the same thing. But depression makes you think things about yourself that aren't true, too."

"I-I thought you were doing better," Nadine said.

I laid back down on the blanket. This time, I was the one staring up at the sky, unable to meet her gaze. "I have been," I assured her. "But it's not gone, not totally."

"You should have told me," Nadine protested, sounding more like herself.

"I wanted to do it on my own," I said. "I thought I could."

She sighed. "Lucas, you've treated me better than I deserve. You've been here for me all year. Let me be there for you."

I took a deep breath and rolled over on the blanket, until I was lying on my belly. I rested my chin on my folded hands and locked eyes with her. "It's not easy for me to open up."

She frowned. "It isn't easy for me, either. Please, Lucas."

Nadine's voice was pleading, so much that it made my whole chest ache. Her eyes begged me to let her in. I didn't say anything for a long time. All I could do was stare at her and wait for the courage to rise within me.

Slowly, Nadine's fingers inched across the blanket, until her hand was on my back. She rubbed it up and down, and I felt comforted by her touch. The hem of my shirt rose several inches, exposing my back to the night air. Nadine glanced downward, and she stiffened. I didn't realize why until a moment later.

"Your mark," she whispered. "I-I've never seen it."

I swallowed. "Yeah. Not the best location, is it?"

She sat up a little and furrowed her brow at me. "What do you mean?"

"Grant joked that it's a tramp stamp."

A smile briefly touched Nadine's lips, which I thought looked really beautiful on her. "Grant doesn't know what he's talking about. I like it."

Nadine began tracing the skull tattoo on my back with her fingers. Her proximity was intoxicating. I loved the feel of her hands on my skin.

"I didn't tell you I was still working through my depression, because I didn't want you to worry," I admitted while she ran her fingers over me.

"It's okay to ask for help," she whispered.

"I didn't want you to see me as weak," I said softly.

"I wouldn't do that. You don't have to go through this alone."

"It's not fair to drag you into my problems."

"But that's what we do when we're in a relationship," Nadine insisted. "It's what I agreed to when I became your girlfriend. You would never let me go through anything alone."

"You're right," I agreed. "So don't push me away."

She went still, and the air felt colder on my skin. "I didn't mean to. I want to help you."

"I wish you could," I said. "I know I'm not working through this as fast as other people might, but I'm going at my own pace. Just let me get there, okay?"

Nadine dropped her gaze to my tattoo and began tracing it again, slower this time. "Then I need to work through my darkness at my own pace."

"Not without my help. I won't walk away from you."

"Then don't ask me to walk away from you!" she cried. "This relationship isn't a one-way street. We have to help *each other*. If I'm going to accept your help with my darkness, you need to let me be there for you with your depression."

The clearing got really quiet as I contemplated what Nadine said. It sounded fair, but it didn't *feel* it. Protecting her was my duty. I couldn't lay a burden on her.

"Worrying about me is useless," I told her.

She was quick to counter. "Worrying about you is all I'm going to do if I don't understand how you truly feel. I have to trust that you're being completely open and honest with me."

Her words struck a chord within me. She wasn't asking for a burden.

I rolled over onto my back and stared up at her. "You're right."

"I'm… I'm what?" she asked, like she hadn't expected me to cave.

"You don't deserve to be kept in the dark," I decided. "I will be more open about my feelings with you."

Nadine pressed her hand to her chest. "And you say *I'm* your starlight. Lucas, that brings so much light to my heart."

I smiled shyly. "I wish I could bring it all, but you do that yourself."

Nadine smiled and leaned down, until our noses were practically touching. Heat flared deep in my belly as her lips hovered just inches above mine. "If you think you're going to convince me I have light within myself, you're going to have to start believing the same about yourself."

She leaned in, and our lips connected. The primal instinct to take her right here overcame me as my heart swelled inside my chest. I wrapped a hand around her neck and tangled it in her soft hair. I dragged her closer to me and kissed her passionately. Nadine returned the sentiment as she crawled on top of me and pressed her body into mine. My hands roamed all over her, and my head spun at the sweet taste of her kiss. I never wanted the kiss to end.

Right here in this moment, the light we spoke of seemed almost blinding. I lived for moments like these, for the undeniable connection we shared that brought me to life. I knew the second I opened my eyes, all I would see was the dark sky above, littered with dim stars. Not a single one could outshine *her*—not even the sun.

In this moment, she glowed, and I knew that even when everything seemed to be falling apart, I had these small moments to live for.

Nadine came up for air, and I couldn't help but ask, "Are we okay, then?"

She smiled down at me. "Yeah, we're okay."

I was mesmerized by her smile and the soft look in her eyes. As if my hands had a mind of their own, I reached up to push her hair behind her ear. My fingers ran across her cheek as I admired her, and she tilted her head toward my hand, as if savoring every caress.

My body yearned for her, and my soul was drawn to her as if the two of us were tethered by destiny. Passion rose within my chest, feeling as if it might explode out of me. Words couldn't do this feeling justice. I was high on the taste of her kiss, and the feel of her body grinding against mine. I wished I could share this feeling with her, to show her exactly how I felt. Maybe I never could... but there were other things I could share with her, pieces of myself she would carry for eternity.

I grabbed her around the waist and rolled her over, until she was lying flat on her back on the blanket. Her eyes blazed with hunger as I climbed on top of her.

"What's going on?" she asked curiously, obviously liking where this was going.

"I want to make love to you, Nadine," I whispered, sharing the raw honesty I never could say before.

She stared at me with soft features as she ran her fingers through my hair. "We can't."

"I know, but maybe I can get close."

Her eyes sparkled with intrigue. "What did you have in mind?"

A blissful smile spread across my face. "Let me show you."

Nadine shivered as I reached for the button on her jeans. She started trying to kick her shoes off in anticipation, but I placed a hand on her leg to stop her.

"Let me," I whispered. "You don't have to work for this."

Nadine relaxed, and I slowly slipped off her shoes, before reaching for her jeans and stripping those off. Her shirt rode up, showing off her skin all the way from her belly down to her toes. My gaze locked on her blue lace panties, and my pulse quickened.

I didn't move quickly, though all my instinct told me to fuck her right here. But tonight wasn't the night for *that* kind of pleasure. Tonight was a night to be gentle, to savor every sensual moment—to make *love* to her.

I roamed my hands over her naked legs, rubbing her muscles softly. She moaned in pleasure as my hands moved over her, and I knew I had the pressure just right. She was in chronic pain, and I thought she might like the massage. It turned out I was right.

Slowly, I moved my way up her body. She shivered under my touch, but never once drew away. She simply relaxed into the blanket, closing her eyes and taking it all in. My fingers reached her thighs, and I turned from massaging her to gently caressing her skin. Her body quivered as I came closer and closer to her panties.

"Is this okay?" I whispered.

"It's perfect," she replied blissfully. "It only tickles a little."

"In a good way?" I teased, tickling her thighs again.

She laughed, and her smile widened, though she never opened her eyes. "In the best way."

"What about this?" I asked. I slipped my fingers under the lace of her panties a half inch, skimming them over her skin.

"Better…" she encouraged.

"And this?" I dipped my head downward and took her panties in my teeth.

"I like the direction this is going," she whispered, sounding like she was in a dream.

I wanted her to feel more of that, to enjoy the blissful high as long as possible. Tugging with my teeth, I pulled the panties down her legs and tossed them beside her pants.

Nadine gasped as my lips met the inside of her thigh. She writhed beneath me, as if begging for more. Inside, my heart hammered like a wild animal begging to be released from its cage. Nadine arched her back, and her breaths became heavy in anticipation.

I kissed her again, higher this time. Nadine couldn't seem to take it any longer. She sank her hands into my hair, pulling on the strands passionately. She spread her legs wider, inviting me in. It totally broke something inside of me, and all my wanting for her turned to desperation. My lips connected with her most sensitive areas, and she gasped in pleasure.

"Oh God, Lucas," she cried.

The sound of my name on her lips—the way she used it to beg for more—did something to me. I forgot all about taking things slow and began running my tongue over her quickly. Her sweet taste filled my mouth, making me go wild. Nadine wrapped her legs around me, and I couldn't help but go deeper, my tongue moving in and out of her as she moaned in pleasure. I wished there was more I could offer her, but all I had was this moment—my tongue exploring the apex of her thighs.

I ran my tongue over her pleasure centers, while I took two fingers and inserted the inside of her, slowly at first, until her fingers tightened in my hair, begging for more. My dick went wild in my pants as I sank my fingers deep inside of her, moving in and out quickly, using her sensual noises as a guide. Nadine arched her back. She was fucking *loving* this, and so was I. I moved faster, pleasing her inside and out. Her moans grew louder and louder.

Then Nadine gasped, and she tugged my hair so hard I had to pull away. But it was so fucking hot, I didn't care. She contracted around my fingers, and I watched her body writhe on the blanket beneath me as she reached her peak. She squeezed her eyes shut tightly, but her mouth hung open, like she was amazed at the way I made her feel.

"Lucas," she breathed as she came down from the high. Slowly, she peeled her eyes open, and she beamed as she looked up at me. "That was amazing."

I smiled. It totally was. Watching her enjoy herself like that... hell, it was as if she'd given me oral herself. I felt like I was on top of the world as I lay on the blanket beside her. "I'm glad you liked it."

She laughed. "Well, that's a tame way of putting it."

I wrapped my arms around her and drew her close. She curled into me, like I was the one place in the world where she belonged. I loved holding her, like I could keep her safe here in my arms.

I pressed my nose into her hair. "You're right," I teased. "You fucking loved it."

Nadine giggled again, then relaxed into me. "I did. And I love *you*, Lucas."

"I love you, too, Nad," I whispered.

Nadine relaxed so much, I thought she might fall asleep in my arms. And I would stay here beside her all night if she did. I pulled a corner of the blanket up to cover her legs. I didn't want to let her go. And so I didn't ask for anything in return. Holding her was more than enough. When I held her, all felt right in the world.

If only I knew perfection like this couldn't last.

nadine

TWENTY

Being with Lucas in a whole new way was enthralling and magical. I'd loved every second of it and was comforted by how close the night had brought us together.

But when I woke the following morning in Lucas's arms, all the events that led to that magnificent night under the stars came rushing back to me. Being with Lucas had been wonderful, but I worried that it was more of a distraction than anything. And now that it was over, I had to face reality again.

I didn't know how to explain to my friends what I'd done. Lucas seemed to understand me, but Talia was pissed—perhaps even frightened. And Grant? I had no idea what he thought of me. I thought about leaving without saying anything. It would be easier.

I didn't return to the dorms after that night. Talia deserved her space, and I didn't feel welcome anyway. I decided to stay at Grammy's over the weekend, and I barely got out of bed. I didn't answer any of the calls and texts from my friends, either.

Eventually, I had to return to the school to get my things. I was packing up my stuff when Talia entered the room. Her eyes lit up momentarily. "You're back!"

"Not for long," I said.

She eyed me curiously. "Are you leaving?"

I frowned as I folded clothes into my suitcase. Isa kept crawling into it and laying on top of the clothes. "I'm suspended," I stated flatly.

Talia crossed the room slowly, like she didn't know what to make of my announcement. Gus followed at her feet, and she sank into the couch. "I'm sorry. I…"

"You don't have to say anything," I told her. "I already know what I did was wrong."

Talia scoffed. "I'm not going to argue that. But why didn't you call?"

I shrugged and didn't meet her gaze. "I thought you wouldn't want to talk to me."

"I called you a dozen times!" she cried.

"I thought you'd just chew me out," I admitted as I dragged Isa out of the suitcase once again.

"Maybe at first," Talia said.

"Chloe took my meds and threatened Lucas. What was I supposed to do?"

"Maybe not beat her?" Talia suggested.

I sighed. "Yeah, I know. All I want to do is pack up my stuff and finish the semester."

"Nadine," Talia said softly. She stood and walked over to me. I didn't want to look her in the face, but she grabbed my shoulders and practically forced me. "Look, I won't pretend like I understand the way you lashed out. It was… frightening to watch. But I will say that I want to help. We all do."

"We all?" I questioned.

"Me, Grant, Mandy, Amy," she listed off. "You're our friend, and you're obviously going through something. I know things have been traumatic for you lately."

My teeth gritted. I shook my head and turned back to my clothes. "Whatever you have to tell yourself. It sounds like you've thought this through. How long was the meeting?"

"Meeting?" she asked.

"You know, the one where you all got together and decided I lashed out because my parents were dead," I stated flatly.

Talia gaped. It was obvious they'd all been talking about me behind my back.

"It wasn't like that," Talia insisted.

"I don't care how it was," I said honestly. "I just want to get out of here for a while. I need some time to think."

"Consider yourself lucky," Talia replied.

I furrowed my brow at her. "Lucky how?"

"Maybe your grandma's place is safer for you right now," Talia suggested. "Tons of people are having issues with their magic. Everyone's afraid they're going to fail their exams."

My eyebrows shot up. "It's getting worse?"

"Yeah, you missed it over the weekend. Two more fights broke out, and the Imperium Council was here again."

I gaped. I'd heard rumors about how people thought this was some sort of curse, but who could be so powerful to cast it over the entire town? Unless it was more localized…

"Is it only at the school?" I asked.

Talia shook her head. "Based on the rumors I've heard, it's widespread all across Octavia Falls. But for some reason it's more localized here. Maybe because we're in so close proximity."

"So the curse spreads like a virus?" I asked.

Talia shrugged. "It's a theory. It wouldn't be the first curse to do so."

"I can't break something this big on my own," I blurted.

"No one's asking you to," Talia promised. "There's still no evidence it *is* a curse. It acts too weird. Like you'll be affected, then get your powers back, then be affected again. It doesn't seem to have any pattern."

I shook my head in disbelief as I calculated what she'd said. I didn't know enough about magical theory to come up with my own guess. "Lucas told me about one of his Magical Theory lessons," I mused. "He said when you overexert yourself, your magic can take time to replenish."

"Yeah, but everyone's not overexerting themselves all at once," Talia pointed out.

"Unless there was something drawing their magic, like the Protection Tree," I thought aloud.

It was a good theory, but Talia shot it down. "The protection spell's magic doesn't work that way, but you might be onto something."

I double checked my suitcase to make sure Isa wasn't hiding inside, then zipped it up and lugged it off my bed. "That's pretty good for a novice."

"You're catching on fast." Talia shrugged, before quickly adding, "You should stay here tonight."

I shook my head. "I can't. I'm suspended."

"Then you're my guest," she teased. "I've really missed having you around. I mean, it didn't help that I was worrying about you. Just one night?"

When Talia said she was worried, it tugged at my heartstrings. I thought for sure she'd be pissed at me. And maybe she was, but we hadn't seen each other in a few days, so we'd both had time to cool off. I missed her, too.

"Okay," I caved. "I'll stay."

Talia and I stayed up playing with her deck of tarot cards, eating popcorn, and listening to creepy music. We didn't read the cards for ourselves—because I really didn't want to hear what they had to say—but we laughed as we read the cards for others.

"You were spot on with Grant," Talia teased as we did a reading on his love life. Apparently, he'd been lonely for quite some time, but was about to find a long-term girlfriend. Or so we interpreted the cards.

"Good for him," I said. "I hope he ends up happy."

Talia's laugh quieted, and she spoke softly. "Yeah. I hope he does, too."

Eventually, I couldn't force myself to stay up any longer. I kept yawning, and Talia suggested we call it a night.

I snuggled up with Isa in my bed and drifted off…

☽

Bricks settled in my gut as I stared up at the painting of Mother Miriam in the Main Foyer. The coals of the fire burned red, though there were no flames. Outside, the sky was dark, and wind whistled through a crack in one of the windows. Though the chair I sat in was plush and usually comfortable, it felt like a rock today. The painting had been slashed three times, and I held the cool handle of the dagger in my hand.

"What did you do, Nadine?" I asked myself. I couldn't remember doing it or what reason I had to in the first place, but somehow, I knew it'd been me. It felt like a worthy revenge on the coven. They were going to kick me out. I had to do something.

"Not like this," I whispered under my breath. This felt wrong. I was horrified,

and yet I couldn't move. Perhaps it was fitting that the coven should abandon me. Then I wouldn't hurt anyone else.

"Are you talking to me?" A female voice came from behind me. It was soft and curious, not dark and sinister like the Nadine who roamed these halls.

I whirled around and was surprised to see Mandy standing there. She wore a black skater dress and high boots.

"Mandy?" I balked, sitting up straighter. "What are you doing here? I thought I was alone."

"Well, you were." She stepped toward me. "I don't know how I got here. I can't control it yet."

"Control what?"

Mandy glanced around the empty foyer. Her eyes traveled over the sconces, then up to the chandelier. No candles were lit, as the only light came from the dying fire.

"I can't control my dreamer powers," Mandy clarified as she spun to take everything in. "So, this is your subconscious?"

I eyed her as her words sank in. "This is a dream?"

"Yes, but don't freak out," she said quickly.

As realization came over me, the scene began to shift. Candles lit all across the room, and the dagger in my hand vanished.

"I'm going to wake up," I realized.

"No, don't do that," Mandy said. "This is... cool."

Her words sounded flat. It wasn't cool. It was a tad bit depressing.

I forced my heart rate to slow and felt myself sinking deeper into sleep. "Why don't you want me waking up?"

She finally tore her gaze from our surroundings to look at me. "You're my friend, and I want to help."

I narrowed my eyes at her. "Help with what?"

She gestured around. "Whatever this is. Why are you sitting in the dark?"

I shook my head. "Please don't go digging. If this is really my subconscious, then it's private."

"Too late. I've already seen it," she stated simply. "Can I sit? I need the practice dream analyzing anyway."

My guts twisted. It wasn't that I didn't want my friend in my dreams. The truth was, I'd been sitting in the dark to hide from the woman who lurked these halls. Now that Mandy had shown up, the lights had come on and she would find us. She would see Mandy's presence as intrusive. I could already feel it. I didn't want her hurting my friend.

Mandy sat in front of the fire and warmed her hands, while I hurried to the nearest sconce to blow it out. But as soon as my breath passed the flame, it lit again. I panicked.

"Look, I appreciate the help, but you have to leave," I stated quickly.

She looked up at me and chewed her lower lip. "Leave?"

"Yes, please leave," I requested, as nicely as I could.

"I don't know how yet," she said. "You'll have to wake up."

"How do I do that?" I asked. I tried instructing myself to open my eyes—to do anything—but nothing happened. I remained rooted in place, staring at Mandy who sat uninvited in the middle of my dream.

"I'm not sure," she admitted. "I'm still learning."

A noise came from down the hall, though I couldn't place what it was. I glanced toward it, but the hall was dark. Worry began to rise in my stomach.

"You need to figure out how to leave," I insisted.

Mandy gaped at me. "I really didn't mean to intrude. But like I said, I'm still learning—"

A maniacal laugh echoed down the hall. My pulse sped up, and Mandy stiffened.

"Wh-what was that?" she asked warily.

"The reason you have to go!" I cried. I hurried over to her and grabbed her by the wrist. "You're not safe here."

I tried shoving her toward the door, but Mandy resisted. She planted her feet firmly in front of me. It was my dream, but we were equally matched for strength. It seemed a little unfair.

"Hold on," Mandy said. "I'm not going anywhere until you tell me what's going on. Are you okay?"

"You caught me on a bad night," I told her. "Please go."

"I'm getting a really bad feeling. Please let me help."

I gritted my teeth. She didn't understand what Dark Nadine would do to her. The laughter came again, this time louder and closer.

"She's coming!" I shoved her toward the door again.

Mandy opened her mouth to respond, but she didn't get another word in. The laughter came to an abrupt halt, and then a voice sounded directly behind me.

"Get. Out. Of. My. Head!" Dark Nadine screamed.

I whirled around in time to see her evil snarl, eyes locked on Mandy. One *second she was standing at one end of the foyer, and the other, she was lunging for Mandy. I threw myself in front of her at the last second and tackled Dark Nadine to the ground.*

"Mandy can stay!" I shouted. "You're the one unwelcome here!"

Dark Nadine laughed from beneath me. "Oh, Nadine," she said condescendingly. "You're the one who invited me here. I'm not going anywhere."

☾

I WOKE WITH A START. The dream was fresh in my mind, though my surroundings eluded me.

I'd fallen asleep in my own dorm—I knew that much. But this didn't feel right. The ground I lay on was hard and uneven, and the air was chilly with a slight breeze. Something moved above me in the darkness, but I couldn't make it out. As my eyes adjusted to the darkness, I realized it was trees swaying in the wind. I blinked a few times and winced as I pushed myself to my elbows. Sleeping on the ground hadn't been kind to me. Every muscle and joint ached as I moved, trying to take it all in.

How had I gotten here?

My gaze swept the forest. I didn't recognize where I was, and it was hard to make out the patterns in the trees at this time of night. It had to be after midnight. The forest was oddly quiet, and the hairs on the back of my neck stood up. I sensed nothing in the trees, and I wasn't sure if that should soothe me or make this more terrifying.

The possibilities went through my head as I waited for my aching body to get with the program so I could find my way back to the school.

Did I sleepwalk? That was the only explanation for how I'd ended up out here. Maybe it was a side-effect of Mandy's dreamer powers. If that were the case, I couldn't be far from school. Problem was, I didn't know which direction was the way back.

I had to try something, though, because I wasn't staying out here in the frigid air all night. I reached out for a nearby tree and used it to support myself as I climbed to my feet. I was barefoot and in my pajamas. Luckily, I'd chosen the warm, comfy flannel ones tonight with the witch hats printed on them.

I scanned the trees for signs of light, hoping I might spot a beacon that would lead me home. The only light I saw came from the stars and moon above. I drew a deep breath. I had to start *somewhere*. I chose a direction and began walking—slowly, because my whole body ached from sleeping on the ground. I took several steps… and then I heard it.

A stick snapped from behind me, and my heart leapt into my throat. The hairs on the back of my neck stood straighter. Though I hadn't seen anything in the woods, I sensed danger was lurking nearby. Could it be a monster, like the one Lucas and I had run into earlier this semester?

The forest had gone quiet, and I wondered if I'd imagined the noise. Still, I couldn't keep the worry from my mind. Adrenaline rushed through me, and I quickened my step.

Another twig snapped, and fear overcame me. This sure as hell wasn't my imagination. I began running as fast as I could through the trees, but it wasn't fast enough. Whatever was pursuing me was coming closer. I couldn't hear it, but I felt it within my bones.

I couldn't bear to think of the possibility. *This better be another dream*, I thought, but my pounding heart told me otherwise. This was real, and if the monster caught up to me, I was dead.

My bare feet moved over squishy moss and then hard rocks. A sharp stick stabbed the middle of my foot, cutting into the delicate skin there. I drew a breath but didn't slow. I didn't know how far I'd run or how long, but I kept on going.

I was slowing down fast, though. My body betrayed me as I sucked in deep breaths. I used nearby trees to support myself as I passed them. I hit a root with my toe and cursed as I tripped forward. I caught myself on a tree trunk, but my next step forward was nothing more than a limp.

I paused to take in my surroundings again. Everything looked the same. All was still—then a rustle came through the trees.

Fuck. I couldn't stand around. I had to move, or fight back. That was my only other option, because if this was a monster, I wasn't outrunning it.

I jumped around a tree, until I was on the other side where I could hide for cover. The footsteps following me slowed. I peeked around the tree and spotted a shadowed figure moving in the distance, but I couldn't make out its shape or size. It was at least as big as I was, for sure.

I took aim and shot a battle orb toward the creature. The second the orb left my hand, my shoulders sagged as my magic drained my energy.

The orb exploded against a tree—nowhere near where I'd seen the shadowed figure. If I thought I could fight back, I was kidding myself. I was already freaking exhausted, and my magic would only drain me further.

As I sat there contemplating my next move, a huge rock slammed into the side of the tree I hid behind. It landed only inches from my head. My heart leapt into my throat, and I scrambled to my feet. Now the creature was throwing shit at me? Fuck, I had to get out of here.

I took off running again, tossing battle orbs over my shoulder when I thought I heard the monster getting too close. But I didn't have time to stop and aim. Each one of them missed.

It was a mistake to use my magic. The more I did, the greater toll it took on my body. I was slowing down—fast. The only thing that kept me going now was the adrenaline coursing through my veins like a raging fire.

The forest began to swim in front of me. I must've been running for a while now. This felt like some sort of sick game. Otherwise, why hadn't that thing caught me yet?

Please, somebody help me, I thought. I wanted to say the words out loud —to yell and scream in hopes that someone would hear me. But I couldn't open my mouth to get the words out. I was too tired from what felt like the marathon I was running.

I spotted a break in the trees up ahead, and I rushed toward it. But the faster I moved, the more fatigue overcame me. The forest spun around me, and the trees blurred together.

My body went limp, and the forest floor titled, rushing up to meet my face.

When I came to, I was lying in the clearing. The dark sky was wide open above me, except for the ends of a few gnarly tree branches in front of my vision. I wondered where the monster had gone, but I was glad it hadn't devoured me.

I went to sit up, but something tugged at my neck, and I coughed. My shaking fingers immediately went to my throat as panic overtook me. I felt a rope, and my panic turned to sheer terror. I slid my fingers under the rope and yanked on it, but it only tightened around my neck.

"I can't... breathe!" I gasped, as if someone might be able to hear me.

"That's the idea," a female voice responded.

I stopped struggling as I realized what this was. The noose was a warning. The more I fought, the tighter it would become, until I was suffocated—or hanged.

Slowly, I turned in the direction of the voice. The clearing was dark at first, until the woman formed an orb in one hand and tossed it into the air. It wasn't the bright, colorful light I was used to from orbs like mine and Lucas's. Instead, this light was dim, with a reddish-orange hue. It hovered in the air above our heads, casting an ominous glow over the scene.

Finally, I was able to make out where I was. The Protection Tree stood in front of me, and I noticed the rope around my neck hung over one of its branches. The woman held the other end, tugging tightly at it every time I moved. The reddish orb illuminated her dark hair and sharp features.

My hands curled into fists. Instinct told me to throw a battle orb at her—a high-powered one that would actually do damage. But before I could, something clicked. She'd just conjured a light orb herself, which meant she had magic. I didn't know what she was capable of.

"What the hell is this?" I demanded. It was then that I realized *she'd* been the one chasing me through the forest. She hadn't been hunting me. She'd been leading me here.

Choe threw her head back in laughter. If I thought Dark Nadine was bad in my dreams, she was nothing compared to Chloe. Chloe was *real*.

The last time I'd seen her, she had bruises all over her face. Her stay in the infirmary had done her wonders, because I didn't see a mark on her.

"Isn't it obvious?" she asked. "I'm here to get what I want. My powers have finally awakened. Your time is up."

Though I was the one with the noose around my neck, I couldn't help but shoot back at her. "Is this some kind of trick—an illusion?"

Chloe tugged at the noose again, shutting me up. Damn it. Even if I wanted to fight back, I wasn't in a position to do so. I had maybe one spell in me right now. I had to time my attack just right.

"Witches can't cast illusion magic, you idiot," Chloe snapped.

"It wouldn't be the first time you stole an illusion spell," I retorted. She'd used one last year to fake my hanging. It was fitting that she might use one again with a noose around my neck.

"Does this feel real enough to you?" Chloe demanded. She tugged on the rope again, and I gasped for air. As her fingers tightened on the rope, I spotted the mark of a Mentalist on her wrist. I'd bet anything her specialty was telekinesis, based on the rock that had flown through the air earlier and nearly hit me.

I spoke through wheezing breaths. "I'm just... surprised you... passed your ceremony."

"Don't be," she snarled. "I actually know a thing or two about this coven."

"Don't forget I'm a part of it," I said in a struggling tone.

"I don't know why Mother Miriam would want you," Chloe said. "Either way, this curse is going to take one of us, and I won't let it be me."

"So that's what you're doing?" I demanded. Chloe had loosened her hold on the rope, enough that I could make out a full sentence. "You're going to hang me—make sure the curse takes me first?"

"This coven needs me!" she yelled. "I'm going to become a priestess one day! I'll serve on the Imperium Council. What will you ever do for the coven?"

"Protect it from people like you," I rasped.

Chloe scoffed. "You think I'm so bad, that *I'm* the mean girl. Take a look in the mirror."

"I do what I have to do to protect myself and the people I love," I snapped.

"So do I!" she cried. "We're not so different. The difference is that *you* can have a life out there. You've done it before. I grew up here, and I've trained my whole life to become a part of this coven."

"My life out there is gone," I argued. "This is my home now. We can both stay, but you have to listen to me!"

"Listen to you?" Chloe laughed. "That's the same thing your grandpa said to mine, before he betrayed him!"

"This isn't about them!" I insisted. "This is about us. We can break the curse. We just have to—"

Chloe yanked on the rope again. "Even if there was a way to break the curse, do you think I'd work with you? My family's already been betrayed once."

Tears began to bead in my eyes. "How? What did my grandpa do?"

"He attacked my grandfather when he tried to take what was rightfully his!"

"And what was that?" I asked. Chloe had piqued my curiosity—I couldn't deny that. But I also had to keep her talking as I calculated my next move.

"Seriously? Your grandmother didn't tell you?"

I felt a sudden stab of betrayal from Grammy, but I realized Chloe was just trying to get into my head. "I'm sure she had a good reason."

"Really? Like your grandpa had a good reason for hiding the Oaken Wands from his own people?"

I stilled. "The Oaken Wands?"

Chloe rolled her eyes. "You just keep proving you don't belong here. You're so ignorant."

I held my head high. "I can be taught. What are the Oaken Wands?"

Chloe looked about ready to lose it. "You really want to know what all this is about? Nicholas Tucker was a criminal. That's why men shouldn't serve on the Imperium Council. He was driven by greed."

"I don't believe you," I countered. That went against every story my mom and Grammy had told me about him. He was kind and a good leader.

"Your grandpa was on the council because he was the only one in his Cast," Chloe said. "They had no other options. The Oaken Wands were a collection of five powerful wands created for the coven. Your grandfather used his power to hide them from the coven, because he wanted them for himself!"

"I don't believe you," I snarled.

Chloe ignored me and continued. "My grandfather hunted down the Mentalist Wand, and intended to give it back to our Cast, but *yours* got in the way!"

I never knew my grandfather, but it didn't matter how Chloe twisted the story. I didn't believe her. Grammy and Mom would only protect the coven, and I had to believe my grandfather would've done the same. "If it's true my grandfather hid the wands, he had a reason. Probably so people like Jeb Olson couldn't abuse their power."

"Who is he to decide!?" Chloe sneered.

"He was a priest!" I cried.

"A priest who stole power from the coven!" Chloe shot back. "The wands belong to the Casts, not the council. It was *your* grandpa who cast the first spell when they fought."

"And *yours* who cursed us!" I reminded her.

"He did what he had to do to protect himself and his family," Chloe insisted. "My grandfather had the Mentalist Wand, but yours took the Curse Breaker Wand, and they dueled. It was his only choice to end things."

"Through murder!?" I snapped. "I guess the apple doesn't fall far from the tree."

Chloe's fingers tightened on the rope. "Not when it comes to this coven."

I wanted to know more about the story—what had *really* happened all those years ago. I couldn't take Chloe's word for it, but she had planted seeds of doubt in my mind. I didn't know who was in the right, or if they were both in the wrong.

But I didn't have time to rehash the past. There was a fucking noose around my neck, and I wasn't going to let this decades-old feud end here. Not tonight. Not with my hanging.

"We can end this," I told Chloe.

"You're right," she said coolly. "We can. You're going to leave Octavia Falls and never look back. I've given you endless chances, but your time has run out. You leave tonight, or you hang from this tree."

"Not like this," I insisted. "I tried to tell you before, but you wouldn't listen. We can break the curse."

Chloe threw her head back in laughter. It didn't sound like her usual laughter. It was maniacal and dark—a laugh that reminded me of my own darkness swirling in my gut.

She has darkness of her own. A shiver traveled down my spine, because I knew she'd kill me. If her darkness took over, she wouldn't question it.

"There's nothing you can say to save yourself," Chloe growled. "So I'll ask you this once. Are you going to leave Octavia Falls?"

I swallowed, even though the noose felt tight around my neck. "No," I stated firmly. "I'm going to—"

I didn't get a chance to finish my sentence. Chloe yanked hard on the rope, and it tightened around my neck. My body jerked into the air, until my toes were no longer touching the ground. I thrashed, as if that might help me break free. But the more I moved, the tighter the rope became. Pain radiated across my neck as it dug into my skin, forming bruises. My windpipe burned, and my chest ached as I tried gasping for air.

I clawed at the rope on my neck as panic swept through me. My darkness rose to the surface, and I let her take over, because I knew I wasn't strong enough to fight on my own.

But even Dark Nadine had run out of ideas. I tried to form a battle orb with enough power to burn the rope above me, but I was exhausted. The magic didn't come.

I formed what magic I could and aimed it at Chloe. It was my last resort. I had just enough power to stun her and get her to drop the rope, but I was spinning through the air and running out of time. Black spots entered my vision, and my heart raced. I took aim the best I could and threw my final spell at her.

Chloe dodged my spell, and the rope slipped through her fingers just long enough for my toes to touch the ground again. I gulped a greedy breath of air, but the noose tightened before I could get my fingers on it again.

Chloe yanked me upward, and my feet left the ground again.

"I'm a… a… Curse… Breaker…" I gasped.

"You'll burn in the Abyss for the lies you tell!" Chloe screamed. The edge to her tone was unlike I'd ever heard it before. It was full of rage and hatred, and that was when I knew her darkness had totally consumed her. She was going to kill me.

I grabbed for the hem of my shirt and yanked it upward, displaying the crescent moon tattoo above my hip. The best I could hope for was that she was curious enough to talk. Otherwise, I was a goner.

"It's… true," I rasped.

Through my blurring vision, I witnessed Chloe's features falter momentarily. She quickly rearranged her face back into a sneer, then yanked even more on the rope.

"It's a trick!" she snarled. "You're just like your grandpa Nicholas! It's no wonder my family cursed yours. You are deceptive and a traitor to the coven. You will be punished in the Abyss, and I will—"

A stunning spell whipped through the air and slammed into Chloe's back before she could finish her sentence. The rope slipped through her fingers as she slumped to the ground. I fell from the tree and landed on all fours. I yanked the noose off my neck as fast as I could. Relief flooded through me, and I searched the trees for signs of my rescuer. It had to be my friends. Talia must've woken and realized I was missing, and they came looking for me. Oh, how I longed to fall into Lucas's arms right now. I could weep at being rescued.

"I'm over… here…" I called out to the darkness, but my voice was quiet and raspy. I hoped my friends could hear me.

I waited for their reply, but it never came. All I saw was another stunning spell whizzing through the forest. I didn't have time to move out of the way.

The spell hit me in the face, sending a shooting wave of pain through my nose. My body slumped to the ground, and darkness consumed me.

TWENTY-ONE

Several Hours Earlier

Finals were just around the corner, which meant it was time for mine and Grant's bi-annual skip day. It'd quickly become tradition after our first semester. At the first sign of clear skies and warm weather, we gathered our gear and spent the day hiking the mountainous portion of the Black Circle Trail at the edge of town. We climbed boulders, before playing a round of disc golf at the local park.

Around twilight, thick clouds began to roll in, and the temperature dropped at least ten degrees.

Grant looked up to the sky. "Seems a bit ominous, doesn't it?"

"It's hardly superstitious," I said, though a chill traveled down my spine anyway. It was as if the town itself was trying to tell us something. I couldn't shake the feeling that dark times loomed ahead.

We didn't get back to the school until after sunset.

"We should get some real climbing gear," Grant suggested as we entered the Main Foyer. "I mean, bouldering is fun enough, but I want my ass in a harness, you know?"

I laughed. "Last time we tried that, you passed out and hung there like a dead fish. You should probably stick with the school's indoor rock wall."

"Apparently, it didn't traumatize me, because I want to try again," Grant replied.

"Yeah," I agreed. "I'd love to get some gear—"

"Lucas!" Mandy cut in front of us, hugging a thick book to her chest. My stomach sank at the worried look on her face.

"What's going on?" I asked.

She grabbed my wrist and began dragging me away from Grant. "We need to talk."

Whatever it was sounded urgent. I turned back to Grant. "I'll catch up with you later."

He gave me a salute. "No problem. I have some swimming to do, anyway."

Mandy's manicured nails dug into my arm as she dragged me to a secluded corner of the foyer. She guided me to a study area with four chairs set around a coffee table, but there was no one else nearby.

"Thank the Goddess I finally found you!" she said breathlessly. "I've been looking for you all day."

I felt the blood drain from my face. "Grant and I skipped. We turned off our phones."

I quickly conjured my phone and turned it on, so I could check any missed calls or messages. "What's going on? Is Nadine okay?"

I could only imagine what had gone down this time.

"I haven't seen her all day," Mandy said. "This isn't about her. You might want to sit."

I really didn't want to, but Mandy had me worried. I didn't want to argue. I sank into the nearest chair, and she sat across from me, placing the tome on her knees.

"It's about the missing boys," she said.

My spine straightened, and my gaze flickered to the book. "You found something?"

"More than I care to know, to be honest," she admitted. "It started last night."

Mandy shot a gaze around the room. The closest students were gossiping by the fireplace, totally oblivious to us. We wouldn't be overheard, but she lowered her voice anyway.

"I'm still learning my powers," Mandy said. "Right now, I can't control whose dreams I end up in. Last night, I saw *him*."

"Daymond?" I asked. I could hear it in her tone.

"I'm not sure *whose* dream it was," she clarified. "But whoever's dream I was in, he knew about the missing boys."

I leaned in. "What happened in the dream?"

Mandy's hands shook, like it was hard to talk about. "This dream felt so real—almost like a memory. I saw a man sitting at a desk, but it was so dark, I couldn't see his face. He was flipping through a calendar, like he was planning something. I saw the boys' names, but he wrote down other things, too—astronomical events like meteor showers and the full moon."

The air left my lungs. "You think Daymond's performing a ritual?"

I'd thought this was all about revenge, but a ritual explained why he'd waited so long between kidnappings—and why Travis hadn't been taken yet. This was dark magic beyond comprehension.

Mandy swallowed. "I think this is definitely tied to some sort of ritual. When I couldn't find you earlier, I went to the library to research. I had to make sure the dream meant something and wasn't just utter nonsense. But the dates line up. You heard their voices on the full moon as the boys died. Both instances coincided with another event—a comet the first time, and a meteor shower the second."

Mandy sounded really frightened, and I was right there alongside her. Murder was pure evil, but using it for dark magic went beyond that. Daymond deserved longer than an eternity in the Abyss.

"That's not the worst part," Mandy continued. "I searched what kind of rituals could be performed around meteor showers and full moons."

I sat up straighter, my eyes locked on her book. "And?"

She flipped open the book. "There are thousands for the full moon, but when you add in other events, it narrows the options. And Lucas… they're bad. Like, sacrifice-a-living-human dark."

My stomach twisted. "What kind of dark rituals are we talking about?"

Mandy's voice shook. "Spells that can prolong life. Ones that enhance your power. These are things witches couldn't normally do, not without the power of the moon and stars to strengthen our magic. They're so forbidden, this book only mentions them in passing. I don't know how they're actually performed."

My hands curled into fists. Daymond wasn't just getting revenge. He was using the boys for his own magical gain. Perhaps even to become immortal.

Mandy's voice shook, and her worried eyes glistened. "I saw him circle a date in his dream. He didn't write down a name, but I knew what it meant. He's planning his next attack."

"When?" I asked desperately. "How many full moons do we have left?"

Tears spilled over Mandy's lids. "There was a meteor shower yesterday… and the full moon is tonight."

I shot to my feet, but my head spun as my heart stalled in my chest. I barely made out Mandy's next words.

"I wanted it to be nothing more than a dream, but I double checked," Mandy sniffled. "His chance is *now*. It's only a matter of hours before he kills his next victim."

Her final words snapped me back to attention. I didn't have time to sit around and think this through. I had to act.

"Thank you," I said in a rush. My feet were already moving beneath me.

"Wait," she called. "Where are you going?"

"If he's going to strike tonight, I have to make sure he never gets the chance," I stated firmly.

That was all I said before I turned from her and sprinted out of the school.

My feet carried me to where I needed to go. I barely paid attention to how fast I ran, because my mind was racing even faster. I had to get to Travis before Daymond did. If he stuck with his patterns of the past, he wouldn't take Travis for another few hours.

Unless he already had him…

I sprinted down the street so fast that the houses seemed a blur. When I finally bounded up the Bennetts' porch steps, I was completely out of breath. I hammered my fist against the door.

Please, Goddess, I begged. *Let Travis be safe.*

I heard shuffling behind the door, then it swung open. Angela Bennett stared back at me, looking stunned by my appearance.

"Lucas?" She knitted her brow.

"Travis," I gasped as I steadied myself against the door frame. I'd run so fast, I could hardly stay on my feet. "Is Travis safe?"

Angela looked horrified. "Yes, he's fine. What's going on?"

"Are you sure?" I demanded.

"Yes, he's right here!" Angela opened the door wider, and I caught sight of her husband and son at the kitchen table. Jude looked worried, while Travis had a look of confusion on his face and noodles hanging out of his mouth. He slurped them up, and I nearly fell over in relief when I saw he was unharmed.

I straightened and spoke more clearly. "You need to leave. Your son is in danger."

Jude stood from the table and came to the door beside Angela. He spoke softly so his son wouldn't overhear. "There's no reason to frighten him. Let's talk on the porch."

Angela nodded in agreement, and the two of them stepped outside. Jude shut the door, but he kept an eye on his son through the window.

"What's going on?" Angela's voice was laced in worry. "Did you find something?"

"A pattern," I told them. Shocked faces stared back at me, before I dove into what Mandy had discovered.

"I know you don't want to leave the coven," I concluded with. "But you can't stay here tonight."

"We'll start packing right away," Jude said in a rush. "Thank you for letting us know."

Jude clapped me on the shoulder before rushing back inside, his wife in tow.

I'd finally caught my breath and felt slightly better knowing Travis was safe… for now. I had to make sure things stayed that way.

I knew Professor Daymond's schedule like the back of my hand. I'd followed him this semester and knew he liked to stick to a routine.

I checked the time on my phone. He'd be on his way home from the school right now. More than once, I'd seen him leaving his house late at night—and usually lost him from there. If he stuck to his routine tonight, he'd make a stop at home before sneaking off at late hours to perform the ritual.

Professor Daymond's house was on a quiet street, tucked deep into the trees to provide privacy from his neighbors. I'd searched the grounds more than once for clues and never found anything. I'd never managed to get through the ward on his house, no matter how many spells I'd tried. Tonight, something felt different in the air. If I could get inside, maybe I could find something to incriminate him before he could carry out his plan.

The house was dark, illuminated only by the full moon. A shiver ran down my spine as an owl hooted in the distance, but I was confident as I approached the house. I didn't care what happened to me. All I cared about was protecting the coven from Daymond.

The door was locked—of course—but all I had to do was overpower Daymond's ward and I could get through. I'd never been so desperate as I was now. Maybe it was enough…

"By the Goddess's power beneath the moonlight, drop this ward and grant me passage tonight." I spoke the incantation softly, but with vigor in my tone.

The lock disengaged, and I sensed the buzz of magic in the air wane as the ward fell away. Smirking in triumph, I twisted the doorknob and snuck inside Professor Daymond's house.

I worked quickly, moving from room to room for obvious clues that would incriminate him. By the end of tonight, I *needed* that proof. I wouldn't let anyone be in danger from him again.

Daymond's house was a little sad. There were no photographs on the walls, and the drying rack next to the sink had only one plate and one fork. Things were tidy, but it was obvious this guy was lonely. No wonder he'd turned to dark magic—though I didn't know what he hoped to accomplish with it.

I stepped into the living room, which was bare of decor except for dark curtains over the windows. Even the fireplace mantle was empty, save for a container of matches used to light the fire.

A piece of metal caught my eye, propped up against the brick. I reached for the long piece of iron and held a fireplace poker in my hand. It was thick and sturdy, longer than my arm, with a sharp point on the end. There was no way to take Professor Daymond down with my magic —not with his power and knowledge—so I had to resort to the next best thing.

I held tight to the fire iron as I moved through the room. Half of the living room was taken up by a sitting area near the fireplace, with a couch that faced a television in the corner. The other half housed a huge desk in front of a tall window, where I'd seen Professor Daymond working late hours when I followed him.

I decided to start at the desk. I subconjured the fire iron, then knelt beside the desk. I conjured my phone and began filming, in case I ran across anything of interest. My phone chimed with a few texts, but I turned my phone to silent and ignored them. I couldn't get distracted right now—not when I was so close.

I opened the top drawer. There, sitting on top, was a photograph of a woman and child in a frame. Judging by the clothes they wore, the picture was taken at least ten years ago. It must be Daymond's wife and son, but why would he tuck the photo away, instead of setting it out on the desk? It was almost like he couldn't bear to look at it—like it was too painful.

I paused on the photograph only a moment, then continued to the next drawer. I knew the calendar Mandy saw in her dream might not be real, but I held my breath, hoping that perhaps it was. It'd be enough to get the police to question him—and hopefully get him off the streets for tonight. If I was going to get Daymond arrested and put away, I needed evidence.

Daymond's files were meticulously organized. I glanced at the labels, but they all seemed to be related to the college. I skipped that drawer and moved on, making a note to come back to it if I didn't find anything.

As I opened the middle drawer, a notebook caught my attention. When I reached for it, I sensed a low hum, like it was protected by magic. I became instantly curious and plopped down in the desk chair to inspect it. I swiveled the chair toward the window so that I could read the notebook in the moonlight.

I flipped it open. I must've been praying for a miracle, because my shoulders slumped when I saw gibberish written all over the pages. It was some sort of code, the words scrambled by the spell cast upon it. I opened my mouth to speak an incantation I thought might break the ward, but before I could get the words out, a door creaked open behind me.

A smile crept across my lips. It was finally time to give this asshole what he deserved. I subconjured the notebook and tucked my phone into my jacket pocket to record the whole scene. I leaned back in the chair, my hands resting calmly on the armrests. The light clicked on above my head, and I turned.

Professor Daymond stopped dead in the doorway. He took in the sight of me for a moment, before his lips curled into a sneer. He had a battle orb at the ready in under a second. It crackled in his hand, but I was too fucking done with this shit to care. This ended tonight.

"You again," he snarled. "How did you get past my ward?"

I shrugged like it was no hassle. "Your ward was weak tonight. You're distracted."

Daymond narrowed his eyes. "You don't know what you're talking about. Get out of my house or I'll—"

"You'll what?" I asked, crossing my hands in front of me. "Kill me like you did the other boys?"

Daymond opened his mouth to retort, but he hesitated. "That's a little extreme, even for you, Mister Taylor."

"Why not me?" I challenged. "You were already planning to take one life tonight."

"Are you on drugs?" Daymond snapped. "What in the name of the Goddess are you talking about?"

My rage exploded. I slammed my hands on the desk and shot to my feet. "I know everything, and you're going to admit to it! I know the Thomases, Millers, and Bennetts caused the house fire that killed your family. I know you took Caleb and Isaac as revenge on their parents. I know you killed the boys on a full moon that coincided with a comet and a meteor. And I know you're planning on getting your final revenge—tonight! What's the ritual, Daymond!?"

I was yelling now, but I didn't give two flying fucks. He was going to admit to everything, and I'd have it all on audio. By morning, the whole coven would know.

But Daymond didn't react as I expected. I was ready to dodge a deadly spell, but his battle orb fizzled out. His hands dropped to his side, and he stumbled back a step, steadying himself on the edge of the couch.

"You... you know who killed my Tonya and Oliver?" he rasped, as if it was the first time he was hearing it himself. The pain of a thousand lonely nights was evident in his eyes.

I narrowed my eyes. What was this, some sort of ploy to throw me off my game? I wasn't buying it.

"Yeah, I know," I snapped. "Don't act so surprised."

"You have it all wrong," Daymond insisted. "Whoever killed those boys, it wasn't me. I never knew who was responsible for the fire that killed my family."

His eyes seemed clear, honesty evident in his tone. Holy shit. Daymond wasn't lying—not unless he was one hell of an actor. But it still didn't add up...

"I saw you in an alley talking about the kids," I growled. "I know you took them!"

"Not the *missing* kids, you twat!" Daymond roared. "*College kids!*"

"So you're going after college kids now?" I accused. "Don't pretend like you don't have a hand in this. You threatened me in the hall when I caught you stealing from the alchemy room."

"Because I thought you were going to turn me in for nightshade!" Daymond yelled.

"Nightshade?" I demanded.

"Drugs," he sneered. "What did you *think* I was stealing? Drug ingredients!"

"Then what's this?" I demanded, conjuring the notebook I'd just found and smacking it on the desktop. "Spells? Rituals?"

"It's drug contacts," Daymond growled, like I was daft. "You think I'm out there murdering people, when all I've done is ferry a few drugs through the student body. My teaching position is hardly enough to provide me with the cushy retirement I deserve."

I was struck dumb as all the pieces fell into place. That night in the alleyway, he wasn't paying off someone to cover up the murders. He was working with another drug dealer. Fuck, I'd messed up.

"You could join me," he offered. "It's exceptional money."

I scoffed. "You *really* think I want to sell drugs? I'm trying to save a boy's life!"

"I'm afraid it's your only choice, Mister Taylor," Daymond said. "Now that you know, I can't have you running off telling anyone. I won't let you ruin my retirement."

He may not be a murderer, but I was disgusted with this man. "You're supposed to protect the coven. Instead, you're getting college kids to deal your drugs for you."

"I'm not *making* anyone buy the nightshade," Daymond snapped. "I'm not hurting anyone. You talk about protecting the coven like it's so noble. Where was the coven for me when they killed my family? As far as I'm concerned, those parents got what they deserved when they lost their kids!"

"You're deplorable!" I yelled. I was done with this asshole.

I didn't even move before Daymond lifted his hand. A red battle orb shot out of his palm, and I ducked instinctively. It missed me by a hair and soared over my head. The window behind me shattered as the orb went through it.

Holy shit, that was one high-powered spell. It could've killed me.

Daymond already had another spell in his hand. I wasted no time and dove for the door to the kitchen for cover. The second orb smashed against the wall, cracking the drywall.

"You know too much," Daymond growled as he came around the corner.

A stunning spell swirled in my palm, and I lunged toward him to slam it into his chest. But Daymond was faster than I was, and he threw up a shield to protect himself. My spell ricocheted and fizzled out at the other side of the room.

Daymond jumped toward me, and I whirled around to make a break for it. He caught me around the ankles, and I went tumbling toward the ground. My hands reached out for anything, and my fingers curled around the back of a kitchen chair. It crashed to the floor with me and knocked Daymond in the side of the head. Blood trickled from the wound, but it barely fazed him.

"So you *are* going to kill me!" I accused.

"You sure as hell aren't going to remember the night."

"Get off me!" I screamed as he tried to hold me down. I yanked my foot from his grasp and slammed it into his nose.

His hands shot to his face, giving me enough time to wriggle out from beneath him. Anger marred his features, and he drew his hand back again, a spell already forming in his palm.

Adrenaline pumped through my veins, and I moved faster than I thought possible. I conjured the fireplace poker I'd picked up earlier and swung it at Daymond like a baseball bat. It clanked against the side of his head, vibrating up to my hands. Daymond's eyes rolled back into his skull, and he slumped to the ground. Potion vials slipped out of his coat and rolled across the floor. It could've been nightshade. I wasn't sure. I wasn't sticking around to find out, either.

I stepped away from his unconscious body, heaving. The fire iron dropped from my hands and clattered to the floor. Daymond was out cold, but he was still breathing.

I scrambled for my phone and ended the video, then dialed the police station. I gave them the address and a vague explanation of what had happened. They promised medics would be on their way and told me to stay put. But I couldn't.

Daymond wasn't the killer, which meant the real murderer was, waiting to claim their next victim. The Bennetts were leaving town, but that didn't mean the killer wouldn't take someone else.

I stumbled out of the house, my head spinning. I didn't even know where to start. I'd been so certain Daymond was behind this. I tried to put the pieces together in my head. A thousand theories raced through my mind, but were quickly shot down by the facts. The moon loomed overhead. It could already be too late.

I made it to the sidewalk, when a car honked and slowed to a stop beside me. I jumped, but then relaxed when the driver rolled down his window.

"Grant?" I asked. "What are you doing here?"

"I could ask you the same thing," he replied. "I've been driving around town looking everywhere for you. Get in."

I didn't have to be told twice. The last thing I wanted was to be around when the police showed up. If Daymond woke, he could have me arrested for trespassing and assault. That would have to wait until after I found the killer.

I hopped into the passenger seat. "It's not Daymond," I rushed to explain to Grant. "The real killer's going to strike tonight, and we have to find him."

I quickly explained to Grant what had happened. "We need to find who's really behind this—before it's too late."

Grant glanced at me sideways. "Any idea where to start?"

"No," I admitted. "I thought everything pointed to Daymond. I don't know who else could—"

"Here." Grant tossed a hardback book onto my lap, before turning his gaze back to the road. "Why don't we start with the families?"

"I've tried that," I reminded him.

Grant's fingers curled tighter around the steering wheel. "They're hiding more than you thought. We need to get the truth."

I furrowed my brow as I looked down at the book he'd tossed at me. It was a Miriamic College yearbook. I flipped it open to a page that had been folded down in the corner. I clicked the light on above my head and eyed the photos. The spread showed photos of the swim and diving teams. There were team photos, as well as snapshots of competitions and team members goofing off at the pool.

"What is this?" I asked. "What am I looking at?"

"Look closely at that photo in the corner." Grant stabbed the yearbook with his index finger. "I was going through swim stats again, gearing up for next week's competition, when I came across *this*."

The photo he pointed to showed a few members of the swim team in suits and caps, posing for the camera near the diving board at school. I leaned in to get a closer look and noticed something in the background. A couple stood in the shadows at the entrance of one of the locker rooms, looking like they were about to kiss. The blonde girl's back was pressed against the wall, and she stared up at the guy with admiration. He wore a swimsuit and had one arm around her. He held the other index finger to his lips, as if the two of them shared a secret.

"Holy shit," I remarked. "Is that Michelle and Keith? Isaac's mom and Caleb's dad?"

"It sure as hell looks like it," Grant replied.

"But Keith and Krista were dating back then," I said, putting the pieces together.

Grant cocked an eyebrow. "Check out who took the photo."

I scanned the caption and saw that Krista had taken it. "They were having an affair, and Krista must've found out. How does this tie into the case, though?"

I was asking myself more than anything, trying to piece it all together.

"I don't know," Grant answered. "But these parents know a hell of a lot more than they've admitted to."

I conjured my phone and began going through my contacts. "Then we're going to get the truth."

I just hoped the truth led us to the killer.

☾

THE SUN HAD SET hours ago, and the full moon was quickly reaching its peak in the night sky. Grant and I waited in the car, watching the parking lot curiously.

"I know what happened to your son," I'd said when I called the families. "Meet me at Coven Park."

It was the only way I could think to get them here—and fast. The park was dark, and the trees rising around us seemed sinister in the night. This was a central, neutral location that was deserted this time of night.

A car approached, followed by a second one moments later. I hadn't called the Bennetts, because I wanted Travis as far away from Octavia Falls as they could get him tonight. But I sure as hell was getting the truth from Krista, Keith, and Michelle.

I stepped out of the car, and the three of them climbed out of their own vehicles. Krista rushed over to me.

"You found him!? You found Caleb?" she cried.

"What do you know about Isaac?" Michelle demanded.

"You're going to tell me what you know first," I nearly spat.

Grant stood beside me and crossed his arms. "We know you've been lying."

Beneath the light of the streetlamp, I saw Keith narrow his eyes. "Who are you?"

"He's a friend," I explained. "If you want to know what happened to your kids, it's time to start telling me the truth."

Krista threw her hand over her mouth to hold in a sob. "We've told you everything."

"You've told me nothing!" I burst. "I *know* your children knew each other, even though you said they never had."

"That's not true!" Krista exclaimed.

Keith exchanged a glance with Michelle. He sighed and placed a hand on his wife's shoulder. "It *is* true."

Krista's eyes watered as she looked up at him. "What are you talking about?"

"We're sorry," Michelle practically begged. "I know we haven't always gotten along, but Keith and I wanted the kids to know each other."

Krista's jaw dropped. "You took Caleb to meet Michelle without asking me?"

Guilt marred Keith's features. "I just wanted him to know Isaac and Travis. We always said our kids would grow up together—and I knew you wouldn't approve."

"So you went behind my back!" Krista raged.

"It was just a few playdates. It was nothing!" Keith reached for his wife, but she yanked her arm away.

"And yet you still felt the need to hide it from me!" she yelled.

"Because I knew how you'd react," he stated.

"The kids had fun, Krista," Michelle insisted.

"Stay out of this," Krista snapped. "It's not about what happened; it's that you both lied to me."

Keith opened his mouth to respond, but I cut him off. "We don't have time to fight. Whoever took your kids plans to strike again tonight. We need to know everything."

Krista glanced between Keith and Michelle, then wrapped her arms around herself. "W-what do you want to know?"

"Everything!" I cried. "Maybe start with how you never turned in that pin to the police, because you thought if Professor Daymond was after your families, you'd have to admit to what you did to his!"

Michelle gaped. "How did you—?"

"It doesn't matter how I know." I pressed my fingers to my eyes. "But Daymond's not the killer—"

I cut off as I realized something. I turned to Grant. "Daymond didn't take the kids, but that pin proves that someone from the college *did*."

Grant's features were calculating. "Who else would possibly target them?"

I whirled back on the others, but my gaze focused on Michelle. "What other connection do your kids have? Is someone trying to get back at you for the affair? Your ex-husband? Who? Who do they plan to take next?"

Michelle laughed nervously. "What affair?"

Krista was sobbing now. "Stop lying! I know! I've always known!"

Keith reeled back. "You… knew?"

"Of course I knew," Krista spat. "And so did Mark. Why do you think he and Michelle divorced?"

Michelle looked stunned.

Keith kept his eyes on his wife. His brow furrowed. "But you still married me."

"Because I loved you!" Krista cried, her whole body quivering. "I didn't mean to hurt our kids…"

My body froze. Was Krista admitting she had something to do with their death?

"Hurt them how?" Michelle asked in a stern, clipped tone.

Krista sniffled as tears rolled down her cheeks. "It was before they were born. I thought Keith was going to leave me. I-I cast a curse upon your firstborn. What I didn't know was that the curse would back-fire and curse Keith's firstborn as well… *my* firstborn."

"You *cursed* our kids!?" Keith shouted.

"It was only a curse of bad luck," Krista said.

"That's why Caleb broke his ankle so many times," Keith realized. "And why Isaac was always breaking things."

"Bad luck!" Michelle got up in Krista's face and spat. "Do you realize what kind of *bad luck* our kids had!? They were taken because of *your* curse."

"Or targeted because of it…" I said under my breath. Everything clicked, and I felt the blood drain from my face. I whirled toward Grant and grabbed him by the shoulders. "The ritual. They must need a cursed sacrifice to perform it—a cursed child. Travis wasn't cursed, which means he was never a target!"

Grant's features fell, and he looked like he might puke. "Which means anyone who *is* cursed could be next."

There were only two people I knew of who were cursed, and I loved one of them like no other. My stomach dropped from my abdomen, and my voice came out a whisper as I considered the worst possible outcome —the killer's next victim. "Nadine."

I barely had a chance to think about the possibilities when my phone rang. My heart leapt into my throat as I saw the name on the screen. "Talia?"

All I heard from the other end of the line was Talia's sobs. "Lucas, I-I don't know what to do."

"What's going on?" I demanded, my heart hammering. Somehow, I felt I already knew what she was going to say. It didn't make it any easier. My blood turned to ice in my veins as she spoke the very words I feared.

"Nadine's gone."

nadine

TWENTY-TWO

My head spun as I came to. For a moment, I thought everything that happened had been a terrible nightmare. But as my senses came back to me, I realized the nightmare was all too real.

The first thing I noticed was the ache in my body. My neck was stiff as I lifted it. I sat in a chair that felt as hard as rock. My arms were tied tightly together behind my back, and my ankles were secured to the chair legs.

It took a few moments for the room to come into focus. It was some sort of library, or a study, perhaps. It was dark, apart from the streaks of moonlight coming through the tall windows on my left. The room was nearly as big as some of the classrooms back at the college—but it was completely trashed. It looked as if no one had stepped foot in here in ages.

Bookcases lined one wall. Some of them had glass doors that had been shattered, their pieces littering the floor. Most of the cabinet doors were missing, while the others hung at odd angles off old hinges. On the other side of the room stood a large desk, but that too had been destroyed. It sat at an angle, with one of the feet missing.

The floor itself was covered in garbage, from plaster that had fallen from the worn ceiling to hardwood floorboards that had bowed upward. Old books littered the floor, and a pile of rusted garden tools lay in the corner. A scythe sat on top of the pile, which felt oddly ominous. Cracks ran through the walls, and wind whistled through the windows. A shiver traveled down my spine, followed immediately by rage-filled heat.

The ropes on my wrists tightened, and something stirred from behind me. A moan came, and I realized I was tied to someone else. We sat back-to-back, a rope securing our arms together. I could feel her wrists pressing into mine.

"Chloe?" I tried to turn my head, but my neck was too stiff from how it'd been hanging while we were knocked out. I didn't know how long that'd been.

Chloe groaned again. "What'd you *do*?"

"I didn't *do* anything! I thought this was your doing."

"Bitch, I was going to hang your ass. Why would I drag you here instead?"

"Where is *here*?" I growled, my anger building by the second.

"No idea." Chloe yanked at the ropes that were holding both of us in place, but the more she struggled, the tighter the ropes became. "Shit, there's some sort of enchantment on these."

Chloe gave up and paused for a few beats, as if taking in the room. I looked out the window, hoping to spot any landmarks, but all I saw were trees. In the silence, I heard something I hadn't caught before.

"Whoever did this is going to—"

"Shh…" I hissed at Chloe. "Do you hear that?"

"What?" she scoffed. "The sound of impending doom? What kind of trick is this?"

I ignored her accusations and listened closer. "I hear something like water… lapping against the shore."

Chloe went still and listened closely. "It's Lake Santos," she said thoughtfully.

My stomach dropped to my toes as I realized where we were. "This is Pinewood Manor—that haunted house where all those people were killed forty years ago."

"Aw, hell no!" Chloe cried. She began struggling at the ropes again, and I winced as they tightened around my legs. "This place is haunted worse than hell. If whoever took us doesn't kill us, those ghosts will."

"Ghosts can't do that, can they?" I asked, my voice shaking.

"I sure as hell don't want to stick around and find out!" Chloe practically shrieked.

"How do you suggest we escape?" I snapped. "You said yourself these ropes are enchanted. The more we struggle, the tighter they get—fuck, that hurt!"

Chloe had tried conjuring a battle orb in her hands, but it seared my skin. She let out a cry of pain as the ropes tightened momentarily around us. They let up the second she dropped her spell. I was impressed that she managed to conjure such a powerful spell, considering how new her magic was.

"Let *me* try," I suggested. I mentally searched my stash, wondering if I had anything useful in it. It wasn't like I carried knives around, though I was starting to think I should—just in case. The best I had was nail clippers. I conjured them and did my best to turn them in the right direction. My dexterity was shit. I dug the sharp point into the ropes and tugged. I expected to hear a few threads snap. Instead, the ropes tightened on us again, so tight that I dropped the nail clippers. My frustration grew as they clinkered to the floor.

Chloe scoffed. "Leave it to me to save your ass."

From across the room, a sharp piece of glass levitated into the air as Chloe used her telekinesis powers. It flew over to us and landed in her hands tied behind her back. She flipped it around in her fingers.

"Ow!" I complained as the sharp glass sliced the back of my finger. "Watch it!"

"You'll be thanking me when we get out of here," Chloe sneered. The ropes tightened again as she worked the glass against them. She sliced for several minutes before I heard the glass clink to the floor.

"It's no use," Chloe complained, more to herself than to me, I think. "There's some spell on the ropes. They won't cut."

"There has to be a way to get out of here," I insisted.

"We'd have to break the enchantment."

"How do you do that?" I asked, my hope surging.

"A counter spell," Chloe said, before her tone turned sour again. "But since we don't know what spell was used in the first place, we can't perform a counter spell. The only other way would be to kill the spell caster."

"Perfect," I said flatly. "Let me do that with my hands tied behind my back."

"Ugh," Chloe groaned. "Of all the people I have to be tied up with, it had to be *you*."

"I'm not happy about it, either," I snapped. "Would cursing the spell caster get us out of these ropes?"

Chloe blew a breath. "Good luck with that. We're still novices. We aren't powerful enough to cast a curse that could kill. We'd need some sort of magical boost."

"Black magic," I stated. It wasn't a question. "Like some sort of sacrifice."

"Exactly," Chloe said. She didn't sound opposed to the idea, but we weren't exactly going to be performing any rituals tonight with our hands tied behind our backs. "This would be a hell of a lot easier if I knew what the fuck was going on!"

"You tell me," I scoffed. "You're the one who lured me into the woods —somehow! How'd you get me out there, anyway?"

I felt her shoulders sag. "Hypnosis."

"Hypnosis? I didn't know witches could do that."

"They can't," Chloe explained. "The magic came from another supernatural race—hypnotists that live in the Grand Canyon region. It's an herb only hypnotists can grow, and insanely expensive. I mixed it in with the fake meds you took. It's a one-time sleepwalking spell that can be activated anytime up to a year after the victim eats the herb. I could've made you sleepwalk wherever I wanted you to go, even made you walk off a bridge. You'd have no choice—"

Chloe cut off as the sound of footsteps approached the room. They came from behind the doors to my right. There were several pairs, and I held my breath.

The door swung open, and three shadowy figures stepped into the room. I didn't recognize them at first, until the moonlight hit their faces. The woman in front had a long nose and gray hair piled atop her head. Beside her were two other women—one who wore cat-eye glasses, and another with long white hair cascading around her shoulders.

My breath caught. It was Betty, Agnes, and Sandy, the women who owned *The Gingerbread House* candy shop along the Catwalk.

Chloe didn't waste a moment. She summoned her powers, and a

pointed shard of glass whizzed through the air, aimed straight toward the first woman's face—Betty.

She was expecting it. The witch caught the glass in her hand and smirked as it cut into her fingers. She seemed amused by the attempt. Blood dripped onto the hardwood, and she tossed the glass aside like it was nothing.

Betty wiped the blood on her skirt. "Your attempts to intimidate are comical, at best."

I caught sight of the scythe in the corner wavering as Chloe tried to lift it with her powers. But Chloe was a brand new witch. She couldn't control larger objects yet.

"What the hell do you want with us?" I snapped.

"The Imperium Council will have your heads for this," Chloe threatened. "My grandmother does *not* take threats like this lightly."

Betty threw her head back and cackled—like a full-on, evil witch laugh. These ladies had seemed so sweet when I'd met them at the career fair. Now the sight of them caused a bitterness on my tongue and made my skin feel as if a hundred centipedes were crawling all over it. They no longer hid the sinister motive from their eyes. They didn't have to.

"Oh, my dear," Betty practically sang as she stepped forward. "You think we took you to intimidate your grandmother? Why would we bother messing with a priestess?"

"Plenty of reasons," Chloe spat. "What kind of ransom do you have out on me? Is it money? Or perhaps legal demands upon the coven?"

Agnes, the one with the cat-eye glasses, laughed. "So naive. I *love* it. Can I have this one?"

Sandy stepped in front of me. She bent to my level and ran a chilling finger across my cheek. "If you get her, I want this one."

"Watch it," I snarled, and she backed away. "Touch me again, and I'll bite your fucking finger off."

Sandy shot me a dark glare that seemed even more dangerous in the shadows. "I'd like to see you try."

"Come back over here, Grandma, and I'll show you what kind of damage I can do," I threatened. I was so pissed I wouldn't hesitate to hurt any one of them.

"If you're not holding us for ransom, what the hell is this?" Chloe demanded.

"Isn't it obvious?" Betty smirked in amusement and crossed the room to the windows. She yanked the dusty drapes open all the way and gestured toward the moon. "What happens on a full moon, girls?"

A beat passed.

"Come *on*," Agnes pressed, clicking her tongue like she was disappointed in us. "You should know this from your classes."

"Rituals," I snarled under my breath.

"Ding, ding, ding," Sandy sang. "Oh, I do love this one."

Chloe blew an angry breath. "What ritual? Why us?"

"For the love of Mother Miriam, don't tell me you put dead people in your candy," I said.

Betty cackled again. "What a wonderful idea! Fortunately for you, this ritual has nothing to do with our candy shop."

"Then what?" Chloe snapped. "You're feeding on the youth of Miriam College to keep yourselves young?"

Betty's eyebrows shot up. "Very good guess, my dear—but no cigar."

"We deserve to know what you plan to do with us," I said. All the while, I was working through plans in my head to escape, but most of them required the use of my hands. Fuck.

Betty smiled, but it was a sinister smile that made me want to stab her in the eye. "My dear, it won't matter after we're finished with you."

My mouth went dry. "If you're going to kill us, then it won't matter if we know."

"Oh, can I tell them?" Sandy bounced her toes, like she was about to tell us a bedtime story rather than recount a scene from a horror novel.

"I *hate* keeping secrets," Agnes agreed. "I've been *dying* to tell someone."

The way she said *dying* made my whole body shiver.

Betty waved nonchalantly. "Fine. Go ahead. They'll be dead within the hour anyway."

Sandy and Agnes laughed gleefully. Sandy leaned down and sniffed me, like she wanted me for her next meal. I told this bitch if she got close to me again, I'd hurt her. So I didn't even hesitate when she got near. I lashed out like a rabid dog, catching her ear between my teeth. I bit down hard and tasted blood.

Sandy jumped away from me, cradling her bloody ear. A moment of shock overtook her features, then morphed into anger. I barely saw her hand coming before it cracked against the side of my face. My head whipped to the side, pain radiating up my cheek.

Sandy shoved her cold fingers into my hair and yanked backward, forcing me to look up at her. "I knew you two would be a handful," she sang, like she enjoyed it.

I narrowed my eyes. "What the hell does that mean?"

Sandy stared down at me, but it was Agnes who answered. "Cursed children can be quite… dramatic."

"How do you know we're cursed?" Chloe demanded.

I rolled my eyes. "Like it's a secret. Everyone at school knows we've been fighting all semester."

"Yes," Sandy said with a smile. "We heard the rumors, but we had to confirm they were true. Remember those lucky lollipops you had at the career fair?"

"They weren't lucky at all," I accused. I hadn't forgotten what happened to me later that day—how Chloe had hexed all my hair to fall out.

"Of *course* they weren't lucky lollipops!" Betty seemed pleased that someone had finally caught on. "They were made specifically to change color when someone with a curse ate them. How do you think we found the other cursed children?"

All the blood in my body drained. "You're talking about Caleb and Isaac," I said breathlessly. I remembered the witches' candy booth at the Halloween Festival last year. They must've used the same ruse to target the kids.

Chloe seethed in her chair, causing the ropes to tighten on us both again. "What did you do to those poor kids!?"

Betty smiled, like Chloe's reaction amused her. "Nothing you weren't about to do to your dear friend here."

Betty reached out and ran her fingers through my hair. I shrugged her off and curled my nose at her. "They killed them," I told Chloe.

Betty's eyebrow shot up, like she was impressed. "You sound so sure."

"Well, you're going to kill us, aren't you?" Chloe growled. "All for… for what?"

"For an *incredible* payday!" Agnes cried happily. "You have no idea what kind of rare magical supplies we're getting for our troubles."

My stomach twisted. "Someone hired you."

"I see why you like this one," Betty said to Sandy as she paced around my chair. "Yes, a ritual to raise the dead is far more complicated than anything we would need ourselves, but we couldn't pass up such a payment."

"Raise the dead!?" I balked. "Why would you—?"

I cut off as a memory tickled the back of my mind. Last semester, my friends and I had a run-in with a zombie in the cemetery. Lucas had said it wasn't necromancy, that it was darker magic. These witches must've had something to do with it.

"We try not to ask our employer too many questions," Betty went on. "This ritual is complicated enough as it is. No need to add in extra issues."

"What kind of issues?" Chloe demanded. I could hear it in her tone— she was gathering as much information as she could, so we could figure out a way to escape. We were both stalling.

Agnes groaned. "Don't get us started. There have been too many."

I smirked. "Humor us."

Betty seemed more than happy to oblige. It was like these women were *proud* of what they'd done and were happy to finally have someone to brag to. It made me sick.

"Have you noticed anything strange about this month's full moon cycle?" Betty asked rhetorically. "It happened to coincide quite nicely with a meteor shower. We didn't realize when we started that the ritual required such an astronomical event. We made a mistake, and had to hold the first boy here while we waited for such an event to occur."

Lucas had remarked himself how strange it was for the killer to wait so long from the time Caleb disappeared. Now it all made sense.

"But that was only the first mistake of many," Betty went on as she paced around the room. "We tried the ritual with him the night a comet coincided with the full moon, but the ritual required a full meteor shower, not a comet. And so, we thought we had the kinks worked out when we took the second boy. But the stars were not aligned that night, for the shower came *after* the full moon. We know now that the brew required for the ritual must be mixed the night of a meteor shower, and the ritual performed under the full moon."

"We were delighted when we found *two* cursed students at the college," Agnes added. "And that you'd both have powers by tonight! We suspect using two individuals with powers will create a much more potent ritual."

"You bitches waited until I had my powers?" Chloe raged. "Well, it's a perfect fucking night for that."

Betty beamed. "How fortunate for us!"

"Why us?" I insisted. "You could've cursed anyone to use in your *ritual*."

"I'm afraid it's not that simple, my dear," Betty said in a condescending tone. "It is the dark energy of a curse that makes the ritual strong enough to raise the dead. Even the dark magic of an ordinary sacrifice is not so strong. A fresh curse wouldn't be as strong as one that was cast ages ago."

"None of this explains how you managed to hide this from the coven," I pointed out. "You're Alchemists. How did you keep the coven from tracking you?"

"A very good question," Betty said. "And one that I'm afraid I'm not at liberty to share. Let's just say… our employer has many tools at their disposal."

Betty glanced out at the moon again, as if gauging its position in the sky for the time. "Now, if you'll excuse us, we have a few final preparations to make for the ritual. Time is running out, and we will not fail a third time."

Betty turned on her heel, and the other two witches followed her out of the room.

I struggled in my chair. Nobody tied up Nadine Evers, and they certainly didn't dodge her questions! "You bitches are going to get what's coming to you! You will rot in the Abyss!"

The door clicked shut behind them, and Chloe laughed under her breath.

"What's so funny?" I snapped.

"For once, we actually agree on something."

I scoffed. "We're going to have to agree on more than that, because we need to get out of here."

"If we could agree, we'd never be in this situation in the first place," Chloe shot back. "You'd have left town months ago."

"I didn't have to!" I cried, yanking on the ropes until she gasped. "I'm a Curse Breaker. I've been trying to tell you for weeks I can break this thing."

"If you're so powerful, why haven't you broken it yet?" Chloe challenged.

"Because I…" I trailed off and ducked my head. "Because I need your help."

"What was that?" Chloe asked. "Nadine Evers needs *my* help."

"Don't let your head explode with that ego."

"*I'm* the one with the big head?" Chloe laughed. "*Okay.*"

"You've been doing everything you can to hurt me since I moved here!"

"Don't act so innocent," Chloe sneered. "You've had your fair share of payback. One of your tricks cost me a hot date."

"That cursed earring?" I balked. "*That's* what you're worried about? Goddess, you're impossible. I didn't mean to do any of that to you."

"Let me guess," Chloe said flatly. "The devil made you do it? That's exactly the kind of claim that should get you hanged."

"Not *the devil*," I snapped. "This curse."

"Did you forget I'm cursed, too?" Chloe asked.

"I didn't forget. Are you saying your darkness made you do those things to me?"

"*My darkness?*" Chloe laughed sardonically. "You talk about it like it's separate from you. What do you think this curse is? A possession?"

"Something like that," I replied curtly.

"Well, you're wrong," Chloe stated. "The darkness you're talking about is yours. The curse just brings it out. You get to decide what to do with it. Every action you took is your own. You've convinced yourself otherwise so you don't have to take responsibility for everything you've done."

I opened my mouth to respond, but I cut off as her words hit me. My stomach twisted at the frightening reality. Chloe could be messing with me, but it didn't seem right given the circumstances. She sounded like she was telling the truth. And deep down, I knew that she was right.

Even Grammy had mentioned something similar in my first curse breaking lesson. *Even if that dark magic is there, a person has a choice whether to act upon it or not.*

All my friends thought I was a Curse Breaker because I'd proven I could resist the darkness. Everything that happened this semester proved that they were wrong. Dark Nadine had taken over time and time again… but only because I'd let her.

My pride crumbled as I caved to the truth. "You're right," I admitted aloud. "That's why I haven't been able to break the curse yet… I've been trying to draw it out of myself as a separate entity. But it's been there so long, I've grown with it. The curse is a *part* of me. The darkness is *mine*."

"Now you're getting it," Chloe said.

I frowned as it sank in. "I don't want to be a bad person."

Chloe chuckled. "Too late. You already are."

Her accusation would normally make me lash out, but my anger felt nearly non-existent as stronger emotions rose to the surface. I had a renewed sense of clarity, which was both comforting and frightening. I relished in the comfort I felt for the first time.

"You know what? You're right. I'm a total bitch," I stated out loud.

I didn't know how admitting such a thing could make me feel so comforted, but it was like I'd been running from the truth for so long. I was relieved to finally stop lying to myself. An invisible weight that'd been lying on my shoulders for so long seemed to lighten the smallest bit.

"I thought I was justified in everything I did to you," I admitted to Chloe. "But I've been nothing but cruel. And… I'm sorry."

I expected the words to taste bitter on my tongue, but they didn't. I felt something break free within me. Though the ropes tying us down didn't loosen, it seemed that something holding me down inside had.

"I-I…" Chloe stammered. She was at a total loss for words. "I guess I've been a bitch, too."

I laughed, but I wasn't mocking her. It was truly comical, the way we'd been fighting all semester, only to end up here together with both our lives on the line.

"You guess?" I asked. "You tried to *hang* me."

Chloe laughed along, like she too found the situation silly now that we were here. Her tone softened. "On some level, I was using the curse to justify my actions, too."

"The curse was never an excuse for anything I did to you," I told her, feeling the truth deep in my belly. "I'm responsible for everything I did. The curse may have made it easier to give into the darkness, but I still did. I made those choices myself."

"Me, too," Chloe admitted. "I know it doesn't matter much anymore, seeing as we're both probably going to die tonight. But for what it's worth, I'm sorry. I actually do wish we could've worked things out."

"Are you just saying that because we wouldn't be in this situation if we'd worked things out?"

"Yes and no," Chloe said. "I'd much rather be back at school in my bed right now, but what I meant was… fighting with you has been fucking exhausting."

"Another thing we can agree on," I pointed out.

The two of us laughed. How we were laughing right now, I didn't know. It seemed insane. And maybe we were. All I knew was it felt good to apologize. At least I could say we worked things out before we died.

Those bindings inside of me seemed to loosen even further. My anger and rage remained, but I had the choice on whether to control them… or to let them control me.

Something else stirred in my gut. It wrapped around my emotions, influencing them and fighting for control. Dark Nadine was struggling to emerge. She was a manifestation of my curse, but I would no longer let her control me. I *owned* my darkness. I *owned* my choices. Dark Nadine would not speak for me any longer. She whispered thoughts into my mind, begged me to take actions that would perpetuate the feud between Chloe and me. But I wouldn't do that anymore. It didn't matter if I died here tonight or made it out by some miracle. I *chose* a different path. I *chose* to be a better person.

Something broke within me, and I felt the curse separate from my emotions within me. It would bind me no longer!

"Dear Goddess," Chloe breathed. "What is *that*?"

I turned my head to the left and gasped. In front of the window, a huge ball of magic had formed. It was made of black wisps, swirling together so tightly the magic was beginning to block out the moonlight.

"The ritual must be starting," Chloe stated, her voice wavering.

I narrowed my eyes at the entity forming before my eyes. It was dark energy for sure, but it felt familiar… like I'd known it all my life.

"That's not the ritual," I replied confidently.

"Then what is it?" Chloe demanded.

"It's our curse," I said breathlessly.

"Our… curse?" Chloe sounded as if she was trying to wrap her head around the concept.

"We're drawing it out!" I realized. "All this time, I thought the curse was wrapped in my anger and resentment, but that was only part of it. The curse lies within our feud. By admitting our wrongs and apologizing, we're fighting the curse. This is a manifestation of it. If we keep this up, I can draw it out even more."

Chloe gasped. "And if you break the curse, the witches can't use us for their ritual."

"Exactly," I stated. "Look, I'm not just saying this to get us out of here, but I get where you were coming from all this time. You were only trying to protect yourself."

"As were you," Chloe admitted. "I kept telling myself I deserved the coven more than you did, but it wasn't like you chose to be born outside of it. You didn't choose for your parents to die, or any of that. I get that this is the only home you have now. I just didn't see a way we could share it."

"I didn't know if we could, either," I replied. "We could've figured it out, though."

The more we spoke, the more magic began to swirl within the ball manifesting before us.

"Maybe if we were never cursed, we could've actually been friends," Chloe suggested.

I smiled at the thought. "I don't even know who I'd be if I hadn't been cursed. But I bet you're right. We would've gotten into so much trouble together."

"Oh, we've done plenty of that," Chloe teased. "Aren't you suspended?"

I shook my head in disbelief. "Earlier this week, my suspension seemed like the end of the world. Now it doesn't even matter. If we make it out of here, I'll take whatever punishment the school board has for me."

"Can I tell you a secret?" Chloe asked.

"Sure. What do you have to lose?"

"You're not going to believe this, considering what I did to you earlier tonight," Chloe started. "But during my Evoking Ceremony, I had a vision where I could either get you thrown out of the school or get you pardoned. I chose to stick up for you."

Her confession floored me. "You did?"

"I told you that you wouldn't believe me."

"I do," I said quickly. "I did something similar for you during my ceremony."

"Really?" She sounded shocked. "What'd you do?"

"Remember that prank you did last semester when you hung a dummy from a tree and it was supposed to be me?" I asked.

"A classic," she teased, before softening her tone. "No, but really, I am sorry about that. I hate that I came up with the idea."

"Well, in my vision, *you* were hanging from that tree," I admitted. "I saved you."

"Wow…" Chloe said softly. "You'd really do that for me?"

"I would," I replied honestly. "I never wanted to kill you. I just wanted to protect myself."

A beat passed before I added, "If you got me pardoned in your vision, why did you try to hang me in real life?"

"I don't know," Chloe said thoughtfully. "In my vision, it was like the dark part of me couldn't get to me. And when I woke, she wouldn't leave me alone. *You have to do this, Chloe. You have to save yourself.* She wouldn't shut up, and I…"

Chloe choked up.

"You hear voices, too," I stated softly.

Chloe sniffled. "She just talks. I choose to give in to her. But it's the only way to shut her up. That's not an excuse for what I did to you, though."

Holy shit, *Chloe* was crying now. A lump rose to my throat, and I knew my tears weren't far behind. I understood exactly where she was coming from. I'd gone through the exact same struggle myself.

"I just thought if I listened to her, maybe the coven would be better off," Chloe explained. "It's common for the priesthood to pass down through families, and with my grandma on the council, there's a good chance I'll be there one day myself. I have so many ideas for how to help the coven—social programs, industry expansion, education requirements. I felt like I could do so much, and I knew I'd never get a chance if the curse claimed me. I thought getting rid of you would let me help the coven in other ways. I thought it was best."

Sympathy swelled in my heart as Chloe spoke. I never thought I could feel anything for her but resentment, but right now, I felt *sorry* for her. It was unfair what this curse had done to her… to us.

"Remember the night I woke up screaming last semester, and the whole hall came out of their rooms to see me freaking out?" Chloe asked.

How could I forget? I was the one who'd caused the nightmare with the potion my friends and I had brewed. "I'm sorry about that," I said genuinely.

"Thanks," Chloe replied. "Do you want to know what freaked me out so badly? It wasn't spiders or zombies or some freaky thing like that. My nightmare was that I didn't make it on the Imperium Council, and you did. In my dream, you basically took over the coven, and everyone turned against each other. You sat on this throne made of thorns, laughing while the rest of us were hanged or burned at the stake."

"I would never do that," I told her.

"I know. But that doesn't make it any less terrifying."

"Why are you so afraid of what will become of the coven if you're not there to run it?" I questioned curiously.

"I don't always agree with the coven's methods," Chloe said. "Burnings and hangings are offensive to the coven, considering what happened during the witch trials. It makes them that much worse when they happen today. But they shouldn't happen at all, and I'm afraid they'll only get worse. My grandma always taught me it would be my responsibility one day to help make decisions for the coven. I wish I could learn how to trust others to protect us."

My stomach sank. "You sound so noble, while I'm over here being selfish and just trying to find my place in the world."

Chloe snickered. "The girl who tried to hang you is *noble*?"

I shrugged. Though she couldn't see me, I knew she felt it. "You saw me as a threat to the coven, and they're more important than I am. You saw my hanging as the one to end them all. I forgive you."

Chloe hesitated a moment. "How *can* you?"

"I guess on some level, I understand. We were both nasty to each other, and if I were in your position, I think I would've done the same thing."

"I'd like to think I'd be able to forgive you if you tried to hang me," Chloe said. "I don't know how I'll forgive myself for going to such extreme lengths."

"You have to trust yourself that you won't go down that path again," I offered. It was something I needed to hear as well.

"I won't," Chloe promised. "I don't know what I would've done if I'd gone through with it. You were right—I'd have been kicked out of the coven for sure. I don't ever want to risk that. I'm here to help people, not hurt them."

"Me, too," I agreed. "I don't want to become like those witches out there. No matter how far I'm pushed, I will fight against evil, rather than become it."

A beat passed as Chloe considered my words. Finally, she spoke sincerely. "Then I forgive you, too."

At her words, the magic before us swelled, growing into a swirling ball twice my height. It darkened until I could barely make out the shapes and shadows in the room. I turned my attention inward, to mine and Chloe's hearts, and drew out the final bits of cursed magic still tethered to us. I winced as the curse fought against me, but after everything Chloe and I had said tonight, its hold on us had become weak.

Finally, the tethers broke, and the swell of magic reached its peak. It diverged into two pieces and shrank, until the magic formed two humanoid shapes. They looked so real as the moonlight glinted off their skin. It was nothing more than a manifestation—a sort of hallucination induced by the curse Chloe and I had worked together to free from ourselves.

Dark Nadine stood tall, glaring down at me. Beside her stood a version of Chloe I'd never seen before. Her raven hair was cut short to her chin, and she had a long scar running down one side of her face. It was almost as if Chloe had inflicted it herself while battling her darkness. The two dark versions of ourselves wore matching smirks and looked like the perfect pair of villains—co-conspirators in the battle Chloe and I fought against one another.

"*You*," the real Chloe sneered at the spitting image of herself. "You have no power over me."

"I do," Dark Chloe replied in a sinister tone. Her voice sent a shiver down my spine, and it sounded even more threatening and sinister than the Chloe I'd come to know. It only made me feel for Chloe more—that she'd been fighting this bitch the whole time. "I've *always* had power over you."

"You don't have power over us anymore," I spat at the two of them.

Dark Nadine clicked her tongue and paced around my chair. I urged to shy away from her, but I forced myself not to move. She wasn't real.

She was made of magic—magic *I* could control. She couldn't manipulate me anymore.

"Nadine," she sang. "All this time, I thought we were getting along and having fun. You're nothing without me."

"She's everything without you!" Chloe snapped.

I smirked at Dark Nadine, who was staring me down in a way that was meant to intimidate and belittle me. "You wouldn't exist without me," I snarled. "I own your ass."

Dark Chloe laughed maniacally. I couldn't see her from where I sat, but I felt her energy pulsing around the room as she paced in front of Chloe. "You two think you're so strong, but you're nothing but puppets."

"You're wrong!" Chloe yelled. "I'm done listening to you. The things I've done in your name are deplorable. You will no longer whisper in my ear."

"And you," I sneered at Dark Nadine. "Your hold on me is over. From now on, *I* decide what's best for me. This curse will no longer bind us. Chloe and I are *both* staying in Octavia Falls. As the sole Curse Breaker of the Miriamic Coven, I declare this curse *broken!*"

I heard the sound of bones snap as the magic of the curse began to consume Dark Nadine and Dark Chloe. The two of them shrieked in unison as I ordered the dark magic to change intentions. No longer would this curse drive Chloe and I apart. This dark magic would become something new—a curse that would not destroy us, but would *save* us.

Dark magic swirled around our counterparts, until they were nothing more than shrieking shadows. I heard the pound of footsteps racing down the hall, and I held on a moment longer.

The doors burst open, and the three witches scrambled into the room to see what was going on. It was then that I unleashed the dark magic, focusing all my intent on the evil witches before me.

"What in the name of the Abyss is going on—?" Betty began, but she cut off as the shadowed remains of Dark Nadine and Dark Chloe sprinted across the room toward her.

The shadows dissolved, until there was nothing left but a mass of unidentifiable dark magic sweeping their way. I couldn't change the energy signature of the curse, as Grammy had taught me, but I *could* change the intent. Tonight, I sought out *justice*. The witches would pay for everything they'd done. Never again would they touch another one of the coven's children. This curse would be the judge of them.

Thick wisps of dark magic slammed into each of the witches. It diverged into three strands, assaulting the women by entering their mouths and noses. Their heads snapped backward, and they cried out in pain as the dark energy entered their bodies. The whole house shook at the sound of their screams.

The last bits of magic entered through the orifices on their face, until the wisps disappeared completely. As if in a coordinated movement, the three of them fell to their knees. Betty made a choking sound, then landed on all fours. She sucked in deep breaths. Her hair had fallen halfway out of her bun and hung in tendrils around her face.

Betty's nostrils flared as she lifted her gaze, shooting an angry glare at Chloe and me. "What did you do to me?" she snarled, clipping each word.

"You've been cursed," Chloe said proudly.

Agnes fell onto her back and screamed out in pain. Sandy gasped, like she was suffocating.

A look of terror came over Betty's face. "You'll pay for this!"

She began mumbling an incantation under her breath, and my veins turned to ice.

"What's she doing?" I asked Chloe.

"I don't know," Chloe said in a rush, sounding as worried as I felt. "Cursing us? Starting the ritual? I have no idea!"

"Sisters!" Betty cried. "Speak it with me!"

Though the witches were in pain, they pushed past my curse and began speaking in unison in a language I didn't recognize. The language sounded Celtic of some sort, with Scottish or Irish roots. It was as if this was some ancient spell only the darkest of witches would know.

The ground shook beneath us, and dust rained down from the ceiling. Chloe and I struggled, but the ropes tightened. It wasn't as much as before, as if the witches' spell over our bindings was degrading.

The witches' voices grew in intensity, and Betty lifted her arms. Wind that seemed to come from nowhere whipped through the room, sending the pages of old books tumbling across the floor. Tendrils of my own hair snapped against my face.

The witches' incantation switched abruptly from the ancient language to English. In unison, they spoke, *"From the depths of the Abyss, I release you!"*

The moment they finished, the wind in the room stilled, but my heart pounded harder than ever. From a room nearby, I heard something heavy land, and the floor quaked beneath us. Then came a ghoulish cry that made my whole body quiver.

Heavy steps sounded down the hall, coming closer and closer at top speed. A hellish creature burst through the doors, and the air left my lungs. I'd never seen anything so sinister in my life. It was as if Death himself had shown up at our door.

There were two creatures. The first was a horse-like monster, but it was made entirely of bone as dark as obsidian. What little flesh remained hung off its skeletal frame and dripped blood onto the floor. Its eyes blazed red, and a row of sharp teeth lined its jaw.

Its rider was even more horrifying. It had the shape of a man, with spindly arms and legs and long nails. The monster was bald and almost completely naked, apart from ripped pieces of fabric draped over its form. Gray, powdery skin hung loose on his ghoulish figure. He had pointed ears and a mouth that was far bigger than it should be, with rows and rows of sharp teeth that rivaled the terrifying teeth the horse bared.

The horse reared upward and let out a chilling shriek that sounded like someone being slaughtered.

"What is that!?" I screamed. I wasn't sure I expected anyone to answer.

Chloe's voice wavered as she cried out. "It's a *sluagh*!"

"What the fuck is a sluagh?" I demanded.

"Monsters of Irish lore," Chloe rushed to explain. "Some stories say they're a rogue form of lesser fae. Others call them sinners who return as malicious spirits. But there's one thing all the stories have in common... sluagh come to steal your soul."

And the witches wanted the sluagh to take ours.

I barely had a second to take in the monster before Betty pointed a twisted finger at Chloe and me. "Get them!"

TWENTY-THREE

Grant and I rushed back to the school the second Talia called. It was past midnight, and the halls were quiet, but we could hear Talia's sobs from the top of the grand staircase. I sprinted down the hall and came to a skidding stop outside her open doorway.

"Tal, what happened?" I demanded.

Talia was such a mess on the phone, I barely got two words out of her. She wasn't doing much better now as she knelt at Nadine's bedside. Talia held the sheets close to her chest, her tears soaking into them. Isa and Gus paced the room, both looking agitated.

"I-I don't know," Talia wailed. "Isa woke me up, and Nadine was gone! I-I tried to use my magic to find her, but I can't make sense of the visions. I called Headmistress Verla at home—she gave me her number after the vandalism incident—but I couldn't get ahold of her. I don't know what else to do."

"There has to be something here—some sort of clue," I insisted. "Nadine wouldn't leave without Isa."

I began rushing around the room, tossing things aside and looking for a clue—any clue. If Nadine was in danger, she'd be sure to let us know *somehow*… right?

Grant knelt beside Talia and placed a gentle hand on her shoulder. "I know how hard this is right now, but you need to take a breath. Your magic won't work unless you're focused. We're going to find Nadine."

Talia wiped her eyes and sniffled. "Something terrible happened. I just know it."

My heart stalled in my chest. "What do you see?"

Talia's breath wavered as she brought the blanket to her nose. She closed her eyes and inhaled deeply, pushing the tears away as she concentrated. "It's really dark, so it's hard to make out. Nadine got out of bed, but she looks... like a zombie or something. It's like she's in some sort of trance."

"Fuck," I growled, my hands curling into fists at my side.

Grant's face paled. "Someone used magic to lure her away."

I raked my fingers through my hair as I paced around the room. Whoever had taken my dear Nad was going to know torture for eternity. I wasn't sure there were enough fires burning in the Abyss to handle such a vile person.

"She had to go somewhere." I couldn't just stand here. I had to move. I had to do *something*. "Tal, can your magic retrace her steps?"

Her sobs had turned to sniffles, though her eyes gleamed when she looked up at me. "I can only see an object's past. My vision ends when she left the room."

"Then we'll follow the trail," I said. "Let's figure out where she went after she left the room."

Talia took a breath and stood. She was wary on her feet, but Grant held her upright. She nodded. "I'll do everything I can to find her."

Talia walked to the door and closed her eyes as she ran her fingers over the doorknob. I shook in my shoes and was ready to race to the ends of the earth to find Nadine. Patience was the last thing I had right now.

Finally, Talia opened her eyes and pointed to her left. "She went this way."

Grant and I followed Talia down the hall and toward the grand staircase. Isa and Gus followed. They both sniffed the air, as if trying to track her themselves.

Talia slowed when she reached the staircase and placed her hand on the banister. I could tell by the way her eyes fluttered behind her lids that she was having another vision. "She definitely went this way."

Talia descended the stairs and hurried to the Main Foyer's double doors. She only touched the handle a moment, and already knew Nadine had left through the main entrance.

Talia's visions seemed to speed up as she discovered a newfound sense of hope. I felt it, too, but it was greatly outshadowed by the worry that twisted in my gut. What if we didn't find her? What if it was too late?

I couldn't let myself think like that. I had to believe we could get to her before she was hurt. I couldn't let anything happen to her.

Talia's visions led us deep into the forest. She knelt down several times to inspect roots or rocks, each one of her visions leading her forward. We were nearly a mile from the school when Talia pressed her hands into the dirt and hesitated.

"What is it?" I asked breathlessly.

"This is where Nadine woke up." Talia glanced around, like she was trying to match the scenery to her vision. "She was really scared and took off running. I think something was chasing her."

Grant's tone wavered. "Let's hope it didn't catch her."

Neither Talia nor I responded. We didn't want to face that possibility just yet.

Talia must've seen something in her vision, because she sprang to her feet and started running through the trees. Grant and I rushed to keep up with her. Though Talia moved quickly, the moonlight illuminated the look of deep concentration on her face each time she slowed. She ran her hands along trees, as if those were the same ones Nadine had touched when she took this path earlier tonight.

My heart raced, but as we broke out of the trees, it dropped straight out of my chest. The Protection Tree stretched high above our heads. The moonlight cast ominous shadows through its gnarly branches, and a noose lay on the ground.

"Dear Goddess," Grant breathed when he saw the noose.

We all stepped forward, like we didn't want to believe what we were seeing. Even Isa and Gus moved warily through the clearing. To the coven, a noose was a symbol we all feared—a symbol of death.

I shook the thought from my head. My Nadine was still out there. I hadn't heard her last thought. We still had time to find her.

I bent to pick up the noose, but Talia stopped me. "You should let me. I need the vision to be as clear as possible."

My mouth went dry as I stepped back. "Please find her," I begged.

Talia's eyes filled with sorrow. It was as if she wanted to promise me she would, but she couldn't bring herself to lie.

Talia knelt on both knees and picked up the noose. The clearing went eerily silent as she fell into another vision. It was longer than the others, the seconds ticking by into an eternity. I held my breath, praying to Mother Miriam that Nadine's thoughts would be kept safe tonight. I couldn't handle hearing her in my mind. I'd done it once before, and it had torn my hearts to bits. Tonight, there were no reapers, and no way to summon them. I couldn't bring her back to life a second time.

Grant shifted beside me, but I kept my eyes on Talia. I didn't know what she was seeing, but the longer we waited, the more significant I felt it was. I didn't dare interrupt her.

Talia tilted her head. She spoke slowly, though her eyes continued to move rapidly, like the vision was still happening. "This was Chloe's doing."

Red-hot rage built up inside of me. I hated that the girls had been fighting all semester, but right now, Nadine's last encounter with Chloe seemed justified. I'd pummel her myself if I found her.

Grant looked confused. "So this has nothing to do with Lucas's investigation? Or is Chloe working for someone?"

Talia gasped.

"What?" I demanded. "What do you see?"

"Chloe lured Nadine out here, but it was personal," Talia said. "She didn't know someone would target them both."

My breath caught. "There was someone else here?"

Talia furrowed her brow, concentrating harder on the vision. "I see three figures. They stunned Nadine and Chloe. Hang on, they're talking…"

Nobody said a thing as Talia concentrated on her vision. All at once, Talia dropped the noose, and her hands shot to cover her mouth. She gasped as her eyes went wide.

"Tal!" I cried, kneeling down to shake her a little. She stared off into the distance, as if she couldn't believe what she'd seen. It wasn't until Isa meowed and dug her claws into Talia's leg that she seemed to come back to reality.

Her tone came out sounding hollow. "Nadine and Chloe were taken to Pinewood Manor."

That was all we needed to hear. The three of us raced to Grant's car, and he took off like a firecracker down the road.

The car's tires skidded across the gravel as we came to a screeching halt in front of Pinewood Manor. The mansion stretched up three stories and looked frightening in the glow of the full moon. Most of the windows were smashed, and I saw nothing but darkness beyond them, as if I was staring into the black pits of the Abyss itself. Siding hung from the exterior walls, and the paint had peeled over the years, save for a few lines of graffiti here and there. Most of the graffiti was only half done, as if something had spooked the artists away before they could finish.

The hair on the back of my neck stood at the sound of the howling wind. Just the sight of the mansion gave me the creeps. On any other night, I'd have run from this place as fast as I could.

Tonight, I wasn't leaving until I was certain Nadine was safe.

Talia had explained in the car what she'd seen in her vision. Those witches from *The Gingerbread House* had stunned and taken Nadine. I was still trying to wrap my head around how they were involved, but I didn't waste time with too many questions. All I wanted to know was where to find Nadine. The rest could wait.

We jumped out of the car. Isa prowled beside me, her big green eyes scanning the trees for anything suspicious. Talia held Gus close to her chest for comfort. She stared up at the haunted mansion and took a step back. Grant was right behind her, draping an arm around her shoulder.

"I'm scared, too," he whispered. "But we have to find her."

"Are you going to be okay?" I asked Talia.

She looked awfully pale. "I can do this. It's just this mansion… there's so much history here. I don't even have to touch it to see that horrible things have happened here."

I didn't think Talia saw anything specific, since her eyes weren't moving behind her lids the way they usually did when she had a vision. Instead, it was an instinctual energy reading. Based on her gift, I could only guess how much stronger she felt it than either Grant or me.

Grant looked over to me. "This place is huge. Where do we start?"

I gestured to the front door. "Let's see if they took her through here."

We climbed rickety stairs to reach a pair of massive double doors. Talia brushed her fingers over the thick brass handles, but she winced, as if witnessing something painful. "They didn't come this way."

"What did you see?" I asked curiously.

She shook her head. "I told you. This place has a dark history."

Grant's shoulders fell, and he spun around to gaze across the property. "Where would they have taken her?" He lifted his hands to cup them around his mouth. "Nad—" he started to shout.

I grabbed his wrists to silence him. "Shh..." I warned. "Remember, we're not alone. If the witches catch us before we find the girls, they might accelerate the ritual."

Grant dropped his hands. "I wasn't thinking straight."

"I can hardly keep it together myself," I admitted. But I had to. "This place is too big to explore the whole thing. We need clear-cut answers. Which means if they didn't bring Nad and Chloe through here, they took them somewhere else on the property. Let's keep moving, and hopefully Tal can pick up on something."

We snuck around the side of the house. Nearby, a private graveyard stretched across the property. Tall tombstones were tilted, as if they may collapse at any moment. I kept my eyes peeled for any signs of a mausoleum, or another building the witches could be holding Nadine and Chloe in, but all I saw were the shadowed outlines of old gravestones.

Isa sniffed the air, then rushed forward, entering the cemetery.

"Isa!" I hissed, but she didn't listen.

"Ow!" Talia cried as Gus jumped from her arms, scratching her. He ran after Isa, neither of them turning back to see if we were following.

I exchanged a glance with my friends. "Maybe they're trying to tell us something."

"Then we'd better check it out," Grant whispered in a shaky tone.

I shared in his wariness. On any ordinary night, cemeteries didn't frighten me. I'd had my Evoking Ceremony in a freaking mausoleum. But at Pinewood Manor, a witch had every reason to be frightened. It was as if I could sense the ghosts watching me. Dread filled my stomach, like malicious spirits might spring from behind the gravestones and hurt any witch or warlock who dare stepped in their path.

Isa and Gus stopped at a fresh mound of dirt and circled it.

"Please, for the love of the Goddess, don't let this be a grave," Grant prayed under his breath.

I hoped for the same thing, but the sinking horror in my gut told me otherwise.

Isa began digging, then shoved her nose into the dirt. She came up holding a piece of fabric between her teeth. A clue...?

"What is it you found there, girl?" I bent to inspect the piece of fabric. As I yanked on it, my heart leapt into my throat. I reeled back as a *hand* came up out of the dirt. It was barely a hand anymore, with a brownish-black complexion and skin hanging off the bones. I dropped the fabric, and the hand fell limply back atop the shallow grave. My stomach hollowed, and Grant gagged from behind me.

"No… no, no, no," I mumbled.

The hand was so small, the size of a child's.

"Dear Goddess," Talia whispered breathlessly. She knelt beside me and placed her hands on the edge of the grave. She yanked back a moment later, trembling all over as a vision of what had happened here assaulted her.

"It's *them!*" she wailed. "It's Isaac and Caleb."

I didn't want to imagine what horrible visions Talia had just seen, even if it had only been a mere glimpse into the past. Though I'd known for quite some time that the boys were dead, it didn't soften the impact of finding their bodies. I didn't know how someone could do something like this to these children—and then just toss them into this shallow grave like their lives meant nothing.

To these witches, perhaps they didn't. I had no reason to believe they would treat Nadine and Chloe any differently.

If I could, I would unbury those bodies and lay them to rest in a *proper* grave. But there was no time for that—or there would be another two graves to dig tonight.

I got to my feet. "Guys, we can't stay. Nad and Chloe are still here somewhere. We have to find them before the witches complete the ritual."

That got both of their attention, and they climbed to their feet. I pointed around the side of the mansion. "Let's keep going."

We left the cemetery and walked along the edge of the mansion. Talia's fingers trailed over the walls, and she winced every now and then, though she didn't say anything. My breath grew shallower the more we walked, as if my worry had taken space within my chest. I peeked in the windows as we passed. There was no sign of life, only one dark, abandoned room after another.

We reached the last window along the edge of the mansion, and something caught my eye. Through the glass in the light of the moon, I could make out a parlor room. An old couch faced an empty fireplace, with a wide area rug placed between them. I expected to see dust and debris, but the room was clean, as if someone had been taking care of it.

I scanned the room briefly, until my gaze landed upon a pile of modern children's toys in the corner—toy trucks, a chalkboard, and various puzzles.

My stomach sank. "This must've been where they kept Caleb. They kept him alive for months after they took him."

Talia touched the window, her eyes filling with tears. It was like she was watching Caleb play and felt the weight of his loss tenfold. "How could anyone—?"

Shrieks erupted through the night, and my whole body turned to ice.

"That sounds like Nadine and Chloe!" Grant gasped.

I ran toward the screams as fast as I possibly could. They were muffled and coming from inside the house somewhere. I turned a corner to the back of the mansion, but the screams stopped abruptly.

"Where are they?" I demanded frantically, asking no one in particular.

I rushed past the windows, looking through each one briefly for signs of life. Chilling fear coursed through my veins. If they already started the ritual, we could be too late.

Each room was as empty as the last. Then I heard a howling cry, like that of an animal instead of a human. It had to be only a few windows down. Isa sprinted faster than I could, but I took off running as fast as I could. Grant's and Talia's footsteps followed, but all I heard was the cry echoing in my ears, drowning out the thump of my pulse.

I skidded to a halt outside a wide, tall window. I barely took a second to take in the scene. Nadine and Chloe were tied to chairs, their backs to each other. Beyond them, three witches looked in pain in the shadows. I recognized them from *The Gingerbread House*—Sandy, Agnes, and Betty. They cowered near the doorway on their knees, as if they couldn't help themselves.

"Get them!" one of the witches shouted.

Glowing eyes appeared out of the shadows, and I made out the sight of a ghoulish monster. I knew it as sluagh, a creature I'd only ever seen in drawings in class. It rode the back of a horse that was nothing but a skeleton and rotting flesh. The eyes of both creatures glowed a matching red straight from hell. The horse-like creature bowed its head and bared its sharp teeth. It scuffed its hooves against the floor as its rider gave orders to charge the girls.

I reacted instantly. A battle orb erupted out of my palm and sailed through the window. Glass shattered everywhere. I leapt through the tall window frame before all of the pieces had scattered to the ground, and landed in a crouch just in time to witness my magic slam into the horse's rider. The orb had to be strong enough to kill any living human being, but this creature was no human. It went flying off the horse and smashed into a bookcase nearby.

"Lucas!" Nadine cried, her voice a mixture of terror and relief.

My heart swelled at the sound of her voice, but it was immediately crushed when I saw the horse aim its red eyes straight at Nadine. Adrenaline coursed through my body so fast, I reacted without thinking. My fingers curled around the first weapon I found, lying just a few feet away from me—a scythe. It fit perfectly in my hands, as if I'd been handling the weapon all my life. I leapt to my feet, but the horse was already charging Nadine.

I acted upon instinct and ran forward, planting myself between the monster and the girls. I swung the scythe upward just as the horse was about to pummel into me. The blade sliced through bone, severing the creature's head from its shoulders. The head went flying, landing on top of one of the witches who was on her knees.

Victory surged through me as the creepy skeleton horse went still, then crumpled to the floor like a puppet released from its master. Though the creature was made mostly of bone, blood spilled out of its vertebrae and pooled on the floor.

"Look out!" Nadine shrieked.

My victory was short-lived. One of the witches raised her hands, and a spell burst from her hands. I didn't have time to form a shield. Instead, I raised my scythe and intersected the orb's path. To my surprise, the blade sliced the orb in two, and the spell fizzled out. I didn't understand why, until I realized the blood of the monster was still on my blade. It must've had magical properties—properties that had enchanted my weapon.

Mere seconds had passed since I'd burst through the window. Grant and Talia weren't far behind. They skidded to a halt in front of me, and Isa and Gus both bared their teeth and hissed. The three of us formed a protective barrier between the witches and Nadine and Chloe.

"You handle them!" I commanded. Grant conjured a potion that glowed green, while Talia formed a battle orb in her hands.

I whirled around to Nadine and Chloe and worked as fast as I could. I dug the tip of my enchanted scythe into the ropes binding them, until their hands broke free.

"Thank the Goddess," Chloe cried in relief.

"How did you find us?" Nadine asked as I cut the ropes around her legs.

"I'll explain later," I said quickly while I worked on Chloe's bindings.

Chloe got free and leapt to her feet. She raised her hands, and shards of glass from the broken window rose into the air, following her command. I'd almost forgotten it was her birthday. Her powers had been awakened.

I grabbed Nadine's hand and helped her to her feet. I stared into her eyes for signs of injury. I expected her to at least look scared, but she stood firm, courage written all over her face. "Are you okay?"

"For now," Nadine replied.

That was all I needed to hear. Battle orbs went off behind me. Whatever potion Grant had brought along must've hurt like hell, because the monster was screeching as if it'd been burnt with acid. Chloe's glass shards must've hit one of the witch's shields, because they bounced off of something and skittered across the floor.

And still, the sounds of a fight seemed insignificant to the sound of Nadine's voice. I'd worried that we'd be too late, but she was well and alive. It was like a blessing from Mother Miriam herself.

I couldn't help it when I flung an arm around Nadine and squeezed her close to me. My nose pressed into her hair, and the chill in my veins seemed to be chased away by the warmth of her body. Nadine took my face in her hands and planted a passionate kiss to my lips. I nearly melted in relief right then and there, still oblivious to the magic whizzing around the room. But Nadine drew away abruptly, pulling me back to the screams and reminding me I held an enchanted scythe in my hand.

"Look out!" Nadine grabbed my shoulders and yanked me downward, just in time for us to avoid being hit by a high-powered battle orb. It slammed into the edge of my scythe blade, knocking the weapon from my hands. I whirled toward the fight, barely having a moment to take it all in.

Grant faced the sluagh. The green potion he'd conjured covered the monster's skin and sizzled. The monster began advancing. Grant aimed battle orb after battle orb at the monster, but they bounced off of him without damage.

The witches seemed to be breaking through whatever spell had left them curled up on the floor. They threw up shields to counteract each of Chloe's and Talia's attacks. The woman in front—Betty—got to her feet. Another battle orb grew in her palm.

"You are nothing but children!" Betty spat. "Your magic cannot defeat us. You will all die tonight!"

I threw up a shield in front of Nadine as fast as I could, but she was ready to fight. She planted her feet in a defensive stance and held her hand up. A blue battle orb glowed in her palm. "Do you really want to take that bet? Burn in hell, you filthy old hag—"

Boom!

Nadine never got the chance to release her spell. The shadow of a man appeared in the doorway, and the air burst around us as he shot off a high-powered defensive spell. The spell slammed into my gut, and the blast of energy sent my friends and I flying across the room. My head cracked against the wall, blurring my vision. Nadine slumped to the ground beside me, gasping for air that had been knocked from her chest. My head spun so fast, I couldn't find my bearings. Nearby, Grant, Talia, and Chloe groaned in pain. Isa and Gus yowled in unison.

The man stalked forward, but I was so disoriented I couldn't completely make him out. He reached for Nadine and yanked her to her feet.

"Let me go!" she screamed.

"Don't touch her!" I yelled at the same time. I scrambled to my feet, but stumbled as I struggled to find my balance.

Nadine conjured a spell, but the man yanked her hair so hard her head twisted to the side. She cried out in pain, and the spell fizzled out.

"I told those witches students would be nothing but trouble!" he snarled.

My stomach plummeted to my toes as I recognized that voice. The killer was a professor from the college, as we suspected all along.

I just never expected it to be *Professor Carlisle*.

I couldn't even process the realization. He'd allowed me to pursue an investigation. Hell, he *helped* me with it. How could he be the one orchestrating all this?

I realized then that it was *his* dream Mandy had seen, not Professor Daymond's.

Anger rocked my body as my vision came back into focus. A headache pulsed through the back of my skull, as if someone was trying to hammer their way through from the inside.

But I ignored the pain. Carlisle dragged Nadine out of the room, and all I could manage to focus on was the need to go after them. Magic began to whizz around the room again as my friends came to. I finally gained enough balance to race after Carlisle. The sluagh and the witches were a mere afterthought. I stumbled into the long, dark hallway.

"You will answer to Mother Miriam for this," Nadine sneered at Carlisle.

"Shut up," Carlisle snapped. "We're completing this ritual, once and for all."

Carlisle shoved Nadine forward. She stumbled, landing on her hands and knees in front of a double doorway. Candlelight flickered from inside the room, casting shadows down the hall through the open doors. He kicked her into the room, and she cried out in pain.

"You won't use her for anything!" I raged as magic formed in my hands. Battle orbs blasted from my palms as quickly as I could come up with spells, each one growing in intensity.

Stunning spell.

Burning battle orb.

Explosive magic.

I managed to distract Carlisle long enough that he stepped away from Nadine, but he threw up shields as fast as I conjured orbs. Each of my spells bounced off his shields and slammed into the walls. Burn marks seared the wall from one of my spells, and plaster exploded from another before the spells fizzled out.

"It was you all along!" I raged as I advanced toward him. For a moment, I hoped that it was some sort of mistake, but the wild look in Carlisle's eyes was nothing short of a confession.

Carlisle dodged another one of my attacks and laughed—like he was amused it took me so long to catch on. "Of course it was me! You had all the clues. You were only too stupid to put them together!"

I threw another high-powered orb. He deflected it with such precision that it ricocheted back in my direction. I ducked as it nearly hit me.

A high-pitched scream echoed down the hall. *Talia.*

"Goddess!" Nadine cried.

I took my eyes off Carlisle momentarily to witness the hesitation in Nadine's eyes. She'd gotten to her feet and steadied herself against the wall.

"Go help the others," I told her.

She didn't follow my instructions right away. A moment of hesitation told me she didn't want to leave. Then another scream sounded, and her eyes went wide.

"I'll handle him!" I insisted. This asshole was *mine.* "Talia needs you."

Nadine knew there was no time to stand around contemplating her decision. She whirled around and raced back to the study to help our friends.

Mere seconds had passed, but Carlisle had already conjured another spell. The dark green magic flew through the air, aimed straight for my gut. I could tell by the way it crackled on the edges that it was high-powered as hell. I threw myself to the floor just in time for the magic to whizz over my head. It hit a nearby wall and blasted straight through into the next room.

Holy shit. That motherfucker could've burned a hole straight through me. Carlisle wasn't fucking around. He was ready to kill on sight.

I retaliated immediately, jumping to my feet and blasting another stunning spell at him. But something strange happened. The spell never reached him. Instead, it hit an invisible barrier and came back toward me. Instead of fizzling out the second I dodged it, it ricocheted *again* in my direction, like my magic had been contained inside an invisible bubble and wouldn't stop until it hit the only target within the barrier—*me.*

The stunning spell zipped around me so fast that I couldn't track it. It slammed into my side, blasting me off my feet. I soared through the open doors beside me and landed flat on my back inside the room where Carlisle had been taking Nadine. It took me a moment to process what had happened. I realized Carlisle had projected his shield around me, so that my spell would backfire. Thank the Goddess it hadn't been anything more than a minor stunning spell. And since I was the one who cast it, my magic could counteract the effects faster.

And still, I couldn't move right away.

I lay on my back gasping, though the rest of my body had been paralyzed by the spell. I stared upward at the ceiling, watching the candlelight flicker off the cracked plaster as I waited to regain control of my limbs again. It took all my strength to turn my head.

I was inside the mansion's master bedroom. A huge, arching window took up the entirety of the wall opposite the doors. Beneath that, the full moon illuminated a queen-sized bed. The bed was surrounded by ritualistic paraphernalia—candles, crystals, herbs, and all kinds of symbols I didn't recognize burned into the floor. On the other side of the room was a fireplace, where a cauldron bubbled over a burning fire.

A shadow passed over my face as Carlisle's footsteps came closer. He stared down at me in satisfaction—like he was going to have fun finishing me off.

"This doesn't make any sense," I gasped through labored breaths. "You tried to help me. How could you be the one behind this?"

"I was *watching* you!" Carlisle seethed as he leaned over me. "I only agreed to the newspaper column because I didn't want you investigating on your own. At least under my supervision, I could keep an eye on you."

"That's why you shut me down," I accused. "Not because you were scared for my safety. You feared I was learning too much."

Carlisle smirked and lifted his foot. The spell that had hit me kept me immobile as Carlisle brought his heel down on my face. Pain shot through my nose, and I immediately felt the bruises begin to form.

"I *did* warn you," Carlisle mocked.

His words came back to me. *Men like Professor Daymond won't hesitate to harm you to protect themselves.*

Men like Professor Daymond, my ass. Carlisle was warning me about himself!

"Then let *me* warn *you* of something, Professor," I said, sensing control of my body returning. "You won't get away with this!"

I conjured a weapon—a knife I'd kept in my stash since the night I was attacked on the street, just in case I had to defend myself. The knife materialized in my hand, and I finally regained my strength. I swiped the knife outward. It sliced across the front of Carlisle's leg.

Carlisle let out a cry and collapsed onto one knee. Blood dripped from the deep wound and pooled onto the hardwood. I leapt to my feet, and Carlisle lifted a hand. I lashed out on instinct and sliced my knife toward him again. This time, it connected with his palm. The spell he'd been about to conjure fizzled away as she screamed out in pain a second time.

"My friends and I won't become your next victims!" I growled.

Carlisle muttered an incantation under his breath. A blast of defensive magic whipped by me, knocking me backward. I landed on my back, and my knife went skittering across the floor and under the bed. Carlisle was already on his feet, pushing past the pain in his leg as he lunged for me.

I grabbed for the first thing my hands could find. My fingers curled around a candle, and I thrust it toward him. The flame seared his skin, and he jumped backward. I took the opportunity to scramble to my feet.

I was so fucking pissed that I slammed straight into him, tackling him to the ground. Carlisle's cancer meds must've been working wonders, because the old man was stronger than he looked. He grabbed me by the collar and rolled the two of us over, until he gained the upper hand. Magic began to form in his hand, until my fist cracked against the side of his jaw. He rolled off of me.

I jumped on top of him to hold him down. I thought I had him, but the next thing I knew, sharp claws were digging into my back, and the screech of an animal pierced my ears. I reared backward and reached over my shoulder to nab the animal. My fingers met fur, and I grabbed a handful of scruff, yanking the animal off me and tossing it across the room.

A gray cat rolled across the floor, coming to a stop next to the fireplace. It struck me where I'd seen this cat before. It'd sat in Carlisle's office so many times, but it'd also been on the street the night I was attacked.

I grabbed Carlisle by the collar, seething. "*You* were the one to attack me that night on the street!"

"Of course I was!" he snapped. "You were getting too close."

All the pieces of the puzzle fell into place. "The healing potion we found near the Bennetts' house—it was *yours*! You were sneaking around that night. You're the one we heard knock the garbage can over."

"So I investigated the kid," Carlisle said like it was nothing. "It turned out he wasn't a candidate for the ritual."

"And my girlfriend was!?" I growled. My fist connected with Carlisle's cheek—not because I needed to defend myself, but because the asshat deserved it, and far worse.

"Why are you doing this?" I demanded. I drew my fist back again in warning. This time, a battle orb crackled. It was powerful enough to burn his skin if I let it.

"I'm doing what's needed to be done!" he cried. "My powers are the only magic within the coven that would ensure the boys could not be tracked."

"How did you do it?" I demanded.

"It doesn't matter," he spat. "You won't live long enough to care. *Suffoco.*"

Carlisle spoke the incantation so fast, I didn't have a chance to react. In the blink of an eye, pain radiated up my throat, as if a fire was burning my insides and an external force was crushing my windpipe from the outside. It was some sort of defensive magic I didn't even know existed— or a type of curse, perhaps. All I knew was it hurt like a motherfucker. Carlisle shoved me off of him, and I gasped for breath on my knees.

A satisfied smirk touched Carlisle's lips as he got to his feet, looming over me. "You seemed like such a smart kid. I see now I had no reason to worry about you."

"How did you do it!?" I rasped again through labored breaths.

"I practically gave you the answer!" Carlisle snapped. "I showed you my powers to misdirect you—to look helpful. But you should've known there was more to them. After all, no Seer in the coven has magic quite like mine."

I sucked in deep breaths, but each one caused the blazing inferno in my throat to intensify. The pain began moving downward toward my gut. Carlisle paced around me, looking satisfied as I clutched my stomach and curled forward. My mind raced with spells that might counteract this one. I didn't have much time, but I had to keep him talking, or he might decide to finish me off before the spell took its full hold on me.

"I'm going to die anyway," I struggled to say. "You might as well tell me how you kept the coven from tracking you."

"I told you my gift was multifaceted," Carlisle reminded me. "I'm a projector. My magic works by casting visions into other people's minds. You can't project onto a projector."

It all made sense now. With Carlisle involved, no one could track him with magic. Mandy's magic must've worked differently somehow, because she'd seen into his dream—like the dream was a projection itself.

"You made a mistake," I realized. "You weren't with the other witches tonight."

"A mistake *they* made," he sneered. "They got impatient and went against orders! Now everything's been ruined."

"What do you mean... *everything?*" I gasped as the pain dipped deeper into my abdomen. "What exactly is your plan? What kind of ritual could possibly drive you to murder members of your own coven!?"

"I had to!" he insisted. "I'd be dead without it!"

"Better to be dead than to be a murderer!" I seethed. "Is that what this is—a ritual to brew your cancer potion?"

"The cancer medication is my *payment,*" Carlisle growled. "Stealing those children was the only way for me to gain the medicine that keeps me alive! I couldn't afford it on my own, even with my salary. I was going broke! The coven didn't *need* those kids. I'm a professor for Miriam College! All the knowledge I've gained will die with me. The coven *needs* that knowledge to survive."

"So write a fucking book," I wheezed. "People die every day. Your life is no more important than those boys you killed. After everything you've done, you're worthless."

I never saw his hand coming. Carlisle slapped me so hard that my head spun.

"You know nothing about worth," he growled. "You're nothing, Lucas."

You're nothing, Lucas.

The words echoed in my mind. It was something I'd heard my father say more than once. A memory tickled in the back of my mind, an incantation Eric had taught me years ago before I even got my magic. It wasn't something we learned at school, but I'd memorized it in case I ever needed to use it to defend myself against my father. I'd never gotten the chance.

It was then that the answer came to me. I pushed past the pain of Carlisle's curse and forced one last breath through my swollen windpipe.

"*Praeligo hostilis,*" I managed to rasp out, though my voice was barely audible.

Carlisle's arms froze at his sides, and he collapsed to the ground. He tried to move, wriggling on the dusty floor, but my spell would not permit freedom. It was a spell meant to bind your enemies. Satisfaction swept through me. I wouldn't let this man hurt anyone else.

As my binding spell took hold of Carlisle, his magic melted away. I regained control of my lungs and sucked in a deep breath. I got to my feet and loomed over him the way he had to me. A battle orb formed in my palm, and I prepared to deliver the final blow.

Carlisle began to laugh, catching me off guard. "What are you going to do? You don't have it in you to kill me."

I paused as his words hit me. *I could kill him,* I thought. It wouldn't take much—a deadly battle orb, my knife to his heart. He had nowhere to run.

But just the thought of stooping to his level—of killing another person, let alone a member of the coven—made me sick. And what would that make me? A murderer worthy of a hanging myself.

Death would be merciful after all Carlisle had done. Caleb and Isaac deserved better. They deserved for their murderers to be brought to justice—in this life and the next.

The law was more important than my personal feelings. As a journalist, my job was to gather and report the facts, not deal out punishment as I saw fit.

I had Carlisle within my grasp. All I had to do was stun him long enough to turn him over to the Imperium Council. He would confess all he told me here, and the priestesses—the highest power in our coven—would decide what to do with him.

It didn't matter to me if he was sentenced to a hanging or a burning at the stake, or if the council allowed him to rot in prison for the rest of his days. I wouldn't shed a tear.

But I'd taken an oath to protect the coven the night of my Evoking Ceremony. And though I didn't believe Carlisle deserved a place in this coven, it wasn't my call to make. I would *not* become a murderer like him.

"I don't speak for the coven," I snarled. "You will confess to the Imperium Council, and suffer their wrath. The coven will decide your fate. I hope you get the death you deserve."

I shifted the intention of my spell and thrust it forward. A stunning spell slammed into Carlisle's face. His features went blank, and his eyes rolled back into his skull. His cat yowled, but Carlisle was out cold.

A scream echoed down the hall. My raging anger was instantly overtaken by a sinking horror. *Nadine.*

Carlisle was knocked out—he could wait. I took off running down the hall to the aid of my friends. What I saw when I reached the study chilled me to the bone. I came to a skidding halt in the doorway. I barely had a second to take in the scene. It all happened so fast that I had no time to fight.

Chloe lay motionless on the floor next to the scythe. I wasn't sure if she was dead or alive. The witch with the cat-eye glasses had Talia by the hair, and her hands blazed red with magic as she lowered the spell toward Talia's face. Talia had been beaten so badly that her face was almost unrecognizable. Both eyes were covered in dark bruises and swollen shut, and blood dripped from a deep gash on her nose.

Grant wasn't far from Talia. He lay on the floor, writhing in pain from a spell the long-haired witch had cast on him. His left arm was bent at an odd angle, obviously broken.

The final witch and their leader—Betty—muttered something under her breath, and the gangly monster advanced on Nadine.

Nadine was the only one still free of the witches' hold. Though she'd suffered bruises all over her body and a gash ran along her face, she remained on her feet. Her gaze flickered between Chloe, Talia, and Grant. I witnessed realization cross her face. Despite the spell cast over them earlier, the witches had gained the upper hand, and they were about to finish off our friends.

Rage unlike I'd ever seen before twisted in Nadine's features. It was even more frightening to witness than the day she beat Chloe and sent her to the infirmary. She was a fire that could not be put out—and that fire would burn every creature who stood in the way of her and her friends.

Nadine screamed as a spell gathered in her hands, then blasted outward at the monster. It knocked the creature several feet away from her. Without missing a beat, Nadine spun toward Agnes, who was about to finish Talia off. Before Agnes's spell could touch Talia's skin, Nadine grabbed hold of the bitch and yanked her so hard that she dropped Talia.

"Go to hell!" Nadine yelled, shoving Agnes in front of the monster.

What I saw next was something out of a horror film. Agnes stumbled into the sluagh, and it grabbed her. Satisfaction was written in its features, as if it would take any soul offered to it. And I knew that it would. The only way to dissuade a sluagh was to place another soul within their path.

Agnes screamed when she realized what had happened, but it was already too late. The sluagh dipped its head and opened its mouth. Its breath turned to red poisonous wisps that instantly took the witch's life. I felt the void of death enter the room.

"This is a cruel death." Her words played in my mind, the burden of her last thoughts handed to me as the Reaper's Apprentice.

Agnes's body slumped out of the sluagh's hands, but an imprint of her form remained, translucent in the moonlight. The sluagh wrapped her soul in his arms. His torn cloak billowed around him, and he rose into the air, defying gravity. A hellish screech erupted from his lungs, and he took off through the broken window, carrying Agnes's soul with him to the Abyss.

"Agnes!" Betty cried.

In a split second, the monster was gone, and Nadine was already onto the next witch. It happened so fast, I barely saw it. Nadine sliced her hand through the air, performing battle magic I'd only ever heard of the most powerful witches casting. Her magic hit Sandy's throat, slicing through it like a cleaver. Blood spurted from the deep wound on her neck, and her hands instantly went to cradle the wound, as if she could hold the blood inside. All it did was run through her fingers like a broken spigot.

Sandy's wide eyes met Nadine's, and she gaped like she wanted to say something. But no words came out—only blood. She sank to her knees, before her eyes rolled back in her skull and she slumped lifelessly to the floor. The spell she'd cast on Grant broke, and he stilled from where he'd been writhing on the floor.

I barely had a chance to process it as another thought entered my mind. *"The coven will come to regret this."*

The feeling of death seemed to permeate into the walls of the mansion.

"My sisters!" Betty wailed, her cries echoing off the walls of the mansion. Magic swelled in her hands as revenge overtook her features.

I thrust out a shield as quick as I could, projecting it between Nadine and the witch. But Nadine was faster than I was. Whatever magic Nadine was using passed through my shield and assaulted Betty. The witch screamed so loud, the walls of the mansion shook. Her back arched, and she fell onto her knees, her features contorted in pain.

"Stop, Nad!" I shouted. I could barely wrap my head around what she'd already done. I couldn't stand the thought of her taking another life.

But Nadine didn't hear me. She kept her gaze locked on Betty as the spell twisted its way through her body, making her convulse at Nadine's feet.

"What are you doing to me!?" Betty screeched.

"The curse I cast upon you was cast with the intent to deliver justice," Nadine told her. "I'm only speeding up the spell. Say hello to your sisters in hell."

"Nad!" I screamed.

This had gone too far. Nadine had taken it upon herself to be judge, jury, and executioner, but it wasn't her place. She'd already gained the upper hand. Betty was vulnerable. We could take her to the Imperium Council with Carlisle—let *them* deal out their sentence.

But Nadine had no intentions of slowing down. That was clear in the rage that burned in her eyes. Nadine's curse took hold of the witch, and it was as if she'd called upon death itself. Horror washed over me like the cold chill of a ghostly haunting as I witnessed the life get sucked straight out of the witch. Her soft, pale skin turned black and began to peel off her body in chunks. Betty's wailing cry of pain pierced my ears, sending tremors down to my bones.

Blood dripped down Betty's clothes as Nadine's curse tore her apart layer by layer. Muscle separated from bone and became goo that trailed down the paths of blood and pooled onto the floor. Her eyes popped from her skull, until there was nothing left but bone, her screams becoming nothing more than echoes in my mind as death silenced her voice.

"This witch is no better than us," Betty's voice said in my head. *"She will rot in the Abyss for her sins."*

I sensed death stronger than ever through the power of my gift. Nausea hit me like a rogue battle orb, slamming into my gut so hard I doubled over and puked. I gagged a few times, before coming up for air. The last I saw of Betty, her bones had transformed to ash, and her whole body crumbled to nothing.

Just like that, it was over.

And yet, it all happened so fast that it felt like it'd only begun.

The images of the witches' deaths played in my mind, their words echoing on repeat. I had wished the worst for these women after what they'd done, but I never imagined Nadine would be the one to deliver their end. I'd been excusing everything Nadine had done this semester, but it was time to admit the truth.

Nadine Evers fucking terrified me.

I was so shocked by what happened that I had to steady myself against the doorframe to stay upright. Nadine took a step toward me, but I held a hand up.

"Don't," I snapped.

Confusion and hurt crossed Nadine's features. "Lucas, are you okay?"

What kind of a fucking question was that? "You just *killed* all those witches," I gasped, the shock still riveting through me.

"I did what I had to do," Nadine said softly.

My girlfriend had just become a murderer, and she was trying to justify it? This had to be her darkness. She wouldn't do something like this without remorse.

"Nadine, you saved us," Grant gasped. He cradled his broken arm to his chest and inched over to Talia. She felt out with her hands until she found him, then clung to him tightly as her whole body shook.

"I don't want to spend another second in this place," Talia sobbed.

Nadine glanced toward the door. "What happened to Carlisle?"

"He's not going anywhere, for now," I answered. "We have to call the Imperium Council and report what happened here."

"I agree," Grant said. "Let's get out of here and let the council take care of him."

Grant's broken arm hung limply at his side, but he used his good arm to help support Talia.

I went to Chloe's side. She was still breathing—thank the Goddess—but she had a huge gash across her forehead that oozed blood. The scythe next to her caught my attention briefly, and I grabbed it without really thinking about it. I subconjured it. Though it was one of the largest items I'd ever stored in my stash, it disappeared immediately and effortlessly from my hand.

I lifted Chloe in my arms and carried her out the window behind the others. None of us moved very fast, as we'd had all the fight beaten out of us inside the mansion. Nadine looked about ready to pass out after all the magic she'd used, and I didn't know how long it'd been since Grant had eaten anything. He tried to stay strong as he helped Talia navigate across the grass, but he was slow and obviously fatigued. Low blood sugar was setting in, and I feared he might pass out as well.

I had the thought to force him to eat the second we got in the car, but we never made it that far. We turned the corner to the front of the mansion, and the car came into view when—

Boom!

A deafening explosion sounded, echoing across the lake. The blast was so close that it rocked the ground beneath our feet like an earthquake. We were all tossed to the ground at the strength of the blast. Chloe landed on top of me, and she groaned as she began to come to. She rolled off of me, but still seemed out of it.

My adrenaline spiked again, and my heart hammered. I sat up, only to see the roof of the mansion begin to crumble inward. The building cracked and groaned as it toppled in on itself.

"Get back!" I shouted.

Chloe snapped to attention, and her eyes widened as she looked upward to see the building falling down. Nadine and I each grabbed one of her arms, and Grant and Talia took off running. We scrambled away from the mansion as fast as we could, until we were finally out of range of the building.

Nobody said anything. We just watched in shock as the walls crumbled. Even Isa and Gus looked terrified, their hair standing on end. It seemed to happen in slow motion, and yet, seemed to take no time at all. Soon, the wing we'd been standing in only minutes ago had been leveled to nothing but a pile of building materials.

"The coven is nothing without me," a voice came into my mind.

Carlisle.

My stomach hollowed. I'd left him trapped inside the building, and the weight of the explosion had killed him.

An orange-red glow emitted from somewhere inside the rubble. It didn't take long for the fire to begin eating away at the remains of the mansion. There'd been a fire burning in the master bedroom fireplace, and it was spreading quickly.

Chloe shook as she gazed over the destruction. The growing flames flickered off the contours of her face. "What just happened?"

"No idea," Nadine said, trying to catch her breath. "Maybe the witches cast some sort of fail-safe spell to cover up everything that happened here."

Nobody seemed to have the energy to move—only watch the blazing fire. We all slumped to the grass at the edge of the cemetery, feeling relieved that the night was finally over.

At least, I *should've* felt relieved. Inside, adrenaline continued to pump through my veins, and I was still reeling in shock of everything that had happened. So many people had died tonight. I'd heard so many thoughts.

These thoughts should've been easy to let go of. They'd come from the most vile members of the coven, and they didn't deserve my attention. But each thought had been laced in unmatched evil that burrowed deep into my gut. Letting these thoughts go would be harder after what I'd witnessed. Forgiveness was not something these people deserved—and was not something I thought I could give to anyone right now.

"Lucas," Grant wheezed, sucking in a deep breath as he shifted slightly. "There's a first-aid kit in the back of my car. Can you go get it?"

"Yes, absolutely," I replied.

I'd only just gotten to my feet when the sound of tires crunching on the gravel caught my attention. We whirled around to see a black vehicle hurtling down the drive. Instantly on alert, I threw up a shield around us.

The car came to an abrupt halt. I breathed a sigh of relief when Headmistress Verla rushed out of the vehicle. She was in such a hurry that she left the driver's side door open. I dropped my shield.

"Dear Goddess!" she cried as she ran to us. "I got Talia's message. We've been searching everywhere for you."

Nadine stood from the grass on shaky feet. "We?"

"The Imperium Council," Verla said. "They'll be here any minute."

Verla reached out and squeezed Nadine's hands, then did the same to me and the others. Tears brimmed her eyes, like she couldn't stand the thought of losing her students. "Thank Alora you're all okay. What happened here?"

"Nadine and I were kidnapped." Chloe immediately dove into an explanation of what had happened and what the witches had confessed. I was only hearing it for the first time myself, and all the missing pieces of my investigation fell into place.

Chloe failed to mention that she'd tried to *hang* Nadine earlier in the night, and Nadine didn't bring it up, either. But there were other parts she left out, too, like how Nadine had killed the witches. It was like Nadine and Chloe had entered an agreement to protect each other.

"We got out just before the blast," Chloe concluded with. "I don't know how anyone inside could've survived."

"I can't believe Professor Carlisle was involved," Verla said.

"He hired the witches," Chloe explained.

"I'm not so sure about that," I countered.

All eyes turned to me.

"He was in on it for sure," I quickly clarified. "But he said something about his cancer meds being his *payment*."

"So… there's someone else out there responsible for this?" Verla asked.

A shiver traveled down my spine. "There must be."

"Did he tell you who?" Verla sounded worried to hear the main culprit was still at large.

"No," I said regrettably. "That was unfortunately the one piece of information I didn't get out of him. I had hoped he'd confess everything to the council, but then… well."

I gestured to the collapsed mansion, but my eyes went to Nadine. I couldn't help but glare at her.

"What matters is that you're all safe," Verla said. "I'll get the fire department and medics out here right away."

"We found bodies, too," I added.

Verla's face paled. "Bodies?"

"In the cemetery." I pointed to where the shallow graves had been dug. "It's the missing boys—Isaac and Caleb."

"I'll inform the police immediately," Verla promised. "I'll be working closely with the Imperium Council to catch anyone else involved. You have nothing to worry about."

She conjured her phone and began dialing. Grant asked Chloe more questions about the kidnapping, and Talia leaned in close as Chloe went into more detail.

Nadine turned to me and took my face in her hands. She felt cold. I instinctually drew away. Pain was written all over her features, and it wasn't because of the physical injuries. She could feel that I was avoiding her touch.

"Are you okay?" Her tone was laced in desperation. "Your face looks pretty bad."

She touched one of the bruises under my eye, and I winced. I'd nearly forgotten about them.

"I'll be fine. It's just..." I glanced toward the others. Though no one was listening to us, I didn't want to talk out in the open.

"Let's talk somewhere private," I suggested. I took Nadine's arm and led her into the trees nearby. I dropped my voice, so we wouldn't be overheard. I didn't know how to admit the truth to her, but the words came tumbling out anyway. "You really scared me tonight."

Her shoulders fell, and she reached out to take my hands. "I know it must've been terrifying not knowing where I was, but I'm alive."

I squeezed her hands, wanting desperately to convince myself I wasn't frightened, but I couldn't do it. "That's not what I was talking about. Of *course* I was scared when I found out you were missing, but what you did to those witches..."

Nadine drew away, her brow furrowed. "You're... *mad* I killed them?" she hissed in a low whisper. "You're pissed off that I got rid of a group of *child murderers* to save our friends?"

I searched for the right words, but couldn't seem to find them. "I didn't realize what your darkness was capable of."

"My *darkness*?" Nadine blew a breath. "Lucas, you need to stop this! You've been doing this all semester. You think my darkness is like some demon inside of me. She *was* separate from me, but not in the way I thought. Chloe helped me realize that every decision I made was my own. I have to take responsibility for my actions. Of course there were times when my darkness took over, but only because I let it."

"No," I insisted. "It'll be different when you break the curse."

"That's just it!" Nadine replied, before lowering her voice again. "I *did* break it. Tonight. Right before I killed the witches!"

I reeled backward. "You... you killed them all by yourself?"

"Yes. I transferred the curse into the witches. I never could've performed that last spell without some sort of external magic supply."

"But you... you," I stammered. If this had been a product of her curse, I might be able to accept it. The curse made her do things outside of her control... right?

"The curse is gone. The voices are gone," Nadine said. "I have to accept that the decision I made tonight was my own. Can you?"

I hesitated. I wasn't sure I could. "To be honest, that terrifies me."

Nadine tilted her chin upward. "It doesn't terrify me. You know why? Because I know now how strong I am. I know what lengths I'm willing to go to protect the people I love. And I will stand by that decision. You said it yourself that I do bad things for good reasons."

"Maybe I was wrong. We could've turned them in—"

Nadine's teeth gritted, like she was getting irritated with me. "I did what had to be done. Those witches were going to kill Grant and Talia."

"The last witch wasn't anywhere near them!" I hissed.

Her jaw dropped, and her voice grew louder and more intense. "What do you think was going to happen if I let her go? She could've killed *you*. She could've killed any of us. I had a decision to make. Are you seriously going to stand here and tell me I made the wrong one?"

Yes, I thought. Nadine had taken things too far. I'd been making excuses for her all semester because I loved her, but after what I saw tonight, I wasn't sure I could keep doing that.

"There had to be another answer," I argued.

"I took the one that made sense at the time!" she growled. "Sorry that's too intense for you."

"Of course it's intense!" I snapped. "You should be using your Curse Breaker powers for good!"

Nadine opened her mouth to respond, but she stopped dead when her eyes locked on something behind me. Horror filled her features.

The sound of footsteps came a moment too late. Slowly, I turned to see the four priestesses of the Imperium Council approaching us through the trees. They wore dark robes that marked them as the coven's highest governing authority. As soon as the words slipped from my mouth, the priestesses came to an abrupt halt.

I wished I could take back the words, but I couldn't. Nadine's secret was out in the open now. The whole council knew.

"A Curse Breaker?" Priestess Margaret gasped.

My stomach hollowed. I'd begun the night intent on saving Nadine. Instead, I'd betrayed the woman I loved.

"This is unexpected news," Priestess Margaret said. "Nadine Evers, the

Imperium Council hereby summons you to the Imperium headquarters tomorrow at dusk. You are expected to be there—or reap the conse-quences."

TWENTY-FOUR

Warm water enveloped me from all angles, but even that couldn't keep the shivers from traveling down my spine. I should've felt comforted to be lying here in the tub in Grammy's bathroom. I was alive, after all. At several points last night, I didn't know if I'd make it until morning. But images of the previous night assaulted me. Parts of it felt like a dream. Other parts felt all too real.

I sank deeper into the tub, until everything but my nose was covered. Thoughts raced through my mind a million miles per hour. Mine and Chloe's feud felt like a distant memory. The curse was gone, and there was no pressure to fight anymore.

The images of the witches dying was seared into my memory, but the images didn't scare me. I'd done what I had to protect my friends. I wasn't ashamed of that.

But there was one thing I couldn't seem to get past—one thing I couldn't bring myself to forgive just yet.

Lucas had given up my secret.

His words echoed in my mind. I'd spent all semester trying to protect myself, and in the blink of an eye, my secret was out there.

The Imperium Council had requested a meeting with me. It was just as I had feared—just as Grammy had warned. The second people knew what I was, they would turn on me.

Maybe I could trust the council. I hoped. But a weight like bricks settled in my gut as I anticipated our meeting later today. I feared what they had in store for me.

At least the council hadn't overheard what I'd done—how I'd killed those witches. Even murder in self-defense would earn me a trial. The fire had destroyed all evidence, and I hoped it would stay that way. None of my friends seemed inclined to share *that* secret. Even Chloe's lips were sealed on the matter.

A knock came at the bathroom door. I didn't notice it at first, until I heard Grammy's muffled voice through the door. I lifted my face from the water.

"Grammy?" I asked. "Is everything okay?"

"I'm just checking on you," she said. "You've been in there a while. Isn't your meeting soon?"

"Yeah, I'm almost done," I told her. I'd slept most of the day, and it was late afternoon already. It felt like I hadn't slept at all.

Grammy had been frantic when I showed up at her house early this morning, before sunrise. My adrenaline had kept me going, but by the time I stepped in Grammy's door, I felt like I could finally give in to my fatigue. I'd passed out right in front of her, and the bruises all over my skin didn't help convince her everything was fine.

It wasn't fine. *Fine* was a lie I'd told myself so long that even in the wake of trauma, it felt true. And that was the biggest lie of all.

Chloe and Talia both had to get stitches. Chloe had a concussion, and Talia's nose had been broken. Grant suffered a severe broken arm and would be in a cast for weeks. Out of all of us, Lucas was in the best shape.

The police had dropped me off, after the medics had cleared me. I knew I should've gone to the hospital, but I had a lot of experience convincing people I was okay when I wasn't. I just wanted to see Grammy. She was a comfort after everything that had happened. Being with her felt *normal* when nothing else about that night had.

I was barely inside for a minute before I broke down in front of Grammy. She'd held me tight while I opened up to her about everything that had happened. I didn't keep anything back—not even about what I'd done to those evil witches.

Grammy hadn't said anything, just sat and listened. There was no judgement in her eyes, just relief that I had made it out alive.

I could tell she was trying to keep quiet when I told her how Lucas had let my secret slip. She didn't want me to be scared of the Imperium Council. But I knew how to read the purse of her lips too well. She was pissed at Lucas, same as I was.

I couldn't skip out on my meeting with the Imperium Council. Such a thing was one step short of ignoring Mother Miriam.

I climbed out of the tub and reached for my towel. Every muscle in my body protested, and my head spun. I wrapped the towel around myself and sat on the edge of the tub, waiting for the dizziness to pass. I'd used so much magic last night, I felt worse than normal. A bout of nausea hit, and I lunged across the room just in time to reach the toilet. I leaned over it and spewed my guts. When it was over, I leaned my head back against the cold wall, shivering. I waited for Grammy to knock on the door and ask if I was all right, but she must've gone to the other side of the house and hadn't heard.

It was probably better that way. She'd try to nurse me back to health, when there wasn't anything she could do. I just had to push through it.

Eventually, I pulled myself up from the floor and wrapped a plush robe around myself. I brushed my hair into a ponytail, but I didn't waste any magic applying makeup. Maybe if I *looked* sick, the Imperium Council would see I couldn't help them.

I returned to my guest room and got dressed, then found Grammy in the kitchen making eggs. She scooped scrambled eggs onto a plate and turned to me when she heard me approach. "I made you breakfast."

"Isn't it a little late for breakfast?" I teased. "It's almost dinner time."

"Consider it breakfast," she said. "You had a long night."

She could say that again.

Grammy scooped the rest of the eggs onto her own plate, and we sat at the breakfast nook together. Grammy's eggs were heavenly, fluffy and perfectly seasoned. I ate slowly, savoring every bite.

After a few moments of silence, she set her fork down. "Nadine."

"Yes?"

She waited for me to meet her gaze before she continued. "I didn't get a chance to say this last night, but I wanted you to know… I'm proud of you."

I stopped chewing as I digested her words. "Proud of me for what?"

Grammy reached across the table, placing her soft hand over mine.

"You went through a lot last night, and you still managed to break your curse and save your friends. You're a much stronger witch than you realize."

I offered her a smile. "Thanks, Grammy. But I'm sure a strong witch wouldn't feel like shit every time she used magic."

Grammy's features fell. "If you need to rest and skip your meeting—"

"No, it's the Imperium Council," I said. "I'm obligated to go."

"Whatever they say to you, we'll figure it out," she promised.

"Thank you for being on my side."

Her lips lifted at the corners. "Always."

I finished my eggs and felt a little better after I ate. Isa and Grammy's cat, Cornelius, were lounging in the living room when I passed. Isa jumped off the couch and rubbed against my leg as I went to the front door.

I bent to pet her. "I'll be back soon, girl. I love you."

I took my car to the Imperium Council headquarters, located on the top level of Octavia Hall. The door was open when I arrived. The room had a vaulted ceiling and dark wood tones, with all types of witchy paraphernalia on the walls and bookcases. All four priestesses sat around a table in the center of the room. A fifth chair sat empty, and a fire burned in the fireplace. It should've given the attic space a warm, comforting vibe, but I shivered when I stepped in the door.

"Nadine," Priestess Margaret greeted. "Please, have a seat."

I walked over to the empty chair and sat. The priestess with a skull tattoo on her wrist—I thought her name was Priestess Charlotte—stood and closed the door.

"There's no need to be nervous, my child," one of the priestesses said. She was the youngest of them all, and though I couldn't see her tattoo, I figured she was a Seer based on the tattoos of the others. That meant she was Priestess Stella. "This is a safe room. It's been enchanted so no one can overhear us."

"I'm not nervous," I lied, holding my head up high.

"Then we shall get started right away," Priestess Lilian said. She was Chloe's grandmother, and there was obvious disdain on her face when she saw me. Even though the curse had been broken, it was clear she still held a grudge against my family.

Although the priestesses tried to appear gentle and kind, I felt uncomfortable in their presence. Lilian's feelings about me were evident, but I suspected the others were simply better at hiding it. Their smiles seemed fake, and their kind, sweet voices felt like a ruse to lure me in. I didn't like it one bit.

Priestess Margaret cleared her throat. "I think it's obvious why you're here. As the only Curse Breaker in the coven, you are the sole candidate eligible to sit upon the council to represent your Cast."

I gaped at them. "You… want me to become a priestess?"

Priestess Margaret nodded. "Yes."

I reeled back, nearly falling out of my chair. I didn't even know what being a priestess would entail, or what kinds of duties I'd be expected to do.

"Officially, you will not be inducted as a priestess until Halloween," Priestess Stella clarified. "As that is the night the veil is the thinnest, all priestess inductions are performed on October thirty-first."

"What would I have to do if I was a priestess?" I questioned. I wasn't sure this was something I wanted.

"Being a priestess is a life-long commitment," Priestess Charlotte explained. "As a priestess, you will be trained in Miriamic law. You will be responsible for creating and upholding laws, as well as representing the coven in foreign supernatural relations."

"Foreign supernatural relations?" I repeated. "Like, meeting with other supernatural races?"

"Yes," Priestess Charlotte answered. "We have many treaties to uphold and are always working to improve relations among various supernatural races."

I mulled over what she said. "I wouldn't have to perform any spells?"

"Oh, my dear," Priestess Margaret laughed. "Of *course* you'll have to perform spells. With a Curse Breaker in the coven, our magic will be unmatched. There are so many spells we can perform now. Our economy and infrastructure could grow ten-fold just by having all five members of the coven working together."

I remembered how I'd been told the space-bending spell on the school had been performed by members of all five Casts. The coven hadn't been able to perform spells like that since my grandfather died. How many spells would they ask me to cast, and how quickly?

"I don't know that I'm cut out to be a politician," I admitted. I'd much rather work in the police force, *enforcing* laws rather than creating them. "What if I say no?"

Priestess Lilian laughed in a way that bordered on mocking. "You misunderstand, Miss Evers. There are rumors of unrest in Malovia. A new king by the name of Elijah Zlodia is being crowned as we speak, and our intel has gathered that he intends to grow the Malovian army. We must take this as nothing short of a threat. We need *all* casts to come together should the fae rise up again. You are the only Curse Breaker in the coven. You don't have a choice."

I didn't get a chance to process what she'd said, let alone object. Priestess Margaret clapped her hands together and said, "Now that that's settled, let's move on to our first order of business. As mentioned, you will not become an official priestess until your induction ceremony on Halloween. But there are matters that cannot wait. Therefore, your training begins today."

I glanced between the four of them. "Other matters?"

"You have heard the rumors affecting magic at the school—how people's magic is disappearing for days at a time," Priestess Margaret said. "It is unfortunately a problem wide-spread across the coven."

"You want me to break the curse," I stated flatly. "To be honest, I don't even know how to handle something this big."

"No, no," Priestess Margaret said quickly. "We have not been able to identify the source of this issue. Initially, we suspected this was some sort of attack from the fae. However, after all the evidence that came to light last night regarding the missing boys, it's been proven that we cannot even trust our own people. We suspect someone in the coven is draining our magic."

"Do you think it has anything to do with the ritual the witches were going to perform last night?" I asked.

"The investigation on the matter is on-going," Priestess Margaret said.

So basically they had no idea if there was a connection.

She continued. "The only way to combat this—whether the threat is coming from inside or outside the coven—is to unite the Oaken Wands."

A shudder traveled down my spine. Chloe had mentioned the Oaken Wands—that they were the source of the feud between our grandparents.

"What are the Oaken Wands, exactly?" I asked.

"The Oaken Wands are powerful relics created during the Great

Supernatural War," Priestess Margaret explained. "There are five wands—one for each Cast."

I was curious, to say the least. "What's so special about these wands?"

"Most wands are merely a tool for focusing and amplifying magic, and can often be transferred from one witch to another," Priestess Margaret said. "The Oaken Wands contain magic themselves, as they were carved from a branch of the Protection Tree itself."

They were carved from oak, I realized. Hence, the Oaken Wands.

"Not just anyone can use them, though," Priestess Margaret went on. "The wand must choose *you*. They work by attracting the power of each Cast to the wand. During the Great Supernatural War, we feared the fae might try to steal our magic, and so the Oaken Wands were created to get your magic back if it was stolen. They were created as a failsafe, if you will."

"You said you wanted to unite them. What happened to them?" I questioned.

"Forty years ago, they were stolen from the council," Priestess Lilian sneered. "By *your* grandfather."

"Lilian," Priestess Stella said with a frown. "You know that was never proven. Are you forgetting that Jeb possessed one of the Oaken Wands as well?"

Priestess Lilian blew a breath. "My husband was only trying to protect them."

"Either way," Priestess Margaret cut in, "the Oaken Wands need to be found. It is the only way to ensure our magic is not threatened further while we investigate the cause and culprit behind this."

"Is there any chance the Oaken Wands were destroyed?" I asked.

Priestess Margaret shook her head. "They can't be destroyed. It's impossible."

I eyed the four of them curiously. "And how do you think I can help?"

Priestess Lilian's lips pressed into a thin line. "Well, your grandfather was the last known warlock to possess the Curse Breaker Wand. Perhaps your grandmother is hiding it."

"You think my grandmother would betray the coven!?" I demanded. Nobody accused Grammy of such things!

Priestess Margaret held up a hand to calm me down. "It was merely a suggestion, Miss Evers."

"The Curse Breaker Wand was never found after Nicholas died," Lilian added.

"Then maybe *your* family has it," I accused Lilian. "It was, after all, *your* husband who killed him over it, wasn't it?"

"You will accuse him of no such thing!" she cried.

I cocked an eyebrow, and Priestess Lilian held my gaze. If they thought I was going to play nice on the council after accusing my family of such things, they were wrong.

"What happens once you have all five wands?" I asked.

"We will have control over all Miriamic magic, as the council rightfully deserves," Priestess Lilian answered, tilting her chin upward.

I crossed my arms. "So you'll be able to decide who in the coven gets magic and who doesn't?"

It sounded like a dark, dangerous road to go down. I didn't think I could support such a thing. Women like Lilian would hand out magic to whoever she felt had "earned" it. After what happened to those boys, the council felt out of control, and they wanted to gain that control back—at the expense of the rest of the coven.

It wasn't a sacrifice I was willing to make.

"Miss Evers, please," Priestess Margaret pressed, her voice turning harsh. "You swore to protect the coven. This is the way to do it. If you refuse to seek out the Oaken Wands, your refusal will be considered a betrayal against your people."

Her unspoken words hung in the air. Traitors got burned at the stake or hung at the gallows. It was the way of the coven—like what they'd done to Nicole Verla when she tried to chop down the Protection Tree.

My intuition about the council had been correct. They didn't want me here because it was protocol to have a Curse Breaker on the council. They wanted to use me... because they thought I had the Oaken Wand they wanted.

But the implications of such power seemed minor at the moment. Of course they were using me, but Priestess Margaret had been right—I'd vowed to protect the coven. Magic was being threatened *now*, and I had a chance to stop the person responsible.

It didn't matter what I wanted. There was only one choice that made sense. I had to accept my position as a priestess, and hunt down the Oaken Wands... before all magic in the coven was lost.

"All right," I agreed. "I'll join the council and help you find the Oaken Wands, so that nobody else gets hurt."

"Very good," Priestess Margaret said with a smile. It felt more sinister than welcoming, though. "I'm glad you came to your senses and want to work together on this. Meeting dismissed."

I was still trying to wrap my head around what I'd agreed to when I left the Imperium Council headquarters. I drove through town on my way back to Grammy's house, mulling it over.

There seemed to be so many outcomes, some of which led to my hanging if I failed to live up to the council's expectations. I wasn't sure I truly understood what I had gotten myself into. But at least if I was on the council, I had *some* sort of power. I wasn't sure it was power I wanted, but perhaps this was what Mother Miriam had chosen me for.

I didn't understand why. I had murdered members of my own coven last night. That didn't make me pure of heart, as a Curse Breaker should be.

But maybe that wasn't what Mother Miriam needed in a Curse Breaker. Perhaps she needed someone who was willing to make tough decisions.

It was clear to me I didn't have all the information I needed. The council had provided me with only the bare minimum. But one thing was for sure. Whatever they planned to do with those wands, I would be there to make sure they were used for good.

I needed a place to think. Instead of heading back to Grammy's, I made a U-turn and drove toward Lake Santos. I parked my car in the lot near the Catwalk and walked the trails until I reached the scenic overlook.

Pinewood Manor was nothing more than a silhouette in the fading light. It looked completely different after last night's explosion. Only half the mansion remained standing. The other half was nothing more than charred remains.

I took a seat on the bench that overlooked the lake, staring out at the mansion. I'd made the right decision last night. I was sure of it.

So why did I feel so conflicted?

I grabbed my phone from my back pocket and pulled up my most recent contact. I held my breath as I waited for him to answer.

"Lucas, we need to talk."

TWENTY-FIVE

The sound of Nadine's voice left my chest feeling hollow. It was like I was drowning as I raced to meet up with her at the Catwalk. Grant had let me borrow his car, and it wasn't a long drive, but it felt like it stretched a hundred miles. Nadine had sounded worried. I had the horrible feeling something bad had happened—or was about to.

I was still trying to understand how the woman I loved could scare me so much. I wanted to run away from her as fast as I wanted her to run into my arms. I couldn't make sense of my own feelings.

I ran down the path, then slowed when I spotted Nadine. She sat on the bench at the scenic overlook, staring out over Lake Santos at what remained of Pinewood Manor.

"Nadine," I said breathlessly as I approached. "Is everything okay?"

She turned to look up at me. There was sorrow in her features, but whatever she was feeling seemed to go much deeper than that. I couldn't read it.

"I'm trying to process everything, but I'm so confused," she admitted in a wavered tone.

I sat beside her on the bench, though we were at least a foot apart. "I feel the same way."

"You're talking about what I did to those witches," she stated flatly. It wasn't a question.

"Well, yeah," I said. "I've excused your behavior in the past, because I thought it was outside of your control. Last night proved that I was wrong. It feels like…"

I held my breath. The words pinched like needles in my throat. I couldn't admit it out loud.

"It feels like what?" Nadine pressed. "If you have something to say, I need to hear it."

I took a deep breath. "It feels like… I don't know who you are anymore."

Nadine's jaw dropped. "I'm the same person I've always been. Did you not expect me to defend myself—defend my friends? I *protected* you last night, and all you did in return was throw me under the bus."

"I chopped a monster's head off to save you!" I countered.

"And how's that any different from what I did?" she demanded.

"I killed a monster from the Abyss. You killed *people*. I heard their last thoughts, Nadine. *This is a cruel death.* They were right."

Nadine's bottom lip quivered. "I didn't call you here to fight about this. I can't sit here and justify it to you, because you obviously won't understand."

"You acted with no remorse," I stated.

"I had to stay strong," she shot back, her tone growing intense. "You think I didn't feel something? I hate what I did, but it was a choice I had to make."

"You didn't have to make *that* choice," I argued.

Nadine narrowed her eyes. "You're right. I could've let those witches kill us all."

"You're forgetting we still don't know who paid them to perform the ritual," I reminded her. "Now we'll never figure it out, because you killed the people who could've given us information."

Nadine's breaths became shallow. "You think this choice was all black and white, but it wasn't."

"I know what kind of choice it was," I snapped. "I had the chance to kill Carlisle, and I didn't."

"Well, aren't you nice and fancy up there on your high horse?" she growled. "I had to sacrifice my morals to do what was right."

"I guess that's the problem. The Nadine I know wouldn't sacrifice her morals."

"Then you don't know me at all!"

My chest compressed as Nadine's voice grew. Initially, I wondered how she could say such a thing, but I realized that perhaps she was right. Maybe I *didn't* know her.

"I don't get you," she cried. "You'd rather let your friends be killed, just to save the lives of child murderers."

"I'm saying *no one* had to die," I emphasized.

"You're a hypocrite," she accused. "You said yourself you'd make whoever did this pay for what they've done. You had a chance, and you didn't do anything! You wanted to hand them over to the council, because you're too much of a coward to make a decision yourself. At least I took action."

"You're pissed I *didn't* kill Carlisle?"

"I'm pissed for a lot of reasons," she fumed. "You told the council my secret. Now they want to use me—just as my grandmother feared. They're going to induct me as a priestess of my Cast."

I furrowed my brow. "Why's that so bad?"

She blew a breath. "I don't *want* to be a priestess! I haven't figured it all out yet, but I don't have a good feeling about this. I don't want to be made into someone else's pawn."

"I never meant to give up your secret, Nadine. You have to understand that."

"Don't call me by my full name like it makes a difference," she spat. "Did you know my threat of expulsion has been dropped?"

I didn't understand what she was getting at. "Maybe Chloe decided to drop the charges."

"She did, but it also reeks of the Imperium Council pulling strings. How much do you want to bet that if they *found* evidence of what happened last night, they'd cover that up, too? It's because I'm valuable to them. Even if I can trust them, once I'm made priestess, the whole coven will know what I am. Then everyone will want a piece of my magic." Nadine's nostrils flared. "As it is, they want me to help them find the Oaken Wands."

"The Oaken Wands?" I asked. I'd heard of them before, but only in the context of lore. I didn't know they actually existed.

"They're supposed to help fix whatever the hell is happening to our magic," she explained, waving her hands as she spoke. "But I don't know how the council intends to use the wands, or if I can trust them. The coven's magic is strongest when all five Casts come together. I'm the only key to the most powerful spells the Miriamic Coven can cast. And I can't be responsible for something so drastic."

Nadine gritted her teeth. "I'm exhausted *all* the time. After the magic I performed last night, I don't even know how I managed to get out of bed this morning."

"That proves you're stronger than you realize," I pointed out.

She shook her head. "Magic makes all my symptoms worse, and I just don't think I can do this. I can't be the witch other people look to."

"If you just do as the council asks—"

"If I do everything they're going to ask of me, I'm going to reach my limits and crack! And if they ask me to do something that could hurt innocent people, and I refuse, I can't say no or I'll be hanged! This is your problem, Lucas. You're too passive. *Just do what they tell you. It will all be fine.* I don't buy that bullcrap."

"What do you mean, I'm *too passive?*" I demanded.

Nadine scoffed. "You sit around doing what you're told. You never take risks."

"Yeah, that's why I investigated the missing kids," I replied sarcastically. "Because I was doing what I was *told.*"

"It depends how much it scares you," she said.

I cocked an eyebrow. "Like what?"

Nadine couldn't take it anymore. She shot to her feet and paced several feet away from me. "*I* do! *I* scare you. The second you saw a glimpse of the real me, you panicked. You put me on a pedestal and think I'm perfect, but that's not fair. You've based all your happiness around me, and that's too much to expect of me. You're not mad because I fucked up. You're mad because I've broken this illusion you had of me. I've proven that I'm the kind of person who makes mistakes, and you can't deal with it. Curse or not, I was at least going to *try* to make things work between us—to give you everything I thought you deserved."

"You *were* going to try?" I scoffed. "What does that mean? You're done trying now?"

"Maybe I am. You seem pretty hell-bent on pushing me away. Did you ever want to be with me, or were you using me the whole time to distract from your depression?"

My chest twisted into knots at the accusation. "That's low, Nad. Of course I wanted to be with you—I *do* want to be with you."

"Then why can't you accept all parts of me, and help me work through the things I need to change?" she demanded. "It's like you don't want a girlfriend. You want a savior who can rescue you from your emotions."

"Are you even listening to yourself?" I yelled. "You're being irrational! If I ever pushed you away, it was because of the Reaper's Shadow curse. I don't want you to get sick—sicker than you already are!"

"So you'd break up with me because I'm *sick*!?" she bellowed. "I deserve better than that."

"You're right," I agreed. "You don't deserve to be cursed."

Silence fell as Nadine took in what I'd just said. I hadn't even realized the meaning behind my words. I hadn't countered her question about breaking up, and I wasn't sure that I could. It tore a hole straight through my guts to even think about, let alone admit... but maybe we simply weren't right for each other.

Nadine's eyes glistened with tears, and she took a step back. "Wait... does this mean we *are* breaking up?"

I raked my fingers through my hair. "I-I don't know," I stammered. "I don't want to break up, but..."

"Don't," Nadine said in a clipped tone. Tears spilled over her lids and down her cheeks. "Don't say *but*."

"I don't know what to do, Nad. You were right—I thought you were perfect and that your darkness wasn't part of you. Now I see that it is. You're not the Nad I fell in love with."

Her bottom lip quivered, and it felt like someone had placed hot coals inside my chest cavity. "Are you saying you don't love me?"

What the hell *was* I saying? Of course I loved her, but...

But maybe that wasn't enough.

A lump rose in my throat. It took everything I had to shove it back down. "I'm not okay being in a relationship where other people are dying for me."

"Those witches *murdered* children!" Nadine cried.

"And nothing will erase the blood on their hands, but..." I shook my head, as if that might erase the images flashing through my mind. "I can't live with myself if you die for me."

Her gaze felt like a knife carving out my insides, one organ at a time.

"So this is about the Reaper's Shadow? You don't even want to *try* breaking the curse?"

"I don't know if you *can*," I growled. We were both so angry now, neither of us could seem to hold it together. "You said yourself magic takes its toll on you. Either way—breaking the curse or giving into it— you could die. I can't keep convincing myself I'm okay with those odds. The only way to save you is to let you go."

It was the final nail in the coffin, and something I hadn't been able to admit to myself until now. Breaking up with Nadine was like hurtling myself off the edge of a cliff. I knew the fall was coming and there was nothing but jagged rocks at the bottom, but I did it anyway—so that she wouldn't have to. Every bone in my body seemed to shatter, tearing through every muscle, ligament, and tendon. Forget the term *heartbreak*. This tore my whole fucking body to shreds.

"The only way to save me is to let me go?" she repeated in disbelief. "You're not afraid of the Reaper's Shadow. You're afraid that things are too real between us, and you're running from it."

"I'm not running from anything!" I cried. "Your mother wanted you to stay safe. The least I can do is make sure you do."

She took a step back. "What are you talking about?"

"It was your mother's last thought," I said. It was a secret I'd kept from her for so long. Maybe it was enough to push her away for good, so I'd stop hurting her.

"You told me she said she loved me," she spat. "Was that a lie?"

"No," I said quickly. "But there was more to it. I thought if you knew, you'd go running into danger."

"I've been in danger since the day I joined this coven!" Nadine raged. "And you just *kept* this from me?"

"I didn't mean to keep it from you for so long—"

"Tell me what she said, Lucas!" Nadine demanded. Her chest rose and fell rapidly as she spoke through shallow, angry breaths.

"She said; *The coven's in danger. Stay safe, Nadine. I love you.*"

Her nostrils flared. "You never thought to mention this to me!? What if she was talking about the missing boys? What if I had known something?"

"Did you?" I asked.

Nadine pressed her lips together, her breath wavering. "No, but that's not a reason to keep this from me. I asked you what she said, and you lied to me. If you kept this from me, what else are you keeping?"

"Nothing, I swear."

She shook her head, the betrayal evident in her eyes. "I don't know if I can trust you. You outed me as a Curse Breaker, and you lied to me about my mother. I guess it *is* time to let each other go."

Saying it myself was one thing, but hearing Nadine agree with me was a whole new level of agony. I'd barely had time to consider it, and the world was already crashing down around me.

I crossed my arms. "Do you really think that?"

She shoved her hands into her hair. "All I know is you're too afraid to love me. You're afraid to be in a relationship. You push everyone away—like we're all going to treat you like your parents did, or leave you like your brother did."

My anger flared, and my hands curled into fists. How *dare* she throw that in my face! "I'm sorry I didn't get over my brother as fast as you got over your parents!"

Her jaw dropped, and tears glistened in her eyes, but I didn't let her speak. I was on my feet in a second. I let the words pour out as anger and frustration consumed me. "You act like you have it all figured out, but I'm not the only one with issues in this relationship."

"Oh, *I* have issues?" She crossed her arms and raised an eyebrow. "Other than giving up my soul for you and being ready to go to hell, what did I do that was *so* bad?"

"Come on, Nad. You're way out of my league. We both know you attached yourself to me because you were desperate for love after your parents died."

Disbelief washed over her features. "I'm not desperate for anything!"

"You just said it yourself," I insisted. "You were so desperate that you nearly gave up your soul and went to hell. Being with me is dangerous for you, and you just keep pushing those boundaries. It seems like I'm the only one who cares about your well-being, because you certainly don't."

She blinked a few times, her eyes glistening. "What are you saying? That I'm with you to *punish* myself? I'm with you because *I love you.*"

"You just want to fuck me," I spat. I wasn't even sure why I said it, but it was out there in the open now. I couldn't take it back.

"If that's all you think this was, then you're going to die alone," she shot back. "We're done."

Nadine turned on her heel and stomped away from me. Within moments, she was out of sight.

I couldn't move. I couldn't breathe. Nadine's words were final. It was over.

I thought I would feel numb, but losing Nadine was like a dagger tearing through me. It was unlike any pain I'd felt before. Tears spilled down my cheeks, and I sank to my knees. It was as if the jagged rocks of that cliff I'd spiraled down earlier were spearing into every limb and crushing me to the point where blood oozed from every pore in my body. Nadine might as well have taken my broken body and cast the most intense, painful spell over it.

Nadine had once been my entire world. She was my sunlight and my stars. And I'd just been cast out into darkness.

I didn't know how much time had passed before I stood and stumbled back to the car. I shook the whole way back to campus, and took the back way in through the school, so I wouldn't run into her. All I wanted to do was hide in my room, where I wouldn't have to face her.

Grant was lying in his bed when I arrived, staring at his phone. Doodles covered his fresh cast. "You okay?" he asked. I must've looked like shit.

"Nadine and I broke up," I said, but there was no inflection to my voice. It still didn't feel real.

"Aw, man, I'm sorry," Grant said genuinely.

"I don't want to talk about it." I flopped onto my bed and threw my arm over my eyes. "Tell me something to take my mind off it."

"Um… this might help," he offered. "Professor Daymond was arrested for dealing drugs."

I huffed. "How long do you think it will be before he reports me for breaking and entering?"

"There are a lot of rumors flying around online, but nobody's mentioned that," Grant said. "He's probably in so much shit, he's trying to cover his own ass first."

I sat up as a slew of thoughts rattled around in my head. "So if Daymond won't be dealing drugs anymore, they won't be a problem around campus."

Grant frowned. "I wouldn't jump to any conclusions. Professor Daymond's confession went pretty deep, and it's *way* bigger than just here at the school. According to the rumors, Daymond's dealers have been trading nightshade with other magical races—specifically the Elementai."

"Why?" I wondered. "I mean, Daymond talked about the drugs making him money. Are the Elementai paying a higher price or something?"

"They're trading the drugs for unicorn hair," Grant said. "Rumor has it, that's one of the main ingredients in nightshade."

"What's so good about it? Why do the Elementai want it?"

"They're in the middle of a civil war," Grant reminded me. "The drug is supposed to boost your energy and make your magic stronger."

My eyebrows shot up. "Oh, wow. No wonder it's being sold at the school. That's a good way to cheat your way through exams."

"Yeah, but there are side effects," he added ominously. "It's supposedly highly addictive, because the withdrawals are brutal. When you come off the stuff, it apparently screws with your magic big time."

My spine straightened. "Screws with your magic?"

"I heard Samantha tried a few doses to get through her mid-terms, but once she went off it, her magic was totally gone for weeks. She had to see a therapist and everything to combat the withdrawals."

"The drugs are stealing our magic…" I said thoughtfully. This had to connect to what the Imperium Council had asked of Nadine.

"Well, you have to be *on* nightshade before withdrawal sets in," Grant clarified. "We don't know that it connects to the other stuff going on. Amy never took nightshade and had issues with her magic, and I'm certain Ryan and the Tarantulas never went *off* it. And we both know if there are drugs on campus, they're taking them."

"We have to learn more," I said with firm conviction. "I don't know what the connection is yet, but there *has* to be one there."

A spark ignited in my chest. Losing Nadine was by far one of the hardest things I'd ever have to go through, but I had to help her, because I was the one who'd put her on the council's radar to begin with. The council wanted Nadine to help them solve this mystery—and I wouldn't let her do it alone.

Nadine had been right. I didn't like making hard decisions. I didn't like taking risks.

It was time I finally learned how, because I was going to help Nadine find the Oaken Wands, catch the culprit behind this, and save the coven.

Nadine was my Reaper's Shadow. I'd pushed her away to save her from my curse, but that didn't mean I wasn't still in love with her.

And that I was going to fight like hell to protect her.

END OF BOOK TWO

Continue on to read a special excerpt from book three: *The Cauldron's Curse!*

Hidden Legends

Read more from the Hidden Legends universe! Each Hidden Legends series takes place within the same world, but in separate and unique societies. Every series stands on its own, and they can be read in any order.

☾

ELEMENTALS, DRAGONS, & MORE

Academy of Magical Creatures by Megan Linski & Alicia Rades

☾

SHIFTERS, FAE, & SORCERESSES

University of Sorcery by Megan Linski

☾

SUPERNATURAL PRISON

Prison for Supernatural Offenders by Megan Linski & Alicia Rades

☾

Never miss a new release! Join our newsletter at www.hiddenlegendsbooks.com/fanclub

THE CAULDRON'S CURSE
CHAPTER ONE

Lucas

Fighting for justice could be hell.

The last three months had felt like an eternity—yet had passed in the blink of an eye. For three months, I'd been investigating nightshade within the Miriamic Coven. Three months, and I hadn't found one damn answer. Three months, and I still hadn't spoken to *her*.

Three months…

The words echoed in my mind as I strolled along the dark street, my hands shoved into the pockets of my hoodie. How had so much time passed by already? How had I failed to gather any answers?

Something was going on with the coven's magic—unexplained bouts of magical suppression. I'd dedicated the last three months to hunting down answers about Black Ivy—or nightshade, as it was called on the streets. It was a magical drug brewed by Alchemists, intended to boost magical powers. But as soon as you went off it, withdrawals set in, and your magic didn't work quite the same. I suspected there was a connection. I just didn't know what it was yet.

It was my duty to find answers. I'd been the one to give up Nadine's secret, to let it slip to the Imperium Council that she was a Curse Breaker.

Now they wanted her to find the Oaken Wands, powerful relics created to restore Miriamic magic should it ever be stolen, though the wands themselves had been lost years ago. I had to help Nadine find out why this was happening in the first place—even if she wasn't my girlfriend anymore.

I stopped at the end of a long driveway and stared through the trees at the house beyond. The quarter moon cast the abandoned Gothic house in shadows. It was the end of August, and yet the night air sent a chill down my spine.

The house always had a sense of loneliness about it, but it'd never felt abandoned—until now. It was Professor Daymond's old residence. It had been empty since the night he was arrested for possession of nightshade. The whole place had been cleared out after everything went down, and it hadn't sold yet. It didn't matter how many times I'd scoured the property —there were no more answers here.

I knew it, but I kept finding myself drawn back here. It was where Daymond had told me about the drugs, and where I'd found his notebook containing his drug contacts. But the book was long gone, as was everything else that ever belonged to the old man. The house was nothing more than a shell, a memory.

I heard the sound of a car approaching. I turned as it slowed along the street. The passenger window rolled down, and Grant leaned across the middle console to call out to me.

"Lucas, I thought I might find you out here." Grant sighed, before adding, "Why do you insist on torturing yourself?"

"I'm not *torturing* myself," I insisted. "I'm looking for clues."

Grant gestured toward the house. "You've been over this property a hundred times. There's nothing left."

I walked up to his car and leaned my elbows on the open window. "I suppose you have a better idea?"

Grant smirked, like he knew something I didn't. "I do. Get in the car."

I had to admit, he had me intrigued. I opened the door and slid into the passenger seat.

Grant stepped on the gas. "I don't understand what you think you're going to find out here."

I watched out the window as the house disappeared from view. "Something—anything. Daymond was the one lead I had, and now he's dead."

It had happened the night following his confession. Daymond had been found dead in his jail cell. The official report called it a heart attack, but everyone knew what really killed him. He'd been cursed.

There was no way to prove it. Curses that could kill were incredibly difficult to cast, which meant someone was fucking *pissed* at him. It was pretty obvious to anyone with a brain that it'd been someone within his drug circle, someone who didn't want the information getting out and pointing back to them. When the Imperium Council caught the guy orchestrating this illegal trade, there would be hell to pay.

"Daymond wasn't your *only* lead," Grant pointed out. "We know other people at the school were dealing."

"I have no doubt the Tarantulas were in on it," I agreed. "We already know they've been dealing drugs since Freshman year and that they stole from the Alchemy department last year."

Grant and I had investigated their old hideout, but it'd been totally cleaned out.

"But it's not a great lead if I can't find them," I added.

Everyone had their own plans for summer vacation. Nadine had been staying with her grandmother. I hadn't seen her all summer, and didn't know what she'd been up to. Talia had spent the summer composing music for her brother's band, and Grant had spent most of his break at the pool.

As for me, I'd been crashing on Grant's couch, as I did whenever the dorms were closed. When I wasn't there, I was scouring the town for clues about what the hell was going on in this place.

But the Tarantulas? I had no idea what they were up to. After news broke of Professor Daymond's involvement, it was like they'd vanished, along with anyone else we suspected of dealing drugs on school grounds.

"The Tarantulas will be back," Grant stated confidently, though we couldn't be sure.

The best theory we had was that they were traveling, probably transporting drugs and making deals with other magical races. We already knew the Elementai were trading unicorn hair for nightshade, thanks to Professor Daymond's confession. But the Elementai tribe was all the way across the country, in California. *Someone* had to transport the goods, and who better to use than a bunch of kids who had nothing to do all summer?

But just because all my leads had vanished didn't mean the drugs had. They'd just gone underground, where the Imperium Council couldn't find them—and neither could we.

"In the meantime, I think I found a lead," Grant said with a smile.

I sat straighter in my seat. "You're kidding."

Grant traced two imaginary lines over his heart. "Cross my heart and hope to die."

"That's great!" I cried. "What's the story?"

Grant placed both hands back on the wheel and smirked confidently. "I was lifting weights at the gym when I heard Frederick James say something about nightshade. I gave him my whole story about my broken arm and how I had to skip out of the championship swim tournament last semester. I managed to convince him I needed the nightshade energy boost for training."

"You said *Frederick James*?" I asked. "That Mentalist who accused Nadine of hexing the school last semester?"

Grant frowned. "Yes, unfortunately. But he's our only lead. Are we going to take it or leave it?"

I sighed. "Take it."

"Good, because he should be at the school any minute." Grant turned down a familiar road, which led to the gates of Miriam College of Witchcraft.

"The school?" I asked.

Grant shrugged. "It's summer vacation. No one's there this time of year. Oh, and I got you something."

He reached into his middle console and tossed me a small electronic device. I caught it and looked over the buttons.

"It's a voice recorder," Grant said. "I figured it'd come in handy with your Journalism major."

"Can't I just use my phone?"

"This is better," he assured me. "It's easier to use and picks up more sound. And the design is super simple, so it's less likely to get any interference from magic. It'll pick up everything."

I smiled. "Then let's make sure we catch a confession on tape."

Grant pulled into the parking lot of Miriam College. The Gothic mansion was huge and stood out from the trees surrounding it. It was late

—near midnight already—but I was used to seeing college kids roaming the grounds. It seemed eerie that we were the only ones there.

We'd just pulled into a parking space when a pair of headlights swept by us. Grant stepped out of the car. The other car sped through the parking lot and came to a screeching halt beside us. James jumped out of an old, beat-up sports car, and the hinges squeaked as he slammed the door. I quickly pressed *record* on my device and shoved it in my pocket.

"Grant, my man!" James sang, as if the two of them had been best buddies since grade school. He was already approaching Grant, but stopped when he saw me climb out of the car. He eyed me, as if trying to decide if I could be trusted or not. "I see we have company."

"Relax," Grant said smoothly. "Lucas wants a vial, too. I assume you have enough for both of us?"

James relaxed and straightened his leather jacket. "Yeah, I've got enough. What's your story, Lucas?"

"A bad breakup," I told him, without missing a beat. "I need to forget."

That wasn't quite a lie, either. I'd spent the summer trying to get Nadine out of my mind. Nothing—not even throwing myself into this investigation as a distraction—had done the trick. Every morning I woke up, the memory of her was there, seeded into the forefront of my mind. Every night I fell asleep, I dreamt of her. I'd been pissed when we broke up, certain I couldn't forgive her for the choices she'd made to protect her friends. Now I knew I'd been wrong, because if I truly thought I could never forgive her—never be with her again—it wouldn't hurt so damn much.

James smiled. "Nightshade can help with that. The euphoria is quite something. How much are you looking for?"

"Depends. What do you have?" Grant asked.

"I can do two vials each," James offered. "You got the money?"

Grant nodded and conjured a wad of cash. "The price we agreed on," he said. My eyes went wide as Grant handed over several twenties.

"That's... quite the price tag," I remarked, choosing my words carefully.

James narrowed his eyes. "That depends on how desperate you are to forget about this girl."

I chuckled, playing along. "Oh, believe me. I want the nightshade."

I conjured what little money I had and began slowly counting out the bills. James's eyes grew hungry at the sight of cash.

"I was just wondering… is there any chance we can get in on dealing?" I asked.

James frowned. "I'm afraid not."

I stopped counting my bills, but he never took his eyes off the money. "There's gotta be a way to get us in. How did you get involved?"

"Can't say," James replied curtly, before quickly adding, "It's boss's orders. Ever since Daymond was busted, someone's been poking around looking for answers. Did you know his house was broken into after he died?"

Guilty, I thought, though I hadn't been the first person to think of it. By the time I got there, all clues about Daymond's ties to nightshade were gone. Someone really wanted to cover this up.

"Who would do that?" I asked innocently.

James shrugged. "Someone hell-bent on getting the drugs out of Octavia Falls, I guess."

Huh. So they had no suspects of their own.

"Is there someplace we can go to get more nightshade, after we run out?" Grant asked.

A good question. They had to have some sort of headquarters… right?

"Two vials should last you a while," James said. "When you're ready for more, you talk to me."

"What if we can't get a hold of you?" I pressed. "Is there someone else we can get in contact with?"

James chuckled. "It's not like I'm going anywhere. I'm not stupid enough to overdose or some shit like that. Look, I don't have all night. I realize you've probably never bought drugs before, but you're going to have to get quicker on the exchange. The last thing you want is to get caught buying nightshade."

I pressed my lips together. I was getting nowhere with this guy. Perhaps money was the only way to get him to talk.

"Will this do it?" I waved a few bills at him.

"Sure will." James took the cash, then conjured four small vials of nightshade. A purplish-blue liquid sloshed around inside them. Grant and I each took our respective vials and subconjured them.

"You sure we can't get in on this?" I gritted my teeth. I was starting to get frustrated with this guy.

"Positive. Boss says no newbies." James pocketed the money. "Before you leave, a word of caution, since you've obviously never used before. No more than a few drops under the tongue at a time. You don't want to overdose."

I narrowed my eyes. "What happens if we do?"

James scoffed, like he found my ignorance amusing. "What happens if you take too much of *any* drug? You'll die."

My mouth went dry. It wasn't like I was going to *use* the nightshade we'd just bought, but the thought of anyone dying over this chilled me. No drug was worth your life.

"Thanks for your business," James said, with a nod of his head. "Oh, and I'm sorry things didn't work out with your girlfriend—Nadine, was it?"

My stomach twisted at the sound of her name. "Yeah," I replied flatly.

James got a distant look in his eyes. "It really is too bad. I hope you tapped that before you broke up."

My hands instantly curled into fists. *"Excuse me?"*

James laughed. "Nadine's totally hot. I mean, she's not really *my* type, but I'd still do her. Since she's single, I might just--"

Thwack!

My fist cracked into James's jaw, and he stumbled sideways.

"Lucas!" Grant gasped.

I already had a battle orb aimed at James's face. "Don't you *dare* talk about Nadine like that! If you even *think* about touching her--"

"Back off, man!" James thrust his hands outward, and a spell erupted from his palms.

It rammed into my chest and flung me backward. My back slammed into Grant's car, and my elbow cracked against the back window. I hadn't been stunned, but I'd be damned if that wasn't one hell of a spell.

I gasped for breath, but reacted quickly, tossing a stunning spell at him. James was fast and ducked out of the way. I didn't waste a second. I swung my knee upward while he was ducked down. It connected with his nose, and he let out a cry of pain.

Grant grabbed for me. "Lucas, stop. This is unnecessary!"

But I'd already lost it. I shrugged Grant off and grabbed James's collar, shoving him against the side of his vehicle. Blood dripped from his nose. He laughed like the fight was nothing short of amusing.

"You were already pissing me off, but *no one* talks about Nadine like that and gets away with it," I growled. "Where are the drugs? Who are you working for? Tell me now, or so help me--"

"Go fuck yourself, loser!" James shoved me off of him, and another spell blasted from his hands, more powerful than the last. It blew me backward so hard I flew off my feet and rolled across the pavement a few times, accumulating bruises. Something clinked to the ground.

James's eyes darted between Grant and me. "You can forget about buying any more nightshade off me. Consider this your final purchase."

I groaned as I pushed myself to a sitting position. It wasn't until James's eyes landed on the ground that I realized with horror what had slipped from my pocket. *My recording device.*

James's eyes went wide, and he flicked his wrist at me. An ungodly pain overtook my body, as if my bones had been set on fire. My back arched as a scream tore from my lungs. Every organ in my body seemed to be ripping apart beneath his spell.

I was vaguely aware of Grant rushing to my side. I heard the sound of tires squealing as James sped out of the parking lot.

"*Fuuuck!*" I screamed, the blazing inferno tearing through me.

All at once, it was gone. The fire stopped, though every inch of my body trembled.

"Lucas, Lucas!" Grant repeated my name over and over. He slapped my face a little, until I tore my gaze from James's car to look at him.

"W-what the hell happened?" I demanded.

"James is a Mentalist," he reminded me. "It must be one of his specialties—tricking you into thinking you're in pain when you're not."

I drew in a greedy gulp of air. "That was one hell of a spell."

Grant helped me up, though I was still shaking. "Come on. We should get out of here before anyone comes to check it out. I bet the whole coven heard you scream."

I stood on shaky knees, then bent to pick up my recording device. I turned the recording off and waved it at Grant. "Thanks for the recorder, but we got nothing."

His shoulders sagged. "I'm sorry. I was sure we'd learn *something.*"

"It's not your fault this night was a bust," I told him. "I'm the one who lost it."

I just hoped it hadn't cost us everything. James knew now that I was a threat. He knew I was coming for him—for all the witches and warlocks involved in the coven's drug trade.

Which meant I had to get creative if I was going to beat them—before I ended up like Daymond, and the drug ring killed me for messing with their operation.

Continue The Cauldron's Curse to solve the mystery!

BONUS OFFERS

Find coloring pages, games, quizzes, and bonus content at hiddenlegendsbooks.com.

Join the *Orenda Academy: Hidden Legends Fan Group* on Facebook for all things Hidden Legends!

Check out the *College of Witchcraft Official Playlist* on Spotify!

Never miss a new release! Join Alicia's email list at aliciaradesauthor.com/newsletter.

About the Author

Alicia Rades is a USA Today bestselling author of young adult and new adult paranormal fiction. When she's not dreaming up magical stories, she's either binge-watching Netflix, meditating, or spending time with her family. She has an unhealthy obsession with psychic characters and writes with a deck of tarot cards next to her computer.